A CLASH OF THREE COURTS

A CLASH OF THREE COURTS

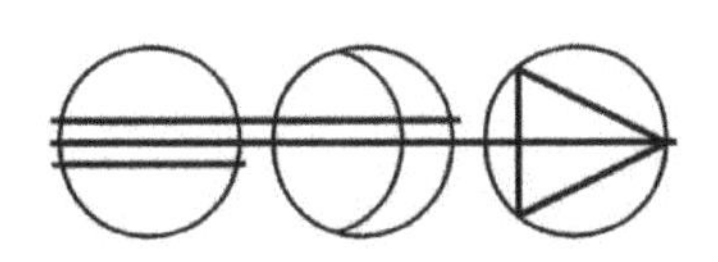

CHLOE C. PEÑARANDA

LUMARIAS PRESS

A Clash of Three Courts

Published by Lumarias Press
www.lumariaspress.com

First Edition published September 2022

Map design © 2022 by Chloe C. Peñaranda
Cover illustration © 2022 by Alice Maria Power
www.alicemariapower.com
Cover design © 2022 by Lumarias Press
Edited by Bryony Leah
www.bryonyleah.com

Identifiers
ISBN: 978-1-915534-01-9 (eBook)
ISBN: 978-1-915534-00-2 (paperback)
ISBN: 978-1-8382480-9-3 (hardback)

www.ccpenaranda.com

CONTENT WARNING

Contains some scenes not suitable for younger audiences. Including scenes of an explicit sexual nature, panic attack, and fantasy violence detail.

DEDICATION

For you, my dear reader

You create the wind in your sails

UNGARDIA
N
W
E
S
Eternal Woods
Inner City
HIGH FARROW
FARROWHOLD
Westland Forest
Sky Caves
Stone Passes
White Peak Mountains
The Black Sea
ALANDRA
LAKELARIA
Dead Lands
To the Western Continent of Salenhaven
Farhin Mountains
NILTAIN

Mortus Mountains
DALRUNE
DALNIRE
Rune Desert
The Dark Woods
Galmire
Dagdune
Valleys of Fenstead
OLMSTONE
VESMIRE
FENSTEAD
Fenher
Silver Forests
CALENMOORE
East Moorlands
Esmire
South Moorlands
RHYENELLE
ELLIUM
VALGARD
Balmore
Fire Mountains
The Southern Gulf

PROLOGUE

A long time ago…

Tauria Stagknight was wholly at peace sitting on the furs and cushions by the fireplace in her rooms, surrounded by various books while she tried to engross herself in the one splayed on her lap. The winter wind rattled the old windowpanes, layering snow on the ground outside in beautiful cascades. She treasured the warmth of the amber flames all the more against the icy storm.

The sound of splitting timber and the occasional burst of fire stars was a soothing embrace to tame her fear of the beast outside. It was why Tauria chose the natural fire to read beside over the soundless cobalt flame she could conjure by magick. Yet the presence beside her distracted her focus more times than she cared to admit.

The Prince of High Farrow lay beside her. Propped up on one elbow, he pretended to be lost inside a book. They'd been silent for some time, but she knew he wasn't reading because of how fast he turned the pages. Tauria bit her lip to suppress her chuckle, wondering if he was simply enjoying the images instead. Something she'd quickly come to learn about the prince was that texts and knowledge weren't his idea of fun, but he was incredibly smart all the same. The way Nik could analyze visuals was admirable. It were as if he created his own stories and outlook without being influenced by a single written word.

"I can't possibly concentrate with you staring at me all the time." Nik's emerald eyes twinkled with mischief as he flashed them up to her.

Tauria's cheeks instantly caught fire. She didn't realize her attention had fallen to him with her wandering thoughts. "Don't flatter yourself," she grumbled, fixing her gaze back on her own book.

Nik thumped his shut, and in thinking he was about to leave her for the evening, Tauria's stomach sank. Instead, though, he shifted the cushions, plumping and fixing them with more exaggeration than necessary. Amusement danced at the corners of Tauria's mouth. Then Nik settled back, his body rolling to face her where he lay. She couldn't ignore the skip of her pulse that his careful adjustment had brought him a fraction closer to where his hand could easily graze her lap.

"Read me yours," he requested.

Tauria's gaze snapped down to his, and his side smile, a partial smirk, momentarily stole her response. The fire that danced across his irises was enrapturing. She shook her head to clear her thoughts.

"You're perfectly capable of reading your own. Perhaps you should choose something with more pictures."

Nik rumbled with laughter, the vibrations creating a shiver over her skin at such close proximity. "I'm trying not to be insulted."

"It wasn't intended as an insult. Simply an observation that you might prefer more visuals."

"So you admit it."

"What?"

"You have been watching me."

As Nik's smile stretched to a grin and his eyes twinkled with delight, Tauria had to avert her gaze in a flush of embarrassment. Some things hadn't changed since the day they met in her home kingdom of Fenstead. Nik's insufferable deviance was one of them.

He shifted onto his back as his chuckling ceased, folding an arm behind his head with a sigh of relaxation. Tauria's traitorous gaze slid back to him, taking in his long form effortlessly stretched out over the furs. She'd requested her handmaidens set up this position so they'd be closer to the fire while the winter nip swirled around the room. Her ability awakened at the restless storm outside with the desire to soothe or play with it. Challenge it. What others experienced as the untamed elements were living entities to her, one with the ability to manipulate the push and pull of wind.

Tauria had learned to find distraction from the humming magick in her veins in reading during particularly bad storms. She'd been alone tonight until the prince's intrusion a couple of hours ago.

"Please, Tauria Stagknight, will you read to me?" Nik drawled. His eyes were closed, and she took that moment to shamelessly admire his broad, toned chest while his arm, hooked behind his head, exposed every contour under his white shirt. His jet-black hair was disheveled, not its usual elegant perfection, and she cherished the sight. Not a prince, but a fae. An effortlessly beautiful male who appeared entirely unburdened by the crown he wore. In this room, she treasured every second, feeling it was the one place they could truly be themselves, locked away from the judgmental eyes of the court.

"If you make one witty comment while I do, you're out," she warned, shuffling to get more comfortable.

Nik grinned but didn't open his eyes as she reclined back, her chest almost level with his head. "Deal."

Tauria bit her lip as she flipped through the pages, until she found a short story to start anew. "And if you fall asleep, you can count on a rude awakening."

The soft whisper of Nik's chuckle caressed her skin. She had to put effort into taming her breath, which wanted to quicken at their close proximity. After a few seconds, she felt her muscles loosen and took a long inhale before beginning. Against the storm the fire played its melody, but above it, Tauria's voice was smooth and unwavering as she spoke, losing herself in the tale to forget everything.

Except him.

Nik's presence wasn't forgotten for even a second, but she was so fully immersed by the world she took them to that she didn't balk under the featherlight impression of his eyes on her. She couldn't be sure how much time passed, but Nik slowly inched closer under the guise of restlessness, and soon only a slither of space remained between them. His breaths blew over her chest, which was bare in the low cut of the gown that felt suddenly scandalous. Then, when his fingers carefully grazed her waist, Tauria's next words stumbled for the first time. She didn't look at him, attempting to continue reading as though it were a mistake. But his hand moved, flattening and curving over her abdomen, torturously slow, leaving a tingling trail that shot to her most desirous parts. Her breathing fluctuated too much to trust her voice wouldn't waver, but her eyes remained fixed on the text.

"Don't stop," he said huskily, sending any response or focus scattering. "Unless you want me to."

Tauria swallowed hard, her heartbeat fast and longing. And then she continued. Her tale took a slower pace while her mind scrambled, reading but not absorbing a single word, because all she could track was his every hint of movement.

With his body now flush to hers, his warm breath blew over her collar. "Do you always prefer for your tales to be filled with romantic notions?"

Tauria shivered, wondering if he'd read the lines over her shoulder. "The real world leaves little to be desired in that respect," she answered, but her erratic pulse nearly trembled her voice, giving away the effects of his closeness.

"Is that so?"

At his mocking tone, she wanted to thump the book shut and send him off. Yet she was gripped by a foolish yearning that seemed to *enjoy* his playfulness. She didn't want him to stop—not really. She kept reading.

His hand on me was a hold of—

"Possession," Nik finished, accompanied by a squeeze of his fingers around her waist, just tight enough to draw a shallow gasp.

"You're being ridiculous," she chastised. Or at least she meant to reprimand him, but her words fell short. Her body was warm. Too warm. Her dress had become so restrictive it was unbearable…with an overwhelming urge to know what Nik's hands would feel like on her bare skin.

His chuckle was a low, entrancing tremor, but he didn't move an inch. "You don't think romance exists like in your novels?"

"Why does it sound as if you've found challenge in that?" For the first time, she found the will to look at him. His smile stretched into a wicked grin, his face so close she didn't dare breathe too hard. She said, "People don't often realize there's a difference between love and lust. They think only one side of the coin is enough." She didn't cower under the intensity that grew in their stare down. "Yet eventually…one always leads to disappointment without the other."

Nik's amusement fell slowly, easing to something far softer. Searching. His eyes fell to her mouth. Only for a split second, but it was enough to make her heart skip a beat. Then he inhaled deeply, his gaze flashing expectantly to her book. "Then I suppose we can consider *that* educational scripture. And *this* a very worthwhile lesson."

Tauria refrained from rolling her eyes. Instead they fell back to the page, about to carry on, when—

Nik's soft lips pressed to her shoulder. She couldn't bite back her sharp intake of breath.

"It's what comes next, is it not? In your novel."

She had no answer for that because she couldn't bring herself to read another word.

Nik's fingers tingled over hers on the book. "Is this what you want?" He slipped away from her palms, which loosened their grip in response. "Seduced by pretty words, hands on your body that know exactly what makes that breath of yours hitch, such longing to hear your desire when they touch you."

As if he knew, Nik's hand slipped around her back just as he pressed against her a fraction tighter. A move so subtle, but it emitted a quiet noise of surprise, flashing a twinkle of delight through his emerald eyes.

"This isn't funny," she breathed in bewilderment.

"No one's laughing, love."

It was too much. He'd made his point, and it was time for the game to be over.

When she felt his lips again over the curve of her shoulder, she couldn't prevent the faint tip of her head, nor the flutter of her eyes. He wasn't stopping. He wasn't retreating. She was waiting for his next teasing remark to expose it all as wicked play.

A cruel voice rang in her mind, chanting how much she wanted this to be real. When Nik flirted and teased, there were times she wished for it to be more than his natural allure. Wished he were drawn to her as much as she was to him. Yet they'd never gotten this close before. Never this careless, unrestricted touching.

"Nik," she exhaled when his mouth pressed to her skin a third time. He'd allowed it to go too far, and in her stomach coiled a thrill that perhaps his actions were true. When she paused to gather her thoughts, she found their scents had become entangled, but she dared to believe she wasn't alone in her rising desire. He straightened his head, and in turning hers she brought their faces so dangerously close it took conscious will not to do something impulsive. "Why now?"

Almost a decade had passed since she fled to High Farrow for refuge. It was only a small measure of time in their long lifespans, and it felt even shorter now the ghost of that desolate day hung over her like a thick shroud. She'd lost everything then, and the only thing that kept her from falling, from *drowning*, under the weight of her sorrow…was Nik. Yet never did he court her—not in the traditional sense. He'd become someone she relied upon, company she clung to like treasure found at the bottom of a barren sea. His green eyes hypnotizing, the pull in them so enticing he could devour her entirely with that look. They sparkled against the firelight as he peered at her through long, dark lashes.

"What if I said it's not just now? What if I said I can't stop thinking about you and that it drives me wild every damn day?"

Nik was such a master of subtlety—slow movements, barely-there touches—that Tauria didn't realize their positions had switched until she lay down and the light impression of his body hovering partially over her sent a spike of adrenaline through her veins. Her mind was so clouded she was losing all sense of herself.

"What if I said that watching your lips move as you spoke so compellingly just now finally made me break? That I've often wondered how they would feel if you allowed me to kiss you."

Her breath almost caught with the need for him to repeat the words she was sure were a mistake. Or a wicked, taunting joke. Yet he remained curious, studying her expression intently for any response to his confession.

"Then I would ask again, why now?" It didn't make sense when they'd had so long before for him to reveal his true feelings.

Nik's expression eased to a pained softness, and he searched her eyes, contemplating. "You needed to mend your broken heart before you could give it to me. I'm willing to wait as long as it takes. I want to help you, and I hope in any way I have succeeded, but most of all, the strength you've regained, the confidence and determination you've taken back with a vengeance…it was all your own will and resilience."

The pride that pierced her heart was like a physical blow, a beautiful kind of ache. Tauria shook her head. "I wouldn't have found my way out of that darkness without you," she said, resisting the urge to reach up a hand to trace his thoughtful face. "You became my light." The vulnerability she harbored deep so it may never be used against her was that she feared without him, that light would be gone, and the unrelenting darkness from a tormenting, desolate past would claim her once more.

There was a flash of shared sorrow in the pinch of his brow, but as his eyes dipped to her chest it mixed with longing infused with desire. "I need to know…" Nik's fingers came up, grazing her skin. They hooked under the thin material at her shoulder, sliding it over her arm, but not enough to expose her breast. "Why did you come to High Farrow, Tauria?"

Her name was a sinful whisper that flushed heat straight between her legs, and she refrained from the urge to find friction and give herself away. Nik's eyes filled with a darkening hunger as he stared at her exposed shoulder. His lips came down to replace his fingers, and Tauria's head tipped back with a breath at the contact that exploded ripples of desire across her skin, tightening her breasts.

"Rhyenelle neighbors Fenstead. You passed through Olmstone to get here. Why?"

Tauria's rising lust threatened the limits of her restraint. "I wanted to get as far away as I could."

"Is that all?" he coaxed as though he knew the truth she swallowed.

Determined not to yield all in fear of what he might do with the knowledge, with her *heart,* Tauria didn't answer. Not to admit what burned in her throat, and not to protest as he shifted closer until she felt enough of his weight on her that she lost all sense and reason. Her rational mind scrambled to push through.

"We can't."

Nik pulled back, and she read the promise on his face. He was ready to retreat entirely if that were her wish. It was so far from it.

Her desire for him had never pulsed so strong. It was as if she *needed* him.

"I'm not free to choose when to be reckless," she said. The truth was an ache in her chest, a twist in her stomach. But she had to think of her kingdom, and that was tied in with her reputation.

Nik searched her eyes, contemplating. "If you were, what would you want?"

Those damned emerald eyes. He could entice her to spill every scandalous thought with a single look. Tauria felt herself slowly coming undone for him. Effortlessly, he was unraveling her tightly wound and well-guarded spool.

"I think you know the answer to that."

There was a flash of something possessive, primal, that sent a shudder through her body, and she couldn't stop the need to tighten her thighs together this time. Nik seemed to notice and carefully challenged that response. His leg shifted, easing between hers to part them again. He never broke eye contact, and she knew his slow pace was in aid of being cautious, to see if she'd object.

She couldn't. Every desire she'd ever felt for him came rushing to the surface all at once, drowning out any hesitation.

"I want to hear you say it." His tone dropped to a gravelly murmur that blew like scattered stars over her skin. His hand met her calf, trailing slowly upward, past her knee, to free her legs from the lengths of her gown. Nik glanced down, and a groan left him as his fingers traced the smooth length. Featherlight. Torturous. Trailing a growing heat up to mid-thigh, where Tauria held her breath to suppress her moan, to stop herself from begging him to reach the ache he caused between her legs.

But that was as far as he went before his hand left her. Nik braced on his elbow beside Tauria, looking at her face with something other than lust or desire. It was soft, searching, and perhaps there was a hint of fear laced in that gaze.

"What are you doing?" She couldn't help her bite of frustration at his retreat from everything he riled in her.

Nik could hardly suppress his amusement. "Abiding by your wishes, love."

"I didn't respond."

"Exactly. You hesitated, but that's okay. I can wait as long as it takes for you to believe my want for you goes far beyond lust."

It was sheer irritation and a severe lack of rationality that drove her next move. With her legs free and Nik still close, Tauria twisted where she lay, hooking one leg around his waist to push him onto his back, where she straddled him. He blinked up at her in surprise, his hands gripping her hips as if he thought she would fall.

"What do you want, Tauria? Forget title. Forget everything but your own desire."

Tauria flared in defiance. Not at him, but her station and anyone who believed she should be robbed of this: her will to do as she desired with her body. "I want…" Her breathing was labored, fighting head against heart.

"Say it."

"You."

Nik inched forward until he was sitting on an incline, supporting her in his lap. Their new position had her feeling his hard arousal against her heated core. The small sound that emitted from her triggered the tightening of his hands.

She broke first.

Tauria moved, needing any sort of friction to relieve that building ache.

"Gods above…" Nik shuddered. The prince stared up at her as though she were more than a princess, awe in his expression as if she were a Goddess. The confidence he enticed out of her through that look alone shattered her shyness entirely as she chased her pleasure. "Look at you," he admired. "So beautiful. You make the sweetest sounds, love. I plan to discover them all."

She kept her eyes on his, face pinching as her pleasure intensified with his words and the way he held her hips firm, aiding the rock of them against him and painting lust on his face. All she could muster was a barely-there nod, panting faster in response.

"You are exquisite."

Her fingers tangled in his dark hair, close to abandon as she used his body to bring herself right to the precipice.

And he allowed her to have it all.

Yet right before she tumbled over that blissful edge, Nik's grip tightened to stop her, and Tauria cried out. His denial left her trembling with her near climax.

"One more move, and you would come for me, wouldn't you, Tauria?" he whispered, right before his lips met her chest.

"Yes," she rasped. She needed it, and he knew it. She felt his smile against her skin.

"Has anyone ever touched you before?"

The question was enough to flush her with embarrassment, shedding light on her inexperience. Did he find it amusing how easily she could reach that end point?

Then her stomach sank with a hideous, shameful feeling as she wondered how many others he'd been with in comparison. Tauria shifted to move off him, but Nik's hold only tightened. Their eyes locked.

"Yes," she answered boldly.

In a quick flash of movement, Tauria squealed in surprise as Nik pinned her swiftly beneath him. His hands trailed over her arms, igniting her skin, until his palms slid against hers and their fingers entwined by her head. The light press of his body was glorious. She longed to run her hands over every hardened contour of him. His soft black hair hovered above his brow as he stared down at her. His green eyes became feral, and she knew he wanted to demand who, but he wouldn't. The challenge grew, and it raced a thrill to incite.

When she couldn't stand that searing gaze any longer, a coy smile eased her defiant frown. "Myself."

An alluring darkness filled his irises, devouring the emerald, at her response. His arousal at the image she painted swirled around the room, and the need to feed her own lust was all-consuming.

"What I wouldn't give to watch you," he ground out at last. Nik leaned his head down, inch by torturous inch, until her lips tingled with the near touch of his.

"Maybe one day you will."

This was power, watching the prince above her fight against coming undone at her words, watching him struggle against the urge to touch her. Somehow, what had awakened between them was a thrilling game: who could seduce the other to break first?

Nik said, "Or maybe you'll surrender yourself to me and allow me to show you the heights of pleasure unmatched by your own hand." Instead of kissing her like she wanted, Nik's mouth traveled along her neck, and she strained against him.

"Bold of you to think you're capable of such thrills."

Nik chuckled darkly against her skin, and her head angled back on instinct. A soft noise escaped her lips.

"You sound eager to find out. Is that what you want?"

She wanted to bite out a retort to shake his confidence, but hers was clouded with whispers of how much she *did* want it. Tauria gave him nothing. Nik only smiled.

"I see." His lips grazed the column of her neck. He shifted his hold to lock both her wrists in one hand. "You want me to make you beg."

Tauria didn't know what to expect from Nik, but this was so much more. His calm composure and torturous touches—they were only the first notes of the song, and she was already molding to his melody.

"I'll never beg," she rasped with the dregs of her resistance.

Nik's hand trailed over her ribs to the strap of her dress he'd already pulled down. She let him slide it farther, all the way, until her breast was exposed. But Nik didn't look down, as though his excitement had heightened only to gauge her reaction as he cupped her breast in his palm, massaging, teasing. Tauria's breathing quickened, bound by his mercy. The connection in their gaze was sensual and challenging, both of them locked in a battle of desire and defiance. Neither backed down. He stopped only to reach for her other strap, agonizingly slow, never letting his touch leave her for a second. Only when she was bare-chested beneath him did he finally look down, and there was a short pause before his mouth descended there.

In his distraction, Nik finally freed her hands. Tauria's arms slipped out of the straps, and her fingers slid through his hair while her chest arched into his assault. Before she knew what she was doing, she'd reached over Nik's shoulders to grapple with his shirt. Reading what she wanted, he let go to lean back on his knees. All she could do was watch, mesmerized, as he reached behind him and folded out of his shirt in one swift movement. The sight of him bare-chested was impeccable. He was honed for battle in every contour.

Beneath the lust, something far softer fluttered in her stomach as he looked her over. Nik was careful as he reached to the front of her gown. The back laces would be bound too tight to slip out of, and it seemed to be exactly what crossed his mind.

"This dress looked beautiful on you," he said in a deep, gravelly tone. Her sharp breath was swallowed by the tear of fabric when Nik effortlessly helped her out from the front instead. "Remind me I owe you a new one."

Tauria bit her lip, completely uncaring about the ruined dress, surprised the action had piqued her arousal instead. Nik's gaze snapped to her mouth, and a flash of hunger shuddered through her body, her hands beginning to cover her chest on instinct as she became acutely aware of her nakedness.

A low sound left his throat as he positioned himself over her once again. His hand took hers, fingers intertwining so perfectly, while his other thumb brushed her bottom lip, pulling it from the hook of her teeth.

"You are beautiful, Tauria. I want—I *need* you to be mine. And in return, I vow to protect you with everything I am. No matter the cost."

When he lowered and their bare skin met, Tauria couldn't help but arch her back with a need to feel every inch of him pressed against her. Her hands roamed his back. His skin was smooth, but every now and then she skimmed over the raised scars of battle. She wanted to treasure and memorize every imperfection. She wanted to taste him, feel him. She needed all of him.

"I'm yours," she mumbled.

Recklessly, perhaps foolishly, she gave all of herself to him without hesitation. But also without regret. She wanted this. More than anything before, she wanted *him.*

"I've waited so long for you," he said quietly. Nik's palm caressed her cheek as he finally brought his head down.

Their mouths met, and something within her that she didn't know was incomplete was forged anew. She wondered in a quick moment of insecurity if he felt it as strongly as she did. The pulse in her chest. The tugging of something soul-deep. It wasn't simply lust or desire. It wasn't anything explainable like love.

Her thoughts were soothed by the way his mouth moved with hers so feverishly. Their bodies harmonized. It was a push and pull, a perfect response to every angle at which they collided. Tauria knew then she didn't need experience to know this was *right.* Every question about what she wanted or desired, what her body craved, what her mind needed…

Nik was the answer.

Tauria,

I trust you are well and the journey passed fast. In your absence, time feels too slow. I've never been good with words, as you are well aware, so I won't write many. I meant what I said in parting.
Please write back.

You are missed.

Nik.

KING'S PAWN

PART I

KINGDOM OF
HIGH FARROW

HOUSE
SILVERGRIFF

CHAPTER 1

Lycus

IN THE THICK of the woods he heard their distant approach. Lycus Warner waited on horseback, knowing they would cross paths here and not wanting to interrupt their farewell with the King of Rhyenelle. Faythe's laughter carried on the wind, and she was the first he spotted on a horse, closely followed by Reylan Arrowood. The brightness in her expression was lit by something the general had said, and it was uplifting to watch despite the uncertain quest they set out upon.

Faythe's amber eyes caught his, and they exchanged a warm smile. "I didn't think we'd have the chance to say goodbye," she said as they came to a halt.

The commanders Kyleer, Izaiah, and Livia gathered around too, along with Faythe's human friend, Reuben.

"I couldn't leave without offering my thanks and bidding you good luck, princess."

Her cheeks flushed with the title. Lycus wouldn't admit he only used it so she'd grow accustomed to the notion she could carry a crown on her head someday. A few close observations were all it took for him to see traits worthy of leadership in Faythe. Traits he admired in his own queen from many decades by her side.

"Thank you, Lycus, for going to her."

Faythe had sought him out, and they'd spent hours in conversation about Tauria. She'd beaten him to it, but he'd been itching to find out news on his queen since Faythe mentioned their close friendship in High Farrow. Lycus couldn't deny the blaring sign of fate that it was time. Time to return to Tauria and hope she'd understand his reasons for staying away for so long and forgive him.

"With all due respect, it is not for you that I'm doing this."

"Of course not. But as Tauria's friend, I'm grateful. She'll need friendship and belief in Olmstone. There is no better time."

Reylan watched her with a pride in his eyes Lycus found admirable. To anyone else, Faythe might appear as no more than an ordinary human, so to have the famous general regard her so highly was baffling, near unbelievable, at first. Until Lycus met her. Until he studied their interactions. What she hoped Lycus could inspire in Tauria during her trials in Olmstone was exactly what Reylan had invoked in her without either of them realizing: an unwavering strength. Though with the pair before him, there was something...*more.* A rare devotion Lycus hadn't failed to notice, which had added a welcome bright shift in his friend since they'd returned from High Farrow with Faythe.

"Send her my regards." Faythe's voice snapped his attention from the observations that came naturally to one in his position. "I believe in her completely to make the right choice for herself and her kingdom, as I'm sure Nik does too."

Her mention of the King of High Farrow was a subtle acknowledgment. Faythe didn't disclose much about their relationship, insisting it wasn't her place to talk about what was or wasn't between Nikalias and Tauria. What Lycus gathered was that it was a long history and far from finished, but he was braced to accept the outcome for better or worse. He knew he would stand by Tauria's choice no matter what.

"We should be going," Reylan cut in softly. Then his gaze locked on Lycus, and they shared a nod of respect. "I'm sure it won't be long before our paths cross again."

He smiled at that. Over the many decades since he'd taken refuge in Rhyenelle, Reylan Arrowood had become one of Lycus's closest companions. He owed a lot of who he was today to the white lion's patience and training, which had helped him to learn what it took to be a highly regarded general like Reylan and his father before him.

Faythe's smile was shadowed with sadness, as though she'd just remembered the uncertain journey they were parting to take.

"I can't wait to hear all about your adventures, Your Highness," Lycus mused lightheartedly.

She gave a short chuckle that upturned even Reylan's usually firm mouth. "We'll have plenty of interesting stories to exchange, I'm sure."

Their gazes met one last time in a silent embrace. This wasn't merely a farewell exchange; it was a promise. When fear flickered in her eyes at the very real danger she could be met with out there, he wanted to be the last person who believed she would triumph in whatever she faced. He watched after her as they turned and began to make paces away.

"Until then, Faythe Ashfyre."

Her horse kept moving, but Faythe's head twisted back. Against the sunlight filtering through the canopy, she was ablaze. Highlights of gold in her hair, sparkling in her amber eyes, flaring in the crimson of her leathers. He couldn't help but marvel at how well she embodied her kingdom's emblem. As though she were born of the Phoenix.

"Until then, Lycus Warner."

CHAPTER 2

Tauria

"YOUR HIGHNESS, PRINCE Tarly Wolverlon requests your company in the atrium."

Tauria Stagknight straightened with the announcement but didn't turn to the messenger. Her eyes remained fixed on the stone courtyard she gazed over while allowing her thoughts to wander. The vibrancy of the forests and meadows wasn't visible from her vantage point, but she couldn't deny the beautifully crafted stone maze was a wonderful tribute to the kingdom.

She took a few seconds to breathe, to drown her anxious thoughts before they could be deciphered on her face. Her divided allegiance taunted that the Wolverlons would see immediately past her guise. Should she discover his alliance with Valgard to be true, King Varlas of Olmstone could never know that he had unwittingly invited High Farrow's ward, the ally of Rhyenelle and avenger of Fenstead, right into the heart of his kingdom.

And she would tear it apart from the inside. Just as they had done to hers.

She hadn't been here long, but a sickness had already settled in her gut, a yearning to be home. Her chest clenched every time she thought of it. Because "home" wasn't her conquered lands of ash and blood. It was him. No matter what became of her time here, she would never forget the century she'd spent prior to this that had defined "home" not as any land. She'd come to associate all sense of the word with Nik. And now this was a test of her resilience. A torment in her mind that wouldn't let him go. Not yet.

But it was hard to move on, to focus on what she came for, when her residency in Olmstone had thus far felt like being locked in a stone cage. Everything was different here. She knew no one. The Wolverlons were…protective. Or perhaps *secretive* would be a more appropriate word.

Tauria twisted to the fae guard lingering by the door, plastering on a smile. "Thank you. I shall go to him."

She hoped the guard would leave her be, but he lingered in the doorway as if waiting to escort her. It wasn't a surprise. She was never alone here. Even her rooms were guarded, and news traveled quickly to the prince if she left their confines. Tauria was quick to question it but was sweetly assured the close watch was for her own protection as a foreigner in their land. She couldn't protest.

As she walked the halls lined with purple tapestries she tried not to be intimidated by the dominating sigil of the two-headed wolf, though a low vibration heated her blood: the awakening of her magick. Her idle fingers weaved wisps of wind at her sides—wind that caressed her skin with the reassurance this was not a punishment. Tauria was here by her own will even if she didn't entirely want to be. She had to keep a level head if she was to make it out alive. And an open mind if she was ever to imagine living a full life here. She couldn't forget that should Olmstone prove to be no threat after all, an alliance with the prince was a smart political move for her kingdom. Yet that prospect felt like phantom shackles tightening around her wrists, silencing her magick. Her fists clamped tight.

The Prince of Olmstone stood perfectly dressed in black accented with his kingdom color, his poise elegant as he awaited her, overlooking the court through a tall glass window. His dark blond hair was longer than she remembered from the time they'd spent together in High Farrow, now resting in waves over his shoulders while half-tied back. As his hazel gaze slid to meet hers his smile was warm, if a little forced. Tauria often didn't know how to feel around the prince who switched moods so fast to keep her on edge.

"You look radiant, Tauria," he said by way of greeting.

She offered a kind smile of appreciation, much as she disagreed with the purple hues that now accented her clothing too in place of her homeland greens. Another measure of *protection.* She was quickly coming to realize protection meant control. Her hand slipped into his outstretched palm, and there Tarly planted a tender kiss.

This was the first summons she'd had from the prince since their arrival a week ago, but she'd been immensely grateful for the alone time to rest and reorient herself as her new surroundings daunted her still. Tarly had been pleasant company on their journey from High Farrow, but only because he'd engaged her in little conversation. Tauria didn't press or pester him, her mind wholly occupied, and she cursed the King of High Farrow many times for it. Their last encounter before she'd left had not silenced itself. In fact, it tormented her on repeat so much she exhausted herself the entire journey trying to suppress the desire that could have shifted her scent and been detected by the prince riding beside her.

I want you to come back.

Tauria wondered with an ache in her chest how much Nik had meant those parting words. Or if he knew just how desperately she'd cling to them. His touch hadn't left her. The impression of his lips still ignited her blood and lingered on her skin. What they'd done was bliss in the moment but torture in the aftermath. Being parted before he could fulfill his promise brought about new heights of irritation and unsated need.

Until you do, I'm going to be thinking of all the shameful things I never got the chance to do to you right here.

Nikalias was wicked. Alluringly, infuriatingly wicked and sinful.

Something huffed a breath against her hand, followed by a wet sensation, and Tauria yelped, spinning around. Fear had her backing up all the way until she was caught by a firm grip.

"Relax," Tarly said gently to assure her the large beast wasn't any threat. It didn't help. "Her name is Katori."

A wolf with a brilliant white coat stood mesmerizing before them. Tauria had seen wolves, but there was something ethereal about this one. She was captured by its silver eyes that seemed to shimmer. It wasn't Tarly's words or touch that soothed her terror; it was the serene embrace she felt within the longer she stared at the beast.

"Why do you have a wolf wandering the halls of your castle?" she breathed, transfixed and unable to tear her gaze from it. She didn't move in caution. It could maul her with little effort if she shifted wrong. But the attention it gave her prickled every inch of her skin with *awe.*

"She's a companion," Tarly said casually, stepping away from her, though Tauria wished he wouldn't in her stiff vulnerability.

She watched as he approached the beast without a flicker of hesitation. It shifted its huge head toward him, and his hand smoothed down over its neck. Tauria's muscles began to loosen as she witnessed the exchange and the complete trust that seemed mutual between them. She'd only known of wolves to be wild and aggressive.

"A forewarning would have been appreciated," she muttered.

Tarly twisted his head toward her, a blond lock escaping his hair tie and falling over his face. "Are you afraid, princess?"

The challenge in those words spoke to her defiance. Tauria scowled as she straightened and found the confidence to slowly approach the pair. Tentatively, she reached out a trembling hand, flinching as the beast inched its head forward as if to meet her touch. When her hand met its smooth white coat, Tauria relaxed and marveled at the experience.

"So you have a pet," she said to detract attention from the nerves that would take time to subdue around Katori completely.

Tarly huffed. "She's not a dog." He motioned for her to walk with him, and she eagerly obliged. "Katori comes and goes as she pleases, but I guess you could say she favors me. Have you never heard of the wolves in Olmstone before?"

Tauria wracked her brain. "Most believe they don't show themselves anymore."

"It's true. I haven't seen Katori in a while, actually. She must have sensed the new arrival and come to see if you were worthy." Tarly's tone took on a teasing edge, but it only riddled Tauria with unease.

Sparing a glance over her shoulder confirmed what she felt as the beast followed behind them. But along with Katori trailed three guards, who offered some small comfort that they could intervene if the wolf decided Tauria was in fact *not* worthy.

"How have you have been settling in?"

Tarly's diversion snapped Tauria back to the present, drawing her gaze out the passing windows. "The lands are remarkable," she answered, not wanting to insult him.

"But it is nothing compared to the vibrancy of Fenstead."

Tauria winced sheepishly, but a smile shadowed his face.

"Trust I am not offended. I might even agree with you. Which is why I asked you to join me." The prince's light touch vibrated over her back, and their eyes met. Tauria didn't ignore the odd skip of her pulse. So far, Tarly had given her no reason to distrust him, no indication he harbored malicious intent like his father.

Tauria hadn't seen King Varlas at all since she arrived—something she found highly uncustomary, and which was on her radar to question when the chance arose. Her inquiries would have to be well-crafted and well-timed, perhaps even dim-witted. She would wear whatever mask was necessary as the slightest suspicion could expose her completely.

"I was thinking about Fenstead," Tarly went on. "I'll admit I have only visited your kingdom once before, for your grand Winter Solstice Ball when you invited all courts. Do you remember?"

Of course she did. Yet the spark of memory only brought forth one person. Ignoring the hollowness in her chest, Tauria offered a weak smile with the dip of her head. "I do. There was so much flamboyancy that night—forgive me if I don't recall many details." She had to avert her gaze, hoping he didn't catch her awkwardness at the topic.

Tarly let go of a short laugh. "You mean you don't remember much of me being there." He called out her unspoken meaning. "I don't blame you. I suppose it was the arrogance of the esteemed High Farrow king who exhausted you that night with his pestering."

She didn't miss the hint of slander in his tone. It was no surprise the Olmstone prince wasn't best fond of Nik. And it was no secret the King of High Farrow reserved no warmth for Tarly. Tauria often found it difficult to keep them both subdued in their dislike for each other. But while she was in the Wolf's domain, she had to play a side.

"Yes, Nik can be…persistent."

"I'm surprised he let go of you so easily to be here."

Tauria wrung her clasped hands painfully. She wondered if his careful prodding was a test to gauge if any deeper feelings lingered for Nik. "I'm not his to let go of," she answered tightly.

"As High Farrow's ward, one might disagree."

"My position in Nik's court was of my will. He knew that."

"Hmm." Tarly's face flexed, so subtle she might have missed it. "I don't believe that was Orlon's view."

"Nik is not his father."

"Nor am I mine." Tarly halted their walk, and Tauria turned to him. Conflict and assessment swirled in his irises. She stood firm, determined not to give any outward indication of her nerves. "I hope you know my father's path of vengeance is not my own. I had my mother taken from me that day in Fenher, but I'm not such a fool to go making an enemy out of those who could help to take down the real evil in all this. The ones who truly killed her."

Tauria shifted her gaze to the guards, curious to see if any of them picked up on the subtle gibe at their king. It was a relief to discover Tarly had seen the madness in his father's brash plan last winter. She swallowed hard, meeting the determination on the prince's face, and for a second she pitied him. Beneath his crown, Tarly was just a fae. One who didn't just lose his mother that day, but in a lot of ways, his father too. To mourn the living was an unfathomable burden to shoulder.

"I know you are not your father, Tarly. It is why I am here."

Tarly's chiseled features softened, and it relaxed her tense shoulders that the dark filter over his eyes seemed to ease. "We're here," he said, his gaze wandering out through the glass doors.

Tauria followed his line of sight, her breath catching. Not far beyond the doors she spotted the single most welcoming color that brightened her mood. Green. It wasn't much, but she spied a beautiful wooden pavilion surrounded by beds of overgrown flowers. She took a step toward the doors but was intercepted by a guard. She couldn't hide her frown of annoyance.

"The guards always go first," Tarly explained, his hand light on her lower back. "Anywhere you go, you allow them to go first. It is for your own protection."

"From what?"

Tarly's eyes flared at her question. "It will take time for your presence to be known and accepted here. We have been over this."

She clenched her teeth, using all her will not to protest the ridiculousness of needing such protection within the castle. They stared off, and when she read his silent warning not to push the matter Tauria conceded with a stiff nod. It wasn't worth arguing over, and as her sight returned to the neglected greenery, she didn't even care anymore.

The guard exited first, scanning their surroundings as she followed behind him. Against Tarly's wishes, she couldn't help herself, and her steps quickened to make it over to the pavilion before anyone else. He said nothing, and Tauria couldn't gauge his reaction because she was already gone, swept away on memories of her homeland as she observed the space. The wood was in need of repair and the flowers needed tending to, but she could already picture how joyous the space would become with the right care and attention.

"My mother loved to come here," Tarly admitted.

Tauria found him gazing over the area with the ghost of treasured memories. When she looked at him, Tarly let his guard slip just enough to show rare vulnerability. It was gone the moment he remembered her presence. What she had come to gather about him was that he was a master of detachment. But under the exterior of a brooding prince, there was a person she could come to understand. They had both lost parents, and Tauria found herself relating to Tarly in the most desolate way. Everyone dealt with grief differently. She was willing to bide her time with one who seemed so accustomed to harboring his emotions within.

"It's beautiful," Tauria breathed as her fingers reached out to a nearby sagging chrysanthemum.

Tarly huffed. "It used to be. No one comes out here anymore. I thought you might like to—" He stopped himself as if kindness was a momentary lapse of his mastered steel composure.

Tauria studied the war flexing his expression. It was one she'd seen before, but on a different prince. In that moment, the thought Tarly and Nik could have more in common than either of them cared to admit crossed her mind.

"I'd love to," she answered, knowing what he wanted to say. Strangely, it pained her to see the quick flash of relief on his face. "I'd love to spend time helping restore this place. It's just what I need. Thank you." Her gratitude was genuine, and slowly, the suffocation that had been closing in since she arrived started to ease with the new purpose, a distraction from her hollow chest.

"Then consider this my gift. You're free to come here and work on the garden as you wish. I'll see to it that you're equipped with the proper materials."

In the look they shared, Tauria believed she glimpsed a crack in his guard. With time, she could learn what melted the ice coating the prince's heart from his tragic past. She could learn to love the qualities she might not always agree with but may come to understand, maybe even relate to. And they would find a way to bloom happy prospects in the midst of desolate memories.

Tauria didn't believe she had a full heart to give anymore, but she could learn to use the pieces that remained and trust that the prince wouldn't shatter what was left.

CHAPTER 3

Nikalias

King Nikalias Silvergriff knew only one release from the cage of his tormenting mind: the swinging of a blade. The resentment in his bones and the hollow feeling in his chest weren't so unrelenting when he released every thought to clashing blades and the awareness of his opposition. It was never a lone guard he fought—he needed more. Perilous odds that gave him no option but to use every last ounce of focus to keep up.

Four surrounded him now, under strict orders not to hesitate in any way. He couldn't be sure how much time had passed when the room was a blur with movement that didn't stop, the sound of steps and steel the only harmony he tuned into in his mind. Nik ducked low, pivoting around the attack of one guard and swiftly kicking his feet out from under him. He fell with a cry before Nik pinned him in a killing strike. Then he twisted, landing a kick to the chest of one who was seconds away from claiming his victory. It sent the guard sprawling, but there was no time for pause or contemplation when the other two were still in play.

He'd come down to the training hall almost every evening. After a day of headache-inducing meetings or mind-numbing catch-ups with various nobles, Nik knew very little entertainment outside this room. Yet it wasn't court matters that drove him down here even against the protests of his body.

It was her.

The thought of Tauria in the arms of another. The danger she could be in knowing he'd willingly sent her there. But worst of all, Nik found crushing resentment in the thought she could be *happy*.

He'd barely lasted a week before he first attempted to Nightwalk to her, if only to be sure she was safe. Yet he was immediately met with a block similar to those he'd taught her to protect herself with using his invasive ability. It was a crushing notion to think she'd set it up to spare him from witnessing her joy in the new kingdom. More specifically, with Tarly Wolverlon.

The next guard's face went blank with ghostly fear, yet Nik couldn't apologize for his pent-up anger while such taunting thoughts screamed to be freed. He was beyond registering what movements he made to fell the guard in seconds. He should want her to be happy. He did. Yet he *needed* to see her, just once. He'd resorted to sending letters, yet none had been replied to so far, and he feared they were being intercepted, or maybe it was just his pitiful desperation for her not to be ignoring him.

"I surrender, Your Majesty," the final guard panted when Nik brought him to his knees.

"Yes," the guard at his back rasped, and Nik found him rolling over in sprawled-out defeat. "Me too."

Reeling back from the quick battle, Nik was slick with sweat, his teeth clenched and breaths painful, but his rage was far from quelled. He glanced around the room, noting all the guards were equal in their submission. Their groans and protests filled the space, and he had to refrain from snapping in irritation at their weakness. It was unfair to push them so hard, but he couldn't help it. Couldn't sate the desperate need to find some distraction for as long as he could. Every time he was forced to retreat to his rooms and the silence took residence, Nik risked shattering from within.

He paced, reluctant to leave the training hall, once the guards had left. His mind was still reeling. Calculating.

"I think you outshine your father in combat skill."

It took everything in Nik not to let go of his groan at the voice that joined him. His eyes met with Zarrius's as he strolled arrogantly into the hall. Nik halted, propping his sword in front of him to stare down at the lord.

"My father was always better suited to the council room." It was a conscious effort to be civil to the one he wanted nothing more than to run through with his blade. Nik's hands tightened over the Griffin pommel of the Farrow Sword.

Zarrius chuckled lightly. "I think we can find ourselves in agreement there."

It was often Nik wondered if Zarrius had equally dark thoughts about him. His dislike for Nik was expertly hidden behind a courtly pretense. But the cracks weren't hard to detect.

"What brings you down here, Zarrius?"

The lord halted below the training platform. His permanent conceited smile always ground on Nik's nerves. "There are some who have expressed concern for you, Your Majesty."

Nik quirked a brow. It wasn't what he was expecting.

"While you have been present in meetings, your attention is not always there. You waste your time down here training harder than even our top war generals."

"What I do with my time is of no one's concern." Nik used a tone of warning.

"As your counsel, I must disagree." Zarrius folded his hands behind him, looking Nik straight in the eye. It wasn't a simple stance; this was a firm challenge. "Your actions impact us all, and since the princess left, there are many who believe your mind has not been centered on the good of High Farrow."

Nik turned stiff to stifle his trembling as he sheathed his sword. He didn't break eye contact with Zarrius as his anger boiled to a reckless force, but Nik breathed consciously. He took deliberately slow steps to close the distance between them, stepping down from the training platform and bringing them face-to-face. Zarrius's throat bobbed, the only faint giveaway he wasn't entirely unthreatened by the king, though his expression firmed. "I don't know what you're implying," he ground out.

"Nothing at all," Zarrius sang.

Nik's eyes narrowed in suspicion.

"I simply come to you in absolute privacy and confidence should there be anything weighing on your mind. I was your father's personal counsel after all."

Yes, as Zarrius liked to remind Nik so often it was insufferable. His jaw clenched tighter. "Then allow me to assure you nothing weighs on my mind."

"Hmm." The tension rose as if they both knew the other was refraining from speaking their truth. "I would just hate to watch this prospective alliance between three courts become threatened should hollow rumors spread."

"What might these rumors suggest?"

Zarrius shrugged. "Who knows what could be dragged up and misconstrued from one's past in bored courtrooms?"

Nik saw no other way to find peace from the lord's circling than to assure him they were close allies in internal politics. "I thought our plans aligned. Yet now you doubt me?"

The lord's eyes flexed, assessing if Nik was being true to him while he came down from his irritation enough to find sense. Zarrius was a game for Nik to master, biding his time while he kept his true feelings buried where no one could reach. He saw Tauria as nothing more than a marker for political gain. Yet she was the most powerful player on the board. A queen under the guise of a pawn.

Zarrius seemed conflicted about whether to test Nik's patience further or accept he was on his side…for now. In the easing of his hard gaze, Nik knew the storm was passing once again. "Of course. You'll understand I only echo the concerns of your nobles, as we have not yet heard a word about how negotiations are progressing with our ward in Olmstone."

"They would not have been long in Olmstone. I expect their initiation letter to come within the week." At least, Nik hoped Tarly would relieve his anticipation with not only information about the potential alliance, but any word on Tauria's safety to ease his misery until he could get through to her. "Trust me when I say I have matters in hand. When I have reason to inform you of anything other than mindless initiation letters, you will be the first person I send for."

It seemed to satisfy the lord, whose mouth curled in cruel triumph. The sight of his satisfaction stirred Nik's violent thoughts. But all that mattered right now was keeping him silent until Nik learned of Olmstone's true intentions. He had to believe Tauria was safe, and that she wouldn't abandon High Farrow to pursue her own prospects without their consideration.

That she wouldn't abandon *him.*

CHAPTER 4

Tauria

Feeling a new sense of purpose and direction, Tauria made her way eagerly to the small pavilion garden the day after her meeting with Tarly. After he showed her the wonderful refuge, she'd reluctantly allowed him to tear her away for a tour of the sculpted grounds instead. But she'd been itching to go back ever since, feeling her first dose of true excitement to begin work on restoring its beauty. Her ties to nature rejoiced from within, her magick already coating a delightful hum over her skin. It would take time, as the Florakinetic talent she'd inherited from her mother was only a kernel compared to her wind manipulation.

Tauria was steps away from the door, but as her hand raised to open it, once again her path was intercepted by a tall form. Her teeth ground as she stared up at the guard, but her scowl was quick to soften when she saw his faint wince.

"You know, I wouldn't tell if we relaxed the ridiculous protection measures. Just between you and me?" She knew it was a long shot.

The guard's sympathetic look reduced her to feeling like a child under surveillance, caught one too many times disobeying strict rules. "It would be far more than my job on the line, Your Majesty." He pulled down on the handle and stepped out, surveying the area that was enclosed by a tall wall overrun with untamed vines.

Tauria followed him out, moved by his words. "What did you call me?"

The guard twisted back to her, confusion pinching his brow. "Am I mistaken in calling you Your Majesty? I did not mean to offend—"

"No, not at all." She cut him off quickly. Her smile stretched to a grin that she felt with a warmth in her chest. No one here so far had addressed her by her Fenstead title, and slowly, Tauria was starting to believe perhaps she wasn't deemed worthy of ruling, always referred to as an idle princess. Even in High Farrow she'd grown accustomed to being their ward. She'd heard the name often enough that she sometimes didn't feel any importance at all, simply another member of court with a pretty standing. Nik had become king, and still she couldn't stop feeling as if she'd succumbed to living in the shadows of who she was supposed to be. His equal. There were times when he'd tried to give her that standing—in her heart she knew this—but it wasn't enough. It was in that moment she acknowledged it wouldn't ever be, because what she needed was not to be granted a voice or power; she had to take those things for herself. While her distance from Nik was painful, Tauria knew this was her opportunity to rise to her name, stand for herself, and take back the control she had lost.

"What is your name?" she asked the guard, which clearly took him by surprise. He was handsome, with blond hair and defined features, but despite his size and station, he seemed timid in the way he avoided her eye.

"Lennox, Your Majesty."

"Let's make a deal, Lennox." She smirked at his perplexed look as she strolled over the crooked stone slabs toward the pavilion. "Out here, no titles, no formalities. Just Tauria and Lennox."

The first hint of a smile cracked on his cheeks, but an edge of wariness remained as he scanned the area. Aside from the glass doors, they were surrounded only by the solid stone circumference of the small garden. Above was a gloriously clear summer sky. The humidity in Olmstone was thicker, and hardly any clouds had broken up the blaring sun all day, yet the attire they'd given her to *fit in* was stiff with corset bones and straight lines. Beautiful but suffocating in this weather.

Lennox seemed reluctant to agree, but he gave a short nod. It was odd to see one so wary of the matter of title and formality, and his reaction instilled a curiosity in Tauria about the Wolverlons' strict upholding of archaic traditions. Her personal guard in Fenstead was a close friend she'd grown up with, assigned by her father as his most trusted general in training. She knew he would have no problem breaking the rules in private. But the ache of memory was a wound she'd long since accepted would never fully heal, and Tauria couldn't expect the same of the guards here in Olmstone.

She faced the neglected greenery. Bracing her hands on her hips, she studied all she could, strategizing on where to begin. Tauria strode right up to the overgrown weeds battling the wisteria.

"Perhaps we should get you some—"

Tauria didn't hesitate to reach for them, ripping them from their roots.

"—gloves," Lennox finished quietly.

She observed the sad flowers that were too wilted to be saved. "No need," she answered, tossing them aside. Whatever she plucked wouldn't be wasted. With her ability, she'd be able to salvage many of the sad blooms; breathe new life into them to be planted afresh. Others could be used for certain herbs and remedies.

This neglected space was desolate and dying on first glance, yet no one knew the infinite wonders and beauty that lay beneath its tragic guise. Tauria was filled with giddy hope and excitement to bring it back to its full glory and make it a beauty people would flock to rather than avoid.

Hours could have passed while she kneeled over the soil, tirelessly digging her way through a small patch overrun with weeds. She had to root them all out or they'd quickly destroy anything new she tried to bloom above them. At some point, Lennox gave her a small trowel, likely fetched by another guard as she was never left alone. She alternated between the tool and her bare hands, enjoying immensely the feel of the cold soil between her fingers. Several times, she fought the prickling in her eyes when the simple act of gardening brought forth treasured memories of her mother. Her Florakinetic ability had been far stronger. Everything Tauria knew, her infinite knowledge of nature, came straight from her mother's heart.

Tauria's knees became so numb she didn't feel the dampness where the earth had soaked through her purple gown. She didn't care for the mess she'd made of herself and made a note to wear more suitable attire next time. Once satisfied with her work, she raised a palm over the soil. Her magick awakened like sand blowing under her skin right to her fingertips. She watched in awe of her own ability as a beautiful bellflower emerged vibrant from the dull soil. Tauria smiled at her first new bloom.

"That's pretty."

The timid voice was quiet, but Tauria whirled with surprise, having spent so long in her own silent thought. Upon spying the small invading form, she was quick to recognize the intruder.

"It's Opal, isn't it?" Tauria had met the young princess before, only once, during the kings' meetings in High Farrow. Her bouncing honey-blonde locks were as stunning as the large blue eyes that complemented her lilac gown.

Opal nodded shyly, and Tauria cast her gaze to Lennox, who shifted uncomfortably as if he'd never been around a child before. She bit back her chuckle at his unease.

"Would you like to join me?" In an attempt to ease the young fae's hesitation, Tauria extended her trowel in offering.

Slowly, a smile split Opal's round cheeks, creating cute dimples on either side. She tentatively shuffled over, accepting the tool, and Tauria saw it as their first treaty exchange.

"How do you make them grow?" Opal asked quietly, her eyes sparkling with wonder.

Tauria's face brightened at her enthusiasm, and she patted the ground next to her. "Come closer—I'll show you."

"I'm not supposed to get dirty. Mother would be mad."

Tauria's smile was partly a wince as she glimpsed the girl's concern. "I won't tell if you don't."

Opal's brightness returned, and she eagerly shuffled over before lowering down next to Tauria and leaning in close. Tauria bloomed several more flowers in the patch she'd cleared. With her new assistant to offer an opinion on colors and arrangements, the bed began to come together more beautifully than Tauria might have achieved on her own.

The afternoon was stolen completely by Opal's keen interest, and Tauria became truly swept away, losing herself in the garden. It had been a long time since she'd last felt so connected to who she was, and for a moment she thought of Tarly, of the kindness he'd extended in granting her free rein over this place, and she planned to let him know just how much it meant to her. Getting to bond with his sister was an unexpected but welcome surprise. She imagined they could spend endless days out here together, the princess her eager apprentice.

"There you are!" A new voice joined them outside, urgency coating the words. In her fine wears, the fae who flustered over the wonky stone path toward them had to be a high lady of the court.

"I'm in trouble." Opal's quiet voice was laced with fear.

"I've been looking for you everywhere. We've talked about this!" When she came to a stop before them, the fae's tone was scolding, but her face only bore concern as she stared down at Opal, who shuffled closer to Tauria.

Tauria rose, wincing at the ache in her knees that was a sure sign she'd been kneeling there for quite some time. "She's been safe with me," she assured the fae with a sweet smile. She could almost feel Opal's relief where she hovered close by.

The fae met eyes with Tauria, her tan skin blanching a shade. "Forgive me, Your Highness." She bowed, still catching her breath. "I am Princess Opal's mentor. She has been warned against leaving my side. I turned for two minutes, and she had disappeared." She targeted her attention on the sheepish young fae.

Tauria's hand went around Opal's shoulders in assurance. "No harm was done. I think we're finished here for the day." She and the young princess exchanged smiles.

The fae gasped, trailing her attention down the length of Opal's dress. "Goodness! We must get you changed before your mother or father catches you in that ruin of a gown." Her arm cast out to usher the princess to follow.

Tauria gave a nod when Opal looked up at her as if seeking permission. "I hope you can join me again," she said with a hint of question.

"She's not allowed to be out here. If her father hears of this—"

"What is your name?" Tauria interjected. It was odd to watch the fae act so concerned over something so trivial. More uneasy questions about the king and queen's strict views surfaced in Tauria's mind.

The fae looked taken aback. "Serena, Your Highness."

"Tauria, please," she insisted, wanting nothing more than to feel welcomed in friendship, not feared by title.

Serena flashed her gaze to Lennox, who tried and failed to look as if he wasn't paying attention, observing the wall instead. The fae loosened her posture, her disconcerted expression easing off. "I didn't mean to sound so harsh and—"

"Like a killjoy?"

Serena blinked, stunned, just for a second before she huffed a laugh, and Tauria was soon joining in.

"You're welcome to join us out here too. This place could use all the help it can get."

Serena glanced at the small garden, not with any inkling of enthusiasm. "We would have to speak with His Majesty."

"Leave it to me." Tauria perked up, dusting off her gown, which was beyond salvation from the muddy stains. "I'll be here tomorrow afternoon. I look forward to seeing you both again."

Serena's nod was stiff, and she looked at Tauria as if she were a foreign plant among the overgrowth. Something twisted in her chest at how oddly her words had been received, as if her kindness wasn't to be expected. She couldn't be sure if it was because of their differing customs; how nobility was regarded in the Kingdom of the Wolf. That, she was still learning for herself.

Serena and Opal left, chatting quietly, and Tauria caught mumbles of reprimand while the princess picked at her ruined gown. Tauria cringed with guilt. She should be the one getting lectured for coaxing Opal to join her. She let out a long sigh as she wiped her clammy brow with the back of her hand and looked down on her work for the day. Her joy burst all over again. It was a small, vibrant bed, but it invited the vision of potential. The distraction of this garden was bliss and exactly what she needed.

"It's getting late, Your Majesty. I should escort you back to your rooms." Lennox's tone was laced with apology.

Tauria tried to answer pleasantly as the guard seemed to know he was to lead her to her most dreaded confinement. "Remember our deal, Lennox," she teased, strolling toward the glass doors with him in tow.

He released a breathy chuckle. "My apologies, Tauria."

As they neared her rooms down the hall, it was a surprise to find Tarly appear around the corner headed directly for them. From a distance, Tauria caught him scan her from head to toe, and the irritation that steeled his face cooled her heated skin. They stopped where their paths intersected.

"What in the damn Nether have you been up to?" he hushed out, not meeting her eye but looking over her muddy state with disapproval.

While Tauria was inwardly stunned by his reaction, she tried to keep a lighthearted mood. "It's just a little dirt. I've been tending to the garden," she brushed off coolly. She was intending to thank him for guiding her to the space that had quickly become a treasure, yet it didn't seem appropriate in this moment with so much ire on his face.

Tarly glanced behind him. No one was around. His hand encased her arm as he began to walk, taking her with him.

"Tarly." Tauria halted abruptly with a flash of anger and tore her arm from his grasp. "What do you think you're doing?"

It was the wrong thing to say. The quick flash of anger in the prince's hazel eyes made her balk, almost yielding a step back. Yet their attention was grabbed by a nearby presence.

Tauria's bewildered looked snapped to Lennox, who carefully closed in beside her. Tarly targeted him with that hard gaze. For a tense couple of seconds, Tauria couldn't be sure what the prince was capable of. Then it winked out, his wrath seeming to defuse so fast all she could do was watch with a fluctuating pulse.

"Sorry," he said though a breath. In the smoothing of his expression, his apology spoke true. Yet she still couldn't comprehend the moment at all. She simply nodded, and he seemed to accept this as her understanding. "It's just not proper for someone of your standing to be seen trailing the castle looking like the stable help."

Tauria winced, self-consciously picking at the dirt wedged under her fingernails and the horrid brown stains all over her gown. She couldn't help but connect Tarly's reaction with Serena's fear of the king or queen finding their daughter in the same state of ruin, but she chose to reserve judgment on his lapse of kindness until she could find out more. She hoped his response was only a warning for how his father could react. But then there was Keira, the queen, whom she had met only briefly in High Farrow, but who in that time had seemed to be quiet and polite, not someone to be feared. Though as a high member of court her whole life, Tauria had both seen and experienced the act of molding oneself to appeal to different expectations.

Tarly gave an exasperated sigh. "I'll assign you a handmaiden to help you bathe and dress." His smile seemed forced, but she returned it all the same. "I would like you to accompany me for dinner in the great hall."

Grateful for the shift of conversation, she nodded. "I would love to." A creeping sense of unease coated her body, and she was eager to retreat. Stepping around Tarly, she barely made it to the corner when his voice carried through the hall to halt her once more.

"In private, you may call me what you want. But in company, respect me by title, Princess."

The words felt like a warning. Tauria didn't hear them as a condition the prince was establishing of his own accord, but rather as a custom of the Olmstone court she'd naïvely overlooked. Despite Tarly's cold tone, she tried not to take his words as an insult. If his father opposed their desire to be casual in public, Tauria supposed she should be grateful the prince had offered to abandon the formality in private. Though the notion of alone time with him coiled in her stomach, and she couldn't be sure if it was through dread or excitement.

CHAPTER 5

Nikalias

SILENCE. STILLNESS. NIK craved both so badly he counted his hasty steps to his private council chamber, though neither seemed eager to greet him as he turned the next corner and met Zarrius instead. Nik suppressed his groan, knowing he couldn't possibly pass the lord with a simple curt acknowledgment. Especially when he was with company.

"Your Majesty, I'm glad we ran into you," Zarrius sang.

Nik doubted it was by coincidence. Coming to a halt where their paths intersected, he plastered on a warm smile, more for the company as his eyes slid to the elegant fae female. Her pine-green eyes were large, blinking prettily with what felt like allurement. She was beautiful, he supposed, with perfectly styled auburn hair, and clearly of nobility.

Zarrius noticed Nik's attention on her, and glee passed briefly over the lord's features. "Allow me to introduce Lady Samara Calltegan."

She bowed respectfully, but her flirtatious gaze wasn't subtle, nor did it leave him for a second. Her family name rang distantly familiar in Nik's mind, and his brow pinched as he thought it over.

"Daughter of Lord Gerat Calltegan, who owns and operates key high trading throughout High Farrow," Zarrius went on when Nik's puzzled look must have voiced his scrambled thoughts. He might have felt sheepish for having to be schooled on one of his own nobles, but truthfully, Nik had very little energy to care.

"Pleasure to meet you," he offered out of nothing more than courtly politeness. "You'll both have to excuse me. I have—"

"I was rather hoping to catch a moment with you."

Nik's eyes flared at the interruption, and he hoped the lord read his warning as he pinned him with a look, which Samara seemed to catch onto by her nervous shift in stance. Nik couldn't feel bad for her; this was his role, and as king he couldn't stand to be talked over by his own lords. Yet it were as if Zarrius wore the crown with his unwavering, arrogant poise. "I'll spare a moment, but that is all," Nik said icily.

Zarrius turned to Samara. "I'm sure you two will have better time to become acquainted. If you'll excuse us for now, my dear."

Samara smiled sweetly with a nod at Zarrius, taking a step to pass by Nik, but she halted instead, staring up at him through long lashes. Nik couldn't deny there was something to be worshipped within such a masterful look of seduction. His younger self would have fallen for it completely. Until her. Unknowingly, Tauria had captured him the first day they met and made the prospect of any other seem almost *sad* in comparison to the thrill and wild desire the princess invoked. Only when the world-shattering prophesy forbade all happiness with Tauria did Nik try to feel again, but it was futile. He led ladies to bed and always ended on false promises when they stayed for company and nothing more. Those nights achieved what he needed them to: they gave Tauria something to resent him for. They kept her at a safe distance from the one person fated to be her destiny and her doom.

"I hope to see you again soon, Your Majesty." Even Samara's voice was tempting, quiet and enchanting.

Nik felt nothing, but he nodded all the same. The curl of her mouth was a promise as she passed. He didn't give it a second thought before he was storming once again for the destination that would allow him a moment of solitude. Yet every step of the lord following behind him stiffened Nik's tense shoulders. He didn't care for Zarrius's presence when he made straight for the ornate chair, slumping into it, no mind for royal decorum.

At his silence once the door had shut, Nik all but snapped, "Your moment is expiring fast, Zarrius." Being in the lord's company often required some strategy, using the right amount of ruthlessness to match but not overpower. The right amount of agreement to tide Zarrius over but not give him the upper hand. The only way to win was to keep the lord on his side. As opposition, Zarrius could ruin everything.

"She is a fine lady," Zarrius commented, not meeting Nik's eye as he paced the room instead. "Of noble name, with a father who has essential ties throughout the kingdom, one of the wealthiest landowners in High Farrow."

Nik leaned back in his chair, his elbow propped on the arm, to press his fingers to his temple. "She is of high birth indeed." He couldn't be sure where the lord was headed with his praise of Samara, but guessing he spoke fondly out of his own interest in her, Nik was eager for Zarrius's rambling adulation to be over with so he could dismiss him.

"Exquisitely beautiful too. Lady Samara is also well-loved by many in court. She is active in affairs. She has been brought up to one day entertain the prospect of an advantageous alliance."

Nik almost breathed in relief, concluding, "Do you wish for my blessing to wed her, Zarrius?"

The lord halted his pacing, and when his eyes locked on Nik's he lost all sense of calm from thinking this was all the lord wished to pester him with. It was in the slow curl of Zarrius's mouth, a cunning gleam before he delivered what he thought to be his latest stroke of brilliance.

"Not I, Your Majesty."

Nik knew the implication then, and it took great will not to react with reckless anger. He got to his feet, not giving Zarrius the satisfaction of seeing it made him blaze with defiance. The prospect of marriage was not something he wanted to entertain anytime soon. Maybe never at all. He couldn't stand the thought of condemning another to such a miserable existence by his cold side. But more so, he couldn't fathom the pain of imagining anyone by his side except the one he could never have.

"I don't remember mentioning I was looking for a bride, nor do I find it appropriate that you took it upon yourself to put forth a candidate."

"With all due respect—"

"It is not *respect* to go behind my back and introduce me to someone I have no interest in."

"Because she is not Tauria Stagknight."

Nik's fury flashed. His fists balled on top of the table. "Watch what you say, Zarrius."

The lord's look was a challenge. "You are not fooling anyone, Nikalias. I stand here as your counsel, not your opposition."

Zarrius had a point. As much as it physically pained Nik to acknowledge.

"If you would only keep an open mind, you'll find what I pose stands to benefit you and this kingdom greatly. The other lords are restless. There has been no news about negotiations in Olmstone, and you have not been as present as you should be. In meetings it is as if you are not there. Around court you are barely seen. The nobles are not fools, and it has been no quiet gossip that your absence has increased since the princess's departure."

The weight of Nik's crown had never bore down so heavily as it did right then. As a prince, his detachment hadn't gone detected when all that mattered were his father's movements. Nik had learned to live in his father's shadow and was content to succumb to his torment there. Yet now the light had dispersed his cover, and in the sudden spotlight, he didn't know what to do. How to act. Where to go. It felt as if everything he did, felt, even *thought*, was tracked and analyzed.

He had been a damn pining fool. And he was not only risking himself, but Tauria too.

Nik straightened confidently, leveling with the lord who seemed to brace for conflict. But that wasn't the strategy at play here. "Perhaps you're right," he said. It seemed to take the lord by pleasant surprise, and like always, as Nik folded his hands behind his back, it was in an attempt to tamp his itch to swing at him. "I've grown up near half my existence with Tauria nearby, and we are close. I'll admit it has been an adjustment to have her gone, but I can assure you I only worry about her settling into a new kingdom all over again."

"As do we all. But I must warn you of the speculation surrounding you and the Fenstead princess."

"You'll understand my concern for her safety."

"As I hope you will understand my concern to protect both of your reputations."

"What are you implying?"

"Nothing at all. But as your lead counsel, I must make you aware of anything that could harm your prospects. It is no secret the two of you were close. Perhaps gossip might suggest…*too* close."

Nik had to focus his breathing. Not out of nerves, but a rising wrath.

"I don't think the Olmstone prince would be so eager to bind his hand to a sullied—"

Nik's hand slammed to the table before he could register the impulsive trigger. Zarrius's eyes flashed to that hand as if it were the blaring answer to his speculation. Nik didn't even give him the chance to speak.

"I will not stand by and listen to you speak of her so lowly. I don't need to convince you or the court, or a damned soul, what was or wasn't between Tauria and me. I'll only say this once, and with perfect clarity: whether she is here or there, no matter who she marries, Tauria

Stagknight will remain under my protection. Her name and her body. Need I remind you and the whole *damned* court that she is still High Farrow's ward, and to spread gossip about her is declared treason?"

To Nik's satisfaction, the lord's throat shifted with nerves. But it wouldn't matter what Nik said. Zarrius was sly and unrelenting in the plans he harbored for personal gain.

"Your protection of her is admirable. Yet it will take more convincing than words to silence these rumors."

Nik was backed into a corner, and the lord knew it—had come to him already with the solution in Samara, a fine candidate for his hand. Yet the idea of entertaining the notion even for a moment twisted in Nik's stomach like soul-deep betrayal. Everything Zarrius proposed seemed in his and High Farrow's best interests, yet Nik couldn't trust him. He couldn't shake the feeling there was always some underlying motive even if he couldn't immediately see it. Right now, he had no choice but to admit defeat.

"You believe my courting Lady Samara will?"

"I do."

Nik gave the lord what he wanted, hating that it was a natural solution. Zarrius wouldn't stop pushing. Yielding to him would give him a false sense of triumph, letting him believe Nik trusted in his counsel enough to heed it.

"She is a highly suitable match. Samara Calltegan would make an admirable queen to the people."

Nik was glad for the table in front of him to lean on for stability. He desired solitude before. Now, he needed it more than anything before his guise came apart completely in the wrong company.

"Thank you, Zarrius." The words burned with how wrong they were. Because the lord took them as Nik knew he would. Agreement. Victory was a suffocating, tangible force that rippled from Zarrius as he added, "I will seek out the Lady Samara at my own discretion."

Zarrius nodded, though it seemed there was no limit to how deep he was willing to sink the blade. "It would be best if you two were seen to be courting."

Nik's heart sank further as he nodded. He had to do this for her. For Tauria. He couldn't risk her reputation being shaken in Olmstone by his own pitiful pining. "I will make sure our appearances are public. But Zarrius, this is by no means my full agreement to what you impose. Samara is a fine lady, but I will not wed anyone solely out of status. I will make my own judgments on who I choose to rule by my side. My decision will be final whenever I choose who will reign over High Farrow."

That insufferable cunning smile came to life. To Zarrius, this was a compromise. To Nik, it was bought time.

When the lord left, Nik only had silence for company as he welcomed his reeling thoughts. At the prospect of this ruse, pretending he sought out a marriage, he couldn't deny there was one person who flashed through his mind. Faythe would make an excellent and willing participant in the game if she were instated as Rhyenelle's heir. Yet he couldn't bring himself to pose the idea out of guilt for the conflict it would stir with Reylan Arrowood. The possessive air Nik had never seen before on the general where Faythe was concerned… Nik kept his observations to himself.

No, he couldn't send word to Rhyenelle with that proposal even as a pretense. He had no other choice but to entertain Zarrius's plan, and he only prayed his heart would learn to tolerate the presence of another who would always feel…*wrong.*

CHAPTER 6

Tauria

TAURIA TUGGED AT the thick purple corset that left little room for movement or even a deep intake of breath. As she winced at herself in the mirror, her handmaiden looked apologetic, helping to secure every torturous ribbon and stiff layer.

"I think the Wolverlons are taking the stone theme of their kingdom too literally," Tauria mumbled under her breath, wheezing with the next tug of strings.

For the first time since the timid human had arrived to help her dress, a hint of a smile danced on the handmaiden's delicate face. But it was quickly suppressed, making Tauria's own mood deteriorate. Faythe would have laughed and added her own lighthearted wit. Marlowe would have come out with something clever, perhaps an insightful tangent into Olmstone's traditions and wears, which she'd absorbed from some obscure book. Tauria was further saddened at the thought of her friends' carefree company she often pined after. She couldn't afford such weak thoughts. Her personal relations would always come second to the good of her country. And it was for Fenstead she would wear her mask of resilience and not allow it to waver in front of the wolf.

Preparing for dinner with Tarly, Tauria tunneled into thoughts of her approach. It was time to put into motion why she was really here. She needed to discover the Wolverlons' intentions, their secrets, before she entertained the prospect of selling her hand to the enemy.

Once she was presentable, drowned in Olmstone purple and clean of the glorious earth that had coated her golden-brown skin from her afternoon in the garden, Tauria sighed at her reflection. Who she looked at was a hardened queen. Her confident hazel eyes didn't betray the sad soul within. Her heart, which thumped to a fractured beat, she didn't think would ever be whole. This was who she was now. Who she had to be.

Tilting her chin high, the Queen of Fenstead left to dine with the wolf.

In the grand hall two figures awaited, already seated around an impressive spread of food and wine. Tauria kept the surprise from her expression as she locked eyes with King Varlas at the head of the table, answering his welcoming smile instead. Both he and the prince stood as she approached, the click of her shoes the only sound resonating through the large room.

"Princess," Varlas drawled, extending a palm to her. He gave her hand a gentle squeeze, not letting her go as they both lowered to sit. "It's so good to see you, Tauria. I must apologize for my absence since your arrival."

Tauria nodded, eyes shifting to Tarly, who displayed very little emotion as he observed them. Her spine locked with the echoes of tension from their rocky encounter earlier. "I'm sure you have good reason, Your Majesty," she answered carefully. Words would be her weapon, if only she could craft them carefully enough that the king might unwittingly divulge something of use.

Varlas slid his hand from hers, reclining back in his grand seat after he reached over to pluck a grape. "Matters of the kingdom is all. I'm sure the day is soon to come when you will understand such responsibilities." The king's gaze flashed to Tarly.

While Tauria sat neutral and poised, beneath the table her fingernails clawed into the wooden arm of her chair. His meaning was so subtle in that look perhaps he didn't expect her to pick up on it: that her hand to Tarly had already been sold. She spoke coolly. "After the near conflicts in the ally kingdoms, I imagine tensions must need to be eased within Olmstone."

Tarly's eyes were daggers, but she didn't meet them. Instead she kept her attention on Varlas, looking for any sign that would betray his words. His pause was contemplative.

"You would be right. My people are unsettled and angry. They don't all agree with our action to surrender."

"The peace treaty is not a surrender; it protects us all against the real enemy. Surely your people must see that it keeps them safe."

Varlas's stare narrowed a fraction as though he were gauging if her words could be taken as a true monarch's and not as the ramblings of an idle princess. Tauria kept her expression neutral. To her relief, Varlas offered a soft smile, reaching for his goblet.

"In time they will. You were not present at the meetings that took place in High Farrow. The fact remains Rhyenelle claims jurisdiction in lands that rightfully belong to Olmstone. The territory dispute has long remained unresolved, and there is not enough land for my people. The towns and cities are overcrowded. We cannot grow food. My people have every right to feel animosity toward our *allies* who have taken land through greed alone."

Tauria didn't just listen; she dissected. The tone Varlas spoke with was personal—too personal. She couldn't help but wonder if his people had truly anything to do with the feelings of anger and resentment that underpinned his speech. "I hope I get the chance to visit the city and perhaps some of the neighboring towns too. We are all allies after all. I am confident negotiations for trade would be heard by High Farrow and Rhyenelle if brought to them." Tauria reached for her cup, her eyes landing on the prince across from her to gauge his reaction. To her surprise, Tarly watched her with what she dared to believe was a hint of agreement.

Yet it didn't seem Varlas was so easy to sway. The king scoffed. "Agalhor serves no one but himself."

"He protected your borders and still offers aid in the face of future conflicts."

"You know *nothing*, princess." His tone dipped low; his eyes narrowed in warning. It was a side to Varlas she had never experienced directed at her, but Tauria didn't balk. Not when it was possible she was staring at her ultimate betrayer if he was found to be consorting with the enemy.

She raised her chin. "I am my father's daughter, Varlas. He would speak highly of your kindness and generosity. He considered you a friend."

"Yet when Fenstead fell, you fled to High Farrow," Varlas cut in harshly.

Tauria was taken aback, but she focused on taming her hard pulse so she wouldn't display her nerves at facing off with a powerful king she felt she didn't know. Not anymore. Since the loss of his mate, Varlas had been an empty shell of his former self, and that fact cleaved something deep inside her. It stole her breath when a face flashed through her mind: emerald eyes that welcomed her home. Imagining them gone forever tore the ground from beneath her all at once, taking her from that dining hall, and for a second she wondered if she was doing the right thing in being here. Nothing about the Kingdom of the Wolf felt right. Not in her heart. But for her kingdom, to see it reclaimed…

Tauria took a long, conscious breath. "That day, I got on a horse, and I fled." She looked to neither royal as she tunneled into her sorrow, reflecting on that desolate day. Remembering exactly why she went to High Farrow. For *whom*. But she kept her face blank, emotionless, so as not to display her true reasons. "I kept going through day and night, not resting, hardly stopping. I rode endlessly because it seemed no matter how far I got I could still hear the echoes of my people dying. Soldiers fighting, innocents slaughtered. I rode and rode, still feeling the heat that torched everything once bright and thriving. Still tasting the ash that became of the lands from which I was born. I kept riding until I couldn't anymore. I wasn't thinking of my safety, or of whom I would seek refuge with. All I wanted was to stop hearing my people dying, and no land seemed far enough away." Her final words were only a partial truth, but she spoke them all the same, unyielding to any emotion that would voice her lie. Because Tauria knew exactly who she sought that day. Somehow, she'd known there was no safer place than with Nik.

The silence that fell was thick and sorrowful. Tauria glanced down at her distorted reflection rippling in the crimson pool of red wine in her goblet, which trembled in her hand. The longer she stared, she saw the face of a coward, her image reflecting in the spilled blood of her people. Her stomach hollowed out completely; her throat tightened with suffocation. She placed her drink back on the table without a sip.

"You are safe here, Tauria." The gentleness of Tarly's voice dragged her eyes up to meet his. They were conflicted. Understanding lay within them, and then a flare of protection.

"Forgive me," Varlas interjected. "I cannot begin to fathom what you went through that day. Though I will admit I always wondered why you never came to me. I was close with your father."

Tauria forced a smile. She didn't remember much about their relationship, only that it was similar to the bond he'd had with Orlon. Her father had trusted Varlas, and for that she had to hope enough of the king her father admired remained after the loss of his mate. Hope to prove every hideous suspicion she had wrong. That he wasn't capable of siding with the ones who killed her parents and took everything from her.

Just as they were about to fall into idle chatter, a lone guard approached the table. His eyes flicked to Tauria just for a second before he leaned in close. His attempt to be discreet was pointless considering she could tune in to every word.

"Your Majesty, there has been a new arrival who requests an audience."

"Who?"

Again, the guard spared Tauria a flash of attention. Her muscles locked in anticipation, wondering who it could be to make him feel the need for such caution around her. Nik wouldn't be so foolish as to come after her so soon. He wouldn't—

"He claims his name is Lycus Warner, a General of Fenstead."

Tauria's gasp couldn't be stifled. Her disappointment that it wasn't who she first thought was quickly dissipated by her world-shifting shock.

Lycus Warner.

His name rang on repeat, her mind refusing to believe she'd heard it right. Because she'd mourned that name long ago, believed he'd died defending his court when Fenstead fell.

Tauria shot to her feet, uncaring of etiquette in her spike of adrenaline.

"We are not done here," Varlas said coolly to his guard while his eyes locked on her in silent command.

Tauria frowned in defiance. "If I may—"

"Sit, Tauria." His smooth order cut off her words and flared her temper like a dismissed child. But her compliance would not be so easily gained now she knew what he intended to keep her from.

"I did not know General Lycus Warner was alive. I will go to him—unless you are detaining me here, King Varlas."

His expression twitched with wrath at her standoff. She couldn't understand why he was so determined to keep her here for the petty feast she had no appetite for. Perhaps it wasn't wise to counter his request. She was trying to play smart after all—had to bide her time and gain his trust. But in that moment, she didn't care. Not when she was in reach of being reunited with her childhood friend. Against her desire, she extended the respect of waiting until Varlas granted her leave, but she stared into his hardened eyes with equal challenge, watching as he battled between asserting his authority and abiding by her request.

"I'm sure we will have plenty of opportunity to dine together again." It was Tarly who spoke as the voice of reason, his gaze sliding tentatively to his father.

Tauria wanted to thank him, and there was a part of her that didn't want to leave him alone with his cold father. The prince's earlier outburst of anger seemed to belong to a different person as he helped her.

The ice over Varlas's expression melted slowly, easing his harsh lines as warmth and understanding returned to him while she remained staring him down. "Of course we will," he agreed, but his words were tight. Relief relaxed Tauria's stiff shoulders. "You will be accompanied by two guards, and several more shall lie in wait. We cannot be certain he does not pose a threat to you or any of us."

Her mouth opened to protest, but Tarly spoke before she could.

"Indeed, it would be wise to take caution after all this time apart." The prince's eyes locked on hers, and the warning was clear. Not anger or dominance, but rather a plea not to push his father. It seeped a chill over Tauria's skin, ringing a faint alarm bell she listened to. As odd as it seemed that Tarly could be *afraid* of his own father, reluctantly, Tauria bowed her head in acceptance of the ludicrous condition. She would meet with Lycus, and it would only be a matter of time before Varlas saw no option but to trust him.

A thrill replaced her unease, and she didn't wait for further permission or pleasantries before following the guard who'd interrupted their meal. Her steps were skips, her heartbeat erratic. She was unable to stifle her giddy nerves and believe that this was real. Over a century since she'd seen him, and she'd long convinced herself he was dead. Tauria tried not to pay attention to the pressure building in her chest as she wondered why he'd kept away from her until now. It threatened to overshadow her joy.

Her steps slowed; her hearing drifted. Her sight fixed, and she stopped walking. Lycus's back was to her, hands clasped behind him while he observed a tapestry at the end of the wide room. There was no mistaking him. Never in her lifetime would she forget an inch of his body.

Time slowed his turn toward her, making it an elegant glide. The beautiful dark skin of his cheeks creased as he smiled, dark brown eyes striking her so deep it was an effort to keep her knees from buckling. Instead she forced her feet to move, just as he began to close the distance to her. His stunning face blurred, and she blinked away the tears pooling in her eyes to take in every feature. His hair was so much shorter than she remembered, perfectly neat and formed in tight dark curls. He was tall—that hadn't changed—but his physique was perhaps more built than she remembered, as though he'd spent all this time in training, never once forgetting they had a kingdom to reclaim.

Never giving up.

They stopped right in front of each other. Neither spoke. Lycus in turn seemed to scan every inch of her. Slowly, his smile upturned into the most breathtaking grin.

And that was the moment she broke.

A whimper left her as her arms flew around his neck, and he rumbled with a soft chuckle as he embraced her back. Tauria didn't fail to notice the shift and high alert of every guard around them, but in her elation she couldn't pay mind to the irritation their overprotection stirred.

"You look well, Tauria," he mumbled into her hair.

Her eyes clamped shut; his voice stole her speech. Because it the first time in over a century she was hearing a voice from her homeland, when so many tormenting days had chanted she never would again. She didn't loosen her vise grip for a long, suspended moment, but it didn't seem he was in any rush either.

When they finally parted, Tauria's feet planted firmly back on the ground after straining on her toes. She couldn't tear her eyes from him, soaking in the image as if it could be a dream. One blink and she might awaken, cruelly snatched from this impossible reunion. Her voice was hoarse with emotion as she said, "I didn't know you survived."

Lycus's face creased in apology. His hand raised, but the guards once again shifted, hands going over their swords. Tauria's pointed look was incredulous as she glanced at them, yet the guards were unyielding.

"I suppose I should be grateful they spare such caution for you. Do not be upset by it," Lycus said softly, offering a kind smile.

She couldn't agree. Not with the notion they considered one of her own court members a threat to her. It was as if they didn't trust in her judgment as a ruler. With her anger stirring, she cast her eyes back to her general.

"All this time…" It was a conflict of heartache and anguish as she looked at him. He would have known where she was. Her refuge in High Farrow was no secret. "Where have you been?"

"We have much to catch up on, Tauria." Lycus didn't react to her broken look of accusation. His smile was bright as he said, "Your friend Faythe Ashfyre sends her regards."

CHAPTER 7

Tauria

RHYENELLE. IT WAS smart of Lycus and what was left of Fenstead's armies to seek refuge there, and Tauria was indebted to King Agalhor not only for his aid and shelter, but for allowing them to stay in his kingdom as they were: Fenstead natives and soldiers, never once forced to change or join Rhyenelle's ranks. Tauria had so much to catch up on, but right now she was eager to hear more about Faythe, having only heard about the cryptic quest Nik had mentioned. She strolled side by side with Lycus, intending to lead him to the garden that had become a distraction from her homesickness and the daunting task of playing spy in an uncertain kingdom. She wanted to tell him everything. She trusted the general completely, yet with the many eyes that surrounded them, Tauria knew it would be no easy task.

"Faythe sets out on her own quest. General Reylan and others accompany her on an expedition to the Niltain Isles," Lycus told her of his short encounter with her friend.

"How is she finding her kingdom? I'm not sure if you're aware of her circumstances, but she's been through a lot."

Lycus chuckled lightly. "Believe me, I think I have heard it all. She's a woman with a remarkable tale. Her presence in Rhyenelle has caused quite a hopeful stir among the people, and I don't think she truly realizes it yet."

Tauria huffed knowingly. Humility was one of Faythe's more endearing qualities, though it made her equally stubborn when it came to accepting her merits.

"General Reylan speaks very highly of her."

With his mention, they exchanged a look. Tauria said nothing, but just like Lycus, she fought a tender smile.

"I have no doubt she is in the safest hands on her journey. She told me of your plans to come here after she spoke with Nikalias, I believe."

There was some caution in the way Lycus spoke Nik's name, but Tauria gave no reaction. Instead, her stomach churned with deep concern for her friend. In a moment of desperation she even considered if she could be of aid to Faythe from here. Nothing her mind could conjure up would help, so all she could do was pray to the Spirits for Faythe to make it back unharmed. She wouldn't accept any alternative when even while apart Faythe echoed Tauria's concerns.

They came to the glass doors, and like always, just as Tauria went to open them, an Olmstone guard obstructed her. She tried not to cringe with embarrassment at being fussed over like a child in front of Lycus. She spared him a quick glance, but all he gave was an assuring smile. His hand hovered over her lower back, but he didn't fully touch her as he made to guide her outdoors.

Halfway down the short path, she said, "I've only just begun, but I intend to bring it back to its former glory." She cast her eyes thoughtfully around the space. Against the stars and moonlight, it was all the more dreary without the color that caught on the rays and turned it breathtaking. In the silence, as she met the pavilion, Tauria twisted around to the general who wasn't so close by anymore. He'd halted, simply watching her, and Tauria frowned in pain laced with joy as the look they shared spoke their words for them.

"I have missed you," he muttered quietly.

Tauria's attention drifted to the three guards spread out around the small space, hating that they couldn't have this moment alone. "You still have to explain to me why you stayed away. Why you allowed me to sit idle and believe that you were dead." She couldn't stop the accusation that slipped into her tone. She hurt with the notion.

"I have every intention of explaining myself to you, but can't we enjoy this moment a little longer?" His smile was careful, and while he didn't look at the surrounding guards, Tauria caught onto his wish to discuss matters of their kingdom in private. She nodded and motioned for him to join her in the pavilion, where they both observed the decaying wood.

"This may be outside of your particular talents," he commented.

Tauria chuckled.

"Tell me, do you still find time to use your Florakinetics? Your wind manipulation is impressive, but it is your weapon. Your talent to play with nature always brought joy to your face."

Tauria's fingers traced the chipped wood in bittersweet reflection. "There hasn't been much opportunity."

Lycus read the lie, and his face pinched in concern.

"My station as High Farrow's ward wasn't all that idle. I still had a role to play in court."

"You mean insufferable ladies to entertain and delirious gatherings to attend."

This brought amusement to her face. "When you say it like that…"

Lycus's laughter fluttered her heart. It was a sound she'd missed so dearly it stole her breath. "I am sorry I've been away from you for so long. But I vow for us never again to be separated now I'm back by your side."

"You could have come to me in High Farrow."

Lycus wandered over to the edge of the pavilion, hands clasped behind his back. He was a marvelous sight, often fawned over in Fenstead. She may have been the princess, but having his friendship often earned Tauria the court ladies' envious gazes. She couldn't blame them, but she'd never seen Lycus as anything more than a friend. A protector. He was the personal guard she'd never wanted while growing up, but whom she had come to love. His father was a leading general, and Tauria supposed his son's age being close to hers gave both their parents the impression he would make ideal company for her while he learned his duty. What her parents had failed to see was Tauria's solitude and retreat to the quiet gardens or libraries was of her own desire.

"Why did you go to High Farrow?" Lycus asked quietly, looking up at the night sky.

"It seemed like the farthest place from everything."

A half-truth.

The moon shone beautifully on his dark skin as she watched him, until Tauria stepped up close, bracing her hands on the chipped wooden ledge. His eyes fell from the sky, and his green irises sparkled as though they'd captured the stars.

"You went because you knew Nikalias would keep you safe."

His statement stumped her entirely. Her mouth fell open to counter the claim, but Lycus smirked as if he anticipated her quick defense.

"I fought side by side with the prince—the king," he corrected. "Many times during the Great Battles. He asked about you often. I couldn't understand his fascination for one he hardly knew. But he wanted to know it all and had every intention of going to Fenstead before everything happened."

A marble formed painfully in her throat as he talked of Nik. Tauria had to avert her gaze, taking a moment to find her composure and fit into the mask she had to wear. Even in front of Lycus. "You're right," she answered, but she kept her tone neutral, factual. "I knew Nikalias briefly from his visit to Fenstead for our Winter Solstice Ball. Believe me, I don't know where his fascination came from either," she mused to defuse the sadness in her heart. "But I went to High Farrow because my father was close with Orlon, and I knew it was far from the devastation I'd left behind. There is nothing between me and Nikalias, nor will there ever be."

His pause of silence itched her skin, knowing there was purpose to his mention of Nik. "I'm only going to ask this so I know where we stand here. I need you to know I'm on your side no matter what."

Her hands tightened because she knew the explanation he was heading for.

"Did something happen between you and Nikalias for you to have come here?"

"My being here is for the good of Fenstead. Olmstone has armies who could aid us significantly. Nikalias will offer aid too, but it is not enough. Securing this alliance could be what we need to finally gain the forces to fight back."

"I agree." For some reason, his response sank with disappointment in her stomach. "But Tauria—" His continuation lifted her eyes. He halted what he wanted to say, deliberating. "Your heart never has to be sacrificed for us to take back our kingdom."

His words tugged on her deep yearning for a way of life tragically out of reach for someone of her status. The look they shared spoke of a hidden meaning between them, but Tauria couldn't admit to any past feelings for Nik. She had to think of her future. She had to put herself first. And while the vultures circled, in the guards around them and the walls that had eyes, Tauria couldn't show an ounce of hesitation for her prospects in Olmstone. Taking a long breath, she let her determination straighten her spine.

"I am here to negotiate a marriage alliance with Tarly," she said firmly, embracing the sure, firm persona expected of her.

"As High Farrow's ward, or as Fenstead's queen?"

"As both. While there are no personal relations between me and Nikalias, I will not forget that I am alive because of his refuge, and I thrived because he did not leave me to cower as a fallen princess, but to rise with a station born out of respect for my role in Fenstead. I owe High Farrow my life, and the least I can do to repay the kingdom is to consider them in these upcoming negotiations."

It was Nik who saved her. Nik who brought her out of the dark and gave her a reason to keep living when she felt she deserved to have died with her parents on the battlefield. It was Nik who inspired her resilience to go on. And he didn't even know it. Tauria's chest hollowed out completely. Her head bowed in sorrowful reflection.

"I have upset you," Lycus said gently. His hand raised to her chin, and while she heard the shuffling of nearby guards, he didn't pay them any notice as he cupped her cheek, forcing her eyes back up to meet his. "I didn't come sooner because I knew that you were safe. Exactly where you should be. I feared that if you knew I was in Rhyenelle, if you knew you still had an army, that you wouldn't be safe anymore. You would want to strike back when it was not time."

Her defiance flared, and she couldn't help but to tear away from him with a pinned look of accusation and disappointment. "Is this all I am to you? Some frail, impulsive princess who doesn't know when she's out of her depth?"

"Tauria—"

"Next, you're going to tell me that I won't be fighting in this war. That I stand to act as a marker alone, a pretty statue to place on a throne earned back by the blood of my people while I did nothing?" A pawn. A piece to be played on the checkerboard of court. In High Farrow, in Olmstone, now, sadness shrouded her mind as she realized even her own kingdom didn't trust her with the crown she thought she wore with confidence, but which now felt like a weight of control.

Lycus's mouth pressed into a firm line. His lack of protest made it abundantly clear.

Tauria huffed a laugh. "It makes sense now." She shook her head, incredulous. "You left your trophy to be cased and protected while you trained soldiers to fight my battles."

"That is what being a ruler is, Tauria. The people need you to live, to lead and restore our kingdom when all this is over. The battlefield is no place for you."

Faythe would fight on a battlefield. The resentful thought swirled in her mind with the heat of her skin, prickling with embarrassment. Though it seemed ludicrous to draw comparisons to her human friend, it shed a light on the fact neither Tauria's experience, nor her will, nor her choices, were appreciated despite all she had trained for and lived through. Her impulses were seen as reckless, not smart. Her will to fight was tragic, not brave. Nothing was enough. *She* was not enough.

"Do you know me at all, Lycus?" She couldn't be sure, not anymore, as the fae she grew up with never would have discredited her so quickly.

"I do. Which is why I knew you would have left High Farrow the instant you found out you had an army to build. You would never have known a moment's peace nor rest until you deemed your forces strong enough to fight back. And let me tell you, it would not have been enough. We still are not enough."

A growing barrel of rage and frustration started to tremble in her body. Her fingers flexed to the tingling awakening of her wind. She was hurt and angry and saddened. There might have been a part of her that knew he was right, that believed in his intentions, yet all she could embrace was betrayal. "I'm not feeble. And I'm not impulsive." Tauria's voice was steady and low while she carefully tamed her magick to cool the heat in her veins. If she were impulsive, she could wreck their surroundings in minutes with her ability. She could choke the air from the lungs of the three surrounding guards if she so desired. Yet she'd never shown that side of what she was capable of—because if her darkness danced with her impulses, Tauria was aware of the deadly weapon she could become. Never had anyone acknowledged that her strength lay in her composure and calculation. Her poise and elegance were not of obedience but skillful observation. In High Farrow, she'd carefully watched and learned the workings of court. To outsiders, she'd lingered in those halls as a tragic princess succumbing to defeat. But Tauria never once forgot she had people to lead home. She trained hard every day despite the whispers that she was a princess, not a warrior. She didn't listen, because for herself and her kingdom she was determined to be both.

Tauria Stagknight would not let her hurt show. She would not display everything Lycus forced to the surface. So she raised her chin, took two calming breaths, and let the hum of her magick fall to silence once more. "You should have had more faith in me," she said coldly, standing firm, unyielding. Tauria would not be the one to walk away in the face of opposition. It tore her heart to want space when they had only just been reunited, but she couldn't stand that look in his eye that battled between wanting to believe in her and protesting that he was right to have kept away from her all this time.

Lycus averted his gaze, along with a small dip of his head, reading in her poise that she had nothing more to say. He began to turn away from her. "I hope to meet with you again soon, Your Majesty. I'll be requesting an extended stay here. Until you send me away, I am yours."

Tauria offered a nod of appreciation. Her brow pinched while she watched his back as he walked away. But she didn't break stance. In their time apart, she had to accept that he'd changed, and she didn't doubt there were moments where Lycus looked to her as a stranger now too. They would have time to talk again, and all she could hope for was to find more of her childhood friend still lingering under the duties they'd grown into and the hardships they'd faced. What hollowed her stomach worst of all was that Lycus didn't realize what he'd enlightened her to. To him, to everyone here, maybe even to Nik, Tauria existed as nothing more than a pawn for High Farrow, a prize for Olmstone, and a trophy for Fenstead.

When she stood alone and let her eyes drift to the moon, Tauria spiraled deeper and deeper into the belief that she had no ownership of who she was anymore.

CHAPTER 8

Nikalias

NIK'S MIND DRIFTED far, transfixed by the vibrant blooms in the flowerbeds as he trailed around them slowly while he lost himself to the memory of his younger days. He heard her laughter and the splashes of the pond water she'd attempted to spray him with.

"I envy the one who occupies your thoughts so deeply."

The gentle feminine voice stole his attention from the uplifting image brought forth by his being out in the summer garden. Nik offered Samara a weak smile.

"I was thinking of my mother, actually. She loved to spend time out here." He caught the faint rose coloring of her cheeks and found the reaction endearing. She'd assumed another lady lingered in his mind. What he tried not to surface, even within himself, was that every time he came out here, his mother wasn't the only person he pictured in his thoughts.

It rose a cruel but beautiful torment every time he remembered his mother's love for the flowers that only blossomed in the summer. Every time he remembered how effortlessly she and Tauria had bonded over them in the decade they got to know each other before his mother's murder. Nik blinked hard to force back the powerful wave of grief and sorrow at that particular reflection. He took a deep breath, turning his full attention to his company.

"What do you like to do, Samara?"

The question took her by surprise. "I—I don't know what you mean, Your Majesty."

"You don't need to be so formal with me. When it's just the two of us, I'd like to think we can be a little more personal."

Samara smiled. He almost did too at the relaxing of her straight shoulders. Nik would never admit or outwardly show that he found their situation equally uneasy. He'd never courted before, not in the traditional sense, his only reputation tied to the courtesans who were seen going to and from his rooms and nothing else. There was no one left around that he cared to tell the truth to anyway.

"As you wish, Nikalias."

He refrained from cringing at the use of his full name, yet as he looked away from Samara in shame, he thought maybe it was better this way—because he had no intention of truly entertaining the idea the fae beside him could be his life partner. He couldn't. The mere thought churned his stomach every time. He couldn't give her what she deserved.

"Shall we head back inside?" he offered to subdue his desolate thoughts.

Samara nodded politely, but he observed a tightening of her expression that indicated her disappointment he'd cut short their time together. Nik wasn't one to deny something beautiful, and Samara was certainly that. He didn't know her well, but he already considered her to be kind and warm, a woman who would no doubt make someone else's life joyous.

Joy wasn't what he deserved after what he'd given up. Who he'd betrayed.

Indoors, Nik didn't fail to notice how closely Samara walked by his side. It was their first opportunity alone together since Zarrius proposed Nik court her. Her hand carefully touched his arm, and while his posture turned rigid at the contact, Nik didn't deny her. Their gazes met, and her sweet smile made it impossible to object. An action with a statement, Samara showed her zeal to earn his favor sooner rather than later when, with impeccable timing, a group of high fae ladies came toward them. Their envious gazes weren't subtle, and despite Samara's arm through his, a few of them tried to catch his attention with idle signals. Eye contact, flicks of their hair, moving their gowns to draw his attention to attributes they had every right to be confident of.

It wasn't out of arrogance Nik knew what to expect; Tauria's many complaints and amusing tales of these ladies' conversations had given him plenty of insight. He couldn't fight the curl of his mouth as he reminisced upon the times when she'd offloaded everything to him.

Unfortunately, one of the ladies must have mistaken his smile as directed at her in the way her eyes lit up, and Nik quickly shifted his gaze in guilt. His eyes landed on Samara, who kept her chin poised high and confident despite the whispering and pointed looks. As they passed the gathering, she pressed subtly closer into his side. Purposeful. Deliberate. She was smart and assertive, and he admired those traits in one with a desire to lead.

The next duo to cross their path unraveled his coils of tension. Jakon and Marlowe were laughing in conversation as they strolled down the hall. The sight of them always brought forth memories of the dear friend he missed. Jakon and Marlowe's presence in the castle kept Faythe's spirit lingering like a warmth in the dark. Marlowe caught Nik's eye first, and she straightened from her lean into Jakon's side. Her smile, as always, brightened the atmosphere. But then her attention slid to his arm, which Samara kept an intimate hold of, and Nik didn't miss the flash of surprise when her ocean eyes lifted again.

"I'm glad our paths crossed," he said tightly, halting as they did and trying not to interpret their stares as judgment or feel Samara's hand like a hot brand in their company. "Allow me to introduce Lady Samara Calltegan."

The humans dipped their heads at her, and Marlowe spoke for them both. "Pleasure to meet you."

"And I'm pleased to introduce you to our town's esteemed blacksmith, Marlowe, and my personal emissary, Jakon."

Samara remained silent for a long pause, and Nik turned to gauge her reaction. Her look was hard to decipher as she assessed the two in front of her. The awkward tension he didn't expect crawled over his skin. "They do not bow?" was all she asked. Her green eyes slid to him, her face a blank mask of ignorance.

It was often Nik forgot many of the court weren't like him or Tauria. Many found it difficult and odd to accustom themselves to the changes he imposed. "That is not necessary," he explained.

"But you are the king, and I am a high lady of the court."

"And they are friends, not servants." He kept the anger off his face, but the bite of his tone he couldn't suppress at the way she spoke of the humans, looking at them as though they were undeserving of his company.

Samara cast her attention back to them, but her expression didn't yield warmth. Nik stiffened, noting how Jakon drew Marlowe closer and didn't hide his frown. Marlowe displayed nothing but patience and warmth on her delicate features—an admirable trait to keep such composure under this level of scrutiny.

"Will you escort me back to my rooms, Your Majesty? I'm feeling tired from our afternoon together." Samara spoke as though the humans were ghosts, her gaze avoiding them as if she could walk straight through them.

Nik's disheartened state of mind urged him to deny her. Then he'd go to Zarrius and make it known he wouldn't entertain marriage with anyone who viewed humans as beneath them. His turmoil at allowing her to shun his friends wreaked havoc on his need to find a way to turn the situation into something more akin with what he hoped to achieve in his kingdom. Coexistence without prejudice. The best way he knew how was to show her their value.

"I was actually hoping to run into you, Jakon. I thought you might join me in the training room." It was all he could think of in the moment. To someone who prized stations like Samara, showing he sought Jakon's company would seem like a declaration of importance.

"We have plans this evening," Jakon muttered, attempting to keep a neutral expression. "How about tomorrow?"

Nik relaxed, relieved when Jakon accepted and withheld the defense he feared he might unleash upon Samara. "Tomorrow then." Nik nodded.

Jakon and Marlowe curved around them without another word, abandoning Nik to Samara's tense company.

"I do not understand your sympathy for them," she commented as they fell into a casual stroll.

"It is not sympathy; it is equality. I hope you'll come to see they're no different from you or me."

"You are a king."

Nik's jaw locked in irritation at her emphasis on his title. His suspicion contemplated her motive: to further exact her own importance by being with him, or to remind him that all he should be seen as was his crown. At her rooms, Nik could hardly keep still, eager to bid Samara farewell, but she didn't turn for her door, instead facing him expectantly. A short silence grew on his agitation, and he watched her, oblivious, until disappointment flared in her eyes.

"Would you like to come in?" she offered as though he should have been the one to ask.

Nik nearly startled, taken aback by the request. "I don't think that's appropriate given how little we know each other." He gave a short nod in farewell before he made to leave.

"Yet it was appropriate with the Fenstead princess."

He felt her call at his back like a blade. It rippled a white fury in him. His jaw locked, and he took a second to breathe before turning back to her. Nik didn't ease the warning that reflected on his face. Wisely, Samara balked—the first slip of her masterful composure.

"You would be wise to keep your voice down. And smart not to mention her again. Ever." He backtracked the few paces to Samara until he'd closed her in against the door. "I look forward to seeing you again, Samara. But I warn you to consider your words before you speak them." His fingers barely touched her chin, and he listened to her uneven breaths, searching her eyes. He saw pride and conviction, but the deeper he looked, he discovered ripples of insecurity within. No matter her motives or wealth or status, she was still just a fae. "Your confidence is admirable though misplaced if you think I don't see your attempt to play cards that won't work in your favor, Samara. You needn't feel in the shadow of anyone, but if it settles your mind, the Fenstead *queen* is as good as betrothed. Don't test me with that again." His hand fell limp as he took a step back.

They shared one final lingering look, his words seeming to swallow her response, then Nik stalked away. He meant every word. Samara had many admirable traits that deserved to be acknowledged and that would take her far. But there remained no shadow to walk in when Tauria never had been, and never would be, his. Each step he took to a vacant destination made that realization sink deeper.

Yet he still needed to know she was safe. Not just in body, but mind. He yearned so truly for that reassurance that every sunrise he wished time would race toward nightfall, when he'd once again try to reach her, grappling with the desperate hope she'd open her mind to him no matter what he'd see about her life in Olmstone. Even if she'd found happiness in the arms of another.

CHAPTER 9

Tauria

Tauria cursed under her breath as a stem snapped in her gloved fingers. It had happened three times now, and she'd had enough. She didn't know how anyone worked in such ridiculous garments or would want to wear gloves instead of feeling the cool soil against their flesh. She ripped each one off with a disgruntled huff.

"Your Majesty—"

Tauria shot Lennox a look of frustration, anticipating what he wanted to say. He winced but continued anyway.

"The prince's orders were very…precise."

She refrained from rolling her eyes. "He's not here, and I can't work a damn minute in these things. It's absurd."

Opal gave a light chuckle beside her, flexing her fingers in the too-big gloves she'd been forced into. It took the fun out of gardening, the carefree excitement of being at one with nature. Serena sat on a blanket in the pavilion to keep from ruining her dress on the sodden wood. She wasn't interested in any of the teachings Tauria had spent many hours engaging the young princess in while they kneeled working on the next flowerbed. Their knees had been spared of a soaking this time with cushions that would be wholly ruined by the time they finished for the day. Tauria had wanted to find pants and a shirt to come out here in, but that idea was refused, and once again she stuffed herself into a purple-accented gown.

But she drew a line at these damned gloves.

Picking up the broken stem, Tauria's palm waved over it, sealing the break as though the stem were new. Opal's gasp of wonder lifted an excited chuckle from her.

"Impressive," Serena commented, glancing up from her sewing.

"Are you sure you wouldn't like to join us? It's very pleasing to bring life to dreary things even without an ability," Tauria offered warmly.

Just for a second, the fae flinched, absently picking at the sewing round in her lap, inside of which she'd begun to craft a beautiful flower arrangement of her own making.

Tauria realized her error. "Sorry, that must have sounded conceited." She laughed awkwardly.

Serena met her eye with surprise. "You have nothing to apologize for, Your Highness."

"Just Tauria, please."

Serena smiled tightly. "As you wish."

Tauria wanted to believe she could befriend the fae, yet she couldn't help but find her conversation stiff. It was as though Serena wasn't engaging, or even here, of her own accord.

"Have you heard the latest whispers to filter through the halls?" Serena asked casually, resuming her sewing.

Tauria hated that she had to confess she'd heard nothing. "In Olmstone?"

Serena huffed. "I think you're the center of all intrigue around here for a while."

Her pulse picked up of its own accord. Dread slicked her skin, but relief piqued her attention, knowing before Serena spoke who would be mentioned.

"They say King Nikalias is courting Lady Samara Calltegan. Though I can't say I'm surprised. Can you?"

It was a test. The first time Serena had given Tauria her full attention, setting her sewing round down on her lap. The name sounded familiar, and with it Tauria pictured the beauty who had a high reputation in High Farrow's court. Yet to Tauria's vague knowledge, the last she'd heard of the lady, her name seemed tied to Zarrius. But that was a long time ago, and she supposed Samara was one of the few fit to claim the hand of a king.

Her confidence sank with her heart. Tauria's eyes fell to the flowers. "Nik doesn't court," she said, but she heard her own uncertainty.

Still, it wasn't a lie. In over a century of knowing him, she'd never once heard nor seen Nik show an interest in courting any lady. He may have flaunted his courtesans, flirted and teased, but he'd never sought one's company exclusively. With Tauria gone, did he now have all the time she usually stole to finally seek out a prospective partner? Regardless, the news seemed so fast. She hadn't been gone for long, and waves of nausea rolled through her gut as she thought of their final departure in High Farrow—and what they could have done before they were interrupted. It meant so much to her, but perhaps it meant nothing at all to him.

"I guess you're misled. Word is they've been seen getting pretty close. Everyone is already calling it a wondrous union."

Tauria couldn't take it. The image Samara painted. Another by his side. Nothing. She had meant nothing to him. She risked revealing too much on her face in the wrong company. Serena watched her like a vulture waiting to devour anything in sight. The slightest flicker of her expression could breathe life to a thousand lies. Speculation. None of them cared for the truth anyway.

"Indeed it would be." Tauria's heart froze over as she steeled her voice. "It's about time Nikalias settles down from his known affairs."

Serena dropped her gaze. Her disappointment added to Tauria's triumph. But she couldn't bask in it while her mood declined. She wished for nightfall to be alone in her sorrow.

"Father never allows me to do fun things," Opal mumbled, stealing Tauria's attention back to where the princess had engrossed herself in planting a batch of thornless roses, which she'd bloomed for her earlier.

Tauria had Tarly to thank for helping her gain permission for the princess to be out here, but it had come with a string of conditions. There were even more guards posted outside the door now, and if she extended her senses, Tauria could detect unmoving forces lingering on the other side of the high wall too. So many watchful eyes she tried to forget as much as possible or suffocation tightened in her throat. Much to her relief, Lennox remained the only one who accompanied them in the garden.

"It's going to take some time to get this place back into shape. I hope you don't grow bored. I don't think I can do it all without you now."

Sparks of joy lit up in the princess's eyes, and Tauria's heart pined for the sense of purpose that straightened Opal's back as she looked over the space. She stared at her own child-self; stared at the loneliness and uncertainty that shadowed one born into a crown so young.

"It's going to be so beautiful. I hope Mother will come." Opal went back to losing herself in the flowers.

This grabbed Tauria's attention. "How is your mother?" she asked. "I haven't had the chance to meet with her since I arrived." She found the queen's absence odd, and it had been high on her list of things to question. The opportunity was presenting itself perfectly, but before the young princess could open her mouth to answer, Serena's voice cut in.

"I think that's enough picking for the day," she said as she stood, dusting off invisible dirt from her impeccable gown.

Tauria glanced up at the sky to gauge the time by the sun's position. "We still have a couple more hours until evening."

Opal had already stood, her face fallen as she shot Tauria a look of apology that didn't sit well in her gut. Tauria frowned, wincing at her aching legs from kneeling for so long as she stood.

"The princess has classes before supper," Serena explained, but she seemed to display no sympathy for dragging Opal away from her small dose of enjoyment.

They were already making their way down the path when Tauria called, "Tomorrow?"

Serena paused, twisting back and offering a pleasant smile. "I shall have to confirm with her mother. She listens to me. I will ask. Though I am sure she has plans to seek you out for herself soon."

Tauria couldn't be sure why Serena so deliberately mentioned her closeness to the queen. She nodded, and her disappointment settled that their afternoon had been abruptly cut short. She turned to Lennox by default, as the only person left. He tried and failed to keep the pitying look from his face despite not meeting her gaze.

"I can't say I'll be of much help, but if you want to stay for a few more hours, I am happy to," he offered.

Tauria's mood shifted at the genuine offer, but she could see Lennox's fatigue and felt selfish for forcing him to stand in his uniform for long hours in the blazing sun. She'd encouraged him to take shelter in the pavilion many times, and he'd politely declined. What he didn't voice was that it wasn't deemed *proper* for him to abandon formality in the presence of nobility. To share the same close confinement of the pavilion with Serena was not *proper* here either. All of it seemed entirely excessive, but it wasn't for Tauria to question foreign customs.

"That's okay. I suppose I should take the time to wash again before I dine with His Majesty. And I should like to seek out my general if he is finished meeting with the king?" Tauria posed it as a question in the hope the guard might have heard word about Lycus, whom she hadn't seen since their rocky reunion days ago. A seed of dread took root that Lycus's presence could shake her prospects with Tarly if they interrogated too deeply into their past together and decided he could be a distraction or sway her affections. No—Lycus wouldn't offer any personal history that wasn't absolutely necessary. At least, it was all Tauria could hope while her anxiety toyed with outlandish thoughts. They had nothing to hide. But Tauria knew in court it wasn't often the truth of the past but baseless speculation that inflicted most damage to one's reputation. She walked side by side with Lycus through the halls as he answered.

"I believe General Lycus is still caught up in matters with the king."

Tauria's teeth ground with thinning patience. "Do you know where they have been keeping him? They have told me nothing."

Lennox's gaze shifted warily around them. Then abruptly, he halted, hooking Tauria's arm, and she bit back her surprise. The hallway they'd stopped in was so cloaked in darkness she could barely make out his expression.

"The walls have ears around here. The Wolverlons aren't kind to inquisitive people. You're smart, Tauria. Don't ask questions—they arouse suspicion. Make statements as if you hold the answers already."

His words were so hushed it took all her focus to hear them. Her heart beat rapidly with alarm. Trepidation crawled over her skin and stiffened her spine. Tauria surveyed the area for herself to confirm they were alone. Lennox's eyes were so dark here, but she locked onto them with a cool warning should she discover his kindness disguised a trick.

"I'll only ask this once: how can I trust you?"

Lennox didn't balk at her gaze. He straightened, and Tauria picked up on a distant approach just as he did. The guard's hand skimmed across hers, and she gasped at its coolness. She spared a glance down at the item he pressed into her palm, and her eyes widened on it for just a second before she tucked it up her sleeve and they continued their casual walk as if the encounter never happened.

Yet she couldn't get that symbol out of her mind. The side-facing stag emblem carved into a brass pin.

Lennox was from Fenstead.

CHAPTER 10

Nikalias

NIK HAD TO ease back centuries' worth of combat training against Jakon. He expected it, but he would never insult the human by admitting Faythe made a better sparring opponent. He supposed she at least had the hidden advantage of her half-fae heritage. Besides, Nik was somewhat grateful for the slower pace. Instead of surfacing his anger only to unleash it, he drilled his focus into careful study, and Jakon seemed eager for tips on how to improve.

"So, you and this new lady…?" Jakon let the question hang with an edge of caution.

Nik failed to hide his disgruntled look. By his order, they were alone in the training room, but Nik spared a glance around them, extending his senses, just to be sure. "It's just for image, that is all."

They clashed swords, and Nik twisted around Jakon, halting in a killing strike that had the human groaning in frustration.

Nik gave a short chuckle. "You're swift, calculating. Have you ever considered your hand with a bow instead?"

Jakon rubbed his jaw as he pondered the prospect. "I did enjoy hunting in the woods, but it wasn't to Faythe's liking. She always preferred something she could throw or swing."

They shared a laugh that seemed to lift the constant heavy shadow clouding them in her absence. Nik lowered his sword, and Jakon asked, "What does having her on your arm say for the kingdom?"

"It was Zarrius's idea," Nik admitted. They exchanged a knowing look, and a mental heaviness lifted to see Jakon hadn't failed to notice the lord's cunning ways. "I'm concerned I haven't done a very good job at convincing the court there was nothing between me and Tauria." As he went over to the weapons wall and Jakon followed, he didn't miss the human's agreement in the way his gaze shifted. "Nor to you or Marlowe, it seems," he accused. Picking a bow, he offered it to Jakon, but he didn't immediately take it. His forehead wrinkled, contemplative, as if he were weighing up his response. "You can speak freely."

Jakon shuffled, giving a quick, bemused lift of his brow. "I never thought I'd come to call a fae a friend, never mind a fae *king*, but I'd like to think through the odds and adversities that's what we are to you. Friends."

"Of course." Nik didn't need a moment to admit that.

"What does it mean…to have a mate?"

Nik blinked, stumped at the swerve of topic. "Why would you ask?"

"To understand. Because as your friends…we can't sit by and watch you make the mistake of a lifetime. And for your kind, that is a long, torturous existence."

Jakon couldn't hear it with his human senses, but Nik's pulse picked up, his guard ready to close him off entirely at the probing inquisition. "I don't know what one has to do with the other," he said. An edge of warning had slipped into his tone as a natural defense. It might have reflected on his face as Jakon balked. Just for a second, until he casually reached out a hand for the bow. Nik's jaw ground at the distraction, but he obliged.

Jakon swiped up the quiver of arrows, casually strolling toward the archery range at the far end. Nik followed him, not forgetting for a second he awaited an explanation for Jakon's odd question.

"What if your mate could still cross your path in this lifetime?" Jakon didn't wait for instruction—didn't seem to need it. Nik observed him with crossed arms as he nocked and aimed with a decent enough poise to be more than a novice.

"A mate is a match of the power we have within. It's not always felt in the heart." When he let the shot go, Nik followed it, and he didn't hide the lift of his brow that it hit one of the middle targets close to the center.

"Good. I just wanted to be sure."

"Of what?"

"That you're not making a mistake because your soul calls to her by some bond of magick, but because you love her. Loved her even before you knew about the bond."

Nik stiffened on instinct, but Jakon didn't register the threatening primal shift in his demeanor like a fae would. "You don't know a thing."

"I'm afraid I know more than I care to know sometimes." Nonchalantly, he swiped another arrow. Nik couldn't decide if he admired his brazenness or if it irked him. "I know more than it feels safe to know, but only because Marlowe does." After letting go of another great shot, he lowered the bow and locked Nik's gaze. "You didn't really think you could keep your secret about Tauria from an oracle, did you?"

Nik cursed internally. Anger twitched his face. Not at Jakon or Marlowe. His irritation flared at feeling like a foolish, pining child. "How long has she known?"

"Does it matter?"

"No, it doesn't," Nik said sharply, but his answer held two meanings. "It doesn't matter who she is. It doesn't matter what I feel. That's not something Marlowe can glimpse in a *vision.* Nor is it either of your concern. You'd be wise to keep silent about it."

Jakon's face held a note of infuriating pity, but Nik didn't get the chance to react as amusement hitched his brow. "Who exactly would we tell? Or who would care to listen to two lowly *humans?*"

Nik winced with apology. "I'm sorry about the Lady Samara's…pretentiousness."

Jakon gave a chuckle. "No need. We knew when we agreed to stay here there would be some opposition."

"Then why did you agree?"

"Because Marlowe is of the opinion our presence, however small, is a step closer to the kingdom you seek to build." Jakon huffed at Nik's expression, creased in guilt for not showing Marlowe enough gratitude. "We don't do it for you, *Your Majesty.*" Jakon's lighthearted mockery of the heavy title invited an unexpected uplift in Nik's mood. "It was Faythe's dream too. I think out of all of us, she was always the most open-minded when it came to the fae we were brought up to fear, submit to. But it's not just for her. As humans we may not live long enough to see it, but whatever children we might have deserve a better chance at a life without fear or divide. They deserve to learn there's strength in the most unlikely of alliances."

Nik nodded with great admiration for their passion for change. Jakon hesitated before following on with the rest of what he wanted to say.

"Are you sure Samara is the one you can see ruling by your side in all this?"

"I believe, like the humans, there are many fae who will come to open their minds and hearts to change."

"That's not what I mean," Jakon said in a way that called Nik out for knowing as much.

"She's of high noble birth. She's beautiful. She would no doubt be a favorable candidate to the court."

"Can you trust her?"

Nik frowned. "She hasn't given me any reason not to."

"What about Zarrius? You said it was his idea to put Samara forth."

Jakon had a point—one Nik had to admit he'd already considered. The human had been present for many of the meetings with the lord in the council room. Zarrius never remained silent, always the one with a plan, an agenda, so all Nik could do to tide him over was agree with enough speculation that he wouldn't seem submissive to his own council.

"Might I suggest something?"

Nik crossed his arms, giving a nod.

"I have no idea how it works, even when Faythe tried to explain it, but would it not be worth Nightwalking through her to be sure her intentions are not being…influenced?"

Nik's reluctance must have been evident on his face as Jakon cringed. "It's not something I would to do to someone whose trust I'm trying to gain. It crosses a personal boundary there would be no coming back from."

"I agree. Though in these circumstances, might it be worth it, not only for your own peace of mind that you're not courting Zarrius in the guise of a beautiful lady, but out of concern for her well-being that this is truly of her own will?"

Nik huffed an incredulous laugh. "I hardly think a lady of the court would need *forcing* into a prospective union with a king."

"I'm sure you don't need me to call out the complete arrogance and ignorance in that statement."

"Yet you just did."

"What can I say? Without Faythe or Tauria, someone has to keep your ego in check."

Nik should have flared at the insult, but he couldn't help but see the humor in the situation. Jakon was brazenly harmless, and there were echoes of the woman he grew up with in that. Faythe and Jakon were like two sides of the same coin.

"I'll consider it," Nik said.

They paced back to the weapons wall, where Jakon set back the bow. "From what I've gathered, you're pretty skilled at ensuring your presence isn't known, and moral enough not to go prying into matters other than those of safety."

While Nik appreciated the attempt to quell the hideous guilt that arose in him at the notion, he wouldn't tell Jakon it eased nothing. His Nightwalking was a weapon. It was invasive, and he'd only had cause to use it when there was threat or suspicion to the kingdom. Or consensually. He'd used it in the past to ease troubled minds and restless dreams, or to aid those who'd suffered so greatly that their last resort was to beg him to take either their memories or their lives.

"I'm glad you two are still here," Nik slipped out in confession. He didn't care how pitiful it sounded. "When do you plan to leave for Rhyenelle?"

The subject exasperated Jakon. "I can't be certain. Marlowe keeps insisting there's client work to be done, yet I hardly see anything new around the compound." A lingering accusation tightened his lips, yet Nik understood it pained Jakon to suspect anything of his fiancée.

"You don't think she is being truthful." Nik didn't make it a question.

Jakon ran a hand over his face, sparing a glance around him as though the blacksmith might be within earshot. "Marlowe would never withhold anything that could put any of us in danger," he said, locking eyes with Nik as if to be sure he knew it.

"I don't believe it's in her nature. Spirit duty or not." Nik's agreement eased Jakon's tense shoulders.

"I just can't be certain what her reasons are for needing to stay, and truthfully, I'm afraid for her."

"She has been distant."

"I'm glad you've noticed. I've been wondering if it's just me. With Faythe gone…we went through a rough patch last time. But she's assured me everything is fine."

As they began to walk out of the training room, Nik couldn't stop the hand that reached up to Jakon's shoulder. As though the gesture jarred them both, he let go, replacing the small comfort with words. "It's often the bravest faces that mask the worst troubles. Don't stop reaching to her. I can't fathom the burden she carries with her gift. I'm sure she will tell all when the time is right."

A heaviness swirled in the air in that moment, a darkness that clouded them both. As though a calm had settled over them before the break of a storm neither one was able to anticipate.

CHAPTER 11

Nikalias

Nikalias Silvergriff stared and stared at the item that had become his eternal torment since the day it came to be in his reluctant possession. His unblinking eyes almost convinced his mind he'd started to see movement between the fine hairs of the black-and-red feather, like tiny embers of flame. He sat deliberating what had weighed on his mind for some time now, ever since Faythe visited him through Nightwalking and took intrigue in the item. A Phoenix feather, she confidently claimed. She was the only person he could think of with the trove of knowledge possible to harbor any fact about the legends of the Firebirds. And after hearing Jakon's concern for her, Nik had been wanting to get a moment alone with Faythe to check in given Tauria's absence.

With a disgruntled huff, he pushed away from his desk, swiping up the damned feather and slinging his black cloak over his shoulders. The blaring sun added smothering heat under the reluctant layer, yet he didn't want to be tracked by guards or seen at all on his venture into the outer town. Luckily, as prince or king, Nik was skilled at eluding his own guard and could roam the town incognito.

He took the underground tunnels, keeping to the shadows of the most desolate paths in town. This route always came with the downfall of pungent scents and dreary gloom, but the unpleasant journey was necessary. He may be king, but explaining his ventures to Zarrius should word travel was not something he wanted to concern himself with.

The blacksmith's compound stood unexpectedly silent when it came into view. Nik welcomed himself stealthily into the back, not wanting to risk alerting any nearby fae if he called out. Marlowe was in the far corner with her back to him, seated at a desk where she appeared beautiful, engrossed in a book. A warm lantern glow spilled over the aged paper and breathed wonder onto her features.

"It must be unusual to visit a commoner's compound, Your Majesty," Marlowe teased as she twisted to look at him over her shoulder.

Nik straightened, taken aback that she'd picked up on his arrival when he'd been predatorily silent and careful. "How did you know it was me?" Taking steps further in, he relaxed within the enclosed space. Nik pulled down his hood, wiping his sweat-slicked brow and scanning the various weapons and equipment in awe. Marlowe was right. His vision tunneled with intrigue on steel partially formed to the shape of swords he'd wielded before, surrounded by the tools to craft them fully.

Marlowe's book thumped shut, pulling his attention back to her. The blacksmith stood but leaned with arms crossed and a mischievous smile. Yet as he met her ocean eyes, he was lost at the distance in them. A hollowness he tried to place.

"You saw me coming," he concluded, blanching at the thought of appearing in one of her *foresights.* The Spirits had no reason to keep track of him.

Marlowe smirked. "Something like that."

A pause of silence settled, and Nik realized she was waiting for him to explain his impromptu visit. He cleared his throat, oddly nervous about the topic he thought to bring to her. He hesitantly reached into his pocket for the feather.

Marlowe instantly straightened from her lax position, taking tentative steps toward him. She didn't tear her eyes from the feather, so many curiosities now filling her irises. He wanted to know what she was thinking, but Nik stayed silent, allowing her to walk right up to him and observe every surface detail.

Nik extended it to her. "I was hoping you could tell me all you know about Phoenix feathers," he admitted, near cringing at the ridiculousness of calling the feather that. Yet Faythe had been so sure despite having only glimpsed a materialized version. And her confidence in its authenticity rattled his thoughts, so much so he couldn't get the damn thing off his mind, much as he despised the sight of it. Despised it for the curse of knowledge about his mate's dire fate it burdened him with.

Marlowe took the feather with caution, examining it so slowly Nik was rooted to the spot, on edge. He flexed his fists to distract himself from the need to press her for information. Finally, Marlowe released a long breath.

"It's real."

"How can you be sure?"

Marlowe met his eye as if assessing if he could handle the truth. "Because I knew you would bring it to me." She handed it back to him, and in his bewilderment, he vacantly took it.

She paced over to a disorganized bookshelf, her hands braced on her hips as she scanned the dust-coated spines. All Nik could do was watch her as she spoke so coolly, with an air of calm.

"It didn't make sense at first," she pondered out loud. "Fire, but not of nature. Healing, but not with fae magick. Abilities heightened beyond what was ever intended. When the Spirits presented such gifts, none were supposed to manifest past a certain strength. There are those more powerful than others, yes, but there is always a limit. No one ability can be altered. Except I kept seeing it. Healers gaining the ability to pull someone back from the cusp of death. Firewielders translating flame to lightning." Marlowe found the tome she was looking for, and Nik moved to aid her when it tumbled down and she winced with the weight of it, but she shot him an assuring smile, adding, "Nightwalkers gaining abilities in the conscious mind."

Nik paled completely at that as Marlowe thumped the large book onto the table, wafting loose parchments and rattling nearby tools. "Like what Faythe has?" he asked.

Marlowe canted her head, heaving open the book to no page in particular. "I can't be certain. Faythe is powerful even if she doesn't have the body to wield it. I don't think she could be matched from her combined bloodlines. But a weaker variation, perhaps. Enough that she should be fearful of anyone with such an extension to their Nightwalking."

"I've had that thing in my possession for near a hundred years. It must not be the real thing, or the legends are false."

Marlowe shot him a playful look. "Don't be so simple-minded. Possession isn't power."

Nik blinked, caught between amusement and bewilderment at Marlowe's casual gibe. A chuckle escaped his lips, and it warmed his chest to see the flicker of brightness on her face, which had seemed cloaked in shadow recently. "How are you, Marlowe?" he blurted, a small frown saddening his features. He may have been consumed by his losses and duties, but he couldn't help but notice the blacksmith seemed…distant. It wasn't what he expected considering she and Jakon were soon setting off to reunite with Faythe. Nik had tried to suppress his envy at that fact. That they were free to leave as they wished while his chains allowed him to stray only so far from his throne. He couldn't allow himself to think about Faythe or the perilous journey she was venturing on right now. Too many desolate outcomes to such an endeavor had him straining to screw the consequences and follow after her.

"I'm well." Marlowe brushed him off and shuffled aimlessly through the pages as if in the hope it would sway the topic away from her completely.

Nik took careful steps closer until they could embrace if they leaned into it. Still, Marlowe didn't look up, didn't stop her page-sifting. Gently, he placed his hand on the book before she could turn another page. It forced her eyes up to his.

"I hope you know you can come to me," he offered, "with Faythe gone and now Tauria too. I was close with both of them, and my door is always open for anything."

Marlowe flinched as if it pained—or relieved—her to hear it. She stared at him, her lips parting and shutting, and for a second he believed she might open up to him, voice what danced on the surface of the ocean that swirled with ghostly trouble in her eyes. Nik didn't envy her gift, seeing how oppressive it could be in such a delicate human. But Marlowe seemed to lose the sense of confliction to share what was troubling her. Every emotion that begged him to find the answer she couldn't speak disappeared in her next blink. It dropped like a weight in Nik's stomach that he couldn't help her. Marlowe held a duty with her knowledge, and it was not for him to press for answers for risk of altering far more than he could comprehend.

Marlowe's voice hummed quietly as she fixed her sights back to the book, and Nik removed his hand. "You are good, Nik. One day your sacrifices will reap reward. Your heart will learn to heal."

He didn't know what she meant by it, but a coldness swept his skin.

"What's going on here?"

Both their heads snapped to the entrance, and Nik had already halfway drawn his dagger. He sagged in relief to see Jakon, but Nik cursed himself for being so entranced by Marlowe's words that he'd failed to pick up on his approach at all.

Jakon stood with a frown of accusation that puzzled him, until Marlowe straightened her back and their arms touched to alert him to their closeness. He took a step to distance himself from her immediately. Humans weren't as territorial as fae, and Nik thanked the Spirits for this, as he was sure he'd be dealing with far more than a look for his proximity to Jakon's fiancée.

"Hey, Jak." Marlowe's voice echoed warmth, her eased expression genuine in his presence. His arrival drew attention to the dull sunlight that didn't filter so strongly through the curtain now. He should be getting back to the castle, but he needed answers about the feather that lay beside the book. Despite all Marlowe had revealed possible, part of him hoped it was nothing more than a hoax, a fake, and that he could discard of the thing for good.

Jakon came to stand by Marlowe's side, and in that second her sad eyes twinkled with happiness, her weak posture found excitement, and she relaxed visibly when his arm encircled her waist. Nik looked away just as he leaned down to kiss her in greeting. He'd long since detached himself from feeling anything about other people's romantic gestures.

"We should be getting back," he said to them.

Jakon didn't release Marlowe, but his eyes drifted to the book. The Phoenix feather still lay on top of it, and he frowned at it in question.

"I came to Marlowe to find out more about it," Nik explained, as he imagined Jakon's surprise to find him out here without reason. He turned his attention to the blacksmith. "Can you find out more? We could meet in my private council chamber tomorrow."

Marlowe nodded. Twisting out of Jakon's arms, she closed the book over on the feather. Nik flinched as she carelessly crushed it within the large volume. She smirked at his reaction.

"For someone who doesn't believe, you seem quite concerned about a dyed pheasant feather."

Nik huffed a laugh. "I guess you can say I've become attached. And maybe your words are swaying me."

Marlowe heaved the heavy book into her arms but didn't bear its weight for long before Jakon swiftly took it from her and she smiled gratefully.

"I trust you to be discreet with this. Don't look into it or display the feather anywhere public. If what you've said so far is true, we may have a great weapon in our hands—if we can figure out how to use it."

Jakon's features firmed, and Nik's fae instincts flared at the hint of threat the human likely didn't even know he emanated. "What are you dragging her into?" he accused.

Nik almost winced. He hadn't considered his request for knowledge could bring danger to the blacksmith. He still couldn't be sure *what* they were dealing with should the feather prove to be real.

Marlowe laid a hand on his arm. "Nothing. It's just research," she assured him.

Diverting the topic, Nik said, "I don't wish to be seen. I'll have to take the underground back to the castle. You two should head back, retire for the night. Research about the feather can wait." He directed this last part to Marlowe alone, knowing she was likely itching to dive back in. Discovering ancient and wondrous things was *fun* for her. Nik merely welcomed the task as a distraction from his fake courtship. From the judgment of his every move. But nothing could sway his thoughts from Tauria, nor would he want anything to—not until he'd heard she was safe and sound.

CHAPTER 12

Tauria

TAURIA SAT ACROSS the table from the Prince of Olmstone. Katori lay by his side, and she was beginning to feel more at ease around the tame wolf through regular sightings. But her awareness and attention flicked to her assigned guard by the door.

Lennox didn't meet her eye once. He stood as alert and laser-focused as the others. As he stared out over the balcony, she wondered where his mind went and if he too dreamed of the vibrant lands of Fenstead as one of her people. At least, he'd led her to believe he was one of her people in giving her the brass stag pin. Such a simple item had doused her with so much strength and relief for what it symbolized, and that morning her fading spirit sparked with determination once more. The emblem of her kingdom was a badge of remembrance and pride that she'd secured within a hidden fold of her dress.

Tauria wanted to get a moment alone with Lennox and had barely slept at all last night with the barrage of questions she had for him. But there was something more pressing that had caused her frequent restless nights since being here.

"Have there been any letters for me?" Tauria blurted. She didn't use Nik's name or mention his kingdom in the hope it would disguise her desperation.

Tarly eyed her carefully with a pause. "No, there have not." So cold, but she couldn't feel guilty for the question.

Her heart sank, but Nik's silence didn't feel right. He hadn't visited her through Nightwalking or sent a single letter, and she couldn't believe he'd neglect to check in so uncaringly.

"From whom might you expect one?"

Tauria felt the careful challenge but didn't balk under Tarly's firm expression. "I would have expected word from High Farrow by now," she confessed. Her heart thumped. She hoped her inquiry seemed detached from her personal yearning so he'd interpret nothing more than political interest. She added, "I hope we can get things moving soon for this alliance."

Tarly's silence often rattled her nerves, accompanied by his assessing stare. The workings of his mind were expertly guarded by his exterior, always keeping her on edge. He averted his gaze, face turning bored. "Nothing of importance or interest is being discussed yet. You have my word I'll inform you about anything of concern."

Tauria didn't see any gain in informing him she planned to send word to High Farrow herself. Nik's name had become a switch to Tarly's irritation. After all they'd been through together, she had to know how he fared despite the twist in her gut that she'd be the one to reach out first.

"How is the garden coming along?"

Tarly's voice stole her attention, and her heart leaped as though she were silently devising a traitorous plan. "It will take some time, but my new helper is very keen to make it thrive again."

Tarly arched a brow. She found his interest endearing.

"Opal is quite the free and wondrous spirit. I have to thank you for helping get permission for her to join me the other afternoon."

At the mention of his half-sister, the smile he wore was one she hadn't seen before. His hollow eyes filled with genuine warmth. Her chest tightened with the realization of how rare this was. The prince wasn't one to surface emotions so easily.

He huffed a short laugh, reaching for his cup. "I had a feeling you two would get along. It's not often she gets to be creative."

Tauria leaned forward. "She loves the garden. I was actually hoping to speak with your father and request she join me whenever she likes." She didn't miss the flinch of his brow as he set down his cup. Her careful inquiry on the princess's behalf was also a tactful test to see if Tarly would shed any information on the king's movements.

"My father is rather occupied. I'm sure it would be the least of his concerns to see my sister covered in a little dirt," he answered. "Though I cannot be certain she won't be disciplined by her mother."

Her mother. So many questions swirled in her mind, and she shifted in contemplation of which to settle on. Tauria studied the distance in his hazel eyes as he mentioned the queen, and on reflection, Tauria couldn't remember her and the prince being even remotely close during their time in High Farrow. She guessed he harbored resentment for the fae who'd seemly swooped in to replace his mother within a century of Varlas losing his mate.

"I haven't had the pleasure of meeting with the queen since I arrived." Tauria decided to push further, but her fist clenched when Tarly's eyes targeted her. The assessment he bore naturally triggered the scraping of her nails over her palm as a distraction. So far, every time she'd been around the prince it was like being on a minefield; one wrong step could trigger his emotional barrier. The dust would once again settle, but it was only a matter of time before her footing stumbled.

Tarly was a puzzle she couldn't figure out how to piece together. Perhaps she pitied him. Her heart saddened with the thought he didn't know how to fix his scattered pieces either. Or had long since given up trying.

After careful contemplation, Tarly obliged her curiosity. "My father has been meeting with some important lords to figure out our kingdom's next movements since the rocky conflicts last winter."

Tauria soaked up every word, storing them for careful consideration and investigation later.

"Keira will no doubt be doing what she does best. Sitting pretty in her ostentatious quarters, gifted and redesigned for her at this kingdom's expense, entertaining young ladies in pointless luncheons to gossip about petty court affairs." Tarly reclined, fingers fidgeting with his knife against the oak table as he spoke of her. His words were coated in aversion. It was clear he didn't care for what Tauria made of them. He huffed a breath. "She's not one to reach out despite the forced pleasantries she might have shown you in High Farrow. I'm afraid she's far too esteemed for such matters now she's back in her own domain. If you desire her company, feel free to wander by the east quarters anytime."

"Desire" was far from how Tauria would describe her feelings, but she was grateful for the knowledge she tucked away for later. She wondered if Tarly realized the trust he was placing in her by revealing his true feelings about Keira, and in doing so, reassuring her the queen's lack of reception wasn't personal.

"Do you like it here, Tauria?"

She picked up her cup, taking a sip as she gazed out over the balcony. "Very much so."

"Hmm."

Tauria watched him as he followed her line of sight, a sarcastic smile edging his lips. "I don't know why you would. Bland colors, stone walls, the heat. Surely it must be a far cry from all you admire about your home."

"I will always favor Fenstead's landscapes, of course. But I admire your kingdom. It's beautifully fitting. I look forward to learning more about the lands."

Tarly gave a single dry laugh, and Tauria's head canted as she observed him.

"You do not agree?"

He still didn't meet her eye, as though he'd drifted somewhere else, somewhere far from them. His long inhale seemed to tumble him back to the present, though his features remained thoughtful. "I prefer the cold, actually."

"I was led to believe Olmstone's winters weren't so."

"You would be right. Does that mean I cannot prefer it?" His stare fell to her then, searching and rare. "I've often wondered if we're all born cursed to desire what doesn't come so easily. To long for what is always just out of reach."

Tarly's words were surprisingly inspiring. Thought-provoking. Guilt started to unsettle her stomach for not appreciating what lay beneath the surface of the cold prince.

He asked plainly, "Do you have plans this afternoon?"

She thought she detected his hope that she'd say no. But Tauria's knee bounced under the table with her giddiness to find some alone time so she could confront Lennox, so she nodded. "I think I might head to the garden if I am to make any progress this summer," she mused lightheartedly, though she had confidence the garden would be thriving in no time if she had her way.

The shift in his expression was unexpected, as though disappointment dampened his mood that she'd want to cut short time with him. Tarly didn't seem inclined to ask her to stay, nor to offer any counterplan that involved her company. His voice slipped back to its emotionless tone, and he didn't look at her. "If that is what you wish."

Part of her wanted to stay. To offer they do something together as his silence seemed to call for it. She couldn't be sure what it was about the prince that made her sympathize with him. Perhaps it was witnessing the effects of the royal court that had weighed her down too. Loneliness. So far, she hadn't witnessed Tarly engaging with anyone. Not a friend or a guard or even the ladies who weren't subtle in their flirtations even from a distance. It was as if he shut out the world completely.

Tarly rose before her sympathy could manifest. It should have been a relief that he was leaving, yet she couldn't prevent her longing to ease the shadows that tormented him. To discover their cause and what it took to chase them away, even if just for a moment.

"Enjoy the gardens, princess. I look forward to seeing the results of your efforts once you've had more time to make significant progress." His words were kind, but they rang with an undertone of pain. He'd told her the pavilion garden was once a spot his mother loved, and in that moment their thoughts might have aligned as she found herself wondering what she would have been like. Tauria had only glimpsed Queen Freya from afar when they'd visited Fenstead. All she remembered thinking was how much her son adored her and resembled her beauty with his dark blond hair and soft features. Only Tarly's eyes were his father's, even more so over the years as they seemed to adopt the same cold detachment.

"I hope I can see you again soon," Tauria called as he made for the door.

Tarly halted, taking a contemplative pause as if debating whether or not to give her the smile that edged his lips. "I'll make sure of it."

Then he was gone.

Tauria didn't get a moment to linger on the sadness that rippled in the prince's wake when her eyes caught on Lennox.

"Shall we go, Your Majesty?"

She scanned the other guards who were positioned further inside. "Yes, but first I should like some exercise after sitting all morning. May we go on a walk of the castle grounds?" The plan was simple but the best she could think of for them to stray far enough away from listening ears.

Lennox seemed to know exactly why she'd suggested the activity, and a knowing twinkle in his eye accompanied his nod. "After you."

Olmstone's grounds were formed of pillars and sculptures. So many depictions were etched into the stone that surrounded them that it took away Tauria's longing for greenery. Occasionally, the beige was broken up by fountains displaying crystal waters or a pond that housed mesmerizing species of large fish she hadn't seen before. Oranges and reds spotted their scales, and she knew if she got closer more color could be glimpsed under the water's iridescent sheen.

Tauria's eagerness for a conversation with Lennox was subdued as she took her time strolling through the grounds taking in the sights that changed at every turn. From her balcony she wasn't able to appreciate the craftsmanship and history surrounding the castle. Into stone, man or fae had carved art or script, and she traced slow fingertips along the warm, gritty texture, brought to life by the sunlight that seemed eager to attract even distant eyes.

They'd traveled far enough now that Tauria was confident in her ability to speak with caution on the topic that had been causing chaos in her thoughts, but she was in no hurry as she approached another large pond. She crouched and decided to sit on its broad rim with the urge to feel the cool water.

"They're magnificent," she muttered, admiring the tango of colorful fish.

Lennox stayed standing. "I believe they call them Coyrico fish. They're considered spiritual. Many come by the ponds to pray or offer their wishes."

Tauria breathed in awe of Olmstone's traditions and religions, finding herself longing to know more. Casting her eyes up to Lennox, her hand shielded her face against the summer sun. He noticed her squinting and shifted to block the rays from her completely, turning him into a dull silhouette. She smiled sheepishly.

"Does the castle have a library?"

Lennox nodded. "It is small and used mostly for the king's personal collection."

Her enthusiasm dissipated at this.

"However, there is the Livre des Verres."

Tauria's mouth popped open. She'd heard of the great library. It was perhaps the biggest and most sought-after trove of knowledge in Ungardia. But her logistics and way with maps had never been her strong suit. She winced as she asked, "Is it far from the castle?"

Lennox chuckled. "Not at all. It's within Vesmire."

The capital city they were in. Tauria's mood lifted immensely. Only, it was quick to dissipate in the knowledge that while the library was close, convincing the prince to allow her to leave the castle grounds would prove a challenge. She'd already felt the weight of the Wolverlons' protectiveness within the confines of the grounds. She'd put it on hold for now. Her leisure activities had to come second to what she came here to accomplish.

With that thought, Tauria scanned their surroundings. They were far enough from the castle that none of the guards would overhear, but while a few roamed the grounds, they still had to take caution with fae hearing. Deeming there were no eyes on them, Tauria shifted the material on her chest to reveal the Fenstead pin she wore.

"Why did you give me this?"

Lennox turned rigid in alarm, sparing a quick glance around before dropping into a crouch. "Why are you wearing that? I didn't give it to you for you to risk wrath by flaunting it where they can see."

"It is not a crime to wear my kingdom emblem."

"No, it is not. But they're testing you, Tauria. They want to know your loyalty does not lie solely in your own kingdom and that you stand to use them for your gain. You need to show them your fealty."

"I will do no such thing." She flared in defense, palms tightening with an effort to keep her voice level. "I hoped that you gifting me this was an indication you were on my side."

"I will stand on the side that will keep you safe. Defiance does not sit well here."

"Then why give it to me?"

His face softened, and she despised the pity aimed at her. "I want you to know you have an ally here. In time, perhaps a friend."

Her anger slowly defused with his words. As it did, maybe she even started to agree with him. Tauria carefully hid her beautiful pin once more. "How did you come to be in Olmstone as a royal guard?"

Lennox shifted, finally sitting down, his knees bent and arms extended over them. "I found myself here after the kingdom fell and all there was left to do was try to get as many to safety as possible."

"Did many…?" Tauria's pulse picked up hard and fast. A creeping terror surfaced her panic, along with flashbacks of memory. But she *had* to know. "Did many make it?"

"I don't have numbers, not even close. I am sorry, Tauria."

Her hand reached out in comfort, but Lennox flinched. His eyes swept their surroundings like clockwork.

"Gossip spreads faster than flame here," he explained.

Tauria swallowed her disappointment. She understood. At least, she tried to. Never in High Farrow had she been made to feel as if everything she did was met with judgment. Yet while there were no nearby lingering bodies, Lennox looked to the stone pillars and walls as though they were the eyes of discernment. He gave a long sigh before he continued.

"I came to Olmstone for safety, but I was of a minority. Most fled to Rhyenelle. I am uncertain how many."

Tauria felt her first wave of hope. If what she had learned about

King Agalhor was true, she hoped the ruler had been merciful in rehoming her people in their time of need. If he was anything like his daughter—like Faythe—Tauria was confident any survivors were safe and cared for in Rhyenelle.

"Do they know you're from Fenstead?"

Lennox shook his head. "It is better they don't."

Tauria frowned. "How so?"

"They're not so inclined to outsiders. Not with the shortage of land and supplies here. Any Fenstead natives who came here wisely abandoned all ties to their homeland."

Tauria's gut twisted with guilt. Shame. That she had failed them so badly it was easy for them to deny claim to their birthland.

"As fate would have it, I ended up exactly where I needed to be. Here—for you."

She turned to meet his gaze, but he was quick to avert it. She wanted so badly to embrace him, to utter her gratitude, as for the first time since she'd arrived…Tauria no longer felt so alone.

"I'm so glad you're here, Lennox. Thank you for all you've told me. Your secret is safe with me."

Lennox offered a small smile. "I promise to tell you anything I learn in the guard that they could be sheltering from you. I think this alliance is exactly what we need to finally move toward what we have all been waiting for."

Tauria's chin rose with a flare of hope. She stood, allowing her mind to conjure the wonderful image of her vibrant kingdom of prosperity. Without apology, without fear. Her breath released long and light. "Taking back Fenstead."

CHAPTER 13

Nikalias

NIK WAITED BY the waterfall in the Eternal Woods, trying to ignore the pining in his heart at the memories that surfaced here. He looked over the space, picturing his days sparring with Faythe. Carefree moments when all he'd believed her to be was a human with a steel will and a unique interest in swordplay. He found himself wondering about her often, imagining the hot-headed, witty human dominating the mighty kingdom of Rhyenelle. He thought it equal parts amusing and unbelievable…awe-invoking. Because he knew with time, the crown could fit wonderfully.

He awaited the arrival of Jakon and Marlowe after craftily getting word their meeting point had changed days ago. He couldn't risk their discussion being overheard even in his private council room. Jakon and Marlowe had already passed the trial to enter the ethereal space last winter, and he was confident it remained a secret to all others considering what dwelled within.

Cracking branches signaled his moment of somber reflection was over. Turning, he spotted his friends emerging through the tree line, hand in hand. Jakon carried the book Marlowe had been in the midst of studying.

"Thank you for meeting me here," Nik said when they were close enough.

Marlowe smiled, pleasant as always. "You were smart to think of this place."

He only felt a fool for not thinking of it sooner. But it took effort to conceal his absence from the castle now. He didn't want to add further speculation to Zarrius's accusation that his mind wasn't on his kingdom.

The blacksmith wasted no time in dropping to the grass and shifting to get comfortable.

"We brought this for a reason," Jakon said, extending a blanket.

Marlowe grinned up at him. "That's for the book." She patted the space in front of her.

Jakon rolled his eyes but spread out the material before laying down the thick tome. Nik couldn't fight his tender amusement. They were an effortless pairing, and their company warmed his cold chest.

"You'll never guess what I found out." Her eyes were aglow with wonder as she flipped through pages.

"She's barely been coaxed away from the damn thing," Jakon muttered.

"It's quite fascinating, really," Marlowe dismissed, too engrossed in her scripture to notice his worry.

Nik asked carefully, "Have you found out if it's real?"

I don't think we'll know for sure until we test what I've found. They say only the Phoenix Riders could feel the pull of true feathers."

"Phoenix Riders?" Nik arched a brow.

Marlowe nodded. "Those with a rare connection to them. During the time of the Firebirds, they were able to form true parings. The Ashfyres were among the first of the bloodlines found to harbor the gift of taming the Phoenix."

It shouldn't have been a surprise, but Nik and Jakon exchanged a knowing look of concern and bewilderment. Was there any limit to the impossibilities surrounding Faythe?

"The feathers lose their vibrancy and power if the Firebird they belong to is killed," Marlowe went on casually.

Nik huffed in defeat, taking a few strides forward to settle against a nearby boulder. "So it has no use."

"Not necessarily."

"The Phoenix birds are long since extinct."

Marlowe peered up at him. Her head canted in challenge. "Because you are ignorant to believe otherwise?"

He hooked a brow at her brazen speech. Even Jakon shifted nervously, inching a little closer to her as though Nik might reprimand her. "Go on," was all he said, the hint of a smile curving his lips to match hers.

Marlowe dipped back to flipping pages until she arrived at the section she searched for. "Like I said, we won't know until we test its capabilities. My visions are true about what the feathers can do. They can temporarily alter and heighten abilities, but being in possession of the feather is not enough. It takes an herbalist to grind it down, a potion-maker to make the elixir, then someone with enough spell magick to activate the amplifier. It's then consumable. The size of the feather determines how many vials can be made, and how long the amplifier lasts will vary depending on the strength of the origin bird."

Nik ran a hand down his face in exasperation. "It will take time to find those kinds of people."

Marlowe's smile made him wary. "I didn't think you would mind considering you were content to simply cling to the feather without discovering what it could do. Or discard it completely."

His brow furrowed in confusion, but Marlowe disturbed the peaceful clearing, already rummaging through a small satchel. Jakon shifted a cautious gaze between them both before she found what she was looking for. She revealed two small bottles sealed with a silver wax, beaming in admiration as the thick red liquid sparkled against the sunlight when she shook them. Nik straightened in awe, staring wide-eyed as he inched closer.

"You found them already?"

"I told you, she hasn't stepped away from the project."

"I know of an herbalist whose husband was a regular client of mine for years. All it took was a trip to the apothecary south of the town."

"When did you go across town?"

Marlowe cut Jakon a look at his concern. "It's hardly a treacherous venture." Even so, she placed a tender hand on his thigh that eased Jakon's face.

"They call it Phoenix Blood." Marlowe shook the glistening crimson liquid. "It was highly prized and entirely illegal to trade. All kingdoms agreed in treaty with Rhyenelle to punish anyone caught selling or consuming it. In the wrong hands…it can grant those with abilities an immensely heightened power."

Nik's attention was transfixed on the bottles. "You said you only found the herbalist and the apothecary."

"Yes."

"So they're not active potions?"

"No. As they are, they might cure someone from a nasty illness, but their true power is in magick."

Nik crossed his arms. "Well, my point remains. The feather is all but useless. No one's heard of practicing spell magick in thousands of years. It's a dead practice since the abilities manifested to be what they are now."

"Or no one's paid them any attention—because what's a lowly spell compared to what the likes of you can do so effortlessly?"

"I'm constantly wondering if I admire you or fear you for your outspokenness, Marlowe," Nik commented.

She let out a delightful chuckle. Setting down the bottles, she reached back into the pack and produced a small wooden box. Nik canted his head, noticing the markings that had been burned onto the wood struck a familiarity.

"I have spiritual blood, and I've been looking into what that truly means. I can receive visions from the Spirits, and they've been getting intense recently." Marlowe's expression faltered as she stared at the box in her hands but seemed to travel elsewhere. Perhaps to one of the foretellings that shifted the mood instantly. Before Jakon or Nik could voice their concern, she quickly wiped her expression, inhaling a long breath before continuing her train of thought. "I thought maybe I could harbor enough to translate it into spell magick."

Nik inhaled a long breath. Marlowe was brilliant. He found himself always in awe in her company. "Have you tried?" he asked.

Marlowe flipped a couple of pages. "Of course I have."

Jakon chuckled softly, his hand trailing down her spine while pride twinkled in his stare.

Nik couldn't fight his smirk. "I'm guessing you had some success, or you wouldn't waste time on such a tale."

Marlowe met his gaze with a confident side-smile. Producing a small knife, she looked to Jakon expectantly. He raised his palm to her in response. "He wouldn't let me use my own blood," she muttered, exchanging a playful look with Jakon. Carefully, Marlowe winced as she cut his flesh.

Nik stood closer, confusion stirring his concern. He watched them both, and a part of his mind concluded—*screamed*—what was happening right before his eyes.

Because he had seen it before.

His eyes were fixed, tracking their every movement as he vacantly closed the steps between them to be sure what he witnessed was real.

Jakon squeezed his fist to gather enough blood before he slowly moved his arm to hover over the box. Marlowe began whispering ancient words without a script, memorized from so long ago when he first heard them. Jakon's blood fell onto the seal, three drops, just as Marlowe finished her spell and all went still.

Nik's heart pounded. The forest murmurs hushed, the waterfall behind them silent. He stared and stared, about to relax his shoulders as it wasn't true. Or Marlowe hadn't succeeded.

But then the seal glowed, and Nik struggled to stay present as it took him to another memory. He couldn't believe what he was seeing as the clasp came loose.

Marlowe had created a Blood Box.

"You bound the magick to it?" It seemed like a ridiculous question, but he had to be sure it was once an ordinary wooden box before the blacksmith got hold of it.

She grinned in triumph as she opened it fully. "Yes. It took some time. I wasn't sure I had it in me at first. It's incredibly draining on whatever kernel of power I have."

"Too draining," Jakon inserted, worry taking over his expression as he tucked a loose strand of hair behind her ear. "She was weak for days afterward. I know what the Phoenix Potions can do, but it's a higher scale of spell than what binds the Blood Box. I've tried to talk her out of being the one to do it."

His protest was understandable. While Nik's pulse raced a thrill to learn they could be in possession of the legendary potion, he couldn't support Marlowe's life hanging in the balance for it.

"It's amazing you discovered all this, Marlowe, but I must agree. We'll track down someone else, or perhaps they'll never come to their true power if the feather is not real. We do not need it."

Marlowe's features firmed. "I can do this," she argued, mostly at Jakon, and Nik gauged it to be something they'd debated hotly before. "It's a weapon we can't pass up. I may not be as good as Faythe with a sword, or a resilient monarch like Tauria, but I have the ability to impact this war as much as anyone. I don't need to be protected, and I don't need to be told what I'm capable of."

Stunned into silence, neither male had the words to counter Marlowe's passionate speech. She was right, and Nik fully admired her dedication to the cause. She saw the grand scale this could reach: a bigger war beyond the possible clash of three courts when High Farrow, Olmstone, and Fenstead negotiated a treaty.

"Thank you," Nik said, glancing at Jakon, who battled a conflict of pride and concern. "Just remember all magick has a well, and that well has a bottom. If you feel yourself getting too close to it, you have to stop, no matter how close you think you are to achieving your goal."

Marlowe nodded in understanding, and upon glancing her fiancé's notes of worry, she gave his thigh an assuring squeeze. "I won't go past my limit."

CHAPTER 14

Tauria

Tauria found herself in the castle's training room, dressed in fighting leathers and armed with the staff gifted by Marlowe. She'd had little opportunity to test out the unique invention from her brilliant friend. She planned to learn the way it could answer to her wind, and she longed to feel the blissful freedom of losing herself in her ability. Tauria didn't track how many precious hours she stole before word of her being in the training room traveled to the prince or king. She hadn't informed anyone of her endeavor. The guards were reluctant, but she was crafty in her words and got them to agree to escort her down here by permission of the prince—a lie she was sure to receive punishment for later. She didn't care. She could handle a scolding in return for the stolen moment of freedom.

Trying to find release from her tormenting mind, she twisted and twirled, her staff a weightless guide to her steps as she imagined a phantom adversary. Her wind breezed gloriously cool against her heated skin while she parried, strands of her bound hair coming loose and catching in the wisps. Her wind weaved through her like a song; it whispered a melody that had her moving in perfect harmony. Push and pull. Yield and attack. The world around her ceased to exist when she lost herself so wholly to her ability.

Tauria finished with a quick whirl, dropping into a crouch as she aimed the tip of her staff into a tail blast that hurtled toward the invading presence. Her intruder anticipated the attack, bracing firmly to absorb the strike while his hands protected his face.

When she stood, Tauria let out a breath of surprise. Lycus straightened, his grin beaming as their eyes met. Tauria's absent steps had already closed the distance, and her arms clamped around his neck when they met in the training ring.

"Where have you been?" was all she could ask, every negative feeling from their tense reunion dissipating in her relief that he was here.

Lycus's grip released her, but his hands lingered on her waist while hers didn't leave his chest. She tunneled into his green eyes for a few seconds before she snapped back into herself. Her cheeks flushed at their closeness, which had extended to an inappropriate length of time.

The general cleared his throat. "The king had some rather tedious *interrogations* for me."

Tauria frowned, her temper flaring. "I was not informed you were under interrogation."

"I didn't suppose they would tell you. Though I understand their need to heed caution around a new presence in their castle. Do not be upset by it." His face softened, and Tauria hated that it fanned her anger more. As though she wouldn't understand from a leadership perspective why such measures were necessary.

"I should have been told of your questioning, and I might have agreed with them. But you are still my general, and I don't care for the king believing he is within his rights to question Fenstead citizens without my say so."

"You are right." Lycus walked over to the wall of weaponry, retrieving an ordinary long staff. When he returned, he spared a cautious glance to the guards down the hall before his voice pitched low and he leaned in close. "We have to be smart here, Your Majesty. From what I've gathered, the Wolverlons won't yield power so easily even with regard to you." He stood so close only a slither of space remained between them, his breath tickling her ear, and in that second, Tauria's pulse missed a beat. Lycus pulled back, but not without locking her gaze with a look that crawled down her spine. She couldn't be sure if he knew what he was doing. If he remembered a time long before their kingdom was conquered when they'd gotten too close with reckless impulse. Far closer than a princess should ever get to her father's general. A match that would never be seen as *appropriate* for a royal. Though it wasn't what she sought from him, or he from her. A curious infatuation, nothing more. "Let's find out if all those years sitting pretty in High Farrow have dampened your skills, shall we?"

The shift was needed. Tauria expelled the memory completely. She took a few deep breaths to cool the heat she blamed on her previous exertion, and then she matched his arrogant smile.

"I can assure you, all those years in High Farrow are about to put you on your ass."

His chuckle warmed her chest. Because it was like hearing home.

Then Tauria realized…Lycus was all she had left. The last person alive she could connect to her father.

Lycus was family.

"I can't imagine the prince was so adept at tuning your ability to your particular weapon," he commented.

Tauria heard the question as a careful test. Lycus sought to gain more information about Nik. She pushed aside the sad feelings that stirred alongside her joy. Getting to reflect on better memories also tugged on the melancholy that had settled in his absence. She angled her staff in a defensive stance to shadow her somberness. "The *king* was always very keen to learn my ways, you'll be glad to hear. Teaching him advanced my own skills." Tauria moved first, and despite the tingling in her veins that longed to release her wind, she stifled it. For now.

"Of course. How is His Majesty fitting into his new role?"

Wood thumped harshly against wood in a series of carefully dealt and avoided attacks. They started slow, getting a feel for each other's movements, which had changed and strengthened in their time apart. Their staffs locked, tips meeting the ground, and they shared wicked amusement.

"You know how nobles are to change. It will take time for him to find assurance in his position while he's being tested, but I have every faith in him."

"You sound like you admire him."

Tauria pushed off Lycus's staff, using her own for balance as she straightened. "I do. Is that so wrong for a monarch to admit?"

He arched an amused brow. "Not at all. I can only be grateful to him that he not only kept you safe but seems to have kept your spirit thriving too. I did worry…"

Tauria's firm shoulders faltered at the drop in his expression. She saved him from continuing. "We both lost a lot that day," she said quietly, and his small nod cut with heartbreaking agreement. "All we can be grateful for is that we survived. The battle may have been lost, but the war is far from over while we still live. I have Nik to thank for keeping me from spiraling into helplessness. He grounded me, reminded me always that while I was the ward to his father, I was still the Queen of Fenstead." Her voice strained with ache. Her head formed a dull throb. Tauria all but whispered, "He never let me forget that."

Lycus took a slow step toward her. "Then I am eternally grateful to him."

Tauria nodded because so was she.

Sensing the dip in her mood, Lycus took a large step back. "You haven't shown me half of what you claim to be capable of."

Her smile lit brightly, thankful the general hadn't forgotten what worked best to divert her emotional spirals.

He angled his staff and braced. "Don't hold back this time. I've been longing to feel the breath of your air."

And so Tauria moved for him. They didn't battle, as this wasn't about triumph. It was a dance of remembering and reconciling. Learning everything that had changed for the better since they were parted. This was catching up on decades' worth of growth and learning and aging. Over a century's worth of pain and sorrow and longing poured out in the way they moved around each other. When they stopped, the last lick of her wind blew across her face, and as her other senses returned, the coldness alerted Tauria to the wetness trailing down her cheeks. The staff fell from her hand, its clatter echoing around the room as her hands raised to her face to muffle her sobs.

Strong arms wrapped her wordlessly, and she relaxed in that embrace. For the first time in a long time, Tauria let down her guard in company. But she wept with joy from having let go of her losses in her movements. Lycus had come to her with hope to see Fenstead reclaimed, and the prospect had never felt so *real.*

An alerting cough stole their attention, and Tauria jerked away from the general, knowing their closeness could be mistaken for something else entirely. They weren't being careful, and if it was—

Her relief whooshed out in a breath at finding Lennox by the training ring.

"You should be glad it is only me," he commented, reading her thoughts in the way he cast a glance behind him. If the prince had stumbled upon them instead, she would have far more explaining to do. Lennox, in contrast, eased a look of understanding. The sympathy in his eyes twinged in her chest but also roused her embarrassment.

Tauria quickly wiped her face, swiping up her staff and positioning herself confidently once more.

"Do I know you?" Lycus asked, his face creased in search of his answer as he strolled a little closer to the guard.

It became a habit to be looking over their shoulders, determining how hushed their words had to be or how craftily they had to speak to elude the constant nearby guards. Tauria didn't think they were entirely safe with their current proximity. Caution made her tense completely when Lennox decided to answer.

"I was a royal guard to the King of Fenstead. It is where I was born."

She gauged Lycus's surprise, then his realization. "By the Gods, what a miracle it is that you find yourself here." A wide grin of disbelief broke on the general's face, and his hand extended out to the guard who hesitated, always shy, always averting his gaze. But then he reached back, and they embraced forearms. Out of respect, as citizens from the same kingdom and with a common goal. The warmth that burst in Tauria's chest to witness the small act stung her nose, her eyes. Because the sight sparked a beacon of hope. Hope of bringing her people back together...then leading them home.

Tauria composed herself, swallowing the hard lump in her throat that formed of elation, not sadness, as they both turned to her.

"I've never seen a staff crafted quite like this before," Lennox admired, trailing his finger down the length of it.

Tauria smirked, twisting it horizontal. "A brilliant invention by a rather brilliant friend." As she tossed the staff into her other hand, her fingers slid across the lever that triggered the steel ends, sharp as any sword or dagger.

Lycus whistled low. "This friend of yours I will definitely have to meet."

Tauria's smile beamed with pride at the thought of the blacksmith. Then her eyes fell, saddened as she wondered how Marlowe fared without her. And Faythe. Often, she worried for both her human friends when their paths stemmed so far from each other now. All that kept her advancing toward her goal without allowing the pain of their separation to set her back was the hope that once they'd triumphed, they would be reunited once more.

"Shall we go again?" Lycus asked softly.

Her eyes lifted as he detected her shift of thought. Tauria rolled her shoulders, her smile arrogant, but her challenge targeted Lennox. "All you've done so far is stand pretty. Is that all it takes to become a guard these days?"

He curved a brow at her playful slander, but his step back voiced his reluctance. "Sparring with the future Queen of Olmstone is certainly a cause for execution."

His words tingled in her stomach, and she found her attention traveling to catch Lycus's reaction.

"She's the Queen of Fenstead first and foremost."

"That is where you are wrong, General."

The new voice that joined them eased in like a shadow of warning straightening her spine. Everyone's attention was drawn to the prince who strolled into the training room. His impeccable royal wears were exquisite on him, but they were also an indication he didn't venture down here to entertain the notion of combat. Lycus and Lennox dipped in a small bow as Tarly got closer.

"Don't fill her head with romanticized notions of what a marriage alliance would mean." He came to a stop, his hands folded behind his back as he stared the general down. The dominance that radiated from both of them thickened the air, but Tauria knew Lycus well enough. He wouldn't stand for the harsh words that came from the prince's mouth, and it was the first time she feared his reactions could provoke Tarly.

Tauria had to stay on the prince's side. She disarmed her staff, the snap of the metal bringing all their attention onto her. She was quick to follow the series of twists that shortened her staff until she clutched it as the size of a long dagger. Even Tarly let go of a flicker of admiration at the weapon. Then his eyes drifted over her from head to toe, and just for a second, she felt the impression of his attention like desire before his features returned to their unforgiving firmness.

"The prince is right," she said sweetly. It took effort to ignore Lycus's incredulous look. She strode toward Tarly. "Together we would be the King and Queen of Olmstone and Fenstead. Neither kingdom would come before the other." Stepping down from the platform, her look softened with effort when she gazed up at Tarly. She didn't break his stare but watched as the firm lines of his face eased. He agreed with her, though he would never voice it. Instead, his eyes flashed to Lennox and Lycus.

"A princess should not be wasting time down here. You could hurt yourself," he scolded.

It took great will to bite down her retort and the flush of heat that rose in her embarrassment. "It is a custom of my people," Tauria explained. She didn't look to her general, but she knew his expression would be straight with anger over the prince's mindless belittlement. She couldn't afford to have him snap on her behalf, just as she couldn't be sure the lengths to which the Wolverlons would go in punishment. It sank her gut to think she couldn't protect him here.

Tarly's cold eyes relaxed. His hand reached up, and Tauria's whole body tensed. His fingers carefully tingled over her cheek, stifling her breath, and the look he claimed her with made her forget their company. "I couldn't stand to see a mark on your face."

She might have believed his words as they were spoken with a low caress. But then his touch left her, as if he'd realized his error in letting his care slip free.

"How would you deal with the gossip and slander from the ladies of the court if you showed up marked and bruised? You have a station, and with that comes expectation and responsibility. This isn't the place for you."

It took tremendous will not to retort. Tauria clamped down on the inside of her cheek until she tasted blood. As much as it defeated her to submit to his words, she tunneled even more despairingly in the company of her longest friend and esteemed army general. Someone she had always looked up to and wanted to prove her strength and worth to. In a matter of seconds, all she'd proven herself to be was the weak and spineless *princess* she appeared.

"Will you escort me back to my rooms?" she asked tightly.

Tarly's smile was barely-there as he nodded, but she could sense his appreciation. His hand slipped around her back but barely touched her as he guided her to leave. Tauria spared one last look over her shoulder.

"I'll meet you soon, General Lycus." She tried not to wince at his unyielding stance and firm face. He pinned her with a look of disappointment he likely didn't realize before it shifted to aim subtle disapproval at the prince's back. Tauria only hoped he saw the pleading in her eyes and would reserve judgment.

CHAPTER 15

Nikalias

NIK NURSED A pounding headache as he looked over the mountain of books and documents—a tedious, mind-numbing side to his reign he'd actively avoided until now. The stacks of confidential, important documents had taunted him in the study area of his office for months since he'd pulled them all together. But he couldn't ignore his duty any longer, feeling if he were a worthy ruler he would do his due diligence on matters he wasn't always present to discuss when his father was king. He had nothing else to occupy his time with after all.

Hours into combing through boring decrees and laws, he was about to retire for the night. Nothing he'd found so far was of concern or required reassessment. Closing his book, the flash of a signature caught his attention on a loose slip of paper that shifted from it. Nik hooked his fingers between the pages, opening the book to pull the parchment free. Because it wasn't his father's sigil and name that immediately caught his attention. It was someone else's. One whose name instantly flushed a heat of rage in him before he even knew why it was stamped next to the previous king's.

Nik read the document, but as he began to filter through words that stopped time and halted his breathing, he rose slowly in disbelief. His eyes scanned every word. Twice. Some three times. His pulse picked up a sprint.

Betrayal.

That was what the entire document was. Betrayal from his father. Or at least a cunning, underhanded sleight from the master of evil Marvellas while she'd stolen his face.

It took a great test of will not to rip the document to shreds in his rising fury. The threat to his reign, even his *life*, that had been kept from him this whole time. There would be copies of something as important as this, likely owned by each and every one of the councilmembers whose signatures also appeared on the decree.

To determine the line of succession should he die without an heir.

A castle full of guards, a crown upon his head, yet his *safety* had been a mockery to him all along.

One lord whom his father favored the most. One with power, wealth, and a far more cunning plan than Nik could have predicted.

He stormed out of the room without a second thought.

It wasn't the lord in question Nik went to confront that night, though it did rage as his initial instinct. When he took a moment to deliberate and calm his wrath, he decided if there was a way to fight fire with fire, only one person might be able to help.

Nik made sure he wasn't being followed and no guards lingered outside Jakon and Marlowe's door. He winced at the late hour but gently knocked in the hope they were still awake. The pause before their answer heated his neck. Because he could hear the shuffling beyond the wood that signaled they were already awake, and it stirred an awkward guilt that he couldn't back away when they tried to avoid answering.

"It's me." Nik spoke quietly and close, adding, "It's urgent."

A few long seconds ticked by, so he was about to retreat, but surprise halted his near-turn when Jakon answered, pulling down the shirt he seemed to have flung on.

"I'm sorry for the late hour, but it's important."

The human's disgruntled features smoothed out but kept an edge of reluctance. He glanced back inside before deciding to step aside and let him in.

Nik realized his error the moment he slipped into the room with a careful check of the hallway. Marlowe sat up in bed, and from the scents swirling in the air, his guilt made the room tense, as obvious as what he'd clearly interrupted. She folded out of the covers, but Jakon was quick to make it to her, helping her into a robe since all she wore otherwise was a nightgown. Nik averted his gaze regardless.

"I won't stay for long, but I found something that couldn't wait. I want to know what you make of it," Nik explained, pacing over to the firepit, where a table was scattered with books and parchments.

"It had better be important for you to be here at all, never mind past midnight," Jakon grumbled.

"It threatens everything," Nik said plainly.

Marlowe came over to him, eyes falling expectantly to the parchment he'd failed to keep from the clutches of his anger. He handed over the creased document, heart pounding as he watched those ocean eyes flick back and forth over it. Jakon glanced over her shoulder with a hard frown.

The blacksmith's eyes rose. "You've only just found this?"

Nik shrunk back at the shame of his avoidance. "It was well-hidden." Not a complete lie.

"I'm not surprised. And you're right. This changes everything."

"It's true and binding then?"

"Without a doubt. Orlon created this long ago, and a majority signatures agree." Her eyes were filled with horror, detected by Jakon, whose hand went around her. "Should you die without an heir…Zarrius will reign over High Farrow."

"That bastard," Jakon muttered.

Nik ran a hand through his hair, awash with a lost sense of confidence. All this time, he'd sat before those councilmembers thinking they retained even a fraction of the respect they had for his father. He'd spoken to them and believed they listened, when all along he played the unwitting fool, keeping the seat warm for the one they truly desired to see on the throne.

It was unfathomable to imagine Lord Zarrius with the crown. A reign akin to Nik's father's with power and divide. Greed and conquer. He couldn't let that happen.

"You have the right to call a new vote," Marlowe said, still scanning every inch of the documents, analyzing what she could while she rubbed her temple. Her brilliant attention was exactly why he'd thought to come to her. "But it would reveal the fact you know about this."

"Shouldn't he?" Jakon weighed in.

Marlowe shook her head, a million thoughts written in her frown. "He's been counting on you not finding out about it for as much time as he can buy."

The conclusion had chilled Nik before now. The blaring target pinned to his back, which he'd walked around arrogantly, *foolishly*, unaware of. "Remove me, and the throne is his."

Marlowe's gaze widened with horror. A small warmth emitted in his chest at her concern. She felt this as more than just the prospect of the kingdom falling to malicious hands once again. Marlowe's worry was that of a close friend.

"Wouldn't he have tried that already? You've been king for months," Jakon said.

"In wait, yes," Marlowe began to explain. "But Nik's not had his coronation yet. This decree would only be binding once he's fully instated. Zarrius is biding his time."

"And I've given him plenty of time to work out how he'll achieve my assassination."

"If there's even a slight gathering of proof he could be behind it, he'll lose his claim. Even his life. This document proves he has the most motive," Jakon said.

"Zarrius is not to be underestimated. He's smart. He'll come up with something convincing to make it look like an accident. Or line someone else up to take the fall." The firm lines of Marlowe's face were calculating.

Nik paced, dragging with embarrassment and disappointment in himself that he hadn't discovered this sooner. It put into question everything he'd done so far as king. No—not a king in the eyes of his nobles. A pawn.

"We have the advantage of knowing this. You can't let them suspect that we do," Jakon said.

Nik's anger soothed at those words. Because the human spoke as if this wasn't just his fight, but theirs. And he didn't know how to voice his gratitude for it.

"I'll see if there's anything else I can find out in other scriptures on High Farrow's law, to be sure there isn't a way to overpower this decree underhandedly. In the meantime, you play the unwitting king, Nik. And if possible, you need to start figuring out who you can trust within your nobles. Perhaps start with those whose names aren't signed in favor of this law. You may have more allies than you think to help tip the scales."

Nik nodded, immensely grateful for the blacksmith's willingness to help. "I agree. Thank you, Marlowe."

Her smile shadowed pity, but her eyes sparked with purpose.

Marlowe enjoyed using her brain to delve into knowledge and wonders. He admired that no task seemed too big an ask.

"Meanwhile, we should look into who could be willing enough or foolish enough to be bribed into committing regicide," Jakon said with a chill.

Nik's spine stiffened with foreboding, wondering if the target might have been placed on his back all this time.

CHAPTER 16

Tauria

Tauria awoke from a dream that was blissful in sleep but cleaved her heart in consciousness. She sat up in bed, knees tucked in tight while she stared out at the moon. Tears threatened to fall as she'd been torn from Nik again even though it wasn't real. She wished it were. Wished she could at least know his lingering embrace really was him through Nightwalking rather than a mindless dream.

She knew the difference. Nik had Nightwalked to her many times with permission, teaching her how to block and what to look out for if he was ever there or they were parted. Tauria had expected him to try by now. Her yearning heart clung to a rapidly fading hope every night she closed her eyes and drifted off to sleep.

His silence carved a void she wasn't prepared for.

Deciding she wasn't getting anymore sleep, Tauria left the warmth of her bed and dressed in casual pants and a shirt. Her plan to pass the night and forget her sorrow might be a long shot if she couldn't elude the guards, but she had little to lose when they'd confined her to the stone cage anyway. She slung a black cloak over her shoulders and grabbed her compact staff, sliding it into the holster she'd made for it. Creeping to the door, it didn't take her long to detect the bored shuffling of guards beyond it. Two of them. Her teeth ground in irritation that she wasn't even left alone in the dead of night. She quickly came to wonder if the guards were a means of keeping her in, rather than to keep any enemy out.

A sense of unease laced her spine as she carefully backed away from the door, not wanting to alert them to the fact she was awake. She didn't think she'd given them any reason to suspect her, yet their watchful eyes made it clear suspicion was the default. Tauria had to work on gaining their trust, having been foolish enough to believe Varlas would be lenient with her as he was close to her father. Perhaps all the Olmstone king saw her as now was not her father's daughter, but her savior's spy.

Tauria liked to believe she was both, as well as her own avenger.

What she planned to do that night would certainly not win her any favors if she were caught. But in her need to find release after her restless night, she was willing to risk it. Her plan was innocent as she only longed to visit the stables. But would this only feed her sadness as it was an activity she often enjoyed with Nik? Horse racing with him was exhilarating, one of her favorite ways to escape and feel…*alive.* When the speed of the beast could whip through her hair and they'd soar like the wind without her having to touch her magick. Even their long days spent roaming the hills casually on horseback were some of her most treasured memories.

She ruled out the regular exit as the two guards outside the door wouldn't be content to escort her to the stables in the dead of night without alerting the prince—or worse, the king. A cunning smile curled her lips as Tauria spun to the balcony doors. As she stealthily stepped out, she carefully glanced over the stone ledge. Spying the two guards below, her fists clamped tight. She refrained from rubbing her wrists, but it began to inspire panic the more she realized she was a prisoner and they'd already anticipated her wind ability would aid her escape with the long drop below. Though she felt flattered they considered her so resourceful.

But they couldn't anticipate the lengths to which she was willing to go for freedom. Glancing behind her, Tauria spared a few quick glances at the distorted rooftop of the castle to calculate her movements. It hadn't stopped her in Fenstead, and it wouldn't stop her here. Her parents may never have found out, but even to this day she knew she had Lycus to thank for helping her evade detection, always able to intercept her sneaking around the castle rooftops. With her adrenaline high, Tauria wasted no time second-guessing before she was scaling the building like a nighttime assassin. Her cloak blended her to the shadows, and she assumed all to be asleep, oblivious to the silhouette darting across the occasional balcony. Tauria didn't fear the distance down, knowing she had her staff and the command of the wind to break her fall. She wouldn't avoid injury, but she wore confidence she could avoid death, and perhaps she'd already reached her breaking point not to care about meeting either.

Her gloved fingers clawed over stone, mind guiding her footing to carefully calculate her way back down a level when murmured voices carried on the wind, grabbing her attention. Tauria braced and flattened herself into the shadows of the rooftop, being utterly still. If she could hear them, there was a high chance they would hear her if she took a loud enough tumble. She strained her hearing. Two voices, and it didn't take long for her to distinguish one of them. Her eyes widened with the quickening of her heart, knowing the King of Olmstone stood within earshot to catch her running amok over his castle.

If she wasn't a suspect before, an iron cage with lock and key would be next if she was found. Still, curiosity got the better of her, and Tauria was no stranger to spying undetected. Albeit she only attempted to eavesdrop on petty meetings her parents deemed her too young for in Fenstead, or games she'd been left out of as a child.

Tauria carefully shuffled across the roof, never dipping into the flood of moonlight as she took the path of shadows. Being light on her feet and stealthy in her maneuvers came second nature to someone with the ability of wind manipulation. She *was* the element as much as it was her.

Finally, the voices grew loud enough that she knew peeking her head over the slant would reveal who she suspected. Alarm skittered over her skin. A sharp chill seeped through her…and her mind screamed at her to retreat, knowing there was nothing good to be gained from whatever meeting Varlas was engaged in out here in the dead of night. But remembering what urged her here, to Olmstone, Tauria couldn't pass up the opportunity to learn something that could be vital to her cracking the suspicion they all thought about him: that he'd truly lost his sanity to side with the enemy and overthrow his allies.

"I think it is time to start setting plans into motion. I'm not a patient male, Varlas."

Tauria didn't recognize the voice, but its dark caress slithered down her spine.

"She needs time to adjust, for us to gain her trust."

"I said we could try it your way, but the clock is ticking."

"And if she doesn't survive?"

"I have the utmost confidence they will. We have tested royal blood before. But with the marriage, we only need one of them to survive. If neither does, then they were both too weak to ever be fit for purpose."

"They? This was not our agreement."

"Maybe not yours, but it has always been mine."

Tauria's pulse jumped rapid, and she blessed the wind for howling loud enough to disguise it and carry her scent away from them without her intervention. She had to get a look to know who he spoke to. Her every hair stood on end.

She had been a fool, content to excuse Varlas's absence as preoccupation with other matters when it was what she should have noticed first. Varlas wasn't ignoring her presence in Olmstone; he was making his own plans for it. The stab of betrayal came as hot as it did icy with a rage to demand why, and in sadness, Tauria wondered what she'd done to deserve it.

"I don't care what it takes. That son of yours doesn't seem to be playing his role too convincingly. By the second full moon I will be here, and I expect to have them both. The ceremony will be spectacular indeed."

Tauria's gloved fingers curled around the peak of the slanted rooftop, halfway to hoisting herself up for a glimpse…

A hand clamped over her mouth and nose, followed by an arm hooked around her waist, and before she knew it, she was twisted and pinned with her back against a strong force. Her cry of surprise halted with the scent that wrapped around her. It wasn't relief but ice-cold dread she felt at knowing her captor's identity.

"Stay silent," Tarly warned, no more than a wisp of the wind.

She would be wise to do as he said, so she didn't struggle or say anything in response. They lay flush against each other on the rooftop, and slowly, he removed his hand from her mouth, but his arm around her middle didn't release.

Still hearing the shuffling of Varlas and his company below, Tauria and Tarly stayed braced in tense silence for a few minutes until they were certain the king had retreated back indoors, and his companion…

The wind was her sixth sense, picking up an intermittent whoosh that disturbed the night's natural flow. Something about it was *off,* emitting a tight shudder. Tauria twisted her head, and maybe it was loose foliage or a flying creature of the night, but in the distance a flicker caught her eye. Wings. Traveling away from them until they were no more than a forgotten fleck of darkness. Her mind reeled, but she couldn't make sense nor order of any of her thoughts.

"Are you insane?" Tarly's hiss snapped her back to the present.

Her whole body flushed at registering their position now the rush of adrenaline had begun to dwindle. As she rolled off him to find a grip on the roof beside them, his hand lingered, reluctant to release her entirely. She eyed it expectantly, and he snatched it back. Tarly's expression lit up, livid.

"From being locked up day and night, I wouldn't be surprised if that's the path I'm headed down," she bit back.

His furrowed brow remained so far from amused. "And if you had fallen?"

Tauria recoiled, stunned that this was his first concern, figuring her spying would have certainly spiked his alarm. She shifted her cloak to expose her staff, though he didn't seem to find it adequate backup should she have taken the fatal tumble. Tauria refrained from rolling her eyes.

"I was only headed to the stables. An impossible venture, it seems, with guards posted at every exit. The drop from the balcony I could have done without the staff."

"Yes, we know."

Her face hardened in accusation. "You know how closely guarded he's keeping me?"

"It's for your own—"

"Protection? That's bullshit, and you know it."

"Is it, Tauria? Look at where you are!"

"I wouldn't be if I'd had a damn choice!"

Suddenly, Tauria's yelp of shock was smothered by his palm once more. The prince moved so fast, his weight pressing against her while he pinned her to the roof. Her spike of fear turned to wide-eyed horror when she picked up on the voices he'd detected before her.

"All will fall to plan, you'll see." Keira's voice pitched horribly sweet and careful, the tone to tame a lion. "Do not forget you have a daughter who could assume the throne."

"You dare to mention such a thing?"

Tauria watched Tarly's face, seeing anger—no, deeper, like building wrath—flex his expression. She couldn't make sense of the conversation, hearing only fragments both with Varlas's unknown companion and now the queen. The only thing she could be certain of was that she and the prince were at the center of whatever storm was brewing.

Tarly met her eye, and his face had inched so close they shared breath when his head angled down. He shifted his weight to allow air to breeze between them, and Tauria shivered with a flash she dismissed as quickly as it arrived.

"I have every faith things will work out how you intended. But we all know the risks. I only meant to assure you there is always a second candidate. One of perfect age to bend to the High Lord's allegiance without the Transition."

"She would not gain us a monarch in Fenstead that their people would accept."

Whatever they spoke of, Tauria had never been so encased with a sense of foreboding that it was an effort to settle her churning stomach. Every instinct roared that she wasn't safe, that she never had been. The guards, the protection, the silence… Tauria was a fool to believe she was ever an active player when she may have walked right into a trap.

Tarly's hand motion stole her attention. He circled her waist as he coaxed her to move. She realized his urgency to get far away from the king and queen was not to be argued with.

Tauria observed the prince, surprisingly light on his feet, darting across the rooftop with an impressive agility she had to admire. He never once forgot about her or allowed too much distance to form between them. She occasionally scoffed at his concern considering she was far more equipped in the sport they'd made of the rooftops than him, but she found it endearing, if unnerving, to glimpse his genuine concern.

Back on her own balcony, Tarly's look switched back to its icy glare as he followed her. He wandered into the games room, and she read his signal to follow before he closed the doors in an attempt to get as far away from the guards' listening ears as possible.

"How did you know I was out there?"

Tarly pinned her with a glare of ire. "You clearly don't know the layout of the castle enough to know when you go dancing across my balcony."

Tauria winced sheepishly. "I meant what I said. I only wished for a damned moment alone."

"And you thought galivanting to the stables in a foreign kingdom—in the middle of the night, need I point out—was the best idea?"

"It is only *foreign* because no one seems to care to make me feel welcome!" The confession blurted from her mouth before she could halt it. She wanted to believe there passed a flicker of remorse in him, but his jaw and eyes hardened to steel. Tarly drove a hand through his messy blond hair that was unbound for once, and for a second, she thought him…beautiful. Carefree.

"You have no idea about anything, Tauria." The tone he fell to, like *apology,* shook her to her bones.

She dared to ask, "Who was your father meeting with tonight?"

"I don't know."

"That's bullshit."

"Careful."

"Why should I be?"

Tarly took slow steps toward her. Steps that felt like the stalking of a wolf. Tauria balked, retreating until she met with a force that caged her in.

"Because you want to live," he said quietly. "Because you want *him* to be safe."

Her heart skipped a beat, and she didn't care that it exposed her desperation as she whispered, "Who?"

"I think we both know who." His hand came up to rest against the wall beside her head. Tauria swallowed hard. "It's okay to admit you care for him. I understand. His father took you in, and you were forced to be around him for so long. He could have had you, but correct me if I'm wrong: he didn't *want* you."

Those words sank soul-deep. Words she'd heard before, only from her own punishing mind. Her embarrassment cooled to pain, but pain heated to anger so fast her hands pushed his chest to put some distance between them.

"I am not his or yours or anyone's to be *had.*" Her indignation matched his. "Is this the part where you tell me you do want me? That I should choose you?"

"This is the part where I tell you you're not that special, princess. That I won't pine after someone who clearly has no interest. Believe me, I am not offended." Tarly moved to the door and made for the balcony. "Maybe I'm even relieved."

Tauria would never yield at the hurt in his words, delivered so precisely it were as if he knew where the dagger was lodged only to twist it further. "You've not exactly made yourself an appealing prospect."

Tarly huffed a dry laugh. "That makes two of us."

CHAPTER 17

Tauria

"I think it's ready."

The upbeat child's voice snapped Tauria's attention from her sulking mood, and she fixed her tunneling thoughts on the flower in her palm. A spindlelily. The red sprouting center against the pure white petals brought forth desolate memories of lives lost as the flower symbolized remembrance on Fenstead lands. Her mind must've been truly spiraling to have created it not entirely of conscious choice as she succumbed to her gloom.

Tauria looked at the perfectly turned bed of soil Opal had achieved alone. Her flutter of pride was welcomed. She mustered a smile at the young princess, who beamed, expectant of her approval.

"You did it perfectly," Tauria said, her somberness echoing in her quiet voice. "What would you like to plant?"

Opal's face turned contemplative until her gaze fell to Tauria's hands. "Those." Her eyes lit up as she pointed to the spindlelily. "I've never seen them before. I've never seen a lot of the flowers you grow. They're all so pretty."

Tauria wanted to match her happiness, but she couldn't bloom a whole bed of spindlelillies in Olmstone. It was Fenstead's mourning flower.

"Oh no!"

Tauria's attention fell to the princess at her alarm, quickly scanning her over for injury. But the princess was unharmed except for a saddened expression, her blue gaze fixed on Tauria's lap. Following her line of sight, her eyebrows rose.

"You can make them die too…" Opal trailed off sadly. It was heart-breaking to see the young fae so upset by the wilted flower. It didn't happen often, but if Tauria's emotions ran too reckless while her ability hummed at the surface, it had the opposite effect on the nature around her. Luckily, her melancholy mood hadn't been dispersed enough to affect anything but the single spindlelily.

"I don't think they were meant for here," Tauria said. But to lighten the mood for Opal's sake, her magick heated her fingertips, encasing the dying bud. They both watched in fascination as it reformed into a white rose instead. "These look similar though."

Opal took the flower with a toothy grin, retrieving her spade to plant the new bloom. Tauria could have grown it directly and saved her the bother, but watching the young fae lose herself in the act of gardening was a nourishing sight she would never tire of. Looking at her now, she started to see echoes of her child-self and wondered if these feelings had swirled in her mother's chest as she watched her.

"Are you all right, Your Majesty?" Lennox's voice carried over to steal Tauria from her painful reflection.

She felt the dampness on her cheeks and quickly swiped at the stray tear that had fallen. Tauria rose from the ground she kneeled on. Serena, who sat in the pavilion as usual, halted her sewing. The fae was often silent but observant, and Tauria couldn't be sure why her presence always felt heavy with the weight of judgment.

"I think I should retire for the afternoon. Or I'll seek out my general."

That seemed to spark interest in Serena. "Yes, I've seen the Fenstead General. He's caused quite a stir among the ladies of the court."

Tauria knew Lycus had taken to training with the soldiers he'd arrived with openly on Olmstone's grounds, claiming he preferred the open air to the private space indoors. She'd watched him a few times but didn't often stick around to listen to his impressive routine or watch as he was gawked at by ladies of the court. She couldn't blame them when the sun tested the warriors for hours, slicking their dark skin and making it all the more alluring when shirts became a hinderance. Tauria didn't believe Serena was excluded from the *stir* she spoke of, nor was she surprised.

"Yes, I can imagine," she mused. She glanced down at the princess who patted the soil she'd planted the new rose in. "I should seek out the prince too."

Looking at Opal inspired the memory of Tarly's rare bright side when he spoke of her. Tauria had so far obliged all his requests to join him, but it roused her guilt that she had yet to instigate any time together. His last words after their hostile run on the rooftops had settled wrong in her chest. She owed it to him and herself to put in true effort and at least *try* to bond.

"I didn't realize you were getting along so well," Serena inquired carefully.

Tauria picked up on the jealous undertone, and her eyes met the fae's. Her envy seemed ridiculous as it was no secret Tauria came here to entertain Tarly's hand in marriage.

"It'll take time to build a relationship, but we're both eager to see what it could bring."

Serena picked at her sewing round. "He hasn't said much about you."

Tauria blinked, taken aback by the fae's boldness to insinuate she'd spent time—*private* time—with the prince since her being here. It wasn't jealousy that straightened her posture; it was a challenge. She couldn't be sure what Serena was trying to provoke.

"He told me I can trust you." Opal's voice sang as she stood, dusting off her beautiful lilac gown. "And he likes it when I talk about the flowers you tell me about."

Tauria's smile was genuine. Warmth eased her tension at Serena's prodding with the knowledge Tarly had spoken of her with his sister. The way Opal's eyes lit up revealed her adoration of her brother. She had to admire the prince for setting aside his dislike for Opal's mother to find love in his heart for his half-sister. No matter how harsh he seemed to everyone else, that part of him was undeniable, and the young fae spoke of him so brightly.

Tauria's pleasant thoughts were short-lived, however, when her gaze shifted to catch the drop in Serena's expression. It unsettled her to imagine romantic goings-on between the lady and Tarly. And now Tauria was a threat in her way of pursuing him. She realized like a fool Tarly's coldness could be brought on by her coming between them. It didn't seem logical considering the match would never be favorable in the king's eye and Tarly had shown little regard for anyone or anything. But she couldn't rule it out.

Tauria asked Opal, "Do you think Tarly would like it if I told him about our day together myself?" Her grin was giddy, and Opal's enthusiastic nod gave Tauria a fresh bout of confidence.

"We need to get you prepared for your classes this afternoon," Serena cut in, her hand on the princess's shoulder as she steered her down the path.

Tauria called out, "I hope you can join us again tomorrow, Serena."

The fae paused out of nothing other than courtesy, casting false kindness over her shoulder while Opal giggled quietly.

Once they were out of sight, Tauria's mood dipped dramatically. She didn't want to make enemies or have her presence become a negative energy. But like in High Farrow, it seemed impossible to stay out of the tangled web of jealousy and speculation that weaved around every corner of the court.

"It'll pass once you and the prince start to make your relationship more public." Lennox walked over to her now they were alone. "They're testing you. To gauge your strength as a leader, and as a couple."

Tauria didn't want to acknowledge that his phrasing twisted unease in her gut. *A couple.* It was why she was here, to find out what could become of her and Tarly. With a flare of determination, she asked, "Do you know where I might find the prince at this hour?"

Tauria cast a hesitant look at Lennox—her third since they'd arrived outside the prince's rooms.

"I'll be right here should you require anything, Your Majesty." With the words, he tapped his chest, and his hidden signal inspired a surge of pride. He knew exactly where her Fenstead pin was secured beneath her bodice.

She gave a nod of understanding at his meaning, *seeing* the assurance on his face before he lowered his gaze in a bow. Lennox would be prepared to damn his guise at a moment's notice if she gave reason. Tauria willed her nerves to be subdued in that promise of protection and knocked twice on the door.

She could barely count her heartbeats before it swung open. Tarly's face offered anything but a warm reception. She didn't have a second to wince before the harsh lines smoothed in his surprise and a warmth eased into those cold eyes. They blinked at each other. The air felt tight, and every word scrambled in her mind, leaving her feeling like a foolish child.

"I wasn't expecting you." Tarly broke their awkward silence, but her stiff shoulders eased when she didn't detect annoyance.

Tauria snapped back into herself, realizing he was patiently waiting for her to explain. "I was thinking about you," she said. "After spending time with Opal in the garden, I thought you might like to—" Her speech halted because in truth, she hadn't thought so far ahead. She had no suggestions for how they might spend time together. It was in that moment she realized she knew very little about the prince—not their common interests or even conflicting ones that she could use to spark *something* between them.

Tarly glanced behind himself, and his hesitation didn't go unfelt, until finally his posture seemed to loosen off and he took a small step to the side. "Do you wish to come in?"

Her eyebrows rose. She didn't expect the offer to come so casually. Then her cheeks flushed at the prospect of being inside his private space. It seemed…intimate. She saw the moment his inner guard started to rise at her contemplation, the fear of rejection slowly firming Tarly's expression and stiffening his poise.

"I'd love to," Tauria blurted.

His guard fell just enough to showcase a partial smile before he stepped fully out of her way so she could enter.

Inside, Tauria's hands clasped in front of her in a vise grip. She didn't know why being invited into Tarly's personal quarters stiffened her body with nerves, as though she knew to tread carefully here. She didn't want to lose the trust he'd offered to her.

Nothing littered the floors, and the grand bed remained perfectly untouched. Hues of deep purple accented the room as she'd expected, but something about the space encased her with a sense of sad *emptiness.* She found nothing of character, nothing personal, and she figured she may as well have been standing in a guest room. The click of the door behind she felt over the back of her neck, curving her posture at the signal they were alone. Tauria's eyes met his, but he lingered in the doorway, watching her with intrigue.

Tauria stifled her fright when movement from the balcony caught her eye. "She stays with you too," she observed as Katori took tentative steps indoors. The wolf walked right up to her, and she reached out a hand when it unashamedly nuzzled into her side. A grin broke on her face, fingers sliding through the wolf's soft fur.

"When she's around. Though it seems she's taken a liking to you. I wouldn't be surprised if she posts herself outside your door instead."

Tauria found comfort in the idea. The wolf's affection felt like acceptance in the kingdom that had so far felt foreign and daunting. Titling her head, she spied something that piqued her interest in the adjoining room as she straightened. "May I?" she asked, casting a gesture toward the next room.

Tarly nodded slowly and took his first steps to follow after her.

In the dining area, she found the first notes of him. Tauria walked the length of the table, unable to fight her smile as she eagerly reached out a hand. "Books," she muttered, taking a small leather-bound book in her hands and flicking open the pages. She lost the fight to her widening smile. "Stories," she added, surprised by the fictional texts.

"They don't have them back in High Farrow?" Tarly asked.

Tauria stole a look. The prince's amusement was rare but so beautiful on his delicate face. He seemed to drop it quickly, and she felt in the pit of her stomach that he was used to hiding whatever kernel of happiness he still harbored in company. Regardless, he walked right up to her, and Tauria's pulse quickened with the short proximity at which he halted. His eyes remained on the books that occupied the whole table, leaving her unsure of where he ate in private. Tarly leaned over, and Tauria's lips parted when his body lightly pressed to her. If the prince noticed, he yielded no reaction. As he straightened, he lifted a book in front of her.

"Gasira Fenrison wrote some of the greatest tales of our time."

Tauria took the offering. "I think I've heard her name before." If she turned her head to look at him now, she was sure the closeness of their faces would heat her cheeks. Instead she tried to distract herself by aimlessly flicking through the pages.

"Do you like to read, Tauria?" The quiet gravel of his voice grated through her internally. Not in discomfort; she *enjoyed* the way he spoke. Attentive, maybe even flirtatious.

She did turn her head then, and their eyes connected closer than they ever had before. For a split second, a flicker of something brought to life those distant hazel orbs. But Tarly didn't let the moment last long enough to grow the tension that formed in her stomach. He pulled back, slowly stalking over to the other side of the table and looking over the various volumes.

"I do. I find it a way to—"

"Escape?"

There it was. The common ground she didn't realize she'd been looking to balance on with him. She should have appreciated sooner how closely their situations resembled each other's. Their lives had always been gripped in the tight fists of rulers who controlled their every public move. She should have seen it, because this kind of escape, like the one found in stories, was what she sought with Nik. Only, she could never be so open about their close bond out of fear their relationship would be twisted by the courtiers to shake their reputation. With Tarly, however, Tauria could be free and open. They could share everything. Yet did it mean that much when they would always be pawns moved by some higher power, their relationship forever painted to be what the people wanted to see?

"Sometimes it's nice to pretend." She aired her thoughts, running her fingers over the delicate pages. "To be anyone but ourselves. To be free of the shackles of our own fates for a while."

Tarly glanced at her with curiosity. "Why did you come to me?"

Tauria's anxiety surfaced at the sway of conversation. She closed her book. "Do I need reason?"

Tarly studied her as though lies could be hidden within her words. One of the first things she'd noted about the prince was his high reluctance to trust. It didn't pair well with the challenge it always was to convince him of anything.

"I hardly think my company has been so inviting as to have made you want to seek it."

Tauria heard his interrogation, his careful test of her motives. It was unnerving to be around someone who always seemed to be waiting for the shoe to drop.

"What makes you believe that?" It wasn't that she disagreed. It was true that being in his company had been...difficult. But his awareness told her perhaps his cold shoulder was deliberate. To hide and protect what little was left of his heart. Tarly Wolverlon was not hateful or cruel; he was lost and broken. Something about that revelation didn't strike her with pity. Instead, she realized with time that she could come to understand him. Another desolate common ground.

Tarly dodged the question. "I trust you've taken no further nighttime rooftop adventures." His hooked brow spoke teasing rather than scolding.

Tauria slipped him a smile. "Not yet."

"Might I warn you, not ever again?"

"Would you believe me if I agreed?"

His chuckle emitted a warm vibration within her, unsettling because she wanted to hear it again. "Not for a second." He took a long pause, staring at nothing in particular while he seemed to contemplate. "What if I happened to tell you my balcony is two up and four across from yours, and that there are many nights when sleep eludes me too?"

An eruption of warmth delayed her response. "Then I might say that balcony is a particular favorite of mine to dance across, and should there be a sleep-deprived prince inside, he would be more than welcome to chase me."

His eyes met hers, heated and twinkling with a rare mischief. Tauria dropped her gaze, a frown forming as she thought of their rocky encounter on the rooftops last week. What she'd overheard...

"Something weighs on your mind," Tarly commented, but he preoccupied himself by flipping haphazardly through a book.

"Who your father was meeting with—I believe they spoke of me. Us."

The prince halted his page turning, but his expression became unreadable. "Is that so odd? Our prospective alliance is something he'll no doubt have great plans for once it's all over and we've taken back Fenstead."

Tauria appreciated Tarly's choice of words, his confidence that she believed was true. He clung to great hope that they would help take back her homeland. "I suppose you're right."

"But?"

Tauria wrung her hands as she began to pace, unsure if she was glad the prince was pressing her further or if she still held reservations about whether or not she could trust him with her free thoughts. "Something seemed...off. And you said you had no idea who he met with?"

Tarly spared a look at the main room as though he were extending his senses to gauge how nearby listening ears could be. His book thumped shut in one hand, and he slowly traced his steps back around the table until he was right in front of her. Tauria's breath held at the close proximity. His hand came up, but he hesitated, searching her eyes as if allowing her to object. She didn't, and her lips parted when his fingers lightly curled around her chin.

"Do you want this? Us?" Those hazel eyes claimed her, and Tauria had never felt more exposed. Vulnerable. As if he could see past every defense she'd built and this had become a test.

"I don't know," she answered honestly.

He didn't release her, and for a moment, she wondered if he intended to kiss her. Tauria's stomach was already knotted at the prospect, and maybe…maybe she *wanted* him to.

Then Tarly's hand fell away, and Tauria snapped out of her trance like a rough awakening. His breath was heavy as he stepped away, and a coldness embraced her.

"We have a role to play here, princess."

"What do you mean?"

"I mean that if you were smart, you would stop resisting."

"I have been nothing but compliant."

"That is the problem, Tauria. You are not making yourself known here, *wanted*. So far, most haven't even glimpsed your presence while you keep to your guard and that garden. I gifted you the space to have quiet moments alone, not to seclude yourself entirely. Then there's you and me…" He trailed off. His jaw flexed as he leaned against the table and crossed his arms. "We don't have the luxury of time. With monarchs, alliances are formed far faster. You've been here long enough now, and we're not fooling anyone."

Tauria realized he was right. And Tarly—this was him helping her. He didn't want to push her into a marriage so soon, but he needed her to at least be aware part of the game was always who could play the best bluff.

"We should make more public appearances," she suggested.

A weight seemed to lift from his expression as though he were glad he didn't have to force his company on her. Maybe she'd been wrong in her judgment of Tarly all along. He wasn't harsh or uncaring. He was… careful. Only, the need to discover *why* riddled her with unease.

"I think we deserve the chance to know if we could find happiness in it all," she added quietly. But it seemed to be the wrong thing to say.

"Our happiness was forfeited the day we were born." Tarly's voice took on a cold edge, a sharpness deeper than she'd heard before. This was personal, and she wondered what had caused it.

She didn't look at him. She didn't need to. She knew the sight would only shroud her in the shadows that seemed to cling to him. "I get it," she said. "I'm not your ideal choice to bind your life to." She tried to hide her twist of hurt.

"Is that what you think?"

"You haven't exactly been subtle in your distaste for the situation. I'm not a fool. I can read when my company isn't desired."

Tarly's touch curled around her wrist when she made to leave, and she snapped her head back to stare him down. There was conflict in his eyes, a raging war that moved his jaw as though he were suppressing what he wanted to unleash. Anger, hatred, warning—she couldn't place it. He let go of her hand.

"Get smart, Tauria. Get smart fast, or it may turn out to be the grave rather than the altar at which we'll finally meet."

CHAPTER 18

Nikalias

Nik paced the endless void of his subconscious mind, the smoke and shadows mocking him as they swirled in his anguish. He'd already tried to Nightwalk to Tauria. Like he did every damn night. But in the hope that perhaps she wasn't asleep yet, he waited like a pining fool to try again.

Every time he stood here, he couldn't help but think the space got darker, the gray and flickers of white that broke up the blackness close to fading out. He didn't know what it meant. Perhaps once the darkness took over, he could embrace a permanent detachment from the feelings that tortured him.

He just needed to see her. Only once. Just to know she was safe. And if she was more than that, living happily and easing in perfectly to her new life in Olmstone…he could live with that. In all this, Tauria's happiness was the only thing that mattered. He owed her that. After all, Tarly could give her everything he couldn't. Nik could almost hear his shadows hiss and torment at the thought, but despite how wrong it felt to wish her happiness in the arms of another, he couldn't afford to be selfish. Not with her.

Nik halted his pacing. It did nothing for his reeling mind. He looked down at the glittering emerald comb that offered the only flicker of light in this darkness. The sinking, horrid feeling of rejection had already settled in his gut whenever he pictured her, imagining that night, how she'd stolen his breath with a mere look. How the world and everything in it seemed dull, lackluster, in comparison to *her*.

He felt the familiar projection as he tried to cross the distance. The strain from trying to leap so far brought on a discomfort he wasn't used to, but he reached further into his well of power, yielding everything without a care about if it would drain him dry. Nik winced with the resistance, but it only lasted a few seconds until he was there.

Except, like every other time, he wasn't met with Tauria's subconscious, but a firm block before it. He was so close, and everything she was lay just beyond that wall he couldn't penetrate. Not without risk of harming her at least. Nik's heart, his soul, withered more and more at the thought of her blocking him. That this was her way of stopping him from playing witness to her thriving without him. And if she discovered anything malicious, only then would she release that barrier.

Until then, there was nothing more he could do.

Nik let go all at once, accepting the harsh tumble back to his own subconscious mind that made him fall to one knee. Nikalias Silvergriff, King of High Farrow, bowed low in his sorrow in the one place he was entirely alone to do so. Then he screamed. His anger, heartache, and loneliness bounded around the space to channel painfully back in through his own ears. He released the pent-up frustration that left him panting. But it was not enough, and he knew if he were around breakable things the room would likely be in pieces by now.

He could hear laughter that wasn't real swirling around him in amusement at his pitiful state. Nik clamped his eyes shut, trying to think of something, *anything*, to distract himself from it.

Then one particular conversation stilled him, and he straightened, remembering Jakon's seed of doubt he'd planted about Lady Samara. More specifically, his speculation that Zarrius could have a hidden motive in bringing Samara to him and encouraging their courtship. In his state of frustration and failure, Nik cast out all wrongful feeling for what he was about to do. This he could do successfully tonight to feel some semblance of achievement and put all doubt to rest.

Standing, Nik thought of her. Focused on her porcelain face, always set in an alluring expression, her voice that of an eloquent seductress, her poise confident, almost dominating. Nik projected into her mind with little effort. Yet just before he arrived to discover the color of her mists…

Within her mind, his eyes snapped open.

Darkness.

Nik felt around, but the block was firm, familiar. His thoughts scrambled because he already knew why. He'd felt the same mere minutes ago.

In *Tauria's* mind.

He took a moment to focus all his Nightwalking senses, reaching and probing through every corner of Samara's mind to be sure it was the same. She was blocking him. But even as he concluded as much, it didn't make sense. Blocking a Nightwalker was not an easy thing to do —especially not with a block as indestructible as the one he faced. He had trained Tauria personally for many decades, dreading the thought of another being able to infiltrate her mind and harm her in the one place he couldn't always keep her safe. So it made sense to assume Tauria's resistance was her own.

Yet with Samara…

Nik knew there was a way to block someone else's mind. He'd supplied such a tonic to Faythe once before, in the early days of controlling her Nightwalking.

He forced himself straight back to consciousness, where he shot out of bed and paced with his reeling thoughts that would make sure no sleep would be had tonight. He didn't want to draw the conclusion his mind screamed at him was true. But it would be foolish to deny it now.

Nik wanted to shout out loud from being constantly surrounded by so much betrayal and uncertainty. He didn't know who to trust or what to believe anymore. All he could do was try to figure out how to gain back the favor of those who had betrayed him before they found out he'd caught them at their own game.

Tauria,

Your silence is loud. Unsettling. The days are long, the nights too short and restless. I had a thought, a childish one really, that while you are far our moon is the same. Look up. I will be too.

No matter what, please let me see you are well.

Nik.

QUEEN'S GAMBIT
PART II
KINGDOM OF FENSTEAD
HOUSE STAGKNIGHT

CHAPTER 19

Tauria

TAURIA LOOKED OVER her reflection in the mirror, her chin poised high, owning the flood of Olmstone purple she adorned like a weapon of obedience. *Give them what they want to take everything I need.* The prince's obscure advice had driven her here. To start making her presence known, and to start gaining some trust and respect.

She walked the halls with confidence, not a princess of Fenstead or the ward of High Farrow; Tauria Stagknight owned the hallways lined with the two-headed wolf emblem like the future Queen of Olmstone. After demanding directions to the queen's preferred quarters, she approached the open courtyard that was scattered with high court ladies. All of them looked at her as she passed, but Tauria marched right past without acknowledgment and entered the den of wolves, primed to strike a new threat to their peaceful hierarchy.

"Your Highness."

A timid voice halted her firm pace. Tauria twisted elegantly toward the lady who was brave enough to speak out when everything about her expression warned against it.

"We were not expecting you here today."

The fae had soft features and pretty brown eyes that blinked too often to be natural. She delicately pinched an ornate teacup, flanked by two others. Tauria gauged her reason for making the remark was that she could be the first to possess the flame of gossip should Tauria reveal anything.

"Does my presence need to be announced or expected?" Tauria asked in a way that had the fae swallowing her nerves. She didn't answer. "I'm here to meet with the queen."

The blonde fae shifted her eyes to her companions as though she was now reluctant to be the one in conversation with her. Fae lords and ladies were often hollow-minded followers. "She is in the middle of luncheon with her close circle. She does not like to be disturbed." The fae hesitated before adding quickly, "By anyone."

Tauria's smile reflected sweet but confident. "Where might this luncheon be?"

Again, looks were exchanged, and she didn't fail to notice several other ladies had irritatingly shuffled closer at the disturbed routine. Their pathetic stares crawled over every inch of her skin, making the deep purple-and-lilac gown itch and weigh heavy. With a quick glance, Tauria noted she was the only one granted permission to adorn the king's colors. Good. Usually, she wouldn't care to be singled out in another court, but this was one she planned to run without the need for a crown.

"In the queen's private section, Your Highness."

The flash of the fae's eyes gave Tauria the right direction. She said nothing in acknowledgment as she took off again. It was what was required of her to assert her rank. Kindness was a weakness in this game, and right now, she was being watched and tested with so much scrutiny that adorning her steel armor was the only way to make it out alive. Only in solitude would she be free to feel, and all she could do was hope her actions in the public eye didn't become too much for her to find solace from within herself.

Tauria spied the small gathering of fae ladies between the pristine white marble pillars that scattered the open space. She identified the queen straight away, her head crowned with silver and amethyst that glittered breathtakingly against her honey-blonde hair. The sunlight highlighted her like a goddess where she sat elegantly in a side lean around a glittering pond. Five others fixed their gawking attention on her while her lips moved with perfect eloquence.

The first to notice her approach was one Tauria had hoped would be in attendance. Serena's eyes widened with a shock that failed to hide her ire. Tauria wanted to learn more about Opal's *mentor*, find out exactly how close she was to the queen as she'd so brazenly claimed. Still, Tauria couldn't deny the sight rattled her nor stop the comparison to herself that threatened to make her poise falter. Just for a second.

When the queen's ocean orbs slid up to pin her gaze, her skin pricked, and it was an effort to keep the confident glide of her walk. She caught the quick flex around the queen's eyes, but Tauria couldn't be certain of her feelings as her expression upturned to a pleasant smile that jump-started her pulse.

"Tauria Stagknight." She drawled out her name sweetly as though being forced to accept her arrival. "I'm glad you finally made your way here. We have been waiting for you to settle in enough to be comfortable with joining us."

Tauria stopped before the gathered party. They all lounged on expensive cushions, surrounded by small foods. If she were honest, she would admit this setting was so far from appealing to her. She smiled amicably, offering a small dip of her head out of mutual respect for the queen. "Had I known, I would have made the effort to come sooner. I find myself feeling welcomed like home in Olmstone." A blatant lie. But told with the masterful courtly façade no one would question. The nature of the ladies before her was to pick and spill gossip and shun any truth if it offered no entertainment.

"My apologies," the queen said. A quick look at some nearby servants had them setting a new place for her opposite the ruler, where a few ladies hastily shuffled aside to give her plenty of space.

Tauria noted even within the queen's close circle they were the only two granted permission to wear the king's colors. Every other fae in attendance wore white or beige. She lowered down onto the cushion laid for her, not breaking eye contact with Keira as she reflected on their brief moments together during her time in High Farrow for the kings' meetings. Then, she'd occasionally felt *pity* for the queen, observing how Varlas didn't seem to return her gestures of affection or care to include her in conversation regarding kingdom matters. She had been silent, obedient, and Tauria had tried her best to engage with her as much as she could to compensate for it.

Yet the fae she looked at now didn't appear to be the same queen Tauria thought she knew. In her own kingdom—or at least in this section that was built like her own private palace—surrounded by those who adored her, *bowed* to her, without the shadow of Varlas, Queen Keira Wolverlon sparked a cunning confidence that rattled her nerves.

"I trust the prince has been keen to occupy your time, as you are here to entertain his hand in marriage, are you not?"

Tauria wasn't surprised by Keira's bluntness, but her nerves flushed at the impending interrogation. All eyes pinned her. The faces of the ladies lifted with envy and intrigue. She had to pick her next words carefully and be selective about what she fed to the vultures.

"His Highness has been kind to show me some of his most admired spots within the castle. Indeed, a union between myself and the prince would be advantageous to both kingdoms." *Don't use his name without title. Make him out to be the dashing prince, not the temperamental asshole.*

Green wasn't a color that suited Serena, Tauria thought, almost seeing flickers of the beast of jealousy pinning her from where Serena sat next to the queen. It was an honorable position, and Tauria saw her claim about being close to the queen was true. But she also didn't fail to notice the quick looks some of the other ladies directed at Serena. Even the queen spared her a flash of attention.

"Have I said something wrong?"

A servant leaned down, and Tauria took the wine gracefully. Her first sip had her biting back a moan, glad for the edge to be taken off her tenseness.

The queen let out a soft chuckle that didn't depict any true humor. "Not at all, my dear. Though perhaps you deserve to be enlightened to the prince's…*reputation.*"

Tauria's fingers grasped her cup tighter.

Serena straightened, a sense of importance angling her shoulders, believing her next words would grant her equal rank with Tauria. "The prince and I have history," she said, locking eyes with Tauria without an ounce of apology or regret. It was an effort for Tauria to keep her face straight at the fae's brazenness. "I don't believe those kinds of feelings go away entirely at the prospect of a forced marriage." The sour notes in her voice were expertly concealed. Perhaps none of the other ladies would pick up on her subtle slander of a royal queen. Yet now it was clear. None of those in attendance saw Tauria as such. Even the queen's mouth curved in an amusement that twisted her embarrassment.

To them, to everyone in Olmstone, she was simply another highly placed lady. A queen of nothing. It wasn't anger that coursed through her veins; ferocity quickened her pulse. This was determination. She was Tauria Stagknight, rightful Queen of Fenstead, and it was damn time people stopped forgetting that. Including herself.

"Hmm…" Tauria sipped casually from her golden chalice. "He has not mentioned you at all. Or anyone else for that matter. We all have a past, but with his keen interest, it has been hard to keep…*composed* around each other." Tauria captured Serena's stare like a challenge. This was how it had to be. Ruthless yet cunning. But despite her outward confidence, Tauria took no pleasure in the faint rose that colored the fae's cheeks at her careful dismissal.

The queen's melodic voice echoed, unfazed by the tension that thickened the air. "I'm sure Tarly is thrilled by the prospect of your hand in marriage. Who wouldn't be?"

Tauria almost smiled, nearly believing the queen she'd gotten to know in High Farrow was still true and harbored a friendship for her. But Keira's next words twisted in her gut.

"Though it is not uncommon for kings to seek comforts outside of marriage."

The ladies around her nodded in agreement. Their judgment was insufferable, weighing on both sides. Acknowledging what this was, her against them, doused Tauria with grief all at once. It was in this moment she realized she was alone. She had no one. Her composure was cracking, but she could not falter. As soon as they glimpsed even a flicker of weakness, they would strike, and strike without mercy.

"I don't wish to concern myself with such matters before I am even wed." Tauria chuckled dryly, leveling with their false kindness. "Shouldn't we all have the confidence to keep our partner's attention? You just need to know how to make them feel what only you can give, but never give it all at once." Then there was his face in her mind, those emerald eyes piercing into hers as she spoke. "Find what makes them yearn for you alone." His breath on her neck, his bare skin against hers. His hands on her... *Gods,* what Nik could do with those hands. "Every male has unique desires, but every female has unique talents. As can be said in reverse." That night they had spent together so long ago was one that could never be matched. Not a single detail had left her mind in her yearning to find pleasure like that again. Completeness. "When two people find a song that can be sung in ever-changing harmonies...I don't believe having their attention sway to discover a new one will be of any concern."

"You sound like you speak from experience, Your Highness," one of the ladies commented quietly.

Tauria snapped back from her lustful trance. Glancing over at the company, she watched a few of them giggle, but they did not mock or belittle her. Their faces were eager for her to go on, and she relaxed at their innocent curiosity.

"Not at all," she brushed off as casually as she could, taking a long drink from her cup as if it would quench a deeper kind of thirst. Tauria flashed a glimpse at the queen for her reaction. Keira yielded very little. Serena sat stunned in bitter silence. Then there passed a sparkle of assessment as the queen tilted her head.

"I hear the new King of High Farrow has a particular reputation with the ladies of his court."

Her statement stirred question. Tauria saw the trap, the queen's attempt to pick up on any hint she might hold a number in Nik's long line of *reputations*. It stung her heart. No—it cleaved it far deeper, because she couldn't deny the fact that she did. She may be a princess, a *queen*, but her mind spun unrelenting in its misery that his night with her he didn't hold in any higher regard than his nights with others who had warmed his bed. Tauria's skin pricked hot. Suffocating. And she wanted nothing more than for the damned luncheon to be over.

"I'm afraid I don't have much inside knowledge of King Nikalias's personal affairs." *Lies*, her cruel thoughts hissed. "I was his father's ward, and the king was kind enough to extend my position permanently when Orlon passed." She couldn't be certain how convincing her factual statement was to hide all true feelings about Nik. To stifle just how close she was to him. Her heart splintered piece by piece, and the queen didn't even realize the weapon she held.

"I envy the Lady Samara who is said to have captured his wandering heart. Perhaps he will take her as his bride," another of the ladies swooned.

A storm collected within. One of sadness for her pining heart, anger at his abandonment long before now, and worst of all, *jealousy*, because despite all this she had never let him go.

All appetite for the delicious food and wine left her. "I don't believe he will be announcing that anytime soon. He faces a lot as the new king." Tauria added a huffed laugh to brush off the topic, hoping it would work.

But the queen's head canted, and for a second Tauria's turmoil swayed her vision, thinking she'd slipped up. As rulers, they were masters of observance, and Keira had experienced far more time in the role than Tauria to decipher every flicker of movement, every changing note of a voice. Under so much scrutiny, exhaustion overcame her in their short company.

"I must admit I wondered why King Nikalias never entertained the prospect of your hand. Surely he must see the advantage in an alliance with a princess, even one who stands without a kingdom."

Tauria's teeth ground together. It was becoming dizzying having to keep swaying the conversation away from the interrogations that seemed endless. She had expected this, and she would be wise to anticipate many more probing observations delivered as innocent questions. She just had to be smart enough to keep her head above water while they tried to drown her.

"Nikalias is smart. He knows High Farrow is better positioned with their ward in a marriage alliance with Olmstone. It could be the start of a great binding between three courts instead of two."

"So you agree." Keira's curved brow was enticing. "You are still High Farrow's ward over and above being the Princess of Fenstead."

Tauria flared with anger, struggling to suppress her ability, which threatened to surface at the constant belittlement. But never so outright as to condemn the queen for being wicked or heartless while she chipped away at Tauria piece by piece.

She would not cower.

Tauria handed over her wine and rose carefully, purposefully, without taking her eyes off the queen. She poised her chin high. "I am the Queen of Fenstead over and above anything else. What I do is for the good of my people and to reclaim my kingdom. I am here of my own will, not any king's, nor will I be moved by the hands of one." She spared a quick glance around at the other ladies, breathing steady with relief and triumph to see their faces had blanked. Perhaps some even glittered with awe as they looked up at her.

Serena's ocean eyes were stony, and her nostrils flared, but Tauria cared little for her opinion. The queen was the only one whose mouth curled almost imperceptibly—in agreement or thrill, she couldn't be sure.

Tauria said kindly, "I'm glad we got this chance to meet. I'm sure it won't be long before we run into each other again." Then she turned and strode from the ensemble, from the highest noble ladies of the court, having only narrowly escaped being swallowed whole by the vultures who were looking to bring her down.

CHAPTER 20

Nikalias

"Come in."

Nik stood by the fireplace in his rooms knowing exactly who was outside his door by the short, timid knock. He straightened as she entered slowly, knowing his summons for her to come to his room would have been a surprise.

"You requested to see me, Your Majesty?" Samara hesitated, lingering at a distance.

With a deep breath, Nik plastered on a smile as he twisted to her. "I did. Thank you for accepting." He might have believed the warmth that scattered her cheeks was genuine and endearing, but there was something pressing at the back of his mind, and he couldn't find an ounce of desire for her to be here. His hands slipped into his pockets as he paced to her.

He studied the nervousness that braced her posture. "Was there something you wished to discuss, Your—?"

"I thought we agreed to abandon the formality," he interjected, stopping when they were nearly shoulder-to-shoulder so he could look down at her. "Especially in private quarters."

Samara's shyness at his proximity and the caress he added to his tone would usually be a surprise from someone so used to receiving attention. It only confirmed what Nik suspected: she really was nervous. Not for his advances, but for what she harbored within.

"My apologies, Nikalias."

"After all, I am not yet king. Not in law until my coronation."

Samara finally peered up. The bait was almost too easy, giving her away in her political intrigue. "You are a king in wait."

Nik's hand raised, and Samara's sharp breath was audible. His fingers barely grazed her skin, but her heart raced to a rapid beat. "Is there a reason you're so nervous, Samara?" he asked in a quiet gravel.

Her chest rose and fell deeply. Her shift in scent he detected faintly of lust, but more so, it lingered with the notes of someone with something to hide. "This is just…"—as he swept her hair over her shoulder, her breathing stuttered—"unexpected."

Nik's hand fell to her waist, and he twisted her toward him. Her doe eyes widened with an edge of uncertainty, but he gauged it had nothing to do with his touch. He looked her over from head to toe. Then he took a step forward, and she backed up one step in response. He took another, and another, until Samara met the wall and he stopped, making no further move to touch her, but his assessment calculated.

"Would you like to stay the night with me?"

The question sent her full mouth floundering, wondering how to deny such a request. "We haven't been courting that long," she got out.

"Many would say it has been long enough."

Samara stayed silent. It was his intention to make her uncomfortable in order to get her to spill what he suspected.

"How have you been sleeping?"

Her throat shifted with her swallow, and it were as if he could see into her mind. Scrambling for a way out. "Well enough," she breathed. "Why do you ask?"

Nik was past playing. His teeth ground as he pinned her with a warning look. "I think you know why."

"You…you haven't been inside—"

"Your mind? No. But I don't suppose you could tell me why that is?"

For the first time, a harshness lined Samara's features. Anger. Maybe even resentment. "How dare you!" She went to slip away from him, but Nik planted a hand by her head against the wall.

"A nightly tonic, is it?" He got his answer in the purse of her lips. "What is he offering you?"

She blinked, eyes shifting from his gaze of warning to the hand that caged her in. "I don't know what you're talking abou—"

"I don't want to harm you, Samara. I don't want to threaten you to get what I need, but I will if I have to. So I'll give you one chance to tell me willingly and trust you will have my protection from him." Nik let the offer linger. In truth, he'd tormented over how to approach his suspicions. "He brought you to me. Why?"

The flicker of her eyes and paling of her face gave away she knew exactly who he spoke of. But still, she didn't speak. Out of fear, perhaps turmoil. Nik was willing to be patient in the hope she'd believe in his will to protect her if she told him all.

"Zarrius will be next in line for the throne should I fall without an heir. What has he promised you? A life by his side—is that it? No. If he had affections for you, I would scent them. I would—" Nik halted his own reeling thoughts as he tried to piece it all together. But a shift in Samara's features had him halting on one particular fact. "You have affections for *him*." Nik didn't leave the fact open to be denied. But in the slight rise of her chin, there was defiance. A protective flare toward him. It was the only answer he needed.

Nik pushed off the wall, huffing a laugh so far from humorous as he paced away, rubbing a hand down his face. "He must have known I would try to Nightwalk to you." His mind scrambled, wondering how to take his turn on the chessboard with the new insight.

"You would never have given your heart to me. Or to anyone," Samara said at last. "Zarrius loves me."

The shadows that circled his chest flared his anger. He slowly turned, hoping those same shadows relayed the message in his eyes. "How is he concealing his scent on you?"

Her lips thinned in protest, but Nik's patience already ran dangerously loose.

"I could have you imprisoned for treason. Executed."

"I have done nothing."

"Conspiring against a king, even unwittingly, is cause for detainment. But that doesn't matter." Nik's tone dipped low. He didn't want to have to use his authority, but to save his kingdom he would do whatever it took. "Remember who I am. Zarrius may have promised you everything, but it all hinges on one crucial fact." Then he saw a twitch of pain as he scanned her delicate face, in thinking the soft-spoken fae he'd come to admire in some respects could be capable of killing… "Tell me something: would it have been worth sacrificing your humanity for?"

Her opposition smoothed from her face, returning it to its soft innocence. "He only said I had to secure your hand. That once we were wed, he would take care of the rest. We could be together at last."

Nik could only pity her for her childish heart. For buying into a romantic tale of playing queen. "He intends to use you, Samara," he said gently, reeling back his own indignation as he knew how his accusation would be received. But if she truly did not know, all Samara had become was a tragic victim.

"You're wrong. You have no idea what we share."

"He needed someone to take the fall for my execution. Someone who could get close enough to pin the motive and blame. He's only been biding his time."

"You're wrong!"

Nik crossed the space, clamping a hand down over her mouth as he detected the rise of her voice. Her eyes widened in horror.

"We can't allow anyone the slightest suspicion there is any foul play here," Nik explained quickly. Reading she accepted her own error, he let her go. "Listen to me, Samara. Maybe his feelings for you are true, but a male like Zarrius will never put anything before his ambition to rise to power." He battled with the protest twitching her face, pleading with him to avoid getting her to see sense.

"He won't listen to me," she whispered like a slipped confession.

Nik couldn't fault her for her heart, just as he couldn't begin to fathom what there was to love in the wicked lord. He backed away from her. "You deserve better."

Her brow pinched at that. "I love him. And he loves me. He wants to give me the world."

"A promise is only hollow words when actions don't hold true. If he loved you, he would never want to put you in any line of danger."

"If I may say something, Your Majesty?"

Nik's shoulders relaxed in the hope he was getting through to her. He gave a nod of permission.

"Lady Tauria—you let her go. Yet Zarrius swears you love her, that in having her wed the Prince of Olmstone you will be at your most vulnerable."

That was what the lord was hoping for. Nik couldn't deny the mere thought did exactly that: weakened him. But Samara didn't know she'd offered him invaluable insight into Zarrius's plans. And his anger boiled to defuse his misery in realizing the lord's movements involved Tauria.

Then it all made sense.

The blocking of Tauria's mind he had been so foolishly content to believe was of her own making. It dawned a cold sweep of failure to think they had always been one step ahead of him when he believed they were behind in the game.

"Is that what love is?" Samara's voice snapped his attention back.

"Yes," he breathed. "It's putting their happiness before your own. Their safety over everything. It's wanting to set them free no matter what it means for you." He paced to the balcony, hands in his pockets as he thought over everything. Every piece of his and Tauria's plan that required sudden reassessment as in rushed a shift of adrenaline infused with a wrath so tangible he wanted to unleash the Nether on them all. Zarrius, Varlas, even Tarly if the prince knew how they were keeping him from being able to reach her. "It's having a darkness you never knew you harbored. Because if anyone tried to harm them…" *Gods*, he had left her there. And now he couldn't be certain what was happening. If she was even *safe.* Nik's hands tightened into trembling fists. "There's no telling what a person might be capable of."

CHAPTER 21

Tauria

THE DAY FOLLOWING her far from delightful luncheon with the queen and her ladies, Tauria sought to strengthen another shaken relationship in her plan to gain influence in Olmstone.

Tarly Wolverlon sat alone on the wide balcony of the atrium where he dined for breakfast. Tauria's pace slowed on her approach at the sight. He wasn't eating, just idly spinning a knife point-down against the table. He leaned back casually in his chair, the sun kissing his tanned skin and lightening his dark blond hair to a golden wave while he looked out over the stone court. For a second, she stared at someone else entirely. Someone she had never met before. Tarly appeared distant, saddened, as though he retired his mask when he believed no one was watching. Then, detecting her presence, his eyes slid to lock on her, and he instantly straightened. The shift of his face was so sudden Tauria took a few fast blinks to be sure she hadn't imagined the last few peaceful seconds before harshness claimed his expression.

She stepped out, the warm summer sun embracing her, and took a deep breath of the dry air, glancing over at the scene Tarly had lost himself to a moment ago. It mapped a breathtaking maze of sand and stone, so much beige but crafted beautifully. Many tall, domed structures could be seen from their vantage point, the sunlight gleamed off the glass to reflect streaks of color.

"I wasn't expecting to see you this morning," Tarly said by way of greeting.

Her eyes fell to him as he rose.

A servant approached to offer her a seat at the opposite end of the table, but Tauria moved to the place beside Tarly's instead. His hazel gaze flickered with surprise, and then a small smile broke his sternness. It fluttered her chest.

"I was thinking about what you said. Spending time together. Being seen as a couple," she began, and she didn't miss Tarly's cautious glance at their surroundings, always careful of who was listening. As much a warning for her as it was a habit for him.

Tarly stepped over, pulling out the seat for Tauria to occupy. She didn't get to read his reaction, but a tense moment of silence turned her stiff. The longer she pondered his offbeat behavior, the more she was beginning to suspect Tarly knew things, or at least held his own reserves about his father's goings-on. Yet he didn't trust her enough to confide in her his thoughts. That became her new course of action: to show Tarly she was on his side, if that was what this was. Him at odds with his father in all this.

"I heard mention of the Livre des Verres and was led to believe it is within close distance of the castle."

Tarly took his own seat with a spark of genuine interest and enthusiasm. "It is. A short carriage ride through the city. Why do you mention it?"

"I wanted to ask if you would take me."

Tarly's brow hooked in surprise, but his hard eyes eased.

"I think the people should see us together if they are ever to imagine this alliance to be true and prosperous." Tauria reached up her hand, tentatively placing it over his on the table as though he might immediately recoil from her touch. He didn't. In fact, she couldn't ignore the small burst in her chest and the tingling of her skin when her hand was accepted and his palm twisted to meet hers.

"I like this idea," he agreed. But Tauria paid attention to how his smile was never fully there, as though he lost his fight to bask fully in a moment of happiness every time. "How about this afternoon? I don't suppose you have any other plans."

"None at all." She gave his hand a gentle squeeze. "I look forward to being able to spend some time together outside these suffocating castle walls."

Observing how longingly his eyes lingered on the world beyond, Tauria knew it was exactly the common interest to explore. Her light humor seemed to work, and she had to put in effort to subdue her awe when the prince grinned. Beautiful. *He* was beautiful. When he allowed joy, however short-lived, to brighten the bleakness that often shadowed his face.

"I agree," he said, but he kept an edge of caution not to give too much of himself away. Tarly's guard was firm, so reinforced she wondered if even he knew how to bring it down. "It's not often we get to leave the castle grounds."

Tauria had to be smart in her inquisition. "You don't visit your people?"

"The capital city, Vesmire, is one of the few safe places we can wander among the people. Don't ask me to take you beyond there, as I warn you now, I will not."

Hot and cold. Tarly was a balance of both that required figuring out so as not to tip the scales too far in either direction.

"Your father mentioned there are not enough lands for your people and that they grow restless."

Tarly scoffed. "He speaks true." He spared a glance back indoors, to where four guards were posted like statues. "But the truth is not often so transparent." It was an obscure thing to say, but the prince didn't look to her, as though he didn't agree with his own last words.

"The stone men…" Tauria trod carefully. "They occupy the passes." She knew this from the kings' meetings last winter. Though she hadn't been invited to attend, Nik wasn't so content to leave her out of court affairs. One thing Varlas had gotten worked up about was his hatred of the Stone Men after Rhyenelle refused to yield land for nothing in return.

"Yes, they have done for some time now, and their numbers grow."

"None of them reside in the city?"

"They are too savage for structured life." Tarly spoke factually. But then he pinned her with a look of wariness and warning that rattled her need to press further.

"Why do they have such a name?"

"Surely you were schooled on other kingdoms besides your own." With narrowed eyes he called her out.

Tauria recited what she knew. "A long time ago, they began as a small group who sought to overthrow the last King of Olmstone."

Tarly nodded, adding to the knowledge. "They didn't agree with the taxes, nor the routine imposed upon them. King Hectas Wolverlon was a ruler of discipline and following. He took great pride in a kingdom that ran systematically. Taxes increased for all no matter their household earnings. Many couldn't afford to live in the city anymore, but it was his belief that he was creating a kingdom of thriving citizens, weeding out the weak and the poor. He wanted Vesmire to become an enviable city of wealth and obedience."

Tauria fixed effortless attention on him, wholly engrossed in Tarly's lesson, which he told it as if it were a fairy tale. The way he spoke was entrancing. She knew vague pieces of the knowledge he shared, but Tarly added so many hidden details of the past.

"The city entered a period of chaos and ruin when many gathered to turn against the king in the fight for class fairness. It nearly brought the city to collapse. They call them the Stone Men because they were too impoverished to afford armor of steel or leather. Instead, they crafted all they could from stone. Weapons, various bodily reinforcements, but never full protection as that would weigh them too heavy. But the weapons they crafted—they were incredible. Catapults, boulders, ramparts. They were very crafty with what they had."

"Yet they never succeeded."

"No, but they came close. King Hectas was given a choice—or a chance, rather—to end the civil war with an agreement. The Stone Men would have the passes, free to live and rule as they wished without his interference, but the treaty also meant they could not demand any goods from the city. Olmstone has long been a divided kingdom."

"Then why is it they grow restless now?"

"It's been a long time. Their numbers have grown, as have those in the city. They have been trying for some time to renegotiate with my father, but he's been too preoccupied to make urgency of it, and they're growing impatient."

Tauria filled in her own meaning with the term "preoccupied," figuring since the death of his mate and with his new path of vengeance it was far from Varlas's priority. She didn't anticipate just how torn the kingdom was, perhaps even on the brink of a new civil war if nothing was done. It shouldn't have been her concern, yet she couldn't deny they all needed the strength of every kingdom to maintain their alliance against a far larger threat. A threat to Ungardia.

"You cannot negotiate on his behalf?" she questioned, but Tarly's face twisted.

"They will not listen to a prince who has no real authority to pass change. Nor is my father any more likely to spare the time to hear it from me."

Her heart stumbled for him. Because whether he realized it or not, in his tone, Tarly slipped the hint that this was far more personal than political. As she watched him, his eyes overlooking the stone grounds, hope weaved through her. An unexplainable *faith* in him that formed her next words, as if he needed someone to say what she saw.

"You would make a great king, Tarly Wolverlon. One who could heal what was broken here."

His eyes slid to hers, holding them. Tauria's pulse picked up unexpectedly, and she wondered if the slide of his thumb against her hand was deliberate. Tarly slipped his guard just to relay a statement that inspired her with its consideration.

"You will make a gracious queen, Tauria Stagknight. One who will reclaim and restore what was taken."

That afternoon, all feelings of reservation dissipated as Tauria skipped out to the courtyard, where a carriage lay in wait. Even her smile was genuine as she met eyes with the prince who waited by it, and when it was returned, her stomach fluttered with excitement.

The walls of the castle had been slowly closing in on her, taking her back to the confinement of the High Farrow court. Under Orlon's rule, it wasn't often she'd found the opportunity to wander the city, and even when she did, it always felt like a mere extension of her stone cage with the city wall shielding any humbler setting beyond it. She was eager to sample Olmstone's diversity in the small hope it might resemble Fenstead or share similarities with the city Nik was trying to rebuild under his reign.

"You look beautiful, Tauria," Tarly said as he glanced over at her, his hand outstretched to assist her into the carriage. It skipped her pulse, and she couldn't help but to admire him back, finding a light shift in his whole demeanor she hadn't seen before. Perhaps getting away from the castle was exactly what they both needed to start building a true relationship. Tauria protected her hope that the prince might let his guard slip while they were away from the walls that had ears and eyes. She *had* to hope because so far, the prince she'd been around was far from one she could picture living happily beside.

In the carriage, Tarly settled in opposite her, his attention unnerving. But he didn't scrutinize her; instead there was a rare look of wonder sparkling within his hazel eyes.

"I can't tell you how pleased I am that we're getting to see the city," Tauria said quietly.

Tarly's look grew pained for a split second before he adjusted his sights on the small window. "I think we are both in need of the fresh air," was all he said.

The carriage jolted forward.

"I had the pleasure of joining the queen for luncheon the other day," Tauria said in an attempt to spark conversation.

Tarly scoffed, his brow hooked in faint amusement as he spared her a look. "You don't need to pretend out here. Or with me. I can imagine a luncheon with Keira was anything but pleasant."

Tauria bit her lip to suppress her smile. Tarly's eyes flashed to her mouth, and the spark of desire in his intense stare had her swallowing hard. She took a deep breath, which in turn seemed to snap Tarly back from whatever crossed his mind. She couldn't ignore the prickling of her skin. Couldn't deny that she *enjoyed* it.

"She has a way with words, that's for sure," Tauria commented.

"I bet she's made a lot of observations about you."

"I don't think she's best fond of me yet."

"She feels threatened."

Tauria blinked in surprise that Tarly would be so bold. But she supposed he had little reason to be careful out here. The guards who trailed them on horseback were likely too far away, and their words would be distorted by the scrape of the carriage rolling over rocks and the clip of the horses' hooves.

"That's a ludicrous notion."

"Is it? You're potentially the next Queen of Olmstone. If we were to wed, her position would become redundant."

"You don't sound like you have the best regards for your stepmother," Tauria tested. But she realized her error with the quick flash of spite that crossed his features.

"My mother is dead. Keira is nothing to me." Tarly's fists were tight on his lap, but Tauria didn't balk. Because it was grief, not anger, that consumed him in that moment. Tauria saw it because she had battled with it many times. She wondered if it was tragic or liberating that their bond might not come from their many shared activities and interests, but from their two dark and desolate pasts.

"I'm sorry," she said quietly, but she knew her words were a feeble attempt to console him. On that day, considering the madness that overtook his father at losing his mate, perhaps Tarly too had become an orphan in spirit. "You don't have to hide from me."

His expression fell. His vulnerability set in. Only a brief glimpse before he composed himself, but Tauria's forehead crumpled with such strong relief to see it. However short, she treasured the significance that whether the prince realized it or not, he'd trusted her enough to let it slip. However, Tauria knew the signs of when a conversation had become too heavy to bear, so she diverted the topic.

"The garden has been coming along nicely. Opal is quite the gardener."

Tarly yielded a small side-smile, adding a welcome lightness to the air of the carriage.

Tauria enjoyed broaching the topic of his sister, finding his care for Opal was the one thing that remained consistent with him. When Tarly found something worth protecting, Tauria was discovering, he kept it hidden and guarded by a part of himself that wasn't touched by darkness. He fought for that against all he had been through that made him resent the world.

"I imagined she would be," he said. "She always has been a creative, free spirit. It's not often she gets to be so hands-on."

"She's very keen to learn and participate, but I can't say the same for her mentor, Serena." Tauria was deliberate in mentioning the fae, and she studied Tarly's reaction with the echoes of her words from the queen's luncheon in her mind.

His expression wiped of all emotion. "I don't expect you'll find many here who understand your ways with nature, Tauria. Do not take it to heart."

"Trust I am not offended," she assured him. "Though she does seem to have a particular…affection for you."

Tarly shifted his gaze to her, and they seemed to assess each other. His jaw flexed, but she couldn't be sure if it was irritation at her statement or the fact Tauria found it appropriate to mention his private affairs. "Does that bother you?" he tested back.

Does it? Tauria couldn't be sure. It dropped a weight in her stomach to realize it wasn't the response she was hoping for. "Your past is not of my concern."

"I don't believe you're curious about my past. Why don't you ask what you want to know: am I sleeping with the ladies of the court while you're here as my prospective bride? Do you think so low of me, Tauria?" He was *hurt.* It wasn't the reaction she expected. But before she could feel guilt, Tarly hit her with more painful words. "Perhaps I have, and perhaps I will. What difference does it make if they're words of gossip or truth? Both are often equally as damaging to those who are too closed-minded to tell the difference."

Tauria didn't know why she felt the need to say her next words. Maybe through Tarly she was beginning to understand, as one monarch to another, court life was lonely. Rumors and claims were relentless. "I believe you."

Tarly pinned her with those hazel orbs, and they narrowed a fraction.

She explained, "If you tell me there is nothing between you and Serena, I will believe you. If you choose to tell me anything about yourself, I will believe you."

"Why?"

His question cleaved something in her chest, as if he didn't expect it. "How can we expect to become anything if we do not trust each other? For our kingdoms, this alliance is everything. But we are people, not just political markers. My parents were not mates. They married out of duty. My father was to become the King of Fenstead, and my mother was a high lady from Dalrune. They weren't best fond of each other at first, only because their union was not of their choice, but slowly, they learned to love each other. They became committed."

"And what if we were to cross paths with our mates?"

Tauria shifted her gaze for a split second of deep-rooted pain. But she forced a smile. "A mate is just a binding of power. I would like to believe that if my parents had crossed paths with their mates, what they found with each other would have been strong enough for neither to want to stray from it. The mating bond can be rejected."

Tarly turned away from her, and the shift of mood palpable through the carriage stole the summer warmth breezing in through the open windows. That chill seeped into her very bones with his next words.

"You wouldn't have to worry about that with me." His tone drifted like a shadow, a distant echo. "My mate is dead."

CHAPTER 22

Tauria

HER FIRST STEP out of the carriage drew a breath of necessary fresh air after the weight of sorrow that had fallen. After Tarly's heart-shattering confession, conversation stifled when he passed off her question about what he meant.

To lose a mate… Tauria's heart clenched with his unfathomable pain. But it was clear the prince wasn't willing or ready to open up to her yet, and Tauria wouldn't press for the story that wasn't her business to know. Except now she felt dedicated to get him to *want* to open up to her. Tarly Wolverlon had lost far more than anyone should in one life. His mother and his mate. She didn't know which loss had come first, and that fact alone burdened her with guilt.

Her hand lingered in his as he extended it to help her out of the carriage, and she offered a smile to portray her gratitude in the hope of dispersing the somber tension. Great relief eased her posture when he mirrored her warmth, seeming glad the conversation could be left behind them in that carriage until he was ready to share more.

"I had them stop a short distance away from the library so you might get to sample the city routes," he said as they began to walk, the summer sun blazing hot and bright—but she wouldn't complain about the stiff materials of her gown that made her wish she were in something more weightless like her wears in High Farrow. "I hope you don't mind." When their hands released, Tarly folded his behind his back.

"Not at all," she answered kindly, observing him through new eyes.

Tarly was a puzzle she couldn't figure out. She tried to imagine a life with days like this. By his side, strolling aimlessly through the streets of his kingdom. What could come to be *their* kingdom. Fenstead too, as she tried to picture him there. What he would look like in emerald green instead. The future she conjured didn't seem all that bad. Perhaps she even found joy in imagining it. As long as she could expel the other face that tried every time to take his place. Dark hair triumphing blond. Green eyes replacing hazel. Tauria swallowed hard, willing her mind to relax the torment. She had to learn to let go.

Katori crept up to her side, and Tauria surged with a new confidence as she ran her hand down the wolf's neck. She was noticing a coincidental routine of Katori appearing when her nerves were rattled the highest.

The city bustled with clusters of humans and fae, adding to the sweltering heat. Market stalls were busy selling wears on either side of them. If it weren't for the guards surrounding them, they would be swept up in the masses. Almost everyone stopped to steal a glance, and she noticed many faces wrinkle with what she could only decipher as scorn as they whispered to their nearby companions. Tauria squared her shoulders to keep her nerves from faltering her confident poise.

The touch on her back made her tense in surprise as she peered up at the prince. He said nothing, but her muscles loosened at the subtle assurance. Tarly didn't mock or abandon her for the attention she wasn't entirely used to. In High Farrow, the people were curious about her presence at first, but quick to accept her or deem her station not worthy of fuss. The more she caught the looks and occasional endings of quiet conversations as they passed the fae here, however, Tauria came to realize she wasn't the only one they directed their unease at. Tarly gave no outward reaction to anything they said or did, so she couldn't be sure if he caught anything or if he was simply used to his people being unwelcoming of their prince.

"They don't seem best pleased by our being here," she commented quietly.

Tarly flinched as if debating whether or not to add thought on the matter. "There are many who blame my father for the failures of this kingdom. The lack of space has led to overpopulation, which in turn means there is often not enough food and wears. The taxes don't help those who have barely enough to survive day to day, but they are needed to keep our defenses strong. If Olmstone doesn't fall by battle, the war may very well cause collapse from the inside out."

Tauria appreciated that he was choosing to share his thoughts on the matter. She saw the opportunity to learn more while he was willing. "So even in Vesmire…they resent the crown?"

"As rulers, it is our duty to protect these people. But it's no consolation for our people to be at peace from war when they're not even at peace with where their next meal will come from."

Tauria watched his face to gauge anything unspoken. His expression hardened as he stared ahead as if unable to bear witness to the scrutiny of his own people. She wondered why he'd offered to bring her here when it was clear in his rigid poise he was far from comfortable.

"Have you ever tried asking for aid? From High Farrow, or perhaps Rhyenelle?"

Tarly huffed a dry laugh as his hazel gaze slid to her, portraying the question as ridiculous. "Rhyenelle will not yield a fraction of land. And High Farrow negotiated plans of aid. My father and Orlon were in agreement, yet I am sure Nikalias will not be so open to their past arrangements."

"Their plan was wholly wrong. To overthrow Rhyenelle…it's blasphemous."

"Is it? Kingdoms have been taken and reclaimed before. Sometimes it is what is necessary to pave a better world."

"You're better than that, Tarly." Tauria couldn't stop herself. She halted, and he turned to her fully. "You are not your father. You already said you didn't agree with his actions."

"Maybe I was wrong to think—"

"You are not."

Surprise narrowed his eyes, and he carefully spared a glance at the guards who'd halted with them. Always so many eyes, always so many rules. It was starting to grate on her nerves that nothing she spoke of with anyone was free or safe. Yet when he chose to meet her stare again, Tauria swore, just for a second, she saw a plea in them. Before the coldness returned and he was turning away from her, not waiting or uttering a word before he resumed his walk.

Tauria rushed to catch up, but her mood had deteriorated, the judgment of everyone she passed weighing heavy. Katori whined, nudging her hand, and she smiled as though the wolf would see her gratitude. She had thought she would enjoy the open air and being outside the castle grounds, yet when it came with so much more judgment, she wanted nothing more in that moment than to be in solitude.

"I'm sorry."

The two words caught her off-guard as they'd been walking in tense silence for a few minutes. "What for?" she asked.

Tarly's hand once again found its way to her, briefly curling around her waist to steer her sideways. Then she spied the grand domed building. It was magnificent. Triumphant. And every negative thought left her completely as she craned her neck the closer they got, eager to glimpse the wonders of such an impressive architectural masterpiece.

Inside was even more spectacular than she expected. The Livre des Verres towered five levels high, with a perimeter balcony that told her the library ventured several levels lower too. Her mouth opened as she scanned the space, heading to the railings. Despite her curiosity to glance below, her eyes cast skyward, spying the glass dome that revealed a breathtaking view of the rolling clouds in the summer sky.

"You should come during the night." Tarly's voice sounded quietly, as if not to disturb the peace that radiated through the space. Tauria met his eye, and he cast his gaze up as he continued. "The constellations are exquisite." Then his sight fell, and hers followed.

A gasp left Tauria at what she spied on the ground far below.

"It's a sundial," Tarly explained. The intricate markings glittered gold. "When one finds themselves lost in scripture, they need only glance down to discover how many hours have been swept away." The way he spoke was so gentle, different. Who Tarly was now was like a tormented soul at *peace.*

Then Tauria realized something. Turning her attention back to the door, she noticed none of the guards had followed them inside. The heaviness that lifted was felt in the loosening of her stiff muscles from being under so much surveillance.

"Not a single weapon has been brought into this library in millennia. It was considered sacrilegious to the Library Masters of Old. They have long since passed on, but the superstition stands that it would be a grave insult and bring bad fortune to disobey them even in death."

Tauria glanced over at the prince, flushing a shade of rose. She had been too engrossed by the wonder of the place to know when he'd stopped to hand over his own sword and any other weaponry he carried. Their eyes met, but only briefly, before his wandered and he shook his head. She might have even gauged it to be out of *embarrassment.*

"Sorry, you did not ask for such a history."

"No, please. I would like to hear more."

As Tarly fixed his attention on her, Tauria held her breath as though one wrong move could trigger the rise of his walls. She was beginning to enjoy the glimpses of what she caught behind them, almost to the point of an infatuation that saw her desperate to keep him present, not shielded.

"What happens to the sundial at night?" Her attempt to entice him to carry on talking seemed to work. The tugging of his mouth was a triumph to see. They both glanced down over the railings.

"The stars appear. It becomes not a time teller, but a constellation tracker."

In an attempt to get a better look, Tauria braced her hands on the wooden railings. Her fingers touched his as she did, and though it might have been intentional on her part, the shiver that quickened her heart at the contact was unexpected, and the look they shared with it…

Tauria stepped away, suddenly overwhelmed by the short, unexplainable pulse that dizzied her. Exploring her feelings with Tarly was part of the plan, but there was always a slither of reservation that drove her to stop any feeling from lingering too long. She had to look away in shame, about to turn from him.

"Her name was Isabelle," Tarly offered quietly.

Tauria was gripped still at knowing who he meant. Catching the fall of his eyes, she found the desolation that swept through his expression, the shadow of loss that darkened the hazel. "You don't have to tell me—"

"I knew her my whole life. We grew up together. But the mating bond can't be recognized before a certain stage of maturity. Even then, if a person isn't ready, they may not feel it when it's standing right in front of them. When I did have my suspicions about Isabelle, neither of us cared to say anything for a long time because it didn't matter. I loved her before it, and I knew I would love her without it."

Tauria's heart struck a hard beat, tightening and tightening for his pain, which felt so palpable. She couldn't be sure why he was opening up to her now. She had to take a moment to tear her gaze from those dying eyes before she heard the worst of the tale still to come. It was this place. Perhaps the only place in his kingdom the prince knew he wouldn't be followed or watched or overheard. Vulnerability faced no mockery in here.

"My father met Keira, and they quickly presented their own child to the world. I thought he had moved past my mother completely, and I resented him for it. I told him I had found my mate and that I planned to wed her, knowing it would infuriate him." Tarly passed her by, walking aimlessly over to the tall cases of books. His sight wandered over the spines as he continued, and she thought by the way he avoided her eye as she followed silently that he might have been afraid of her judgment. "Isabelle was a lady of the court, but she was considered low in station compared to me. I didn't care. Never. But I am the prince, my father's only son. I was born with a hand to sell for political gain, and that is all. Mate or no mate, my father never approved of her. So he did the only thing he knew that could drive us apart. He exiled her and announced her an enemy of the crown, never to set foot in Olmstone again upon forfeit of her life. He didn't care for my threats to follow after her. My father and Keira had Opal. She was only a babe, but one day she would be old enough to succeed them. But my father has never been the same since losing my mother. He stopped seeing me as a son or even a person, only as a right and a marker that was his to move."

Tauria couldn't find any words, didn't even think she could find her voice from the tightening of her throat and chest. The prince's past was so dark and full of misery—so much more than she anticipated to find behind such an icy exterior.

"When Isabelle left, my father made sure I was imprisoned in my own rooms. But in the days he thought I sat succumbing to defeat, I was biding my time. Learning the guard rotations, gathering what I could and storing whatever food I could spare. Nearly a week went by before I saw my opening, and I took it. I got on a horse and I fled, intending to leave it all behind for good. The crown, the wealth, the safety. None of it meant anything without her. I tracked her scent. I would never forget that scent. Until I found her."

Tauria halted while Tarly continued to the end of the hallway of books. Her eyes pricked, and her bones chilled. She watched the muscles of his back lock through his finely tailored jacket when he halted too, but he didn't turn back to her. She braced for the grim ending to his story.

"I tracked her scent all the way to a burned-down building, and within it…she had taken her own life. Her body was beyond recognition, but my mother's necklace lay against the remains." Tarly reached into his pocket and pulled out a sparkling amethyst hanging from a gold chain in the shape of—

"That's the mark of the healers," Tauria identified. The gold etching of a swirl striking through itself flashed her memory back to an old teaching.

Finally, Tarly met her gaze. "You did not know my mother had healing capabilities?"

Her silence and raised brow announced her ignorance. The small smile Tarly offered fluttered her with joy to see despite the sorrowful tales he shared.

"She harbored a very weak essence of the ability, but she was fascinated with the practice. She loved helping people. She told me a lot about Lakelaria—where some of the best healers learn and originate from—and how she always believed it was where she would live out her days if it weren't for my father. It wasn't just duty that bound her here. She could have rejected the bond, but they fell in love." It was a somewhat tragic example of one being torn between two polar desires. Tarly's hand closed around the necklace tightly. "Isabelle didn't know what it meant, but she admired it when I told her. If I was to spend the rest of my life with her, I thought that was what my mother would have wanted. For me to gift it to her." He shook his head, blinking slow. "I should have known… I should have *felt* her die. She took her life as though I was worth dying for. As though I was worth anything."

She watched his fists trembling, and while she hesitated in fear and uncertainty about what the prince was capable of when his emotions consumed him, Tauria couldn't help her careful steps toward him. It wasn't like approaching a snake with a will to strike; it was like advancing toward a creature who could lash out in *fear.* Yet she kept going, her heart thrumming—but so was his. Tarly fixed his sights on his empty hands as though they presented all he felt within. She couldn't fathom the pain that coursed through him at having to revisit that world-shattering vision. Tauria was grateful he'd shared his story with her.

When she stood right behind him, her hand was raised but she contemplated. She paused to study every flicker of his movement, so taut, for any sign he would balk at her touch. Tauria slowly placed her hand on him, and his spine straightened a fraction from it. But he didn't retreat.

"Can you look at me?" she coaxed gently, not speaking too loudly or moving too fast in case he closed himself off to her all at once. She didn't know how long he would allow her to slide in past his defenses.

There was some debate in his hesitation, the war he waged constantly within himself, not knowing if he should let people see there was a person beneath the crown. Because that was all his father had led him to believe he was.

But then Tarly did turn to her. His hazel gaze claimed her with a broken plea, and it shuddered straight through her. Before she could listen to her reservations, her hand moved up from his chest, over his neck, until his angled jaw was within her small palm. All he did was watch her with that heart-wrenching look.

"What do you see?" he asked quietly.

The question emitted an ache in her chest. He seemed to long for an answer that would counter everything he felt within. Tauria searched those lost pools, contemplating.

"I see someone worth everything."

His brow flinched at that. Tarly took her wrist, and her stomach hollowed when he lowered her hand away from him. She watched as the ice that had thawed reformed, and she almost believed she'd said the wrong thing. But in the reflective gaze he cast to the ground before he walked away, Tauria knew she had said the *right* thing, only because she'd seen that look before.

The look of someone who didn't know how to accept love but needed it. Craved it.

She had seen that look before in Nik.

CHAPTER 23

Nikalias

"I can't."

Nik's fists were tight and trembling as he stared into the lake of the Eternal Woods. After relaying all he'd discovered about Samara to Jakon and Marlowe, the blacksmith had wasted no time in delving into her own research to form a counterplan against Zarrius. Now, hearing Marlowe's plan at his back, he was awash with dread and a horror so overwhelming nausea filled his stomach.

"It's time, Nik," she encouraged.

"I can't," he repeated, twisting to her. He couldn't suppress the harsh bite of his tone at what she was insisting of him.

Jakon straightened from his lax position against a rock by the waterfall, edging closer to Marlowe. Nik didn't pay him any mind as Marlowe's ocean eyes displayed nothing but pity and patience.

"Why?" she asked quietly.

Nik flexed his fists. "I think you know why."

The confident lift of her chin confirmed as much. "I can't tell you what to do, only what I've found. What you choose next… I think you at least owe her the truth before you do something neither of you can reverse."

His breaths were heavy with defeat. Fear. He shook his head. "I can't risk it."

Marlowe's eyes dropped, weighted with sorrow, but ultimately, she believed in her plan. "It's better to have options. I'll need something to bind the spell to."

"Even that you can't be certain will work. If I do this, there's no guaranteeing she'll be safe."

"That was never a guarantee from the beginning," Marlowe said firmly. "Even now, you haven't been able to get one response from her. You can't Nightwalk to her. Is this really such a reckless plan when it will set you both free?"

Nik vacantly shook his head. "There's no going back from it." He felt backed into a corner. This day he knew was always destined to come.

"I think that's the point," Marlowe said carefully. "It's time to start looking forward. Whether you defy or bow to fate, it is your choice."

CHAPTER 24

Tauria

WATCHING LYCUS AWKWARDLY examine a book brought amusement Tauria didn't expect that afternoon. During their past hour in the Livre des Verres, they'd wandered down many rows of bookcases while he'd trailed her.

"It's not going to detonate," Tauria chuckled.

Lycus smirked, sliding the book back onto the shelf. "I don't understand your fascination."

"You became a leading general, yet you can't recognize when the greatest weapons are right in front of you."

"Books?"

"Knowledge," she specified. "And stories. Words hold power, Lycus. They can cut and love and inspire. They can break from the inside out."

"When did you get so wise, Tauria Stagknight?"

She smiled to herself, unsure why Nik's face surfaced in her mind. Tauria shook her head, standing with a book splayed over her palms.

She'd been hoping to find something on kingdom lineage, but she'd gotten caught up in the rows of fiction. The book she was looking at now brought forth thoughts of Tarly and how it might be one he would enjoy—at least judging by her glimpse of his messy dining room collection.

Lennox trailed after her and Lycus, arms heavy with books she'd chosen to take back to the castle. He'd been insistent on carrying them for her.

"You can put those down for now. We may be here some time," Tauria said to him.

"I'll head out to the front with them," Lennox agreed.

Tauria winced sheepishly, sliding one more onto the pile before he left.

"What do you hope to find?" Lycus asked.

Tauria wasn't sure. After her first visit here with Tarly yesterday, it hadn't felt right to ask him to escort her back so quickly. In truth, she didn't know what to say to him. How to console him after all he'd confessed to her. She needed some time to figure out how she could help a soul as tragically lost and burdened as the prince.

"I'm looking for kingdom histories," she muttered, stopping to glance at more spines.

"I may not read much, but I don't believe great monarchs of the past would be documented in books with titles like"—Lycus titled his head, squinting at what she read—"'Of Hearts and Ruin: A Forbidden Love.'"

Tauria was caught between amusement and the creeping heat on her cheeks. She pulled the book with a flash of memory. *Then I suppose we can consider* that *educational scripture. And* this *a very worthwhile lesson.* "You should read it," she quipped, not giving way to the bittersweet recollection. "You might learn a thing or two." She let the implication slip into her devious look as she tossed it at him, hearing him catch it as she sauntered away.

They climbed two spiral staircases, coming to more towering shelves that Lycus complained all looked the same. Yet to Tauria, every row opened a bright new wonder. She wanted to explore it all. Lost and blissfully distracted among the books, she didn't realize when Lycus strayed from her.

"Up here," he called.

His voice made her jump with its disruption to the peaceful silence. Her eyes darted to find him. Lycus leaned over the balcony with Lennox, beckoning for her to join them. She cast him a scowl for the fright.

A level up from her, Lycus leaned against a table filled with a tower of books, arms crossed, his quirked brow amused. Lennox lingered by a bookcase a few rows away.

"If we want to stand a chance at making it back for supper, I thought it better to ask where your particular area of interest was shelved." Lycus straightened, thumping a hand on the tall pile.

Tauria wouldn't admit the thought to seek out a scholar had crossed her mind, but she was eager to steal as many hours as she could in the space that wrapped her in comfort and safety. "I wish I'd never asked you to accompany me," she teased. It was a lie. After all, the alternative would have been several Olmstone guards.

Tauria lost herself in scripture that stole any care for time. The table was now consumed by open tomes, and her fascination made her flip pages with record speed to absorb as much of the trove of knowledge she'd discovered as she could.

"Do you know why Fenstead's emblem is a stag?" She echoed the trivia to Lycus, who was leaning lazily over the railing.

He groaned. "We're really going to spend the afternoon reciting history?"

Tauria rolled her eyes. "People often forget this detail as the emblem is always woven into tapestry or carved into brass. But it was prophesized that Ahren, the Silver-Antlered Stag, would *choose* the first King of Fenstead."

"That beast is a myth," Lycus huffed.

"Not according to Jerriah Stagknight. It was said that the beast could recognize one fit to rule and would live to serve them. Ahren revealed himself to Jerriah, guiding him right to Fenstead's heart of Calenmoor, where the castle would be built. When Ungardia was first divided into kingdoms, the rulers were chosen in many different ways. For Fenstead, it was having Ahren by his side that made our people believe in our king. Not for his triumph in battle or any means of conquer; it was in the peace and prosperity he promised the land. The values we've come to uphold to this day."

Lycus's smile was bittersweet. "Sometimes values must adapt to survive in this ever-changing world."

His meaning wavered her spirit. In the war that had seen their land conquered, their peaceful nature was Fenstead's downfall.

"I don't believe that's true," she muttered somberly. "We will rise, and we will fight to regain what was taken from us. But we're not weak for seeking peace first, even if it left us unprepared."

They shared a look of hope and trust, and as if they were agreeing no one would be forgotten, both of them slid a look at Lennox, who paused his page-flipping a few meters away. They said nothing. They didn't need to. Her chest burst with pride all over again that they were here. Tauria had forgiven Lycus for staying away, choosing to be grateful instead that he was alive and they would fight for their kingdom together.

She took a long breath to ease the heaviness that had begun to settle. "Do you know why Olmstone's emblem is a two-headed wolf?"

Lycus chuckled, a bright sound that brightened the silence. "You're not about to convince me those exist."

Tauria giggled, and it felt so light that the sound halted in her throat almost immediately. She frowned down at her book, realizing with a heavy heart it had been so long since she'd genuinely *laughed.* She cleared her throat. "It's symbolic, actually. The wolves have long been companion animals in Olmstone. They're wild and dangerous, but it's said they can be tamed, and many natives forged great bonds with them long ago. When Olmstone was in need of a ruler, there were two favorable candidates, but they were vicious enemies. It was decided trial by combat was the only way—a fight to the death. Darellas and Galnaith fought as ruthlessly as their hatred ran for one another. Darellas was about to be victorious, but just before he could drive his blade through Galnaith to finish the trial, Galnaith's bonded wolf launched into the path of the blade. Wounded, the hound didn't back away from protecting Galnaith. Darellas knew there was no winning the crown without a kill, and he planned to cut through them both. Until his own wolf stepped in, siding not with him but against him, protecting their enemy defiantly."

"So the beast had a change of heart," Lycus drawled. "How poetic."

Tauria shot him a disgruntled look. "A lone wolf is prey. They hadn't realized it before, but their wolves were of the same bloodline. They were two powerful beasts, yet even they knew strength was in a pack—in standing together. Galnaith saw that in the way his wolf didn't back down. He read the meaning. He won fair and square without the kill that was supposed to be inevitable. When they put their hatred aside, they realized how much common ground they shared and became such close allies that once Galnaith Wolverlon was declared the first King of Olmstone, he instated Darellas as his closest advisor. The two-headed wolf is symbolic of that union. Two leaders who harbored so much opposition, discovering what could become of working together when they put that hate to rest."

Stealing a look, it surprised Tauria to find Lycus lost in thought. Until he took a deep breath, letting go of his brief admiration.

"They'd be turning in their graves to see their kingdom now. It seems the current leaders of Olmstone don't take wisdom from their own history."

"Varlas lost his way a long time ago," Tauria agreed.

Lycus shook his head. "I mean before him, when the land was divided with the Stone Men. It sounds a lot like the tale in your book. Except they chose to remain hostile to one another, unaccepting of their different ways of life, and drove apart the people."

"The Stone Men have a leader?" Tauria's interest piqued. She hadn't heard about this from Tarly.

Lycus nodded. "I've met him once. Only in passing. During the Great Battles when they helped defend Olmstone's borders with Rhyenelle. Chief Zainaid, they call him."

Tauria leaned away from her book, wholly engrossed by—and a touch envious of—Lycus's experience.

"What they've made of the Stone Passes is remarkable. Despite their name, they're a very welcoming people. But I wouldn't want to challenge them. They're fiercely protective and ruthless in battle. You spoke of the wolves—you'll find the bond far more common with them compared to us here in the city. So far, the prince is the only person I've seen to have such a connection to the animals."

The wheels of Tauria's mind were turning. Minutes passed as she scanned the book, no longer reading a single word. She braced a hand on the table, sliding her gaze back to Lycus when a plan came to her that could lead to nothing. His brow curved up at whatever he saw in her expression.

"I don't want you to ask questions, but I need to know how confident you are in your messengers to get word out of the city without detection."

Lycus's eyes flared with the desire to press for information, but her expression warned against it. "I can guarantee it," he confirmed. "No one will know."

"Good. I'll have my letter to you by tomorrow. It will not end well for any of us if you are wrong, Lycus."

They stood there as a queen to her general in that moment. They would always be friends beneath their titles, but they were both learning that friendship had to come second.

"You have my word," he promised.

Tauria gave a nod of appreciation. Her shoulders relaxed, and her intrigue began to call her back to the pages around the table once more.

"How much longer do we plan to stay here?" Lycus all but complained. He stretched backward over the railing.

Tauria huffed, but it was humbling to watch him act the most casual he'd been since he arrived. "You don't have to stay. I have Lennox."

All he gave was a disgruntled sound, only moving to lean more comfortably against the wooden railing. Tauria bit her lip against an amused smile.

She continued to flip through pages until her father's name made her halt. Her brow pulled together as she traced the letters. The page was dedicated to him, but her mother's name was not present. Her heart clenched as she read about him, nausea and sadness returning as she pictured his face.

"I don't remember his laugh," she whispered. "He could erupt a room into bright echoes of it, yet…I don't remember what it sounds like."

Lycus mirrored her sorrow, and she couldn't be sure why she'd shared the thought.

"I always feared I would forget what they looked like, but it's far more treasured things that have become distant over time. I should have clung to those tighter."

"You might not see it, but I think you'll find a lot of those things live on in you, Tauria. They would be so proud of you."

Her brow pinched tightly. "I miss them."

Lycus was by her side in an instant, his arm draped tenderly around her shoulders, and she leaned into him. "Me too."

Sorrow and guilt consumed her almost enough that she was about to skip forward—until something caught her attention. Tauria read over the page, her frown turning to confusion as she tried to make sense of it. She leaned away from Lycus.

"Lakelaria," she mumbled. Dates, events, were all vague, but to her memory… "My father told me he'd never been there before." She turned to gauge his reaction.

He seemed unfazed, giving a shrug as he read over her shoulder. "It would likely have been for some political business. A short trip not worth the tale."

"Yet someone thought it was, enough to put it in here."

"Scribes and scholars document all kinds of useless information."

"Nothing noted is ever useless, Lycus." She flipped to the next page. "There has to be a reason." Tauria paused her reading to recall, "I remember learning about the kingdoms when I was younger, and I found Lakelaria to be particularly mesmerizing. After class, my father put me to bed one night and I asked if he had any stories of the land of ice and snow. I asked about the queen, who was powerful and ethereal in depictions, yet he wouldn't tell me anything. In fact, I didn't think much of it then, but it was as if he was *disturbed* by the topic."

Lycus perched on the desk. "Perhaps there was a conflict during his visit."

"Sounds plausible, but why not speak of it?" Tauria wished she'd thought to ask her mother. She noted the dates inscribed next to her father's visit, confirming it was after he'd married her mother but near fifty years before Tauria was born. Yet her mother was not mentioned anywhere in the king's visit to Lakelaria. It didn't make sense. Tauria's fingers fumbled over the pages, trying to find something to explain what he'd achieved during his lone trip. What she discovered began to slick her skin with an unplaceable dread. "He frequented Lakelaria," she whispered because she didn't want to believe it, knowing nothing good ever came from such a well-guarded secret. "Until I was born," she concluded, finding this was when his documented visits each decade stopped.

Her mind raced with the discovery. Nausea overcame her, and she had to step away from the text, unable to keep searching.

"Do you want me to?" Lycus asked softly.

Her breaths were hard, but she met his eye. She didn't have to answer as he'd already moved over to the book, scanning and flipping through a couple more pages. Tauria couldn't take it. She began to pace, her mind already calculating without the need to read on.

"Always to the castle," she thought out loud. Things were sliding together. "Always alone." Her hands ran down her face, and she halted, shaking her head. "Always to see the Queen of Lakelaria."

"I don't think that has anything to do—"

"What if they were mates?" she breathed.

His frown was puzzled as he continued to scan the book. Lycus shook his head. "It doesn't say that anywhere. This is simply a tracking of royal movements over the centuries."

"It makes sense," she continued anyway. "Why else would he be so infatuated with going there? Yet he'd already married my mother and knew the importance of duty. But what if his heart called to another when it was too late?"

"Does it really make much difference to anything?"

Tauria couldn't be sure. There was something unshakable in the memory of how closed off he'd been about the Kingdom of the Water-dragon. She needed to look into Lakelaria, the queen…

"You've been requested back at the castle for supper, Your Majesty." Lennox strolled toward them with the announcement. Tauria hadn't even noticed he'd slipped out to hear it.

Already, this discovery was a huge distraction from all she balanced in simply trying to stay afloat in Olmstone. Tauria decided to ignore her itch to delve into her blaring thoughts about what she'd discovered. It could mean nothing at all, and for now, that was what she had to believe. Chasing secrets of the past had to come second to battling the growing darkness of her present.

CHAPTER 25

Tauria

TAURIA WAS DRESSED and cloaked, equipped with her compact staff as she stealthily made her way out onto the balcony and took to the rooftops. The steady nighttime air wrapped around her body and soothed her mind. The task of hopping and climbing took her complete focus, and she was glad for it, enjoying immensely the freedom and adrenaline that coursed through her at dancing across the night.

Upon a particular balcony—two up and four across—she added an extra layer of arrogance to her skills as she toed her way across the stone ledge, adding the flair of hops and spins without even knowing if the prince was awake to see it. Tauria smirked in amusement as she made it to the end and continued her journey across the roof. She had no destination or even any intention of finding a way down. Perhaps all she would do that night was enjoy the wind whipping around her from the height and glorious openness, free of any eyes as long as she was careful not to go too close to where a perimeter guard could look up.

After scaling the roof a bit higher up, Tauria came to a section of the architecture that had enough of a flat level where the slants met that she could perch on it. There she watched the glorious moon surrounded by twinkling stars and let her mind drift. All she thought of was what it was like to be nothing. No one at all. She thought of what it would be like to have endless days and nights of this with no one to care or reprimand or judge. It was a freeing notion, but also…lonely.

It was in that moment Tauria realized she didn't hate who she was. Not her station nor the life she'd been born into. She loved her friends. She loved her memories of Fenstead. All she longed for was to have it all back. The thought that twisted her gut so terribly was that no matter how much strength and resilience she gathered, there was always the lingering taunt she would never see her lands again.

Tauria was encased with the awareness of Tarly's presence moments before he sat, so his cautious, hushed voice wasn't a surprise when it traveled to her.

"Thanks for assuring me I wasn't about to follow a true nighttime bandit over the rooftops." He settled down next to her, and she was glad he wasn't scolding her like she'd sheepishly braced for.

She turned to him with a mischievous smirk, and it was uplifting to see it matched on his own face.

"The added pirouettes were a nice touch."

"Who said night thieves don't dance?"

"Maybe they'll start. It was certainly an enticing coax."

Tauria grinned, and it was an unexpected feeling. Perhaps jarring that Tarly brought humor to the night instead of his usual gloom. Her smile fell, immediately guilty for the thought. Tarly shouldered more burden that she could possibly imagine. Losing a mother, then a mate, and having a cruel father tied to both. She found herself understanding him, *wanting* to get him to open up to her and know she surfaced no judgment.

"Couldn't sleep?" he asked, staring out at the moon.

Tauria studied how it added a youthfulness to his features. An innocence. As though being up here was a temporary reprieve from his demons. Two strands of hair that didn't fit into his half-tie framed his face, turning golden in the moonlight. "No," she whispered in answer to his question.

When he turned to her, his hazel irises glowed with such peace that it was as if she didn't know who sat beside her. He looked so unlike the brooding prince she knew. Tauria thought the echoes of his desolate past would be tense between them, but it seemed sharing the story had only liberated him. Their stare held for more thoughtful seconds of silence, building on something that made her conflicted with the will to move closer and the ever-present protest of what could become of them if she gave in.

Tarly flinched, reading something unspoken. He saved her from her inner turmoil when he broke, casting his sights back over the beautiful city. A landscape of buildings that glowed at night—not glittering like Caius City, but glowing with a warm hue that reflected off the natural stone and high, glass-domed roofs that stretched on with no end from their vantage point.

"Was there a reason you all but invited me out here?"

"You implied you'd follow me regardless."

"I think we both know you're more than capable of evading my detection, especially now you know exactly which balcony to avoid."

Tauria huffed. "Good to know you have confidence in me. I was beginning to feel insulted."

"I think you're capable of far more than any of us can prepare for." His belief in her was unexpected. Tarly didn't turn to her, and in the way he cast a hard gaze at the stars, perhaps he was regretting letting that thought slip.

"Can I trust you?" She felt foolish for asking, but in all her observations of the prince, one thing Tauria believed was that his true self surfaced when he knew there was no possibility he'd be seen or overheard.

"Since you have to ask…would you truly believe me if I said yes?"

He had a point. Tauria couldn't be sure.

Tarly huffed, taking her silence as answer. "Maybe you should begin by asking why you *don't* trust me."

"You haven't exactly been the most warm and welcoming since I arrived."

"Fair enough."

"Why?"

Tarly didn't respond, and the silence that settled between them told her not to press. She studied his expression. He was contemplating something. As though her question had made him debate if he could trust *her*.

"My father plans to push the engagement. He wants to make it public."

Tauria recoiled. "There's no engagement yet to push. I haven't heard a thing about the proposal or kingdom treaties to even consider the marriage."

"He's not a patient male, Tauria. And we are not granted the luxury of having our personal relations considered in this."

"This isn't what I came here for."

"Perhaps not. But it is what he invited you here for."

Tauria opened her mouth to press further with the sense of dread that washed over her. Tarly pulled himself up into a crouch before she could speak a word of her scrambling thoughts.

"I need to show you something," he said as a coax for her to follow, giving her no choice as he was already darting away with surprising stealth.

Tauria kept close to him, using all her focus to copy Tarly's footing as they dashed through the shadows, only slowing when they had to scale up or down or spare caution to the guard rotations far below. Occasionally, Tarly would pause to offer aid, which was always met with disgruntled protests about how Tauria was far more agile in the sport than he. But regardless, each time his hands went to her waist or her arm in an attempt to help, a short thrill raced over her skin from his attention.

Tarly went first, slipping in through an open window. Tauria had no clue about where it could lead, but she had to follow him if she wanted answers. Without realizing it, she *was* slowly coming to trust the prince. But she could never give away that fact, or it might be twisted as a weapon later. While she couldn't be sure how deep his loyalty to Varlas went as his son, she had to keep an edge of caution around him.

Indoors, they came to small room and slipped inside. It was nothing more than a quaint sitting room, the scent of musk and a coating of dust over everything signaling it hadn't witnessed love or light in some time.

"Did you recognize the hall outside? Do you know what section of the castle we're in?" Tarly quizzed.

Tauria frowned, trying to recall. They seemed vaguely familiar, but in all the matters she was dealing with, exploring the castle wasn't high on her list. Now she felt like a fool for it as she read the reprimand on Tarly's face.

"Remind me to get you a map," he grumbled.

"Why would I need one?"

He walked over to a sad, neglected bookcase. It dampened her mood to see the books discarded and unloved. His hand reached up as if to take one of the thick spines, but rather than the book tumbling off the shelf, it hung there, emitting a loud creak, and Tauria gaped at the discovery.

It was a hidden door.

She met Tarly's smirk, just before he pulled the case away from the wall and it groaned against the stone floor. "Not afraid of the dark, are you?" he chided at her ghostly look.

Tauria snapped her mouth shut with a scowl. What she didn't want to admit was that it wasn't the dark she feared…it was the thought of the stone tomb this could become.

"How do I know this isn't a trap?"

"I think there are far easier ways I could entrap you, princess."

"I think you underestimate me."

"That might go both ways."

They stared off in their matched stubbornness. It was a test, and he knew it. Tauria questioned his trust, and this was him forcing her to admit that. Even within herself, as she took her first steps toward him to seal what she might have felt all along, Tauria couldn't explain why, but somehow, she *knew* Tarly wasn't like his father. He wasn't vengeful even though he'd suffered the same loss as Varlas. The loss of a mate. Tarly was cold, detached, with nothing to lose and no desire to gain.

She didn't break his stare until she stood in front of him, waiting to follow him through the slither of darkness that stiffened her spine. She caught the quick easing of his expression and could only decipher it as *relief.*

Before either of them risked spilling kindness to ease the tension, they both slipped through the gap to become engulfed in darkness. Neither of them spoke. Tauria's fae sight adjusted enough to keep her from colliding embarrassingly with the narrow, bulging walls. All her senses were on high alert, but all was soundless, save for the faint shuffle of gravel beneath their feet. Her veins heated, awakening her magick in her panic about the air becoming restricted. She didn't know how many minutes passed while she focused solely on taming her wild fear of confinement and keeping tethers on her wind as it surfaced in natural defense.

"Would you stop that?" Tarly hissed. "You're creating a horrible draft."

Her fists clamped tight in an attempt to stifle it, but her wind gently chilling the air around them was soothing to her senses. "You're an ass," she muttered, feeling the caress of his answering smile in the dark.

Then Tauria picked up on another movement that couldn't be attached to either of them. Tarly twisted toward her, and she made out the silhouette of him pressing a finger to his lips. More light filtered into her vision, and as they turned, a pool of it flooded the next hall. A welcoming embrace that only marginally loosened her square shoulders.

Three metal vents lined the wall, and her curiosity had her passing the prince to catch a glimpse. Her pulse picked up with the memories that flashed through her, reminding her there wasn't anything desirable to be discovered in hidden passageways. They took up a vent each, but glimpsing below, it wasn't shock or horror Tauria was enchanted with.

It was awe.

The room was beautiful, but darkly alluring only in its decoration. Rows of benches filled the space under the balcony, and as she cast her eyes up, the roof was entirely domed glass like the throne room. Moonlight flooded a tranquil glow over every delicate obsidian decoration. A couple of servants loitered around the space as though preparing it with one death rose at a time. That was the name given to roses of such a color, said only to bloom on land touched by darkness.

Tauria was transfixed. She didn't detect him when the prince came up close beside her. So close she felt the graze of his body as he leaned in to peer out through the same vent.

"They've been at it for weeks," he said, so quiet she could've missed it under the shuffle of her shoe.

"What are they preparing for?"

"What do you think?"

The answer seemed obvious. "A funeral?"

Tarly smirked. "Is that what you'd consider our wedding day?"

Tauria couldn't surface any humor. Or a witty remark. Or anything while ice chilled her spine, making her skin crawl with the worst sense of dread she'd ever felt before. *Run.* That was all she could think upon witnessing the preparations. *Run home to him.* Because there was nothing joyous or exciting about the ceremony to be had in that room. Its beauty was a guise, a coaxing from something dark and sinister.

"How long have you known about this?" she whispered, eyes transfixed on the hollow faces that floated around the room like wraiths. There was something not right about them. Tauria's eyes tracked one female. They were all fae. She was arranging an assortment of black roses with an expression that looked like watching the living dead. She turned her back, and when Tauria's eyes caught her shoulder blades…

Her gasp was smothered by Tarly's hand. His other arm wrapped around her middle, and they both stilled. It was then Tauria caught the flicker of movement. Like smoke easing from the shadows.

When he emerged, a creeping sense of *wrongness* slithered through her chest. All she could think of when she looked at the intimidating fae male…was death. He was made of it. He was a harbinger. The way he moved was careful, as if every step was a challenge to those who dared to look into his black, depthless eyes, and if they did, he could consume them entirely with a single look.

Tauria's heart was a hard beat, but the thump of Tarly's heart against her back was a sure comfort she depended on in that moment to keep her present. To remember it wasn't a cage with bars through which she stared at the dark being.

"This will be a ceremony to be remembered for millennia." The dark male's voice doused her cold and swayed her with nausea. Not at death's caress that spilled from his tongue. But because she recognized it.

In the way Tarly's grip slackened, she knew his shock was true.

"I beg of you, High Lord. I need more time."

Tarly backed away from her at the new voice, and the air dropped to freezing point without his warmth.

Varlas walked carefully up the aisle as though approaching his master in the way the fae—the *High Lord*—stood atop the dais, hands folded behind his back to make his posture all the more dominating. He looked at the king as though he were no more than one of the servants tending to the venue.

"I gave you a month to no result. You allow them to rule you like children. We do this my way now. Come next full moon, we will begin strengthening the line of monarchs."

Tauria's lips parted in shock, horror, a fear so all-consuming she couldn't move. She thought she caught a glimpse of something dark, like shadows, growing over his shoulders. Sharp-tipped…*taloned.* Her mind scrambled but couldn't form anything of logic or sense to make her sure she was awake and this wasn't some unfathomable, ghoulish nightmare. Then time slowed as the fae's face began to angle, his gaze ready to cast up.

Tauria was pulled away from the metal shield completely and strapped to a solid force. Tarly wrapped her, but she couldn't move if she'd wanted to. Her mind raced with the inconceivable, the utterly damning scream so loud in her mind it was Tarly's hand over her mouth alone that kept the sound from being unleashed in her terror.

Because the being below wasn't fae.

Tauria knew she should get out of there.

Run.

Shadows with talons. Wings.

Oh Gods.

The female's back…two hideously torn stumps at her shoulder blades.

Wings.

They were dark fae.

CHAPTER 26

Tauria

Tauria was in her rooms, and for once she didn't want to leave. Not now she knew the horrors that crawled every corner of this castle, into whose path she might step if she did. She stared out over her balcony at the night sky, trying to get her mind to thaw from its hopeless frozen state. After what she and the prince saw in the spy passages yesterday, she knew she should leave or try to warn Nik. It was true. All of it.

Olmstone was siding with the dark fae.

With Valgard.

It was a betrayal so deep-rooted her pain had turned to numbness. Suspecting it didn't make the blow any less. Tauria knew the risk she'd taken in coming here, and since making her discovery she didn't regret her choices. Nor did she intend to flee. Her plan, while she spoke it to no one, remained the same. Nik never would have agreed to let her go if he knew her path of vengeance.

She paced her rooms not out of fear, but calculation, knowing even if she had to start in the flames she would avenge Fenstead. And right now, she was within reach of her ultimate enemy. Varlas would get what he deserved too, but she wasn't entirely devoid of care in her rage to remember he'd once harbored goodness. That, she would mourn.

Through her tunneling thoughts, Tauria's wind surfaced, rattling against the glass panes with the spook of the shadow that dropped to her balcony. She cursed her skittish mood. She'd been so distracted in thought she hadn't detected the prince before his intrusion.

"Are you trying to alert every damn guard?" Tarly hissed as he welcomed himself in, quickly pulling down his hood as if she still wouldn't know it was him.

Tauria winced. "Sorry."

They'd agreed to meet tonight. Following what they'd witnessed, they both needed some time to work out their thoughts first.

"Let's go," he whispered. Because they couldn't be sure their words were safe here.

They settled on the rooftops where they'd met last night. Silence fell between them for a long moment. It was thick, frightening, and cold.

"Did you know?" she began, needing to be sure. "Any of it?"

Tarly knew what she meant. While he didn't meet her eye, the disturbance on his face was too deep to be false. "No," he answered. "I saw them bringing in the death roses and I couldn't imagine what for, so I tracked them to that room, but it was always under strict supervision. I wasn't allowed in. My father has completely closed himself off since returning from High Farrow last winter. I knew nothing of what he was up to. I didn't care. We haven't had a nice moment between us since my mother died, in truth. I let go of my father a long time ago." He spoke so calmly, honestly, but it was with a detachment that tugged in her chest.

"He's consorting with Valgard," Tauria said.

Tarly's fists tightened in his lap. "It seems so." He did look at her then, and it was rare to glimpse his fear that was so laced with concern.

"You're not safe here, Tauria. I don't think any of us are, but you have a chance to leave."

"I'm not leaving."

His eyes flared, returning to their harshness. "I didn't just show you that passage to glimpse the ridiculousness of the ceremony they're planning for us that's likely to never go ahead." His tone was bitter, hurt, and it was then Tauria realized Tarly never had hopes of her agreeing to the marriage. He never believed she would want him. Guilt didn't seem appropriate for what sank so deeply in her stomach. "I took you there to make you aware of some interesting spy points throughout our castle, tunnels intended to circulate air, except the destination only ends in one place. Outside."

Tauria blinked, stunned. Tarly had given her a route to safety even before they'd discovered what awaited them. He was willing to set her free…

"Did you ever have hopes for this marriage?" She couldn't be sure why she asked, but she found herself on edge for his answer, wondering how miserable she must have been to have brushed him off so convincingly.

"Perhaps I did," he said. "Perhaps I still do."

The flutter of her stomach was conflicting. A battle of guilt and flattery.

"But not by my father's terms."

"It would always be by his terms."

"Not if we play him at his own game."

Tauria frowned. "You just told me I should flee, and now you want me to stay and marry you on our own terms?"

"I gave you a means of escape should all Nether break loose," he snapped. He regained his composure at her recoil. "Why must you speak of a marriage to me like it's a forced duty? Is that all you would ever see us as?"

Tauria thought over his words. With them came flashes of what a future with him could entail. By their will, it didn't seem so awful. A life she had once had to consider before, when their match was favorable to Varlas and Orlon. Did they have the same plans before? It made sense to assume so. She and Tarly had been targets for far longer than they thought.

Tauria took a few calming breaths to defuse her panic. It made no difference now. "You haven't exactly romanced me," she mused lightly. It was a relief to hear his huffed laugh. "I'm still not understanding your plan."

"We've been seen in the city together, around the castle. What is only a few ventures out to us means everything to people looking for something to be hopeful for."

Tauria supposed he was right, but she was swept with a sinking feeling. Would word have traveled to Nik? That she and the Prince of Olmstone were getting…*close.*

"For once, the rumors will ride in our favor, and we'll announce my proposal to you to my father tomorrow."

Tauria's heart nearly stopped. And broke. Because an engagement announcement *would* travel fast to all kingdoms. To High Farrow. "We'd be giving him everything he wants," she breathed. It seemed to be his father's goal—the dark fae's goal—as they prepared their ominous ceremony without either of the heirs' knowledge.

"When someone has everything they want, their focus is swayed from acquiring it. Our engagement grants us the upper hand to ease the pressure. Varlas will think it's merely a waiting game to see us wed. It will give us time to turn the watchful eyes on them instead and figure out all we can about their plans for this union, and—" Tarly halted, and it was the first time she'd ever seen the prince look truly *fearful.* "I don't want to scare you, but what we plan to do will be dangerous, and what we might discover may be harrowing should our fates truly fall in their hands. I don't know what the dark fae are capable of, or what someone like the High Lord could possibly seek to gain from us, but I highly doubt it's simply to wed us and see us politically controlled. Something's coming. Something dark and changing."

And it bore down heavy on them upon that rooftop. A frightening uncertainty. A looming dark fate.

"So we fake our engagement," Tauria concluded vacantly.

"Who says it has to be fake?"

Tauria turned to him. His face was unusually soft and searching, and he might have inched closer at some point as their bodies now nearly touched.

"At least the formality will be. But maybe you'll allow me to romance you through it all."

Tauria released a quiet giggle, a genuine bout of giddy humor that heightened in her desperation to quell the horror and fear encasing her. For what was to come, for everything they had discovered.

"I mean it, Tauria. This can be our choice. It starts with trusting each other. I know I haven't been the most forthcoming, but I promise to be on your side, against my father if need be."

Tauria took a deep, contemplative breath. She looked away from him and cast her sights to the moon. A life with Tarly was starting to feel easier. It was a challenge to find out what made him and what broke him, but anything worth treasuring was worth fighting for.

"Yes," she said, pushing down any reservation that threatened to take root in her choice, letting go of the face that sprang to mind as she made her decision. "I will marry you, Tarly Wolverlon."

CHAPTER 27

Nikalias

NIK CLUTCHED THE desk so hard it was an effort not to split the wood and give away the all-consuming anger that coursed through him. The voice at his back was a distant, irritating murmur, relaying the information like a dagger through his heart although it was written on the parchment his eyes bore holes through.

Tauria's engagement.

He had no right to feel the invitation to celebrate their union at the Summer Solstice Ball was a mockery, yet his demons—one of which was real in the form of Zarrius—were laughing. The lord behind him didn't try to hide his sly undertones as he spoke cheerfully of the *joyous* announcement.

"It has come together far quicker than we could have hoped for. I can only imagine how well the prince and princess have bonded."

Nik couldn't stop Zarrius's words from twisting and twisting in his chest. Not without the risk of jealousy pouring out in his tone. He didn't doubt his excessive gushing over the announcement was a deliberate probe, daring Nik to break. The lord knew far more than he allowed Nik to believe, and that was the way it had to stay.

Jakon stood by the side of the room as they'd been in casual conversation before the lord's interruption. Aside from insisting on Jakon's dismissal—which Nik had declined—Zarrius was otherwise pretending he didn't exist. Nik slid him a glance as he straightened, glad for Zarrius's lack of care as the human could hardly suppress his knowing wince. Nik blanked his face. Picking up the parchment, he turned to the lord.

"Indeed. What a grand celebration this will be." *Engagement.* Reading the word over and over again, he numbed himself to it, only to see his own plan written between the lines of the invitation in his grasp. Nik took a long breath, setting it aside. "Have the scribes write back with confirmation of my attendance."

"Is it wise for you to leave your kingdom for a ball at this time?" Zarrius inquired carefully.

"Yes." Nik brushed off his concern. "I see it as the perfect opportunity to introduce my own fiancée to our neighboring courts."

Jakon's shift of surprise was subtle. Nik hadn't told him of his own engagement because truthfully, it had only come to mind in the heat of this moment. This could work to his advantage. He had every intention of going to the damned ball, but only to confirm Tauria's willingness and safety in the plan when he'd yet to receive a single reply to his letters and his Nightwalking was still blocked. Something wasn't right, and his frustration was collecting, reading to unleash in a storm they wouldn't be able to brace for if he discovered she'd been mistreated or her hand forced in any way.

"Advise that I will be attending with Lady Samara."

"I did not know you two had come to such an agreement so soon."

"Royal engagements happen fast. The people will rejoice in this hopeful change for the kingdom. Two rulers are stronger than one."

"I agree. Though might I say, the court hasn't seen much of you two together?"

Nik's smile was falsely arrogant. "I'll admit we prefer our private time," he implied as confidently as he could, though the thought of it filled him with guilty unease. "Expect Lady Samara to be seen by my side more often, Zarrius."

The lord didn't seem as pleased as Nik had hoped. Doubt was written on his face, and Nik understood it would take far more for his brazen plan to seem convincing.

"As it turns out, I believe my fiancée is expecting me now," he said by way of dismissal. Truthfully, he only needed to find her urgently to inform her of the ruse she would unwittingly play a key role in. Nik only prayed she was willing to help.

"Very well," Zarrius said, lingering a suspicious gaze.

Nik kept his expression neutral. His muscles were so stiff it became painful, anticipating the lord might turn back and out every lie he'd spilled from his mouth. He'd hoped the lord would slip up with his personal feelings for the one who was supposed to be his lover, yet Zarrius yielded nothing. No jealousy at Nik's insinuation they'd shared a bed. No anger that he'd secured the hand of his most treasured secret. He had to assume, with great relief, Samara was playing her role well in convincing Zarrius of how things were progressing.

When the door clicked shut behind the lord, Nik's head fell back. He stared at the ceiling, trying to calm himself down, trying to piece together his scrambled mind to figure out what in the Nether he was thinking.

"Congratulations." Jakon's voice cut through his racing thoughts.

Nik's head lolled, pinning him with a disgruntled look.

"I would have brought an engagement gift," he went on, fighting his laughter. "Should I ask Marlowe to craft the ring at least?"

Nik groaned, running a hand down his face. "I need to go to Tauria, and having it known my hand is also committed for all intents and purposes will keep suspicions at bay while I'm there. Zarrius will also believe his plan is advancing."

Jakon nodded, but his amusement didn't vanish.

"Stop enjoying this."

"I have no idea what you're talking about, *Your Majesty.*" But then sympathy eased into Jakon's expression. "You know she will hear of it before you get there. Not from you."

Nik couldn't hide that the thought twisted his gut. "There is no other way." A part of him wanted Tauria's engagement to be true and happy so the false news of his own wouldn't hurt to hear from outsiders. But there was a larger part, a dominant, dark part, that was too selfish to accept that happiness for her unless it came from him.

"I guess you have travel preparations to make," Jakon diverted carefully. "I'll keep an eye on Zarrius while you're gone. I'm not much influence without you here, but your nobles often underestimate what a well-paid network of servants can pick up."

Nik smirked at Jakon's secret insight. He couldn't reprimand him for essentially turning his castle staff into spies if they were daring enough to risk their positions.

Jakon was at the door as Nik called, "The ring." He rubbed his tight temples to relieve some of the tension of this twisted reality in which he was living. "I'll need the damn engagement ring."

CHAPTER 28

Tauria

It didn't take long. News of a royal engagement spread faster than wildfire. Gossip bred from it, some tales romantic, others scandalous, many humorous. Tauria had never had more attention fixed on her wherever she went than now. To everyone here, she was the future Queen Consort of Olmstone. But she didn't let her unease surface for a second. Tauria Stagknight, dressed wholly in the vibrant purple of the kingdom she would soon reign over, marched confidently through the royal halls. Stares of awe, jealousy, and curiosity followed her every move, right until she made it to the queen's quarters.

This time by invitation.

Tauria had been expecting it, having no doubt Keira would have a lot to say about the engagement. It had been joyously announced by King Varlas the same morning they went to him following their rooftop proposal, a tale that could one day be romanticized despite the circumstances surrounding it. They couldn't waste time when it seemed darker forces were at risk of winning the game before their sleight of hand.

Katori had been waiting outside her rooms that morning and followed her. Tauria was grateful for the ally who soothed a lot of her anxiety. Sometimes the wolf's presence yielded a nod of respect from those she passed who might otherwise have questioned her.

Gliding into the brilliant, open marble space, Tauria spotted Queen Keira effortlessly reclining on her side in an elegant chaise longue. Ladies she remembered from her last unpleasant visit circled her on cushions, always positioned below Keira so they appeared to be worshipping a goddess as they fixed their awe-inspired faces on her.

Keira's blue eyes slipped up to meet Tauria's, trailing the length of her as she took in her appearance. The royal wears of Olmstone. She adorned the sigil of the two-headed wolf. The flash of ire on Keira's face wouldn't have been detected by any of the others, and perhaps they wouldn't understand what it meant anyway. That the two rulers now matched in rank. At least, Tauria was granted the same order of protection and respect now she was considered a prize to the kingdom.

"The beast is not allowed in here," Keira said by way of greeting.

Katori's head dipped a fraction, a stance that invited a growl, but the wolf remained silent. Tauria ran a hand down her fur.

"By all means, send her away," she answered casually.

Tauria didn't command the wolf. She had never tried or even thought to ask Tarly if she responded to any commands like she'd seen trained dogs do before. Yet Katori seemed…*different.* Every time she met those shimmering silver eyes, she couldn't help but feel unease, as though Katori could think and assess for herself.

Keira didn't get the chance to spill any more disfavor for the wolf when small footsteps sounded.

"Tauria!"

The squeal of her name was startling, and she turned just in time to catch Opal as she collided into her side. Her chest burst with warmth at the bright reception, so welcoming in contrast to the judgment that tracked her from the ladies.

The young princess gasped as he stepped away. There was no hesitation when she stepped up to Katori, who nearly matched her height, and raised her hands to stroke her. The burst of giggles when Katori nuzzled her head against the princess sparked a grin on Tauria's face. From their exchange, she assumed they'd met plenty of times before.

"When will we get to go to the gardens again?" Opal chirped, eyes wide and full of adoration as she beamed up at her.

Tauria opened her mouth to promise her it would be soon, but the queen's voice eloquently carried over her before she could.

"Come here, my dear," she commanded.

The princess's face fell, her small shoulders deflating a little as she let go of Katori. When she sat by her mother, the queen ran a hand down the length of her honey-golden curls.

"I don't think the garden is an appropriate place for you."

Opal said nothing, but the protest fell on her innocent face as she fought against speaking to sit poised and silent. Tauria couldn't stop her intervention at the suppression that felt wrong.

"She is well-protected in the gardens and under my supervision."

All eyes fell to her, and she didn't have to meet any of them to feel the air tense as if she spoke insult. Tauria smiled sweetly at the queen, never letting her confidence falter. A slight crack was all it would take for someone like Keira to slip enough to break her.

Tauria addressed the young princess directly as she said, "I'll be heading out there tomorrow afternoon, if you are free to join me."

She caught their faint intakes of breath. Incredulity. She had to refrain from casting her irritation over all the ladies for adding flare to the matter. Keira's reputation was what she valued the most, and the subtle overpowering of her authority was likely ten times worse in front of her precious company. But Opal was old enough to make decisions for herself, and perhaps Tauria couldn't help but see her own child-self in the young fae, hoping to instill the same independence and courage her own mother had inspired in her.

"Perhaps the fresh air would do you good, my child," Keira cut in before Opal's eager words could spill. Her switch to agreement was a tactful grapple with the reins of her authority. "Madame has informed me your classes are lacking. A couple of days away from them might clear your mind." Her hand continued to stoke Opal's hair, and Tauria couldn't be sure why the movement made her uneasy. As if she were admiring a well-tamed cat, not her own child.

She had to shake her growing irritation. "You invited me here, Your Majesty?"

The queen's smile was feline. Enticing, but striking with alarm. "Join us, Tauria." It was not a request.

A chair was brought over for her by the queen's silent command. Keira was being strategic, granting Tauria the respect she would now be owed. Tauria sat poised but couldn't help feeling like she was being placed on trial rather than included in casual conversation.

"Your engagement has caused quite a stir." Everything Keira did was careful, analyzing. "I'll admit I'm surprised it came around so soon."

"We didn't see reason to wait."

"Hmm." Keira sipped from a golden chalice. "I didn't know the two of you had become so close."

Tauria was right to feel cautious as she had been placed in this chair to be the center of focus to the audience around them. She wondered if any of the ladies detected the challenge—the careful interrogation the queen had set out this afternoon. Tauria's eyes fell to Serena for the first time, and her gaze was nothing short of green envy. She didn't take the slightest satisfaction in it. Perhaps she even pitied the naïve fae for thinking she stood a chance with the prince when Varlas would never allow it.

"Tarly and I had a history before now. And our private meetings since my being here…well, I suppose you could say they helped draw out our feelings for one another far faster."

The ladies turned giddy, wide-eyed and bright-smiled, eager to hear of her scandalous affairs with the prince.

"Can you tell us more?" one of the fae asked, shifting on her cushion to face Tauria instead.

The flex of the queen's eyes alerted Tauria to the fact she didn't take attention being stolen from her very well. Not when it was in Tauria's favor. She smiled, slow and triumphant, knowing one by one she could take each of them from her if she desired.

But this wasn't her. Tauria would not allow herself to become like Keira.

"The prince is…passionate," she offered, emitting a few excitable squeals from the small group. "But a lady never tells. Let's just say there are many ways of finding pleasure without giving all."

It was like watching children, the way they exchanged looks and their cheeks flushed. They would never know—no one ever would—that she had surrendered herself to another prince long ago. No one could know. Thinking of Tarly now, it filled her with shame to admit as much. Their engagement may be a ruse, but she couldn't deny there was a part of her that thought she owed him that truth at least.

"The King of High Farrow has also been courting Lady Samara for some time."

Tauria's gaze snapped to Serena, and her blue eyes were filled with iron daggers that pierced her. As she sipped casually from her cup, the fae *knew* it could gain a reaction from her.

She tried to keep her composure, casually stating, "He's been known to return many ladies to his company."

"I envy Lady Samara. She is said to be blessed with the beauty of a Goddess," another gushed.

Tauria's stomach clenched. Tighter and tighter. Nik had never sought the company of any high lady with an esteemed reputation. To hear Samara's name again arose pitiful disappointment.

"It is true." The queen drew everyone's attention to her, but her eyes fixed on Tauria. "I am surprised you did not know. I thought you and the king were close enough that you would be among the first he would personally inform. But here we are."

Keira knew exactly where to strike. Unable to touch her status here, she went for everything Tauria was supposed to be in High Farrow. In front of the best audience of all, Keira made it known that she was nothing to Nik. What hurt so badly it stole her breath was that Keira didn't need to say a thing for Tauria to realize it, *feel it,* for herself. She struggled now more than ever to bite back the flood of emotion that pierced her heart, her soul. And Tauria near shattered at the queen's next words.

"The announcement was made around the same time as yours. A fitting coincidence." Her smile was beautifully cruel. "Nikalias Silvergriff is engaged to Lady Samara Calltegan."

Her stomach turned, and she longed to be anywhere but here. Anywhere with eyes. Because breathing was suddenly difficult.

"He plans a trip here for the Summer Solstice Ball, and to negotiate what you and Tarly's marriage alliance will bring for us all. His new bride-to-be will accompany him." Keira delivered each word like the piercing of a needle. Over and over. Tauria couldn't even find it in herself to maintain her placid façade. She cared too deeply. Hurt too truly. When she had no right or reason to be so overwhelmed by her feelings at this knowledge.

He was coming. But not for her. Nik would arrive to witness her in the arms of another, but that was nothing compared to the image that branded itself in her mind of Samara by his side.

"Are you all right, Your Highness?" one of the ladies asked, genuine concern written on her face.

Tauria couldn't fall apart, not within the clutches of the vultures. She glanced into her cup, mustering a nod as she handed it off to a servant. "I don't think the wine has taken well," she muttered, knowing it was a poor excuse, but she didn't care. She needed anything to grant her escape.

"You have only just arrived. I was rather hoping to discuss your dreams and desires for your wedding. I'm sure our king won't give you much time to delay."

Tauria managed to meet Keira's look and find it darkly amused. Knowing. Did the queen know everything? About the dark fae, about whatever plans Varlas had that involved them all.

Too many questions. Too many thoughts. She needed it to stop. And all of it did—in the presence of a sadness so strong it hollowed out everything else. Her eyes fought the burning that threatened to expose her feelings. She kept her face straight, devoid of emotion. A masterful guise of collected royalty. She stood on weak knees, forcing a pleasant smile.

"Thank you for all the congratulations. I look forward to meeting again to discuss more exciting plans for the big day."

The ladies nodded with wary acceptance. Tauria didn't think her tone was true to her words, but she had no choice now but to turn and seek freedom from the suffocation that closed her throat. Her teeth clenched tight as she marched, frustrated that she wasn't able to handle it better. That Nik's claws had a deeper grip in her heart than she'd ever cared to admit. Tauria headed to the one place she could feel any semblance of peace. Lennox was hot on her tail along with Katori, but he said nothing.

In the garden, she went straight for the pavilion. Stepping into the wooden structure, her tears finally fell. She kept them silent despite the pain that constricted her throat, balling in her chest. There wasn't enough air in her lungs despite it swirling around her, answering to the slip of her magick that blew wisps of hair across her face. Tauria clamped her eyes shut, biting down on her lip so hard the copper tang of blood filled her mouth. Her fists trembled at her sides to stifle the dangerous release of her wind with her barreling emotions.

I want you to come back.

She let out a choked sob, grateful Lennox had stayed by the doors and not come any closer. "You lied," she whispered. When her eyes opened, her chest was hollow. Releasing everything all at once, Tauria fell to the bench of the pavilion, defeated. Her disappointment was heavy—in herself for reacting so strongly to Nik's engagement. She had no justification for her sorrow, and maybe she even felt selfish for it. He wanted her to come back, but he didn't want *her*.

Tauria leaned her head against the wooden structure, gazing up at the sky with only lost thoughts. Tormenting memories that occasionally released more silent tears. She watched the clouds roll and disappear. The sun crossed the sky. Her eyes fixed into position as if she weren't even grounded anymore. Day fell to twilight; the sun welcomed the moon along with its dancing stars. Tauria didn't move. Lennox didn't approach her, nor did anyone else, and she was glad for it. Katori emitted frequent quiet whines for a while but then fell silent at Tauria's lack of attention.

She wanted to believe she had no right to find heartache in the news of Nik's engagement. Their fates aligned, just not with each other. But what tormented her on repeat was that he seemed to have forgotten her entirely. Not a single letter, not one Nightwalking visit. She wished she harbored the same gift, riddled with past jealousy that Nik and Faythe had shared that bond. The ability to see each other, talk, feel, within the private space of their subconscious minds. Nightwalking was never a possibility for her.

Tauria was so confused, wondering what she was missing, feeling Nik's actions were so out of character to leave her questioning everything. She wanted to believe in him, at least until she could speak with him. But in her resentment she wished to never see him again.

"Tauria."

For the first time, her tired eyes fell. But she didn't turn to Lycus, too ashamed for him to see the weakness staining her golden cheeks.

"I hoped to find you after your meeting with the queen, but she informed me you left many hours ago. I then got the impression the white beast wanted me to follow, and—" Lycus must have sensed her pitiful mood as he closed the distance between them.

She took a deep breath, trying to straighten, but winced at the pain of her dormant muscles. Lycus was next to her, his hands reaching out as though she might tumble off the low bench she'd tucked herself upon. His fingers grazed her bare arms, their warmth sending a tremor through her, alerting her to the chill that had befallen the evening.

"What happened?" His frown was hard when their eyes met, and she cringed, imagining the sight of herself that he took in with growing anger. Lycus had already undone the ties of his jacket, and she barely had the energy to protest when he shrugged out of it and slung it over her shoulders.

Tauria mustered a vacant smile but didn't voice that as much as she appreciated his concern, she desired to be alone. Out of guilt, shame, sadness… She wanted more time to succumb to it all before fitting back into her mask of resilience for the world.

Lycus sat close. Almost too close to avoid speculation, and Tauria hated the glance she spared to the door to gauge the guards' reaction.

"I dismissed Lennox. The other guards are changing rotations."

It was a relief. And she enjoyed the moment of peace. "I'm fine," she whispered, knowing she would emit an awful croak if she tried to speak properly after her long day of choked silence.

Lycus huffed. "Hardly."

She couldn't stand to look at him. And while she felt guilt for her closed-off silence, it wasn't strong enough in that moment to force the mask back on. Not yet. She liked to believe she didn't need it with Lycus, who had seen her emotions break before. He knew her better than anyone. Or he once did. It was another sorrowful dagger to think that might not be true now time had torn them apart.

"Do you want this, Tauria?" Lycus's question was careful, personal.

She continued to observe the stars as she answered honestly. "I don't think this has ever had anything to do with what I want."

"That is why I ask."

She met his eyes, and they were focused with determination. Lycus studied her as though ready to go to war for her. "I want to reclaim all that was taken from me. I want to avenge my parents. This is how I do it."

"It shouldn't take sacrificing your happiness."

"It should," she snapped. Lycus didn't balk at her tone, and Tauria straightened, uncurling her legs off the bench. "Fenstead soldiers sacrificed everything for me, for the kingdom. As their queen, I will do whatever it takes to make sure it was not in vain."

"What does your heart say?" Lycus was prodding at a wound that had been torn right open. Her breaths came heavier as she refrained from unleashing her dangerously loose emotions on him. She knew control. And poise. And suppressing her true feelings. It wasn't often she felt it all…slipping.

"My heart is with Fenstead." Her words were bitter and ice-cold.

"You are more than that."

"You should leave, Lycus." No one deserved the release of all that was growing and ugly within her right now.

"We can find another way to rise our court. We have been building and strengthening our armies in Rhyenelle, and I am confident they will ally with us when the time is right. Listen to me, Tauria." Lycus kneeled in front of her, taking her hands, and the determined look he pinned her with overshadowed her anger and made her pulse race. "I will help you leave here undetected. I will get you to Rhyenelle, and we can decide our next movements from there. On my life, I promise you that. Just say the word."

Her eyes widened as she scanned her surroundings in disbelief that he would make such a suggestion—one so traitorous to the kingdom they stood in—when she'd all but signed her hand already. "Are you mad?"

Lycus laughed, but she could only stare at him, incredulous. Her fear spiked—for his safety should anyone overhear his proposal.

"I didn't come here to advise you into this marriage against your will. I came because when I heard of it, I knew I would put every plan and action into place should I find it not to be of your volition. To tell you we have another way that won't sacrifice your choice in this."

She shook her head. "You can't be certain. An alliance to Olmstone is a powerful gain."

His full lips firmed. "Let me help you, Tauria."

Her head was spinning. She could leave…but did she want that?

Tauria felt an unexplainable pull to the side of the garden where she knew Katori lingered. The wolf watched her. It was odd to imagine emotion on the beast, but she was patient and understanding, her first welcoming sign in Olmstone, and somehow, she was tied to Tarly. The prince was cold, often harsh and hard to get through to, but he was also broken and lost, and Tauria couldn't be sure of when she'd come to care for him enough to balk at the thought of being another person who left, abandoning him to his silent existence. Then there was Nik… As much as she wanted to despise him, she couldn't ignore that her leaving to seek refuge in Rhyenelle would be equivalent to abandoning any alliance she had with him. She would no longer be High Farrow's ward.

"I don't want to leave," she whispered vacantly, thinking over everything. She was being a fool. The general before her offered everything she'd desired when she stepped onto Olmstone territory. But so much had changed in that short time. Tarly was changing, finally opening up to her piece by piece, and maybe it was her bleeding heart that thought of them as two matching, desolate souls.

"You don't mean that," Lycus accused.

She met his hard eyes with pleading ones. "I do."

"Tell me you love him."

Tauria didn't miss a beat. "I love him."

His eyes flared, but he read something between her words. "Not Tarly," he concluded.

Tauria rose slowly, and Lycus let go of her hands as he stood. "You stayed away from me for so long because you didn't believe in my ability to make choices. To make political movements for Fenstead—"

"That's not true."

"You *left* me, Lycus. You let me believe for over a century you were dead!" Her voice rose, finding the outlet for some of her bottled-up hurt. "You may believe I was sitting idle in High Farrow, but there hasn't been a damned day I haven't thought of taking back what was lost. *I* didn't give up on me. This is me continuing to put Fenstead first. I managed just fine without you, and I don't need you now." She delivered her words without apology. Tauria was beyond listening to those who thought they knew best for her when all they wanted was for her to run away or hide.

"You truly mean that?"

Tauria swallowed hard, despising the ache she'd clearly caused him, but she could do nothing but own her words as a ruler, not a friend.

"I do. I want you by my side, Lycus. But unless you're here to help me fight—to advise, not hide me—then maybe we've learned where our true stations should be."

The flash of disappointment he wore cleaved straight through her, a sign he was deliberating. Tauria hurt at the thought of Lycus leaving. He was the closest tie she had to her parents and homeland. Yet in that moment, it was clear time had made its mark. Lycus thrived at being a general leading armies; she understood his instinct to shield her. But that was not what she needed from him, and she'd laid out the decision for him to make: stand with her here or return to their armies in Rhyenelle.

CHAPTER 29

Nikalias

Nik stared and stared at the box on his desk. His chin rested on his clasped hands. He'd sat there for some time in quiet reflection. He knew what lay within. When he'd first found it locked away safely within the private council room, once his *father's* space, Nik was conflicted with sentiment.

A short knock sounded, and he called for the person to enter as he stood.

"You asked for me?" Marlowe's presence was always a humbling warmth that eased the heaviness of a room.

"Yes. Thank you for coming."

Her approach was careful, her gaze full of sympathy, much as she tried to avoid his eye. "I heard about your engagement." She dipped a hand into her pocket. "I can make you something better if it's to be permanent…or, I mean, if you two are—"

"I don't need anything elaborate," Nik assured her.

Marlowe extended the ring to him as she approached, placing it into Nik's palm. He studied it briefly. It was simple and elegant.

"It's beautiful."

"I made some adjustments to one I already had. I hope it'll suffice. I don't know what the fae are used to. I can fit a bigger stone or add more if you have any—"

"I appreciate your care and attention, Marlowe, but may I ask to borrow your talent for detail once more for something far more precious?"

Her unease lifted, a bright eagerness straightening her posture, and it was a joy to watch her eyes come to life at the ask. Yet Nik was warring within about whether to follow through with his request.

"You asked for something to bind the spell to. This is not my agreement, but you're right. It's better to be prepared." He reached behind him, picking up the small box. Nik frowned at it with bittersweet sorrow before he extended it to Marlowe.

Reading his expression, she was hesitant as she took it. Marlowe paused, meeting his eye, and all he gave was a nod of permission for her to open it. Her brow raised as she stared inside. "Remarkable."

"It's my mother's," he confessed. "But can you make an adjustment for me as well?"

Marlowe's condolence fell on her face first. Then her smile broke. "I would be honored."

Nik took a deep breath, a sickness settling in his stomach. Yet he couldn't get the blacksmith's words from his mind. Her advice in having options, no matter how damning one was, was smart.

"I want to oversee both being done, if that's okay with you."

CHAPTER 30

Tauria

THE FOLLOWING MORNING, Tauria was on edge as she sat rigid across the breakfast table from the prince. Her emotions were still running high from the day before, and what she'd said to Lycus remained a lingering conflict. She'd wanted to seek him out that morning but had been swiftly called to breakfast with Tarly.

Her choice to stay in Olmstone hadn't changed. She'd made a commitment to Tarly to see if there could be something real under the ruse of their false engagement.

"You're quiet this morning," he commented, picking at the grapes on his plate. She noticed his appetite seemed to be lacking also.

Tauria braved lifting her gaze to him, not wanting to spill her turmoil over the traitorous proposition Lycus brought to her. One that could have him in serious trouble if anyone overheard. Instead, she allowed an accusation to surface that had been tantalizing her all night. "Did you know Nikalias plans to visit for the solstice?"

Tarly didn't answer straight away. She didn't need him to. His confirmation was in the way his eyes lingered on his cup before he idly picked it up. His insufferable, icy-cool demeanor was back, and today she might just be too far gone in her indignation that she would match it.

"I did." He spoke factually, with not an ounce of emotion, as though he knew Tauria would unleash enough for them both.

"Why wasn't I informed?"

"We didn't think you needed the distraction. Nikalias plans to visit with his bride to discuss High Farrow's part in the alliance between us as you still stand as their ward."

Tarly used the word like a dagger. *Bride.* And Gods, did she feel it. Not the making of a fresh wound; all he could do was deepen what was already so close to carving out her heart completely.

"Yes, I am," she gritted out. "I had every right to know he was coming."

"You would have known when it was necessary."

The gaze they shared was a challenge. One she couldn't back down from this time. Not with the tethers to her composure straining toward breaking point.

"I'm not so hungry this morning," she ground out, rising from her seat. It was the most composed way she could handle this without letting loose the vulgar string of words she finally wanted him to have. The pulse in her veins was a sure warning her magick was straining beneath her skin. She needed a release.

Tauria began to make her way inside.

"Where are you going?" Tarly called after her.

"To train. Don't try to stop me."

"With whom?"

"I'll find my general." Perhaps getting to unleash their frustrations physically would help them work through the knot of their relationship. She wanted more than anything for them to come to some agreement, to learn the changes they had matured into…

"General Lycus left earlier this morning."

Her heart stopped with her steps. He wouldn't. Tauria made sure her frustration was written on her face as she twisted back to the prince. He remained seated, calmly reclining.

"Left for where?"

Casually, Tarly reached for something on the table beside him, extending it to her. Her eyes narrowed on the parchment as though it would detonate if she took it. Curiosity got the better of her as she strode for it.

"He told one of the guards to give you this."

"Yet you have it."

"Yes, because you could not be found last night."

She'd taken to the rooftops in the restless night to rise her despair to the moon. Tarly gave her a subtle knowing look, and she wondered if they'd discovered her rooms empty and he'd covered for her. Why he wouldn't trespass on her above the castle as he had done so many times, she'd never ask to know.

Tauria took the note, unfolding it. Her breathing was quick, her heart a hard beat, as she caught words but not whole sentences. Meanings but no sense. It was there, all right there, yet she refused to believe it. "He wouldn't leave me," she said with vacant denial. Her eyes couldn't stop roaming the page, looking for a mistake, a sign, for new words to appear that would assure her it was wrong or temporary.

"I think he knows you're in good hands here, with plenty of soldiers and generals to protect you. He is better off strengthening Fenstead's armies back in Rhyenelle."

"He wouldn't *leave* me." But her eyes burned because her mind had accepted the truth even though her heart couldn't.

Lycus had left her.

Just as Nik had left her.

Alone at the mercy of the wolves.

"I saw the general leave on his horse this morning with some others he arrived with, Your Majesty." Lennox was careful as he sank the final confirmation.

But it was enough to shatter her entirely.

"Why don't you sit, Tauria?" Tarly spoke carefully, as if approaching an easily spooked deer, as he rose.

Tauria didn't realize she was nodding, because the alternative was to erupt with the emotions that barreled into her. She continued to comb the letter again and again, refraining from the urge to enclose her fist around it instead. Someone touched her hand. Tarly guided her to sit next to him. She couldn't protest. Silence. Composure. It was the only way to tame the storm that heated the surface of her skin, prickling her fingertips. She was so hollow. And lost. And alone. She wanted to demand why the fates had made it so when it seemed no matter how she played, who she loved, everything was always destined to come crashing down.

Tauria couldn't tear her eyes from the parchment that lay beside her. She couldn't give Tarly an ounce of attention as she read and read again. His voice blurred around her until she'd read it enough times that her emotions had dried, her acceptance settling in. She didn't draw attention to her hand curling carefully around the paper until it was scrunched completely in her fist, knowing it would meet flame the second she was in her rooms.

The hallways weren't equipped for the unleashing of Tauria's wind. In her anguish and sadness she couldn't contain it. In the training room at least she was left to swing her staff freely.

She wasn't alone, of course, but Lennox and a couple of other guards took shelter in the hallway alcove. If it kept them back and their eyes off her for a blessed moment, this was even more reason to surrender to her surfaced magick. Tauria pushed herself harder than she had in so long, hoping it would drain her to a dangerous point. Sweat slicked her skin; breathing cut her throat like spears of ice; her muscles ached and protested. She embraced the pain, welcomed it, needing anything to counter the agony she felt in her unrelenting mind.

"You're going to harm yourself," a voice called out over the clamor of weapons she shook with her blasts. It wasn't a voice she wanted to hear, and her anger only flared at Tarly's attempt to interrupt her. Likely to once again remind her she was weak, and that the training room was no place for a *princess.*

Tauria pretended not to hear his approach, but he would have known she did in the slight faltering of her movements. She blocked him out to continue her dance, a push and pull with the air. Her staff switched hands, spinning, swiping, striking, in time with her footing that had long since tuned itself perfectly to the song of the air. She didn't step; she glided. She didn't turn; she twirled. And the air—she was its master.

Her feet left the ground with her next jump twist, her staff poised skyward to be brought down by the pull of gravity in a long vertical strike. When she expected to cut through air, the harsh vibrations of her staff connecting with something equally as unmoving flared challenge. There was nothing kind or warm in her eyes as she glared at the prince through their locked weapons. She spared a glance to notice he'd picked an ordinary wooden staff. And she was about to test if he knew how to use it.

Just before she pushed off him, she swore she caught a twinkle of *amusement.* Not in mockery, but as though he found entertainment in the act of sparring when he'd so far shown no interest in it.

"I won't go easy on you," she warned. Not because she wanted to direct her rage at him, but because she couldn't.

"Neither will I." His shadow of a smirk almost triggered one on her own face.

Then Tarly's eyes became a mirror. Ones that looked back at her with a familiar lost desolation, except he'd learned how to live with it. If there was anything she could learn from him, it was how to go on with a shattered soul.

Tarly moved first. Unexpectedly. She'd begun to tunnel into pitiful thoughts. Wide-eyed at his swiftness, she glided to avoid the swipe of his staff in the nick of time. In turn, her own cut low to catch his legs, but it seemed he was light on his feet.

"Okay, prince, any other talents you've been hiding?"

Tarly released a chuckle, and she was glad for the distraction. A flicker of light in the dark. "Careful, princess. It almost sounds like you're giving me a compliment."

They exchanged a couple more maneuvers. Not in battle, but in careful calculation of each other's movements.

"You do make it difficult to form them."

"Maybe I like being the bad guy."

Tauria canted her head, pausing her pacing. She propped up her staff. "I don't think you're the bad guy, *Your Highness.*" She emphasized his title with the warning he'd once given her.

He quirked a brow, finding humor as he picked up on her gibe.

Tauria took his moment of distraction to her advantage. She added her wind as she attacked. A long swipe, angled to the second and sixth points of a star. She spun to add force. "I think you're selfish."

He braced, absorbing the impact. Tauria shifted, one foot sliding back as she jabbed forward.

"Fair observation," he mused, spinning his own staff. It slammed at an angle with the ground, knocking hers, but she was already moving again. Frustration rose at his agreement. Her staff whirled between both hands, collecting air, before she twisted it, bringing it down in a powerful vertical strike. Tarly braced in the nick of time, his staff thrust above his head to meet the impact. His teeth clenching with a hiss was a victorious sound.

"You're pompous."

"Perhaps."

He answered every one of her attacks, which intensified with anguish as they moved faster around the ring.

"Arrogant." The ferocity of her strikes amplified. "Bitter." She honed in on him with a lethal focus. "Emotionless *royal!*"

His chuckle was the final trigger to her violence, and her next maneuver collected the wind in a strong gale, but it was her hand that cast out in her firm stance to send it hurtling toward the prince. Tarly wasn't just knocked off-balance in the ring. The horror of her error sank before he fell after seconds of travel through the air. Her head snapped to the guards racing into the room. Lennox in the hallway stared at her with fear ghosting his expression.

Before they could reach her, the prince on his knees raised a hand, and they all stopped advancing. Tarly groaned, rubbing his chest as he rose to his feet. Her hard breaths filled the silence as she waited for his retaliation.

"You really think I'm emotionless?"

Tauria blinked, bewildered he wasn't reprimanding her for the blow that was beyond training limits.

When he was close enough, he smirked at her look. "It's going to take more than that to hurt me, princess. Want to go again? You don't seem finished."

"What are you doing?"

"Sparring."

"Here, Tarly! What are you doing here with me?"

He took steps to her, which she straightened her spine to track. Her anger slowly dispersed in the gaze they shared. Because she couldn't understand the softness in his eyes. And didn't know if her quickened pulse was at the distance that slowly closed between them with his careful approach or the dwindling adrenaline of combat.

When the prince was close enough to touch, she didn't flinch as his hand came up. Slowly, his fingers brushed a loose strand of her hair, trailing from her temple to her chin.

"I'm sorry that he left you," he said so quietly she wondered if he hoped the guards wouldn't hear it. "But I won't."

"Because you have no choice."

"Because I understand."

Her brow pinched at that, and she felt a new connection with the prince. One of sorrow and loneliness—but misery loved company.

"Perhaps we're not so different, Tauria."

CHAPTER 31

Tauria

The King of High Farrow's visit came around faster than anticipated. The whole castle was abuzz in anticipation of his arrival later that afternoon. Tauria still couldn't place her feelings. Part of her hadn't wanted to leave her bed when the sun coaxed her awake. Or leave her rooms this morning after being dressed in Olmstone purple. But seclusion was a luxury she would never be granted.

Nik would be escorting his new bride-to-be—a concept she had never thought would settle with him—and now it all seemed to be happening so fast she could do nothing but succumb to the hollow truth. While she was making moves here in Olmstone, Nik's plan all along had been to secure his own alliances for High Farrow.

Tauria stood alone in the atrium, but several groups of ladies also lingered around the space. She tried not to pay them any attention, but their stares pricked her skin, and the occasional remark or judgment she couldn't block out, so she'd stood with a rigid posture for the past hour. She was brought here like all the other court ladies to await the arrival of their esteemed guest. Tauria looked out over the stone courtyard as she lingered by the tall windows.

"The prince has left you here?" The question came from a lady she didn't know the name of. Tauria's gaze cast behind her, to where three others watched the one brave enough to speak to her with a giddy thrill in their eyes. Tauria couldn't muster anger or embarrassment that they thought to test her as if she were one of them.

"My fiancé has other matters to attend to before the arrival of our guests," she said factually, with just enough of a warning not to press further.

"It's just we couldn't help but notice Lady Serena is also absent." The lady's smile was courtly, but with a hint of suggestion for Tauria alone to pick up on.

Tauria hated the gaze she subconsciously trailed over the room to confirm Serena wasn't present. The fae's lingering implication wasn't subtle. And at hearing the quiet chuckles of her companions, humiliation flushed her body. She turned her full attention to the fae.

"Do you have something you wish to inform me?" Tauria kept her tone level and her chin high. She had dealt with the prodding of ladies on their incessant quest to stir gossip many times, though it never got easier to accept it was often at her expense.

Lennox lingered a few paces away, and she caught him shifting closer.

"Not at all. I just thought you might know where they both are. We've been waiting on Lady Serena all morning."

She almost pitied them for finding this the height of entertainment. Anger flexed her fingers. But as she opened her mouth, a voice traveled to them.

"There you are."

Tarly walked toward them, unusually casual and *warm* as his eyes fixed on her. It was the first time she'd ever seen him in a public court setting, Tauria realized. His guise was wholly convincing as a dashing prince who bore no burden. She felt the suffocation of that disguise in her throat as Tarly looked her over deliberately. A twinkle of adoration skipped her pulse at the attention she wasn't used to. Then he smiled at her.

Tauria couldn't show an ounce of her surprise. She mirrored it.

The prince's gaze eased to a cool indifference when it shifted to the lady who'd approached her. The fae's demeanor changed completely, and while Tauria was glad for Tarly's presence, it irked her that this was what it took for the ladies to finally offer respect.

"Your Highness," Tauria said in greeting.

When he reached them, Tarly's arm didn't hesitate to curl around her, his hand settling on her waist, and in reply she shifted closer, angling her body into him. They were supposed to be amorously in love after all.

"You were supposed to be escorted straight to me, not here. I've been looking for you all morning," he said, and she could do nothing but play along.

"I've missed you."

Tarly met her gaze, and the fluttering in her stomach was unexpected. He gave no forewarning when his fingers caught her chin, angling her head back before his mouth came down to meet hers. In her shock, but still wholly aware of the audience they had, Tauria leaned into the kiss. It was soft and short. When they parted, all she could do was stare, and maybe he read her bewilderment as his head titled close to her ear.

"Actions can silence, while words can be twisted in any which way." His warm breath blowing down her neck made her shiver. His hand remained on her face when he pulled back, and the love in his eyes was so believable she almost fell for it. "Come," he coaxed gently. Tauria slipped her hand through his arm as he began to lead her out. "This is not the waiting place for a queen."

Her heart—she couldn't tame it.

Tarly said nothing by her side as they stood on the portico patiently awaiting Nik's arrival. She could only hope the gentle murmur of the other court members, along with the faint whistle of wind, disguised her erratic pulse. She wasn't sure what consumed her the most: the part of her that didn't know if everything that had happened since they'd parted would tense the air between her and Nik, or that despite everything, she *longed* to see him.

Tarly held her close, just like he had before, and she didn't protest. There might have been something in her that was grateful for the comfort. Whether Tarly knew or suspected her jittering nerves or not, he only cast her a small side-smile before fixing his sights down the length of the courtyard.

Just then, she caught the ripples of Varlas's scent before he stepped out to join them. Casting her attention toward him, she saw the king's face was bright but forced. Queen Keira followed a step behind him, her hand over the shoulder of Opal. The young princess met her eye for a brief second, and the smile they exchanged was a welcome acknowledgment.

Finally, the last to join them brushed her side. Katori sat proudly beside her, and she wondered what she'd done to gain her companionship in the most nerve-wracking of moments. Her hand reached down in grateful acknowledgment.

"Your engagement has already created a hopeful spirit throughout the kingdom," Varlas said, sparing them a glance. His eyes lingered with a sparkle of triumph at Tarly's arm around her.

Tauria forced warmth onto her face, playing the role of lovestruck princess. Her hand slid up to Tarly's chest, and his own hand enclosed it as he met her doting eyes. "We couldn't be happier," she said.

"I am glad. It was always my hope that you would find your own happiness above what might be gained politically."

Liar. The resenting thought blared in her mind, but she kept the accusation from twisting her expression. Tarly's grip at her waist felt like silent agreement, and he refused to meet his father's eye at all.

Before the king could say anything else, the distant clamor of hooves stole their attention. Tauria's spine straightened, and the prince sensed it as he drew her closer. Her hand slipped from him, suddenly rattled by inner conflict at his closeness. Appreciating his comfort while anticipating their approaching company felt *wrong.*

Tauria breathed, making it her only focus as the horses came into view. Three of them. She was quick to notice there was no carriage in sight. But she didn't care because one horse cantered ahead, and even though they were no more than a dark silhouette, she knew who it was.

Nik rode to them alone. It was a momentary selfish reprieve to see Lady Samara was not one of the others on horseback.

Everything went quiet. As if a line ran between them alone as she tracked him, silencing the world. His dark hair was defiant against the sunlight. Eternal night was all she could think of. His wears were black under the billowing deep blue cloak. Closer, she took in his cut features, exactly as she remembered. Their time apart hadn't been long, not really, yet she couldn't let go of her sense of unease that she would be meeting with a stranger.

Nik pulled his horse to a stop in front of all who awaited him on the portico. He didn't need a cavalry to assert his status or dominance. The King of High Farrow dismounted the obsidian horse in an elegant glide. It was in his poise: graceful yet commanding. In his features: unyielding with a challenge. Nikalias Silvergriff didn't falter or hesitate in a single move he made.

"Welcome, Nikalias." Varlas spoke for them all, stepping forward to greet him as he ascended the steps. "We are pleased to host you in Olmstone, but we were informed you would not be alone on your trip."

The two kings embraced forearms in greeting. Tauria couldn't tear her eyes from Nik, studying every flicker of his expression, his movement, as if he would give something of his feelings away. Nik had yet to look at her, and the hollowness in her stomach at that was sickening. She felt a fool for clutching at the hope she would be at the forefront of his thoughts upon his arrival. And she despised the hurt she felt in the way he didn't immediately seek her out.

"I am not alone," Nik confirmed. The first notes of his voice doused her with emotion. Her brow flinched with it, and her clasped hands tightened painfully.

He prefers the openness of horseback, she thought.

"But I find making a journey on horseback far easier. Lady Samara travels not too far behind by carriage."

Even in their short time apart, Nik *had* changed. He'd grown far more into the position of king since she'd left High Farrow. Her chest swelled with pride to watch his confidence, but it was dampened by the thought he'd thrived without her.

The fact he refused to travel in close confines with his fiancée was another selfish relief. Tauria had to remember she too was engaged and couldn't allow any foolish past feelings for Nik to surface and shake her ruse with Tarly. Even to Nik, it had to be real. Believable. Despite the wrongness and churning in her gut. Despite everything that screamed at her to tell him the truth.

Just then, his eyes slid to her for the first time. Emerald orbs connecting with something inside her that trapped a whimper in her throat and strained every muscle that yearned to go to him, to feel him, just for one embrace. The impact of missing him fell all at once, a wave she never could have braced for. Nik revealed no outward emotion. Not when his gaze flashed to Tarly, then down to the prince's hand on her. He gave nothing to indicate their closeness bothered him. Instead, a smile curled on his perfect face as he turned to them.

"Allow me to offer my congratulations," he said to Tarly with a forced kindness she doubted any other would notice.

"Likewise." Tarly took Nik's extended arm—an amicable formality for the crowd, nothing more. But Tauria turned rigid at the tension in their exchange. "I look forward to meeting your fiancée."

"As do I," Tauria cut in.

Nik's attention snapped to her, and she kept her chin firm, her eyes meeting his. There was a *challenge* resonating between them. Until he wiped it, and she grew suspicious at the new curl of his mouth.

Nik removed his riding glove then offered his hand to her. That was deliberate. Unnecessary. Perhaps even uncustomary. A thrill knotted her stomach because Tauria knew him. Every twitch, every habit. Sometimes, she even believed she knew him better than he knew himself. He was restraining his irritation at having to wear a façade for court eyes, and damn, if it wasn't satisfying to glimpse his wavering emotions.

Her palm slid into his with deliberate slowness as their eyes locked in silent battle. Tense. Thrilling. But she made no further movement, ignoring the shivers that raced up her arm at the contact of their skin. A faint flare in his eyes gave away his discontent that she hadn't left Tarly's side to greet him.

"It's good to see you again, Tauria," he said, and the low gravel of his voice was almost enough to make her barrier crumble.

"And you, Your Majesty." It was a twist in her own heart to address him so formally, and in the tightening of his hand, she believed it was a pain within him too.

It was better this way. Smart not to give away so many personal feelings while every set of Olmstone eyes was fixed on their reunion, vultures who would pick apart anything that might reveal they harbored feelings for each other beyond a ward and her king.

Nik glanced down. "Interesting choice of pet," he mused.

"Why don't you come closer and call her that again?" Tarly enticed.

Tauria giggled quietly as she stroked Katori. The wolf didn't drop her stare from Nik, but she showed no opposition to him. In fact, Tauria thought she saw curiosity. She was lost in thought, straightening up again, so she didn't expect the softened attention Nik fixed on her. Her wide smile fell slowly when she noticed it. For a few seconds of suspended time, they seemed to forget about their company. She wanted to know his thoughts as she glimpsed the male she knew so tenderly when they were completely alone.

The approach of more horses was a lashing back to the present. Nik snapped his head around, turning to the carriage swiftly. Watching him walk back down the steps was a harrowing sight, knowing who he eagerly went to retrieve. The ornate carriage was opened swiftly when it halted, and Nik was already there, his smile warm, reflecting in his eyes as they landed on its occupant. He extended his hand for a white-gloved one to slip into it.

Tauria had met Samara before in High Farrow. She was perhaps one of the highest stationed ladies—high enough to be fit for a king. Yet to Tauria's vague knowledge, she'd seen her before on the arm of Zarrius, a High Farrow lord she knew Nik wasn't best fond of.

Nik retuned with Samara, and Tauria didn't miss the attention he gave her so completely. His arm slid around her, and pride danced in his eyes as he presented her to the court. "It is my absolute pleasure to introduce Lady Samara to you all," he announced, and she believed it. His adoration for her.

Tarly's hand caressed her side, but when she looked up at him, his eyes were fixed on the happy couple. She eased under his touch, folding into him. Her hand slipped over his front in acknowledgment.

As if she'd spoken to announce the movement, Nik's eyes flashed to them, hard and emotionless as he took in their intimacy. Tauria didn't know why this had become a game. Feeling each other out with their respective partners was wrong but enticing. She smiled coyly, and no one else would have deciphered the spark that flared in that emerald stare.

"Well, we have a grand feast prepared for your arrival. We don't want it to go to waste," Varlas announced.

Tauria couldn't be more grateful to be past the awkward greeting, hoping the clamor of the dining hall would disperse the attention.

As was customary, Varlas led the way, Nik by his side as they were engaged in idle chatter. Tarly guided her to follow after them, his hand never leaving her, and she was glad for it. Her eyes didn't linger on the elegant hook Samara had on Nik's arm. Rather, as she watched Varlas and Nik converse, she was too wrapped in her fluctuating emotions, remembering with a daunting chill…

Nik knew nothing yet about the dark fae or Varlas's collusion with their High Lord. He didn't know the evil with which he walked at that very moment.

CHAPTER 32

Nikalias

IN THE GRAND dining hall, it was an effort to keep his gaze from Tauria, made all the more challenging by the fact she was seated directly opposite him. He didn't get a choice, and he couldn't decide if the seating arrangement was made in consideration of him and Tauria desiring closeness in their *reunion* or if it was a test. He had to pretend for the sake of the court, but he wanted nothing more than to have her alone so he could express how deeply he'd missed her and that it frightened him even now. His mind kept snapping his attention toward her as if she might vanish in a heartbeat. She was finally right within reach, yet every interaction, every touch they shared, was watched with eagle eyes.

The feast was in full swing, yet though he kept his blatant stare off her, Tauria occupied his thoughts. Or at least, she *and* the prince did. Every touch he laid on her, every smile he triggered. Maybe it was bitterness at seeing her thriving and happy here with his own eyes, but Nik's mind taunted him that their affections were far more than necessary. She knew it would rile him. When Tarly's hand took hers over the table, Nik's tightened around his goblet. He set it down with more force than necessary as Tauria chuckled at something that wasn't even mildly amusing.

He wanted it all. Her laughter, her smile. He was a selfish bastard for thinking as much, but her happiness...he wanted to own that too.

"They have been treating you well," Nik observed when their attention fixed on him at the accidental disruption.

Her smile was forced, almost goading, with the faint lift of her brow. Nik knew her. Better than anyone in this damned place ever could. He knew her habits and braced for her.

"Yes, they have. It's been effortless feeling welcome here."

Lies. Her eyes flared a fraction as if she'd heard him. Or perhaps she knew it too.

Tarly's hand moved, and though the table covered them, it wasn't hard to detect it lay over her thigh. Tauria's lips parted, and Nik swore to the Gods for his fists that tightened to a white-knuckled grip on his chair against doing something unjustifiably reckless. He couldn't give a reaction. Not even when she held his stare and he felt it like an enticing dare. Nik took a second to breathe.

Leaning back in his seat, his arm draped over the back of Samara's. He spared her a glance, and his softened gaze was true as he assessed her ease at the situation. Her face was kind, and as they'd planned, her eyes filled with love and adoration.

"I must say, the news of your engagement came far sooner than we could have hoped for," Nik said, fixing his gaze back on Tauria and Tarly. It was a small flicker of dark satisfaction to watch her calculate his closeness to Samara. More than anything, he wanted Tauria to be happy, yet doubt was taking root in his refusal to believe in her contentment with the prince beside her.

"Considering the news of yours came sooner and far more unexpectedly, are you really surprised?" Tauria bit back, bold and without apology. Like a true master.

Nik had played this game many times. And with her, he might just enjoy this one as their time apart put each other to the test. He reached for his cup, taking a nonchalant sip. His emerald eyes danced with assessment, flicking between her and the prince. He let Tauria know through his look alone that it would take a lot more to convince him. Her teeth ground with the adorable but slight twitch of her jaw in answer.

"It was an easy decision," Tarly chimed in, leveling with Nik's cool demeanor, and it grated on his ugly primal instincts. "When the match you are presented with comes to find feelings so effortlessly." Tarly cast her a look of admiration, and Tauria's cheeks colored faintly with her genuine shyness at compliments.

"It would seem so," Nik responded, trying to seem pleased.

Tauria shifted her gaze to Samara, who had so far remained silent. "I trust the journey wasn't too taxing," she said. "Considering you were spared of Nik's company."

Tarly's smile widened in amusement while Nik's eyes snapped to her. He couldn't let his ire give her triumph. His arm moved from around Samara's chair to take her hand instead as he twisted to give her his attention. It wasn't just an act; he felt her rigidness in her touch and sought to ease her tension under the scrutiny of so many royals. Samara was the only other who could feel and place the emotions between him and Tauria.

"It was well, Your Majesty," she answered, straightening. It was a relief to watch her confidence grow to play along.

"There's no need for the title," Tauria assured her.

"You were not so specific on the length of your stay, Nikalias." Varlas's voice carried down the table.

Nik schooled his face, irritated by the need to engage with anyone else while his emotions thinned to a hairsbreadth. "Only a week. We are looking forward to the solstice celebrations, but most of all I came to discuss the proposal for this alliance in person." Nik slid his gaze to

Tauria, hoping to read guilt or at least acknowledgment with his next words. "Letters would take far too long, and I assume the happy couple will not want to delay their union." He wanted to confirm Tauria had received his letters and chosen to ignore them. He struggled to fight the rise of his pulse, because when she showed no reaction, he wondered if she'd truly been so enamored by Tarly to care or if she'd never seen them at all. The latter was easier on his heart, but it also planted the first kernel of dread in Olmstone if she'd never received a single one.

He stored that away for now, needing to hear it from her to be sure.

Nik announced, "I have a gift." He beckoned over one of his guards, who approached, presenting a small box. Nik stood, and it was opened as he did. He reached inside it to bring to light a beautiful, delicate bracelet, a stone with an opaque surface that seemed to trap the shadows adorning the center. "For my ward—an engagement gift. I hope you will accept this as my eager congratulations." Nik's palm upturned to her. "May I?"

Tauria blinked, dumbfounded by the gesture. He refrained from reacting to the glance she spared Tarly, and the nod he gave in return as though she needed permission. Tauria stood, her palm sliding into his, and her barely audible breath was a musical note. Nik forgot for a moment where they were when their sights connected as though they were the only two in the room. Then he was slow, careful, securing the bracelet around her wrist and lingering a second longer to push the boundary of what was acceptable under the guise of formality.

"It's beautiful," Tauria said. The break of their stare felt like a lash of reality in their current company. "Thank you, Your Majesty." The title she used settled wrong, a formal acceptance and nothing more. Tauria barely flashed a smile before she sat down again.

Nik couldn't give way to the sorrow that began to rise in his hollow stomach. He had a role to play that would always call for the suppression of anything human and real. He firmed his shoulders, plastered on an arrogant smile, and cast his attention down the table as he took up his seat again. "I am looking forward to sampling Olmstone's summer solstice celebrations. Samara and I were most excited when the invitation came through." He had to divert the topic to distract from the need to circle around the table to get to her. Gifting her the bracelet had inspired something sad and reflective in Tauria, and his need to comfort her though no one else could detect her shift was damning when he could do nothing.

Varlas nodded with glee at the mention. "I am glad you could attend. After the ball, I look forward to our meetings the day before your departure to finalize negotiations before this marriage goes forth. It will accelerate things pleasantly, you being here in person."

"As were my thoughts." Nik's agreement was tight as he sat back in his chair and reached for his drink, sliding his gaze to Tauria. "Why waste time when it seems we are all in agreement to make this final." He wondered if the pain in his chest was felt in isolation as he read those hazel eyes, searching far deeper with a longing to pick up on any hint that this was not of her will. The marriage—his heart squeezed with the slow dawning that it was already set in motion. His mate sat before him and within perfect reach for him to claim, yet he would have to watch as she wed another, and with that fact…

The countdown to setting her free once and for all weighted time as an anchor to drowning. The anticipation of how all this could end.

"No, we wouldn't want to delay it," she agreed quietly.

CHAPTER 33

Tauria

THE CHANCES OF being granted alone time with Nik were slim to none. They wouldn't be entirely alone. And with what she had to tell him, she couldn't risk listening ears. Like the guards posted outside her door right now.

It was the dead of night, and Tauria put effort into keeping her restless pacing silent. There was only one place she had discovered to be safe, and it had the added bonus of being wide and open enough to subdue her raging thoughts.

Tauria was scaling the rooftops without another thought. The only reason she'd waited so long was her attempt to figure out another way to get to Nik. She didn't know what room he occupied, and it would be no easy task to find out with the winds shifting constantly above them all. Even then, Tauria was reluctant, not sure if she would be able to handle what could surface if she were to find Nik and Samara in bed together. Heartache. *Jealousy.* She desperately shook the mental image and the hideous feelings they stirred that she had no right to. It was to be expected, she supposed, even though she and Tarly didn't share a room. For a moment, she blanched at the idea being suggested as a way of maintaining their guise.

Tauria gave up before even attempting to scout out Nik's rooms. She couldn't bear it. But the exertion was not wasted as it helped to relieve some of her pent-up agitation and release her permanent cloud of sadness. She closed her eyes against the howl of the wind, enjoying the resistance in her body at the particularly strong currents. It was bliss and freedom tangling in her hair, awakening her magick that heated her skin against the chill. A small smile crept onto her lips, leaving her feeling weightless in mind and body.

In an instinctual reaction, Tauria drew her staff, swiftly extending it to midsize for close combat with the presence that arrived deliberately stealthy behind her. Whirling around, she didn't hesitate to bring it down on the intruder, but it was halted by a firm grip.

Emerald eyes blinked at her in surprise, and Tauria's deep frown released with her own dumbfounded expression.

"What are you doing out here?" she demanded in a breath of relief.

Confusion folded Nik's brow. "I was of the impression you were looking for me."

She was, only she couldn't figure out how he knew it. Or that she was out here. "Did anyone see you?"

He smirked, releasing her staff. "I might not have your ability, but I know how to be silent and evade detection."

Tauria bit back her retort. "What about your bride?"

A slow curl made its way onto one side of his mouth, and Tauria immediately cursed her tone that gave the bastard the impression she cared. "You sound jealous. I wonder how your own fiancé would feel about that."

"Your arrogance is astonishing."

His grin only widened. Tauria couldn't stop her impulse despite where they were. She summoned her wind and targeted him.

Nik braced for it just in time to absorb the blow rather than have it force him back. It was dangerous; one wrong slip of footing could be fatal with the distance down to the ground, but in the flash of his eyes, it was as if he were goading her.

"Why did you come?" she demanded.

"Like I said, I thought you invited—"

"To Olmstone, Nik! Why did you come all this way?"

His expression firmed. "How have they really been treating you, Tauria?"

She recoiled, not expecting the question. All it stirred in her was resentment and rage. "As if you care," she sneered. "You haven't bothered to check in. Not once. It wasn't until the announcement of your *engagement* that I finally realized why, and I might have understood. Yet I had to hear from court gossipers about it instead."

Nik winced, but she wouldn't fall for his false sincerity.

"I might have even been happy for you despite my surprise. You make quick work. But I was humiliated to be one of the last to hear the news, as though I meant *nothing* to you or High Farrow." Tears burned in her eyes, her voice rising with her indignation, and she knew it was dangerous as they stood on open ground. She couldn't find it in herself to pause and extend her senses to check for any nearby presence.

Confronting Nik now…her heart was breaking all over again.

"You didn't reply to my letters."

Tauria blinked and shook her head. "I haven't heard from you at all." She recognized Nik's anger. Sometimes she even feared it—never for herself, but for what could become of something in the path of his wrath. So rare, as though he reserved it with the will to unleash the Nether on anything that threatened what he kept closest to his heart.

Nik closed the step of distance she'd pushed between them, and she wanted to retreat, but her breath caught, and she couldn't. His voice fell quiet and personal. "I need you to—"

"I see you got my note."

A new voice had them whirling around. Nik stepped in front of her, but his arm halted before it could curve around her.

It was no threat. And his near touch didn't go unnoticed by the prince who strolled across the narrow flat of the roof toward them, pulling down the hood of his cloak for the wind to catch the waves of his blond hair.

Nik slumped with irritation instead, stepping away from her. "It was you?" he asked.

Tauria cut in over their shared look of distaste. "Does someone want to explain?"

Tarly's eyes shifted to her. "I knew you would come dancing up here with restless thoughts after the events of today."

She shrunk back sheepishly, but Tarly only smiled knowingly as he walked toward her, nearly brushing Nik as he passed him. His arm slipped around her, and she had to wonder if it was to gain entertainment from the reaction Nik would strain to suppress.

"And I knew *you* wouldn't come if it were by my invitation," he explained with a pointed look at Nik.

"Now I'm confused," Nik muttered, taking up a casual lean and folding his arms against a tall structure of the roof. His gaze kept subtle track of Tarly's hand on her.

Tarly blocked him out to say, "I think it would be best for him to know what we're up against here. In case my father doesn't plan to spare High Farrow this time."

It was unexpected, the prince's trust, and there might have been a part of her that was guilty of not appreciating the many layers Tarly kept hidden.

Nik straightened from his position immediately. "You're in danger?" The threat that seeped into his tone targeted the prince, and Tarly flared with the challenge. Even on the open rooftops, the pull for dominance between them was a familiar suffocation.

"We were right," Tauria cut in before they could begin another round of bickering. "Marlowe was right. Varlas was never sated in his need for revenge."

Nik slid a cautious glance toward Tarly. Tauria flared in defense. "He's on our side."

"I'm on no one's side," Tarly amended. He let her go, and his expression firmed. "I may not agree with my father's methods, but I don't believe he is entirely driven by his own vengeance anymore." It was the prince's turn to lean back against the wall. The shadows engulfed him, adding to the darkness that filled his voice. For a second, there might have been understanding in Nik's eyes before he blinked and it switched to accusation.

"No offense, but we can't really trust your judgment on the matter."

"Do you believe Orlon's actions were his own?"

"Our fathers are nothing alike."

Tarly chuckled without humor. "Is that how you live with his death on your hands?"

Nik advanced, but Tauria was quick to step between them. Tarly didn't move an inch, but his remark flared Tauria's anger, and she shot the prince a warning look behind her.

"We know that Orlon's free will was taken by Dakodas and controlled by Marvellas," Tauria said.

"And how do we know my father is not experiencing the same?"

Tauria turned to him with sympathy. "I don't believe he is. Orlon killed his own mate—" She winced at a sharp pain in her chest, refraining from the desire to apologize to Nik for the memory of the dark secret she'd wrongfully kept from him. "He had no mercy or warmth left. Varlas may be harsh, but he's still grieving. Not to mention his eyes—they aren't black and depthless like Orlon's turned."

Tarly didn't look at her. His hard gaze cast out over the horizon, a guard she knew all too well pulled over his emotions.

"So what have you discovered?" Nik asked with a note of bitterness as he spared a glance at the detached prince.

Tauria took a long breath. "Our suspicions are true: Varlas is consorting with Valgard."

Nik's eyes blazed; his jaw twitched. "You're coming back with me."

"No, I'm not."

The prince met her gaze then, a flicker of surprise crossing through his eyes as he looked between her and Nik. As though he'd expected her to take the first opening out of here.

"You can't stay here like willing prey," Nik flared. His step toward her was halted when she snapped a cold warning at him.

"It's not as simple as that. And I don't need you to decide my movements, Nik. I won't run. Never again."

Nik battled with understanding and his overprotective nature. His icy gaze occasionally pinned Tarly as though trying to find a target for his anger out here. It was becoming dizzying to be caught in the middle of them.

"He's real, Nik." The fear in her voice was enough to grab his attention. "It's true, all of it… The High Lord Mordecai lives. We don't yet know what he's capable of, but he's planning something, it involves us, and he's using Varlas to get everything into place for it."

Nik calculated, the lines of his face deepening, his eyes growing cold. "Your engagement?"

"Is real," Tarly cut in.

Tauria swallowed hard against the will to protest, wondering why the prince would trust him with the knowledge about his father but not want to disclose the truth of their engagement. Nik cut him a look, and then his eyes swept over her. In those few seconds, despite whatever words were fed to him, Nik seemed to have decided his own truth in what he observed. Her heart squeezed, wanting desperately to know if he believed it so easily.

"You're giving them exactly what they want?" Nik concluded with a careful, teetering wrath.

"Yes," the prince answered nonchalantly. "This way we can tide them over. Find out when they plan for the wedding to happen—"

"And then what?" Nik snapped. "Dangle her life before them when you don't know what in the *damn* Nether they want with her?"

Tauria was conflicted between flaring to her own defense or consoling the fear for her that he'd slipped into that statement.

Tarly's blaze of irritation rippled at her back. "I only thought to warn you, Nik." He was bold as he pushed out of his lax position, stepping close to her. "You don't need to concern yourself with her anymore. She's safe with me." His arm found its way around her again, and she tried not to react. There were times she had come to find the prince's touch a comfort to her nerves, but right now, in front of Nik, her stomach knotted while her mind screamed at the wrongness of it all. Because it wasn't a move of comfort now; it was a statement to the king who challenged the prince in a deadly stare off. "You should concern yourself with your own fiancée. But when you go back to High Farrow, I thought you'd like to be aware, in case there are dark forces lingering in the most unlikely of places in your kingdom."

Tauria watched the war across Nik's face, believing the hurt she felt within was an essence of his, but she was thankful to the prince for what he had shared.

Nik nodded in appreciation folded with defeat. "Take care of her."

"I can take care of myself," she answered before Tarly could.

Nik's smile was only half-there, but it was warmed with pride. "I know." He turned from them without another word.

Her body turned rigid in resistance against her mind. And Tauria wondered if there would ever come a time—in years, centuries—that it wouldn't inflict such pain to watch him walk away.

CHAPTER 34

Nikalias

He didn't want to be here.

Not surrounded by flamboyance and loud music. Not standing with a plastered-on face of celebration for the gathering crowd around him. Not courting Lady Samara next to him, whose grip was like a hot brand. A statement.

She wasn't here yet. Tauria had yet to make an entrance, and her absence drew attention to the fact the prince was missing too. Nik's posture had remained so stiff it was near painful. It was all he could do to suppress the rage he battled within, having no right to feel so much at witnessing her with Tarly.

And they were happy—or at least, they were fantastic at making the court believe they were. Nik had to breathe consciously and think of something, *anything,* else or he risked damning his composure.

He felt her before he saw her. The world always silenced in her presence as if nothing else mattered. His heart knew exactly where hers beat. Through the cluster of bodies, he saw her. As if she were a diamond among coal, his eyes caught the magnificent sight with unfaltering ease. The gold accents adorning her pointed ears glinted against the lights, and her warm brown skin was aglow. The gown she wore was a waterfall of silk that accentuated every curve and exposed a long, slender leg when she moved. Even from this distance she drove him wild.

In seconds, the sight of her had obliterated any composure he thought he could maintain. The color she wore was beautiful but *wrong.* Maybe it was his own pitiful resentment that circled the bitter thought that the deep purples couldn't compare to the homeland greens that painted her to life. Or the elegance she embodied in royal blue.

"Everything okay?" Samara's voice was quiet as she squeezed his arm.

Nik shook his head as if she'd snapped him from a trance. Just as well, because when he looked to the lady she'd followed his line of sight, her eyes lifted to his with pained understanding. He hated it.

"Do you need another drink?" Nik diverted.

Samara glanced down at her near empty cup and nodded, handing it off to him.

"Feel free to dance, Samara. I don't wish to bind you in my selfish company all evening."

She smiled gratefully. He'd noticed her gazing longingly at the partner dances as many times as he'd declined her coaxing to join in.

Nik needed a distraction and headed over to the side of the hall where servants lay in wait with wine. He set the cups down on a tray just as the song was getting ready to change, but before it did, he couldn't help but to pick up on the murmurs of adoration. He knew who the crowd spoke of.

Retrieving two full cups, he turned back. Lady Samara had found a partner already, and her smile seemed bright and genuine as he led her onto the dance floor. It drew Nik's gaze right to her. Tauria. Who was also being escorted for a first dance with the Prince of Olmstone while many around them gushed and watched in awe. Nik downed one glass, passing it off, and kept hold of the other as he walked, unable to tear his gaze from her through the crowd until he met the dais and they halted in the middle of the dance floor.

Dressed in similar colors and attire, they looked…*good* together. Tarly leaned down to say something in her ear as those around them took their positions for the dance to begin. Though the crowd was loud, as her grin broke wide and mouth opened he could hear her laughter. But the bright sound passed a fleeting cloud of sorrow as he considered how effortlessly the prince could pull it from her.

"Join me, Nikalias," Varlas's voice rumbled behind him just as the band began to play.

His attention broke from Tarly and Tauria with a snap of awareness. Once again, Nik cursed his error, hoping his fixation on them hadn't been interpreted as anything other than admiration for the happy couple. He had no desire to seek company with Varlas now he knew the darkness he was in collusion with. But this was still a game, and he mustered his best poker face as he stepped up to join the seated rulers. He offered a short dip of his head in acknowledgment of Keira by Varlas's side, and the child seated with her. Opal, if he remembered correctly.

"How are you finding our celebrations?"

"You've outdone yourself, Varlas. It will certainly be a solstice to remember." His lie was smooth and pleasant. He hated everything about the damned ball. It was even more suffocating and extravagant than those back in High Farrow. Court jesters weaved through the crowd trying to draw coin in exchange for cheap tricks. Fae wine was consumed endlessly, so many were acting on enhanced confidence. Sultry, unashamed touching. Dance after dance without pause.

"You do not wish to participate, Nikalias?" The queen's elegant voice was curious, and he followed her sights to where Samara stepped and twirled in the arms of another.

"I'm a little out of practice," was all he could respond as his grip tightened on his cup. Because his gaze was quick to shift from the one who should bear his attention. It was as if his mind were Netherbent on tormenting him all night as his eyes landed on Tauria and Tarly once more. She was exquisite. Completely and utterly mesmerizing as she moved like the wind she could master. He'd never forgotten how beautiful she was when she danced, but seeing it all over again after so long didn't fail to take his breath away. Tarly, to his credit, kept up with her. But it was clear she was leading the dance. The song moved as if it were hers; as if she controlled it too in the way she had the perfect move for each note.

Every instinct within him flared with a hideous, dangerous possession as he tracked everywhere Tarly's hands touched her without trying. Their dance was intimate, their expressions believable, as if they were in love. Nik's hand on his cup clenched so hard he risked shattering it, but it was all he could do to keep his trembling stifled.

She is mine.

It was a cruel chant that would never relent. But seeing her now… this was the happiness she deserved. The love he had never been able to give her. Tarly could. And for Tauria, he couldn't resent the prince for coaxing out the genuine smiles that graced her face now. Never had a more soul-tearing realization sunk him to these dark depths he feared there'd be no climbing out of.

My mate.

But that didn't matter. It *couldn't* matter. He had to let her go. Set her free. She deserved this.

The song reached its final climax, and Tauria spun with the aid of Tarly. Over and over. Her gown fanned, and there was never a more ethereal sight. On the final beat, Tarly's hand caught her around the waist, and they halted. Her chest rose and fell deeply, clutching him as she peered up with a heated stare.

My mate. My mate.

As the other couples began to break apart and find new partners, Tarly didn't release her. Instead, his hand took her chin, and Nik's whole world seemed to halt in the presence of a rage so all-consuming he had no choice but to act.

He should have known there was no way he could watch her body move for another, witness hands on her that were not his. Only he knew what made her breath hitch. What inspired her hazel gaze to flare with a desire that spoke sinful thoughts.

He shouldn't have come here.

Nik finished his second drink before passing it off. The king asked something, and he thought he uttered a response before his feet were moving. The voice that screamed in his mind to stop him before he did something reckless that could ruin everything—he slammed a hard barrier against it before his steps toward her faltered.

For just one moment, just one night, he had to remember what it felt like to embrace her. Dance with her. One last time.

CHAPTER 35

Tauria

IT HAD BEEN too long, and Tauria had forgotten how much she loved to dance. That when she moved through the air with the aid of song it felt as blissful as being on open rooftops with her ability.

Tarly's undivided attention remained on her when their dance came to an end, his arm firmly around her waist, bringing their bodies flush. But there was something in that hazel stare—something she might have caught a flicker of before, except now it was full and without restraint. His hand tilted her chin and her lips parted, heart thundering. Because the awe in his eyes this time she believed to be real. The way they'd moved together she couldn't deny weaved with true passion. The dip of his gaze to her mouth skipped her pulse.

He wanted to kiss her.

This kiss would be real. True. And there was a part of her that yearned for it not only after the high of the dance, but maybe in a desperation to know if she would feel something from it.

It only took seconds for her unease to return. It had surfaced strongly with every touch he'd laid on her from the moment they stepped into the hall. Her heart immediately called to another, to Nik, who she knew stood at the far end watching her as she couldn't stop herself from stealing glances at him.

"Can I kiss you, Tauria?" Tarly's question was uncertain, as if he too pondered exactly what she did. The same desire to know if a fire could spark between them.

Her breaths were shallow, her pulse erratic, as the distance between them had already begun to close. She couldn't do it. Not here and now. Not with *him* nearby and while a pitiful yearning to be in his arms instead tightened her chest.

But there were more pressing eyes on them. Waiting to catch a crack in their relationship. Searching for some kindle to light into flame. Tauria realized what being in power meant. People wanted to see her rise but would relish in the entertainment of tearing her down.

Tarly kept angling his head, the gentle hum of gushing whispers slicking her skin with the awareness that this was what their audience wanted. This was a silencing of the speculation about their lack of affection.

But she couldn't do it. Couldn't do it. Couldn't—

A dark, smooth voice that would never fail to race down her spine cut in through her racing thoughts and froze her body in place.

"May I have this next dance with my ward?" Nik's tone strained with the need to ask Tarly.

The prince didn't immediately look at him, and the tension that grew shallowed her breaths. His jaw twitched with ire. Tauria should decline, or at least find the will to surface the irritation that might have been expected at Nik's intrusion. But all she could embrace was her relief.

Finally, Tarly released her. "If that is what she wishes," he responded tightly.

Tauria's pulse began to make her feel lightheaded. Knowing how close he was, she scrambled to compose her wild thoughts, juggling the performance of being on stage with the will to surrender to her true emotions. She spared three long breaths and slipped back into a cool mask of indifference with a fear that the moment she had those emerald eyes so close, she would be his. And the challenge would be to convince the world otherwise.

"I can spare one dance," she said, not giving Nik the satisfaction of a warm reception.

Tarly's touch lingered on her. The prince flashed his gaze between them as though in reluctance to leave them alone. But not in jealousy. Tarly eased a warning as if in reprimand.

She thought nothing more of it when he slipped away and Nik was suddenly before her. Nothing else mattered anymore. No other dancer, no other king. No other time or place. Tauria looked up at Nik, not breaking eye contact but letting go of a shallow breath when his hand slid across her waist. Slowly, carefully. Torturously.

"Is that all I am to you?" she hushed out. "Your ward."

He drew her closer, more than was necessary, and she had half a mind to say as much. "You want to hear the truth?" he said, shifting their stance, and she allowed him to guide her. "You have never been my ward. Or my subject. Or my princess. You are my equal, Tauria. In every way, you shine brighter than the moon I've watched change in the sky since you left, knowing it was the one thing we could look upon all the same. Is that pitiful of me?"

Tauria's mouth parted; her eyes pricked with tears. The party around them eased away until it vanished in their personal sphere. His confession was a reassurance she didn't realize she'd needed all this time. Tauria had spent so long yearning to prove herself, but now she saw…it was never needed with him.

She had no words with which to respond.

Nik leaned into her, green eyes full of stars. "I trust you'll remember this dance," he said with a low, husky gravel, his fingers grazing her upper arm, trailing down and igniting her skin with ripples of enchanting need, until he reached her wrist and took her hand.

"What are you doing?" Her adrenaline spiked. Because while he was careful, every touch was deliberate, unnecessary, but *damn,* if she didn't crave every single one.

"Dancing."

"You know that's not what I mean."

"What do you mean, Tauria?" His mouth curled with a devastating small smile that stole any response. Or breath. Her name rolled off his tongue in a caress as seductive as his hands.

The song began, and Nik was right: Tauria did know the dance. The song. The night that flashed to her mind immediately, so all she could do was stare at him wide-eyed.

"You remember," he said softly, arrogance falling to something far more treasured.

Her face pinched with the wave of emotion to be back there. In Fenstead during their Winter Solstice Ball. It was both painful and so joyous to return to in memory, if only for a few minutes. One dance. It was not slow; rather, this dance was often a test of compatibility between partners. No room for error or they risked the embarrassment of stumbling in front of the crowds who would halt all other engagement to watch those brave enough to attempt it. In Fenstead, Tauria had chosen him as her partner in challenge. Never did she think he would have his time to test her back.

"We shouldn't," she said, but her tone wasn't convincing with the protest she intended. Tauria was afraid of the dance. Not for lack of skill or confidence. She was afraid to feel everything that would devour her whole in bliss, only to end in misery. Once they stepped off the dance floor, the show would go on.

Yet she'd already surrendered to him. As she leaned into him and braced for the music that would move them just as it had that night.

She didn't know how many other couples were braving the dance because in her mind…there was no one else. No one but him and her and these few precious minutes in which she forgot all else.

"I hope you can keep up after all these years," she said quietly.

Nik's smile broke into a carefree grin, and it stung her nose, her eyes, to see it. She'd missed it so much. "I think you should speak for yourself, love."

Two glides followed by a spin he led her through, catching her again without falter. They twisted; she spun. Each time, their bodies separated only to return flush again, the sensation pulsing a new thrill that rushed her steps with adrenaline. Every time she spun, her gaze instantly snapped back to his as if he was her orbit. Tauria could find those beautiful emeralds in any room, any crowd, and they would never fail to stop the world.

The song was in her bones, flowing through her movements that harmonized so precisely with Nik's. When they danced, when they touched, there was never a more perfect answer. It was clear now more than ever as she followed Tarly's dance with this. The prince was a fine partner, and she had enjoyed the dance they shared. But this…it was an unexplainable push and pull, a force so undeniable it was painful to resist and a pleasure to embrace.

Nik hooked an arm around her waist, and the breath left her lungs in time with her feet leaving the ground when he lifted and turned her. Looking down, she saw his eyes glittered with awe. *Pride.* Then she landed light, breaking into another twirl aided by his hand above her until their bodies came together again.

It was exhilarating in the pulse through her veins. Passionate in every shot of scattered stars when skin met skin. *Freeing* in the air that wrapped around them, sending them dancing as if through weightless clouds.

But it started to become more than expected. Too much. Something in Nik changed; a dangerous ferocity in the way he moved had her quickening her pace to keep up. Not aggression, but a consuming passion. His hands moved over her body with careful calculation. Touching skin, rousing a lust in her she couldn't stifle. Because he was seducing her through that dance, and he knew it. Maybe her own hands over his neck, his chest, his strong arms, was more than what was necessary too as she gave herself over to him and the music without restraint or burden, needing this one night to free her own want and desire.

Their next maneuver brought her back flush with his front.

"You are exquisite, Tauria." Nik's breath down the column of her neck fluttered her eyes. "In a world less cruel, you would have been mine long ago."

Her eyes burned, but she was spun away from him again, the song nearing its end and reality creeping in so fast she had to bite back her whimper.

Nik's large, strong hands gripped her waist for the final turn, lifting her. Tauria braced against his shoulders and kept her eyes on him as he lowered her slowly despite his face beginning to blur. When she was set down and the music had faded, a single tear escaped her, but Nik's hand brushed it away before it could be seen.

"I could have been yours from that first night." The confession slipped past her defenses as a barely-there whisper, but at the same time she jerked with the harsh sounds of applause that erupted and hopefully swallowed her words. Tauria looked around, her face instantly flushed as she saw they were the only couple left on the dance floor with a thick crowd of onlookers.

Oh Gods.

What had they done?

She was overwhelmed with the attention, wondering if the desire she felt was only between them and not decipherable as anything more than a skillful dance. Her eyes caught on a group of ladies—Keira's ladies—whom she recognized. They leaned into each other, whispering, giggling, eyes darting between her and Nik.

Tauria's vision swayed. She couldn't stop the glance she spared at the dais. Varlas had stood from his throne, his face hard, accusatory, as though they'd broken the alliance before it had even been formed. Keira reclined elegantly in her chair, her smile feline, eyes twinkling in delight. Everyone's reactions had protests forming in her throat, daring to spill ungracefully to convince the room Nikalias was no more than a past acquaintance. It was a truth and a lie, and Tauria didn't know how to salvage the moment with so many eyes of judgment on her already.

"Relax, Tauria. Breathe," Nik said gently, sensing her rising panic. A calmness lapped within her—a familiar sensation she grappled with. Before she could step out of his embrace, Nik leaned down to her ear. "Meet me on the rooftops tomorrow night," he whispered. She shivered at the vibrations down her neck, beginning to shake her head, but his hand tightened on her waist. "Please."

She pulled back from him, floundering for words. She wanted to deny him, but the ache to accept was stronger. So she made no promise.

"You were wonderful, Tauria."

Tarly. Thank the Spirits. It was the grounding she needed from her hazy mind.

Nik stepped away as the prince approached. Tauria was too stunned, too confused, by all that was swarming her mind to register Tarly's touch. He took her hand to guide her farther away from Nik. One hand slipped to her waist to angle her toward him. The other raised to her face as he…

Tauria's noise of shock caught in her throat when Tarly's mouth pressed firmly to hers. Stunned utterly still, it took her a moment and some gentle coaxing from him for her to realize what was happening.

Actions can silence.

Tauria's eyes closed, and despite every muscle turning to stone she leaned into the prince for that kiss, yet again to silence the growing speculation surrounding her dance with Nik. But still, it felt so wrong. Every inch of her skin crawled, her eyes burned, and her heart broke all over again knowing Nik watched, his confession still a battering ram to everything she'd accepted he didn't want from her. Those words gave way to something hopeful but damning…

Doubt.

Tarly broke the kiss but didn't release her. His fingers trailed her cheek lovingly. All for show. All for the vultures that circled and whispered and waited to pick them apart, piece by piece.

And she was coming to the realization that was all her life would ever be. A show for others.

Murmurs and gasps stole her attention, and she followed them to where many party members were heading out to the balconies. Relief was a flood that relaxed her posture as the attention dispersed from them. Tarly's hand took hers for her to follow him. But she couldn't help the glance she stole behind her, wondering what Nik's reaction to his affection would be.

Their eyes met, and she saw Nik hadn't moved. Not an inch. His whole posture loomed tall and rigid, his gaze dark, and everything about him in that moment made her tremble with an expected thrill.

Until Samara came up to his side, lacing her hand through his arm and seeming to snap him from whatever turbulent thoughts he battled. It was Tauria's turn to feel the rise of something twisting and ugly in the pit of her stomach as she witnessed their closeness. Samara coaxed him to follow her outside with the others.

Tauria looked away, but as they stepped outside she forgot everything at the magnificent sight. Through all the flamboyance and conflicting emotions, Tauria had completely forgotten what made this solstice so unlike any other. The solar eclipse was underway, an event that would be marked in history.

Yet as she watched the moon drift over to devour the sun, a cold chill began to creep over her skin, prickling like ice crystals despite the heat, along with a creeping sense of foreboding in her stomach she couldn't understand. Tarly guided her to the stone railing as the crowd gave way for them. And with an arm around her, they cast their gazes up to watch the beautiful solar event.

Yet as people gasped in awe and the day began to darken, the warmth of the summer air was stolen from Tauria completely. Still, she fixed her sights on the dark orb as it met the sun. Her heart raced as if she needed to stop it, stop *something*, but it was as if the eclipse were shuddering through her with dark laughter.

"Are you all right?"

Tarly's voice was distant, but she noted his concern. She couldn't respond. The sound of the crowd drifted away on the wind until she was left with nothing but the drum of her heart.

Then, when darkness fell all at once…

Tauria's gasp was silent as a ringing filled her ears. Her hand braced against the stone at the sharpness that twisted her chest before scattering over every inch of her skin, a force so dark and final subjecting her to a passing embrace.

Death. All she could think of was *death.*

Her hand idly rubbed her chest as ice coated her. The total eclipse would only last minutes, but time had suspended to seem untraceable. Tauria felt herself drifting into another realm, a void that seemed…*wrong.*

Then all at once she crashed back to the present.

Her stumble back to reality was masked by Tarly, who held her tighter. Tauria's surroundings started to come back into clarity. Sound returned to her. She met Tarly's perplexed gaze, blinking vacantly as she tried to process the gods-awful feeling that had ensnared her entirely.

An instinctual pull claimed her sight, which landed directly on emerald eyes of concern and *fear.* Nik was already staring at her, the happiness and cheer around them in conflict with the ghostly fear that tunneled between them in that look. Time stood still, keeping them focused on each other while everything real seemed distant. It was all the confirmation she needed to know Nik had felt exactly what she did.

It was a relief to know she didn't imagine it. The pull to him now was so strong she was leaning into her first step…

"Tauria." Tarly demanded her attention.

Snapping her gaze to him, she saw the prince had followed her to where her attention was fixed, and his wrinkled brow gave away his assumption about her stare down with Nik. Yet she didn't have it in herself to convince him otherwise, and Tarly's irritation only bewildered her more—because it was confirmation he hadn't experienced the same thing.

"I'm not feeling well," she got out, and it was the truth suddenly as nausea rocked her stomach. "I just need a moment alone."

The sun began to peek through as the moon gave way. Tauria had to get out of the mass of people or she was at risk of fainting with the echoes of that unexplainable dark energy. As she weaved through the crowd there was only one name, one person, who flashed to the forefront of her mind. A dear friend. An impossible human. And she couldn't be sure why she suddenly feared so deeply for Faythe.

Tauria managed to slip through a side door but was caught by a firm force. She didn't yelp in surprise but immediately relaxed into the scent that embraced her. Nik's hand slipped under her chin, forcing her eyes to meet his. He didn't have to ask; the concern swirling in his own irises as they scanned every inch of her face made her brow pinch. She wanted to embrace him, but she was paralyzed by the awareness anyone could find them here and make a thousand speculations to fan the flames of gossip.

"I'm afraid," she whispered, because she could never hide anything from him.

Nik released a breath, glancing behind them before this hand trailed the length of her bare arm, sending a shiver over her skin that quelled some of her fear before his hand took hers. "Come," he said quietly, the pull on her arm driving her to follow. Or maybe it was the spike of adrenaline at their reckless touch. A giddy thrill that awoke her.

She shouldn't allow him to lead her away, but her steps skipped to chase after him. She should tear her hand from his, yet instead, their casual grip became an intimate entwining of fingers, so natural she couldn't stop it. It was impulsive. *Gods,* she wanted this one night to let go of everything poised and perfect. Let go of her false life that was a live entertainment show for others.

"Where are we going?" she asked, breathless with adrenaline as they wound through dark halls, abandoned while the solstice ball was in full swing.

"Somewhere I can have you alone."

CHAPTER 36

Jakon

JAKON SAT ON the familiar rooftop, his arms around Marlowe in quiet reflection about how often he'd watched the same view of the town with Faythe. They seemed like distant memories now, but not a day went by where he didn't think of his dear friend.

The streets below them were rowdy, so he and Marlowe had come up here for a moment alone someplace where they wouldn't miss out on the solstice celebrations entirely. Jakon leaned his head back in contentment, meeting the tall chimney he was propped up against. His fingers ran idly up and down Marlowe's arm, but his thoughts were more anxious than usual, so he could hardly muster conversation.

Marlowe shifted, turning until she was straddling his extended legs. "What's been troubling you?" she asked quietly, her gentle hands slipping over his chest.

He offered a weak smile, tucking a strand of hair behind her ear. "Nothing gets past you." They shared a sad look as though some kind of mutual longing hollowed through them. He knew what it was—or rather, who. Jakon took a deep breath. "Since the day I met Faythe I've always had this urge to protect her. More than what she needed sometimes, but I can't explain why I feel…*tied* to her." He frowned, looking out over the obscure array of buildings. "I've been wondering about my parents too. Sometimes I think my final memory of them isn't right."

"You said your parents died of the same illness as my mother," Marlowe stated, and he knew that tone meant she pondered something. "As soon as she was discovered to have it, my father took me. All I remember is crying endlessly when we were forced to take refuge in the blacksmith compound, hoping once it passed we'd be reunited. My father never told me how deadly it was. How many lives were being claimed by it. I should have known."

Jakon's arm encircled her, his hand caressing her cheek. "I'm sorry."

She shook her head as if it would disperse the cloud of sorrow. Taking his hand, her troubled eyes met his. "I only say this because you didn't have that escape. No one took you away when your parents fell ill. You stayed with them, yet…"

Jakon nodded, confirming they thought the same. "I've always harbored this guilt. Living under the same roof, sharing everything—how did I live without a single symptom?"

Marlowe's hands trailed over his neck, those eyes of wonder scanning his face with a small but breathtaking smile. "You're a miracle," she said.

Jakon laughed, his lips pressed to her chest. "Hardly," he mumbled. "I'm not much, but I'm yours, Marlowe. And that's enough for me."

"You're more than you take credit for, Jakon." Her brow pinched tightly. "I'm concerned for Faythe too," she confessed, reading what he didn't need to say. "But we will see her again."

The truth was, ever since Faythe left, there'd been something unsettled within him. A wrongness at being parted that he hadn't been able to shake.

Just then, something cold overcame him. Marlowe's spine curved a fraction with an intake of breath that set him on high alert. "What is that?" he thought out loud, not expecting an answer, but it was something of a reassurance that she seemed to feel it too.

Marlowe turned to glance skyward behind them. "The eclipse is about to start."

He followed her gaze, expecting to be awed by the sight of the moon approaching to devour the sun. Yet as his eyes fell on it, the world began to quieten. Jakon straightened, taking Marlowe with him as she sat in his lap. His heart quickened as his skin grew slick. "Something's wrong," he muttered, unable to keep his eyes up.

"Jak..." Marlowe's hands tightened with her concern.

Yet he couldn't feel her. A wave of something dark and claiming lapped within. A ringing filled his ears. Marlowe spoke words, but it was as if his head were underwater. The day was slowly devoured by night, inch by inch, as the moon triumphed. Memories barreled into him, and he clamped his eyes shut.

Flecks of gold.

His parents.

Faythe.

Dizziness lapped at him, but Marlowe's distantly frantic voice while she shook him had him fighting to stay conscious. He lost that fight as his heart raced to a dangerous point, fire erupting in his chest like he'd never known before. Like a blade.

Then, as darkness stole the day, a darkness so final stole him.

Jakon was hurting badly, his skin slick with a cold sweat, but he was flying. His vision came and went, blurry, but in his misery the clear blue sky was a freeing sight. He hoped he could fly higher, above all pain and burden.

Instead he was falling, but he didn't have the strength to save himself or even care. Expecting to hit the ground hard, it was bliss when he landed softly against grass that smelled so fresh. It was then he realized someone was carrying him. Arms slipped from under him.

Jakon fluttered his eyes open, wondering if it was his mother. Yet as he pictured her face, all he could see was how weak she was, just like his father. They were sick. And it seemed he hadn't been spared.

"What is it you come for?" a voice echoed, and he thought it was a Spirit come to take him away.

"He's just a boy. I need your help," a woman he'd never heard before replied.

Jakon's head lolled, and he tried to focus his senses. He heard water. No—something louder that thrashed the element. His vision came around again and he spied the waterfall. It was big. He'd never seen one before. Then he tried to look into the lake he lay beside, and what he saw numbed some of his pain to awe. The river glowed. Small balls of light danced and chased below the surface. He wanted to touch them.

"You come to bargain."

"What will it take?"

"Saving the boy will require his life being bound to another."

"Who?"

Jakon didn't know what they spoke of. He didn't really care with his body so weak, his mind drifting slowly while he watched the glowing orbs.

"He will be bound to her in duty. If she falls, so will he. Mortals live their lives with a natural instinct to protect themselves, to survive. He will not know it, but as his life depends on the safety of hers, his courage will rise to protect her at all costs."

"Who?" the woman bit out again.

"I think you know who, Heir of Marvellas."

A pause of silence.

"Not her."

"Then the boy shall die."

Jakon's hand finally dipped into the lake, the coolness so sharp it took away some of his fever, just for a few seconds, as he attempted to catch the orbs that darted away from his touch. Something pressed to his forehead, and he managed to shift his head. The woman leaned over him. His eyes squinted against the light, wondering if her golden irises were real or just a reflection of the sun.

"You're going to be okay," she told him tenderly. Her voice was soothing like his mother's, and his heart pined for her the most in his sickness.

Why had this woman taken him?

Where were his parents?

He couldn't speak any of it while tiredness sealed his lips shut and breathing became difficult. Darkness drew in to eclipse the day, but with it his body didn't hurt anymore.

The last words he heard came from the woman who must have been his own Spirit to guide him away: "Do it."

Her cries awoke him. Jakon startled with a gasp, eyes snapping open, but he winced against the dim light.

"Jak!" Marlowe's voice broke, spiking his panic.

"Shit, Jak, you scared us."

Jakon blinked slow as he rose, confusion swirling at hearing that unexpected voice. His eyes fell on Ferris crouching by his side while Marlowe helped him to sit.

"What happened?" He scanned Marlowe, his hand raised to her face—wet with tears—scrambling to piece together what he could have missed to cause her such upset.

"You—your heart…it stopped," she choked.

"I heard her frantic calls for help," Ferris muttered. "Seriously, I couldn't find a pulse for a good minute either."

Marlowe's arms wrapped around him, and he held her while she cried. "I'm sorry," was all he could say in his bewilderment. "I don't know what happened. We were watching the eclipse, and it felt…"

"I felt it too," she whispered, not letting him go. Her terror ached within him. "But not like you did."

"Do you know what it was?" he asked carefully.

Marlowe pulled back, her beautiful face sad, apologetic. She shook her head.

"Well, since you'll clearly live, I'll take this as my cue to leave," Ferris drawled, standing.

"Where have you been?" Jakon asked. Not that he cared, but it had been some time since he'd seen the redheaded bastard.

"Here and there," he answered with a sly grin. Jakon shouldn't have bothered asking. "I'm thinking of taking to the seas. The town has become somewhat boring in recent times."

"No new *Gold-Eyed Shadow* to earn your riches?"

Ferris chuckled. "Not even close. I don't think they'd believe me if I told them Rhyenelle's secret princess fought in those caves. An amusing tale, and I hope to see her again to enjoy it with her." Jakon understood Ferris's way of wishing Faythe well though he was too stubborn to voice such care outright.

Alone again, Jakon's hand trailed down Marlowe's spine in comfort when she leaned into him. The eclipse was still underway, and while he had come back to consciousness, a dark chill had not left him, settling with the echoes of a beckoning force that felt so final.

"I don't know what happened to you, but I plan to figure it out with what I do know."

Jakon took a deep breath. "You once said a change was coming." He searched those ocean eyes. "It involves Faythe, doesn't it?"

Her answer was there in eyes so troubled the ocean in them seemed depthless. "It involves us all."

CHAPTER 37

Tauria

THE COILING HEAT in her stomach tingled lower and lower. They climbed two staircases until Nik led her to a set of glass doors and onto a balcony. Outside, Tauria's eyes fluttered with the caress of the wind, so much more freeing without masses of people surrounding her to witness the eclipse. Her hand slipped from his as she approached the stone railing. She didn't need to extend her senses to hear the distant chatter of the crowds two levels below. She looked up at the sky. The sinister unease that had riddled her before didn't return, but the echoes of it—the question of what it could *mean*—lingered in her mind.

"What do you think it was?" Tauria broke their silence without tearing her eyes from the solar event.

"I don't know," Nik answered, but it was as if his thoughts were elsewhere, and she turned to him.

Nik was by the door, watching her with a restrained darkness. It was one of defiance and longing, prickling her skin with its claim. He took a single step forward, and it sparked a current of electricity between them. Her pulse skipped when he took another.

"I thought I could resist you. At least until—" Nik stopped himself.

Tauria's lips parted, but she didn't know what she wanted to say. They moved like magnets, attracted to each other, but she'd begun to feel some resistance and knew to keep her distance. Nik stalked toward her, and she backed up until there was no escape with the stone her fingers curled around right behind her.

"Anyone could find us," she rasped, but each one of his slow steps flared a heat that didn't care for right or wrong. The look in his eyes, a breathtaking sparkling green against the fleeting sunlight, was dark and devouring. Possessive. She might have glimpsed it before, but never so open and raw.

"I should have known there wasn't a chance in any realm I could resist you. Not with how exquisite you look tonight. Not with how entrancing you were as you moved on that dance floor."

Tauria's back curved. A small part of her knew she should stop him. But she didn't.

Nik halted, searching her eyes, her face, lingering on her mouth. When he didn't receive the protest he awaited, his hand slipped over her waist as he leaned into her, and Tauria's sharp inhale was audible. Because she was all too aware of the party gathered below their very feet. Defiant, the scandalous thrill of that fact only heightened her rising desire.

"We can't do this," she got out, but it spoke no real protest. She *wanted* this. And maybe in taking control of what she wanted she didn't leave room to question his motives.

"Do what?" His voice was a low, husky mummer as his lips inched toward her skin.

Her hands tightened against the stone with the heat that gathered between her legs. She wanted so badly to tangle her fingers into his midnight hair instead as she trembled with restraint.

Nik pressed into her tighter, and it was all she could do to keep from curling her hands into his jacket. She tilted farther back over the edge. The rush of dangerous excitement that they could be caught if anyone below happened to lean out and look up…it made her chest rise and fall deeply with lust.

"I didn't come here for this ridiculous solstice ball. I didn't come here to negotiate this treaty."

Her heart thundered. His hand slid around her back, and inch by inch he drew her closer as if they could become one.

"Then why did you come?"

A pause. A long, searching pause charged the power between them.

"For you, love."

Tauria's breath caught. Twice now he'd spoken that name she only remembered from their one treasured night of bliss, never to hear it again. It didn't make sense that it fell from his mouth now, but in that moment, she wasn't sure she cared about anything except the need to be reckless. Impulsive. Knowing the moment they stepped indoors, they'd be back onstage, their lives an act for everyone they fooled down below.

His face slowly inched toward hers, and while her mind screamed with question, Tauria's desire roared to drown out all reasoning about why this was wrong. Because nothing had ever felt so right.

Nik's head angled until the tip of his nose grazed her cheekbone. "You feel it," he whispered. Her breath stuttered from her. "Gravity is so freeing when you just…let go."

Her brow pinched, and she tried to nod.

Nik's hand slipped in through the cut of her gown, and her gasp tightened her fists when his fingertips trailed a featherlight touch along her thigh.

"Why are you doing this?" she rasped with fleeting rationality.

Nik inhaled, long and deep. "Why does the sun rise each morning and the moon cross the night? Why does fire devour and ice preserve?" He drew back, impressing his gaze on every inch of her face before holding her with eyes that promised the world. "Some things are unstoppable."

She breathed out, longing to be reckless for once. "And when the moon meets the sun?"

Nik smiled slowly, eyes dipping to her mouth. "Time—it doesn't count."

That was all she needed to hear to silence that final note of guilt. Tauria gave over to every instinct, straining on her toes, her fingers slipping through his hair as they collided. The raw passion that clouded over them in an instant had her forgetting everything but him. Not the people below who might be able to hear the small noises Nik drew out of her with his roaming touch over her body. Not her ruse with Tarly that perhaps was never truly believed by Nik. Their hands could be sold, but their hearts had already made their commitment long ago. Hers had never sung with so much glee than in this forbidden moment of surrender.

In her need to be impossibly close, her leg felt the cool breeze as it slipped free of the high slit in her lilac gown. As if Nik knew, without breaking apart for a second, he trailed heat from his fingers along her thigh, drawing a soft moan out of her against his mouth. A plea, a beg, uncaring of how indecent or shameful it was. Where they were. *Who* they were. It didn't matter. Something low and entrancing vibrated in his chest right before his hand hooked under her thigh and he drew it around him. Nik's hips moved against her. The angle had him pressed against her core, and it was maddening how much she wanted him then. It was so wrong, so reckless.

And she loved every wild second.

No longer a composed princess. No longer an esteemed monarch. Who they were was nothing more than two unburdened, unforgiving souls. Among all the pretense in their lives they deserved this, no matter what it meant when their skin cooled and their masks were replaced. Out here where anyone could see—they could be caught in the act and there'd still be no taming the wildfire that would erupt—it only made the ache tighten between her legs.

Nik's hand trailed higher on her thigh, and she could hardly stifle the breathless noises that caressed her throat with where he was headed. She began to feel lightheaded from the shortness of breath paired with her rapid pulse, anticipating his touch. And then his hand halted, so close to her apex she almost came apart. He pulled out of the kiss with a groan.

"Tauria," he said against her lips, the low murmur pure lust, "you compose yourself so innocently, so beautifully, for the world around you"—as he trailed his mouth down her neck, a heated sensation curled her fist in his hair—"so no one might suspect how wickedly sinful you really are. Why does it not surprise me to find you bare under this dress?"

She bit down on her lip to stifle her squeal of surprise when Nik hooked his hand around her other thigh, lifting her until she sat on the wide flat of the railing. Her grip fell to his jacket tightly as he leaned into her again. The danger was exhilarating, both relying on his hold to prevent a fatal fall, and more so, hearing the crowd below, utterly oblivious to their reprehensible game right within their reach.

"You enjoy this, don't you, love?" Nik's gaze blazed wild and claiming. The warm breeze filtered his dark hair across his forehead, his green eyes lit up, and there was never a more breathtaking sight. "The fact that anyone could lean out over the balcony below, and all it would take is a glance up to see you." His hand trailed up her thigh again. He never broke eye contact. "But that's not enough. It's the thought of them seeing what I'm doing to you that excites you, isn't it? By the Gods, Tauria, the things I want to do to you right here."

She couldn't tell him to stop. She didn't want him to stop. Tauria didn't care how wrong it was or why he was doing this now; when her life was a parade for others, her desires silenced to display what was proper for the court, she wanted this night to defy everything that was expected of her.

A spike of awareness skipped her pulse, a presence she detected that would soon find them, and there would be no need to speculate on what they were doing as their position left nothing to the imagination. Yet despite the distant approach, Nik's head dipped, and Tauria's sharp inhale curved her spine when his lips pressed against her bare thigh.

"Nik," she breathed. They had to pull apart. They'd be caught, and there'd be no reasoning with the outcry that would come from it, no matter who stumbled upon them.

He laid a second kiss higher, and her legs tried to clamp together, but he eased them apart around him.

"Someone's coming." But despite her words, the pulse in her ears, the tingling of her body, drowned out the protest. She didn't care. She didn't want him to stop.

"Thrilling, isn't it? The thought of being caught in such a scandal," Nik said, the vibration of each word shooting straight to her core. As if he knew it, he didn't stop talking. Words of praise. Of awe. Of desires that painted vivid images in her mind and peaked her pleasure with the want for them to be real. "You're so composed and polite for the court. If only they knew…"

Her breathing quickened and her head tipped back. Her fingers wove through his hair as if to guide his mouth right to where she wanted him. Something warm and building formed in her lower stomach, crawling slowly over her skin.

Tauria shuffled, desperate for any friction as she climbed and climbed.

His third kiss landed at the top of her thigh, and his breath blew across her slickness under her dress, so close to her apex his wicked torture paired with the adrenaline brought her right to the precipice without him even needing to touch her. It was so unexpected stars shot behind her eyes, which clamped shut. Nik's arm circled around her back as she trembled, his mouth claiming hers to muffle her cry.

She barely had a moment to process what had happened when, as her shockwaves began to subside, Nik lifted her down. Her legs were boneless, but he didn't release her until she straightened, her breathing rugged, and finally she found the will to look at him. Bewilderment widened her eyes, but awe and triumph danced in his.

His knuckles brushed her flushed cheek. "So beautiful." Then he took a long breath as he leaned back and scanned her over. "I hope you remember how to behave, love."

That snapped her back to their surroundings.

Oh Gods, she'd let him…

Yet he hadn't done anything except tease and entice her. And that was enough. Her face heated, but not with embarrassment. It was an experience she would never forget—one her mind and body already craved to do again. So reckless, brazen. So sinfully, incredibly wrong.

That presence she'd detected grew stronger, and Tauria straightened, scrambling to piece herself back together when Nik had scattered all her thoughts and decency in minutes. She assessed herself, fixing her gown though it remained all perfectly intact. She couldn't shake the feeling that what they'd done was written over every inch of her.

"You're engaged," she said in bewilderment.

Nik caught her chin, searching her eyes, reading while also straining to tell her something through that firm look. "So are you."

It was unspoken, but the meaning lingered there. He'd suspected all along it wasn't true. Just as she kept her reservations about the believability of him and Samara now she'd watched them together. Only, she couldn't be sure of how much of it was false. Or *why.*

Tauria jerked away. The intruder was so close, nearly within trespassing distance. When she recognized who it was by their scent, she gasped. Her panic reached a sickening point as she realized one crucial thing.

Scent.

They could compose their appearance, but what they'd done would be as good as confessed when their entangled scents gave it away.

"This could ruin everything." It was all she could think.

Nik stepped away from her, putting an arm's length of distance between them as he twisted to look out over the balcony.

"There you are."

Her head whirled to Tarly in the doorway, but her thundering heart stole her speech. She waited on a knife's edge for him to call them out. To immediately detect every reckless, scandalous touch they'd shared.

He didn't. Tarly continued to stroll over to them. His gaze flashed to Nik, who kept his back to the prince, but ultimately his attention was on her. The trail of his eyes down her body stiffened every muscle. She was so tense it was painful. Still, nothing of accusation seemed to be decipherable on his expression. Nothing at all.

"A moment alone?" Tarly's tone was accusatory as he approached, calling out her excuse for leaving the ball and catching her not only with company, but *alone* with Nik.

Her mouth opened, but her words floundered.

"You can escort her back. I only stole a moment to catch up with my ward after seeing her slip out, but we're done here," Nik said, turning to Tarly, his cold expression so sudden and masterful.

The two of them stared off for a few tense seconds while Tauria stood like stone, as if Tarly would see right through the lie. It was a welcome release of anticipation when he broke, his face softening as he upturned his palm.

"You've been missed."

Tauria looked to his palm. She didn't know why she spared one glance at Nik. She didn't regret what they'd done, but fixing her attention back on Tarly, who waited patiently, she was awash with guilt. There was clear tension between her and Nik, and he was channeling it into hostility rather than the scandalous truth. It was brilliant. And a relief. He didn't even spare her a glance, and his lack of desire to be around her was so believable it clenched her chest.

Tauria firmed her own expression. She'd been taught her whole life how to disguise her true feelings, which right now meant the comedown from her high of lust and adrenaline. Sliding her hand into Tarly's, she allowed the prince to lead her back indoors, giving no promise to the King of High Farrow that she would see him alone again.

CHAPTER 38

Nikalias

The eclipse had ended, but Nik couldn't be sure how much time had passed since Tauria left him on that balcony. He hadn't followed them back to the party. He'd needed a moment to accept the choice he'd made. One that, for better or worse, would set him and his mate free.

Nik hadn't known what he would do when he first arrived. He'd wished there were another way. He'd screamed and tormented within his own mind so much that he didn't care what became of himself, but Tauria did not deserve this.

"You've missed most of the celebrations." Samara's voice was careful as she stepped out to join him. He'd detected her hesitant approach minutes ago.

The King of High Farrow stood watching the twilight grow, a beautiful diffusion of pinks and oranges reminding him of summer blooms. Tauria among the flowers…his mother…blissful, carefree days he yearned for instead of this cruel twist of fate. "I've never been a fan of the flamboyance," he commented, not turning as she stepped up to join him.

Her deep breath was one of understanding. "What will you do?"

It was the agony of that question that had rooted him to this very spot since he'd watched Tauria leave with the prince. A decision that was sealed into place the moment she looked back at him one final time. Just as she did at the gates to High Farrow's castle.

"What I should have done a long time ago."

CHAPTER 39

Nikalias

IT HAD BEEN two days since the Solstice Ball, and by next morning, Nik would be leaving Olmstone. He'd barely heard a word of the final council meeting he attended. He rolled his neck in the high collar of his jacket, his skin prickly with a horrible itch, yet he maintained his outward composure, staring at the wolf king as he relayed his final thoughts on the hollow treaty, believing they were all still mindless fools to his game. Nik didn't care for that either, as all he could think about was Tauria. What he had to do, and how he would be leaving her. Each minute counted down to his dreaded declaration.

"I am glad we have all these matters settled to enable us to move forward with the marriage as soon as we can make preparations," Varlas said. The first words to travel in clarity when conversation had distanced to a murmur in Nik's mind in the past hour.

The phantom clock struck its final beat. Nik wished it would still his heart too, which threatened to expose the sound of it breaking. The air was too thick to breathe; the world was lost. But this was what they had to do. The grand finale of the show they'd been born into.

"There is one last thing," Nik spilled.

Tauria's eyes were on him. It took everything in him not to meet them with apology. Varlas's brow lifted in surprise, but all he gave was a nod for Nik to continue and address the council.

His chair groaned across the floor as he rose, drawing all eyes to him while he looked over everyone. Nobles with faces hungry for news or gossip, anything to add flavor to their otherwise miserable existence, as long as it was not an infliction upon themselves. Standing above them all was a move of importance, establishing what he was about to say as no small matter. His eyes fell to Tauria, or they meant to, but all he could focus on with restrained irritation was the hand Tarly held in comfort. She kept her eyes down for as long as she could, displaying her disinterest, or hatred, toward him. But when Tauria forced her sights up, those sparkling hazel pools were a conflict of absolution and heartache.

The room fell silent, but it buzzed with a static of charged anticipation. Nik took a long, deep breath.

"I haven't been completely honest in my reasons for coming here, as what I have still to settle is of a highly personal and important matter. But it affects us all."

Her precious heart picked up tempo, and he wished he could help her. Comfort her. Yet instead, he stood to break her.

"We are allies, Nikalias. I trust whatever it is we can settle this matter together," Varlas assured him.

Nik gave a stiff nod. He couldn't take his eyes off her, willing her to read his apology as their surroundings left him no choice but to appear heartless and cruel. "Tauria Stagknight is not only my ward…"

Time slowed to a crawl.

But he'd made his choice.

"She is my mate."

At his declaration, Tauria's lips parted. Tarly's hand left her, and the gasps swirled like shadows of judgment and shock over Nik's bold statement. He couldn't place her feelings, but it was all he focused on. Anger—no, rage. That seemed more appropriate. Expected. Not at the secret he kept, but the humiliation of hearing the term thrown out so casually to a room of royals and strangers. As though it meant nothing.

As though *she* meant nothing to him.

Tauria rose, and he wondered if anyone else could feel her wrath as tangibly as he did in the glare she kept on him.

"This is an unexpected shock indeed," Varlas said, his tone matching the general mood of disbelief. "You did not know, Tauria?"

Her eyes flexed with embarrassment. "No," she gritted out.

The king released a long sigh. "And you, Nikalias. How long have you known this?"

He winced in apology for her alone while his expression steeled for those gathered. "A while," he said coldly, tearing his eyes away from her daggers of anguish. "It is not a bond I was willing to server so brazenly until I knew there would be no use for it. As you know, a rejected mate bond cannot be undone." His chest was tearing open from the inside out.

"And you waited until now?" Varlas interrogated, his tone sharp with an edge of suspicion.

Nik's confidence was unwavering. "I did not want to mention it upon my arrival and sway concentration away from the matters that will advance our kingdoms forward. This is the final obstacle in the way. I came to Olmstone to secure this alliance, yes. And that starts by severing the bond between Tauria and me so we are free to marry with our hearts instead."

"Then get it over with," Tauria sneered like venom.

He deserved the agony of the soul-deep wound that tone touched inside. His fists were tight at his sides, straining from letting slip the arrogance he had to wear for the vultures of the court.

"Varlas, if I may request a moment alone with Tauria."

"I don't think that would be wise," Varlas answered cautiously.

"It is a sensitive and private matter, as I'm sure you can respect."

"I do. But I also know the pull of a bond is a powerful thing." A brief flicker of pain quietened his voice. "I think for both of your protection, it would be best if this was overseen."

It was an effort not to protest further with the flare of insult. They weren't children in need of observation. Nik thought the anger and disdain that coated the air between them would be assurance enough, but Varlas wasn't going to agree to their complete solitude.

"I don't require alone time for this," Tauria muttered icily. She didn't wait for anyone's permission or to glance who would be sent to follow them as she stormed from the hall.

Every step she took was agony to watch. His heart beat, but only in halves. Then Nik followed her, wondering how he was going to bear leaving this kingdom as half a soul.

CHAPTER 40

Tauria

TAURIA LED THE way into the pavilion garden. Her chest was heaving, struggling to grapple her tethers of control and not break down completely. She halted before the wooden structure. Faintly, over the pounding in her chest, she felt only Nik lingering at her back. But she knew someone—or several people—would have subtle eyes and ears on them from behind the glass doors.

Nik approached carefully, but she couldn't bear to look at him as she spoke.

"All I can think of is…how could I have been so dim-witted to have missed it?"

"You're not—"

"Until I realized it's because of you. It all makes sense now." She turned to him, the first betrayal of her shattered feelings slipping down her cheek. She didn't hide how deep the wound cut her.

Nik's face was desolate.

"You knew what I was to you since that night we spent together.

Perhaps I might have suspected it too, but you were so good at convincing me I was wrong. Neither of us voiced the word. *Mates.* Yet we both knew it. And you led me to believe I was simply a pining fool, another one of your fawning *courtesans.*" She was trembling with the pain when the light of clarity shed on their mess of a relationship. Nik took a step toward her, but Tauria backed up one in response. It wasn't without resistance on that tether between them, and she bit back her whimper. "I don't want it," she whispered. "But you never had desire for it anyway. Just a bond of power, right?"

"Wrong."

Nik's voice was so broken she struggled to keep her composure. He was fighting against spilling more; his eyes faltered as though remembering the spectators who watched them.

"Don't do that," she pleaded quietly, defeat so close to making her buckle.

Nik took another step forward, and against the moonlight she glimpsed silver lapping around his eyes. Tauria had never seen him cry. Not when he lost his mother, nor when his hand was forced to kill his father. Nikalias Silvergriff had been through so much and never once shed a tear in company despite his misery.

"Do what?"

"Don't act like this is *easy* for me." Her voice rose with indignation. "Don't pretend I didn't wait for you. For decades. Staying by your side when you didn't deserve it…you didn't deserve *me*."

"You're right. I don't. I'm not sure I ever have or ever will."

"You're a coward," she gritted through a pained sob. "A liar."

"Yes."

"You're selfish and cruel."

Nik only nodded, but each of her words emitted a wince from him that she felt like a dagger. His pain—she felt it all.

"Stop agreeing with me!"

The air around them stirred with her rising anger. That he was submitting with no resistance.

"I can't."

"Then tell me *why!*" She couldn't stop the flash of lost control as her hands cast out and her wind collected around them. Nik shielded his eyes, but she uncomfortably reined in her magick that trembled her body.

"I love you."

Nik's voice could have been mistaken for the whisper of her wind, which silenced immediately at his words. Her arms fell and her face blanched, disbelieving she'd heard him right.

"Before I knew what bond binds us, I fell in love with you. For your resilience, your patience, for every flaw and every triumph. I love you enough to set you free."

Tauria was shaking her head. She didn't believe he would confess this now. It only served as a cruel and wicked torture.

"I've wronged you in more ways I could ever atone for. I pushed you away in my arrogance and selfishness. Perhaps in my denial. I don't deserve you, and I never will."

Something soul-deep cried out painfully, stealing her breath and stilling her heart as she anticipated his next words before he spoke them.

"Reject the bond, Tauria."

Breath left her body. She fought a refusal to ever inhale again. "There's no taking it back." Her tone was a betrayal of her anger, and she despised the plea that sounded in it.

Nik's nod cleaved her world in half. "It's for the best. For both of us."

Her lips trembled, and she pressed them tight. Tauria knew what she had to say. The words circled and tormented and danced like ash on her tongue, threatening to spill. She could do this. For him, for Fenstead—she *had* to do this.

"I wanted it to be you," she confessed, knowing she wouldn't get another chance. Knowing it didn't matter anymore. "I wanted to take it all back with you by my side at the end of it all."

Pain. So much pain filled those emerald eyes as he whispered, "I know."

Her heart pounded with defiance.

Her mind scrambled between protest and anguish.

Her body went taut all over, fists clenching so tight the sting of her nails cutting her palms was a welcome distraction but not nearly enough to counter what tore her soul in agony.

Tauria's lips parted, her tears falling, as she began to recite the words she could never take back. Words that would change everything.

"With the Gods as my witness and this by will…" Her voice croaked. She lost all strength, all bravery, as she stared at the image that would haunt her for the rest of her days.

Nik's green irises glittered with misery, his broken heart etched on his perfect face. Yet he nodded for her to continue. Approaching tentatively, he unsheathed a short dagger. His cold hand took her trembling one, pressing the hilt to her palm and closing her fingers around it. "It's okay," he whispered.

He let her go.

Tauria took a few seconds to surface the world-shifting statement. She looked at the blade wavering in her tight grip, reflecting the tranquil moon and stars. Tauria spared a slow blink to calm herself and then angled the edge across the flesh of her palm. Her warm blood trickled down her fingers, droplets falling to the stone floor. Tauria spilled the blood that should have been his to claim…to sever all that could have bound them eternally instead.

"I reject the soul-bond to Nikalias Silvergriff, King of High Farrow, first of his name. I release both you and me from that which binds us, so we may be free to choose our own fate of power and heart."

Nik clenched his teeth, slowly falling to one knee as though the bond were being severed agonizingly within. But he made no sound. He kept his eyes on her, tears falling, until his head bowed in defeat. Tauria couldn't bite back the sob that left her. She approached him one last time and couldn't stop her other hand as it reached out to cup his cheek, forcing those lost eyes to stare up at her. The moonlight flooded his features, turning them beautifully soft. Vulnerable. Her thumb brushed the wetness there, and Nik's hand closed over hers, a ghost's touch against her warm brown skin.

"You are free, Nik." Tauria lifted her chin, her gaze catching on Tarly beyond the glass door. His face was stony, utterly unreadable. She assumed he'd heard every word. The prince's gaze only fell to Nik for a second before he twisted and walked away.

Her hand fell limp. "I don't want to see you again," Tauria said, her voice stripped of any joy, any semblance of her former self. "Go back to High Farrow. Forget about me. We will both learn to move on from this."

Squaring her shoulders, Tauria left him on his knees, each step away weighted with world-shattering sorrow. A void had opened in her heart that would never be filled. Not without him. Her silent tears flowed, unable to get the broken image out of her mind. But she raised her chin, filling that hole with determination to do what she had to do.

Tauria left Nik, and she didn't look back.

CHAPTER 41

Tauria

Tauria watched the flood of royal blue preparing to leave from a balcony overlooking the front courtyard. Maybe it was cowardly of her to insist she couldn't bear to face Nik after last night. But for once, she wasn't fought on her request.

She stared after the horse Nik took off on. There was a pain in her chest that strained with every measure of distance. She'd spent every minute since parting with him tunneling into a cold numbness. It was the only way to see this through.

Tarly's presence was at her back, but she didn't turn to him as she watched Samara being helped into the carriage that would trail after the king.

"Shouldn't you be seeing to the send-off?" she asked calmly, trying to muster some semblance of normality.

"My father is handling it just fine." He strode up to her, and with his tentative steps, it was odd to imagine the prince was *afraid* to trigger her emotions. "It would be a ridiculous question, so I won't ask how you're feeling."

Tauria's mouth faintly curled with gratitude. "I won't bother to lie and say I'm fine."

Tarly huffed a light laugh, coming to stand beside her, but they both watched the ensemble below. "Are you sure you know what you're doing?" he asked carefully.

"I don't think any of us know that."

"That's a fair claim."

She inhaled a long breath. "This is what is best for our kingdoms. Even Nik knew duty would always come before all else." Tauria shifted her full attention onto the prince and immediately realized her error in his wince. "I'm sorry, I didn't mean—"

"You're right," he cut in icily. "I was a young fool for what I attempted to do. But I guess fate has a way of steering us onto the right path when we sway. Even by the most desolate means."

Tauria didn't respond. Didn't have any words of consolation or agreement. Side by side, they had become two lost and tragic souls. She had thought she would cast the prince away the moment he came looking for her, yet now she was *glad* for his company. His heart had not thawed for her, and maybe it never would. But she had begun to realize despite this that hers might have matched his all along.

"I'm sorry I never told you about my past with Nik. We were young and foolish. It was one night and nothing more." Tauria spoke the truth with ease in her acceptance now.

"I can't say I'm surprised. But we all have past mistakes. Don't be sorry for it."

The word "mistake" didn't settle right in her stomach, but she gave no outward reaction. Instead, she found herself asking, "Can I trust you?"

"This again?"

Tauria smiled, and it echoed genuine playfulness.

"I meant what I said to him." Tarly stared after the King of High Farrow with an expression that was hard to place. "I don't know what we'll discover here, but there's a darkness rolling in. I showed you your way out, and if it ever comes to it, I expect you to take it and not look back. Not for me."

She shook her head. "I can't promise that."

"You can, and you will. If not for me, nor for him, then you will for Fenstead, or your parents' sacrifice so you could live will have been for nothing." Tarly cut deep and without hesitation, meaning to strike her with a will to survive, but it was overcome by the stabbing of guilt. The prince cast his eyes over the courtyard one final time, and she followed his gaze just in time to see the spec of Nik disappear completely.

Tarly twisted from the balcony, hands sliding into his pockets as he made to leave. "Take a few days to heal, Tauria, but don't let your guard down for a second." His voice was a hush in the wind. "I'll find you soon."

CHAPTER 42

Nikalias

King Nikalias Silvergriff stormed the halls of his castle, needing to be away from eyes, ears—everything. He wasn't sure he could tame the storm within him should he come to face anyone before he had a moment to calm and compose himself.

The journey back was torturous, every single step farther away from her building the hot rage that coursed through his veins now he risked damning every detrimental consequence to turn back. For her. Every marker of distance he felt with physical, painful resistance.

A blonde head came into his view down the hall before his private council room. He halted before opening the door, locking eyes with Marlowe. All she gave was a small dip of her head. There was an understanding, a *knowing,* in her ocean-eyed look of pity that told him she knew. It was done. And there was no going back.

Without a word, Nik almost took the door off its hinges as he entered the room and slammed it behind him. He paced to the window and tried to soothe his mind, but it was hopeless. Storming to his desk, there was no hesitation before he scattered everything on it to find some outlet for his frustration. No—*rage.* So new and raw he didn't know what to do with it.

I didn't have a choice.

Nik paced again. His breathing was heavy. He needed to distract himself from every primal instinct that roared within him at how wrong it was for him to be here. To be so far from her.

Then he halted, gripping the table so hard while his head bowed that splinters caught in his fingers. He raised a hand, needing to undo the ties that felt suffocating around his neck. Not out of tightness, but for what they concealed.

His fingers slowly moved.

His teeth clamped down so hard they almost broke when he felt it.

Because he felt *her.*

When his touch lingered over Tauria's mating mark.

He may admire Tauria for her spectacular display in the garden, but Nik knew…it wasn't all an act. The words she spoke may have been for the audience that surrounded them in that moment, but they were so convincing because they were true.

There'd been a long moment when he didn't think he'd even get the chance to voice his plan while he awaited Tauria on the rooftop the night that followed the Solstice Ball.

But she'd come. She always did.

It was a night he would never forget, both tormenting and treasured. Every emotion and secret that had poured from them both, what they'd done together in the forgotten room she led him to. Then the life-changing sealing of that which now bound them eternally.

Every blissful, elated high of that moment had been cruelly short-lived.

And this new primal, damning need to be near her was all-consuming when he was the exact opposite. The distance between them now was inexplicably maddening, especially layered with thoughts of

Tarly's hands on her that trembled Nik with unjustified murderous desires toward the prince.

The mating bond was the only sure way for Tauria and Nik to harbor a line of communication that couldn't be taken from them. Nightwalking was not an option if they would always be suspicious of him.

And it was for their kingdoms that they'd done it.

It had been Marlowe's plan. Her brilliant idea was not only a means of keeping Tauria safely in contact with them, but a way of ensuring both their kingdoms had two monarchs in the way in case anyone tried to take the other. Still, with the sense of foreboding that surrounded the concept—*mating*—Nik had instantly refused the idea before he left for Olmstone. It wasn't until he saw her, spoke to her, that everything changed.

Suddenly, the world quietened as he felt the gentle pull within. In his desperation, Nik dropped every mental guard, opening himself completely to the bond as Tauria's essence echoed through him and Nik breathed in reprieve. At hearing the first notes of her somber voice, his eyes clamped shut, and he leaned against the desk.

"What I said…I didn't mean it, Nik."

He bowed his head while he clutched the desk so tightly he faintly heard it crack. His arms were stiff. She should be here, by his side, where he could protect her. Touch her. *Gods,* the insatiable rise of desire to feel her again and close himself off to the world for endless days and nights could kill him…

"Yes, you did. But that's okay. I plan to have forever to make amends with you, Tauria."

Something like pain weaved with agreement filtered through the bond.

"Be safe. Until I come back for you. I love you."

Tauria,

I see how much you have grown and how you stand proud on your own. Though do not take my leaving as goodbye, I am here still and should the stag meet the wolf your call is answered.

I am so proud of the ruler you have become. You florish in Olmstone purple, but when it meets the vibrancy of our home, only then do you represent the queen you were born to be.

Lycus.

END
GAME
PART III
KINGDOM OF
OLMSTONE
HOUSE
WOLVERLON

CHAPTER 43

Three weeks earlier
Tauria

Tauria lay in bed, but her traitorous mind wouldn't ignore the beckoning call she felt. The irritating pull of Nik's words, which rang on repeat from the previous night.

Meet me on the rooftops.

With a huff of frustration, she tumbled out of bed. Dressed, she continued to pace, deliberating. She didn't owe him anything, and she agonized in a tug-of-war between her head and heart. Giving him what he wanted rang with weakness.

That was what Nik was. Her infuriating, maddening weakness.

And the bastard knew it.

Every thought was pushed down in anger as she scaled the roof. Nik would get what he wanted, but her presence would be far from inviting. Tauria had succumbed to the need to see him alone again one last time. She couldn't deny there'd been unspoken words between them, and she knew they wouldn't be granted another chance like this again before he was set to return to High Farrow in two days. And tomorrow would be filled with long, grueling meetings to lay down the treaty for her marriage alliance with Tarly.

Before she tracked Nik down, Tauria wanted to enjoy some alone time soaring over the rooftops. She retrieved her staff at her waist as she ran, toeing over narrow edges and leaping over small gaps. Olmstone's castle was built like an alluring assault course for one with her ability. The wind was alive, and with her willingness to harness it she felt it embrace her with a welcoming caress.

She raced the wind. Challenged it. Then became it.

Her staff twisted between her hands over her head to catch an updraft as she leaped between two flat planes that would be too far apart for her to attempt to jump without her ability. Her landing was silent and graceful, but she didn't pause. Coming to two slanted roofs, she hopped with feline stealth between them, her staff pushing the air to aid her, and it was like rowing through an invisible stream. Faster and faster.

In her high of adrenaline to keep from toppling from the fatal height, Tauria didn't know when she started to cry. Her breaths cut like glass up her throat when she finally halted abruptly, and the exertion caught up with her all at once. If she weren't aware of the guards surrounding her from far below, she would have screamed. An unexplainable bubble of emotions she couldn't make sense of barreled to the surface.

"It's been a long time since you've let yourself go so thoroughly."

She didn't want to hear his voice. But she needed it. Just like every other time. It was the only balm that could soothe the wounds that tore afresh. Her failures. Her hopelessness. Her losses. Everything that screamed what she buried so deep just to carry on.

That she was not enough. Not worthy.

Tauria didn't move to pin Nik's location while she caught her breath and let her tears dry out without a sob. He'd witnessed her lose control to all she barricaded before. It was ugly and exhausting, but he always knew exactly how to approach her. Now, it only roused her anger and clenched her pain. Because she longed for it. For him.

Tauria spun, riding the high of her indignation. Her eyes or her heart knew exactly where he stood cloaked in shadow. "Was it all a lie?"

Nik stepped out for the moonlight to catch him. The sight made her rage with conflicting emotion, but above all…she hurt so deeply she thought she might stop breathing.

"I want you to come back." She echoed his words from High Farrow, uncaring that her voice broke to crumble her mask. "Was it all a lie?"

"No."

"So, what…? You wanted me by your side as a trophy alongside your new queen?"

"I know I don't deserve it, but I need you to listen to me. Just hear what I have to tell you, and then every choice is yours."

It didn't make sense. A game—that was all this was to him. And she was the fool in play.

"You're not safe here," he said, taking a step toward her.

Tauria stood firm. "We're the ones who told you of the threat, Nik. You don't get to pretend as if you suddenly care."

His brow furrowed while closing the gap another step, and she tracked the shortening distance. "Did you truly believe I abandoned you?"

Tauria huffed an incredulous laugh. "Well, you certainly have been keeping yourself occupied."

"They've been blocking your mind, Tauria," Nik bit out harshly.

She blinked at the darkening anger that clouded his face.

"After all we've been through, how could you think I would leave you here without checking in at all?"

Because it's easier to believe. "What else was I supposed to think when the moment I left you were *courting* someone else?"

"Are we going to pretend you haven't been doing the same?"

Tauria tightened her lips, almost spilling the falsehood in everything about her seemingly budding relationship with Tarly. She had no reason to keep it from him—except for in petty defiance.

"That was always clear. I never lied to you about my intentions here."

"Yet you kissed me back. In High Farrow and here. Both times you could have said no, and I would have obliged in an instant, but you didn't."

Nik started to close the distance between them. He was so close that she knew she should back away, but she couldn't. "Is there something you wish to tell me?" His tone rumbled low. A dare. Enticing her to confess.

"I could ask you the same thing." Her sharp intake of breath was swallowed by the wind when she felt his hands skim hers. Not to hold, as they continued to travel upward, over her forearms, past her elbows. Tauria and Nik never broke eye contact, strong with intensifying anguish and frustration.

"When the news came of your engagement, I had to see it for myself. I had to know…" A muscle in his jaw flexed as he watched his hand on her. "Is there somewhere we can go? Someplace no one would think to trespass on us for a while?" he asked quietly. Thickly.

She wanted to push him away, but the voice was distant compared to that which screamed for her to close the space between them. It should be wrong, but nothing had ever felt so right.

So against all, Tauria nodded. She could give him this—a moment to explain. As for what would become of them after…she only hoped he wouldn't break her once and for all.

Tauria led them with stealth and caution over the rooftops until they slipped in through the window Tarly had once guided her to. Her escape route. Inside the small, forgotten room, she shook with a sense of unease in remembrance of the hidden passage beyond the bookcase her eyes landed on now. Extending her senses revealed no one around or down there.

She turned to Nik just in time to watch him close the door, but then he dipped for something in his pocket. When he raised it to the wood, a small pulse of light emitted from its center, a shimmering essence that seemed to expel from it, which she would have missed if she'd blinked. Her mouth fell open when Nik let it go but it stayed in place.

"It's a concealment stone." Nik answered her questioning look. "No one can hear a thing past that door or these walls. We can talk freely."

Tauria's hard expression returned despite her curiosity about the strange object she had never seen nor read about before. "I don't think that will be necessary for what I have to say."

"Why didn't you give up on me, Tauria?"

It wasn't what she was expecting, and the sudden shift in conversation had her scrambling for an answer to his question. The same question she'd asked herself a million times already and knew she didn't have an answer to give.

"I had nowhere else to go."

"I pushed you away. I was cold, and perhaps cruel."

Tauria gritted her teeth, hating his encouragement for her to lash out. Or maybe it was enlightenment at how much of a pining fool she'd been and he'd known it all along. Was he mocking her for it?

"Yet you still never gave up. You could have shut me out completely after all I put you through. Do you think I didn't know how much I hurt you every time you witnessed someone entering my rooms?" He was goading her to break. "Do you think I didn't notice your look of resentment, of sadness, yet I did it anyway?"

"Stop," she pleaded.

"I *wanted* you to hate me," he continued. The knife was turning, and she was bleeding freely. "I pushed and I pushed, but you still came back. You defended me, consoled me. Why?"

"Because I had nowhere else to go," she repeated.

Lies.

Nik knew it. "You're very clever, Tauria. Surely you've thought it. At least once, you have suspected it."

Her heart was pounding, her mind swirling with so much confusion and pain it was dizzying.

"Say it."

She shook her head in denial. His eyes narrowed with rising intensity. The distance between them closed in. It wasn't conscious effort; it was gravity. Their own invisible pull. She'd tried to fight it so many times, but it had always been futile.

"If you won't then I will."

"Please—"

"Mates."

She never would have thought a single word could hold so much power. That it could awaken her with clarity but cut her down in an instant.

Nik's voice fell, careful. "You've known it too. Some part of you has always known."

She might have nodded were it not for the shock that stifled her movement and froze her blood with an icy chill. As though this were a piece of information that had been locked away, entombed, for over a century in her refusal to believe it. That fate could deal her such a tragic hand as to be the mate of someone who didn't want her.

"You're a damn fool, Nikalias," she muttered with a shake of her head.

Nik's brow lifted. Tauria was pulled in by those emerald eyes, but not by the bond. Maybe she'd always known why they felt like home but refused to acknowledge what they reminded her of.

Fenstead. The color of her kingdom encircled his pupils.

"It means nothing," she whispered in defeat.

Nik's expression turned to a blank, stunned.

"It means nothing... because it was always *you,* not a bond, that made me come back despite everything."

His eyes fluttered. Pain. He didn't want to hear her truth for the guilt it rose inside of him, but she didn't stop.

"It was you who helped me rise when I fell and never let me crumble again. You teased and tormented and were a royal pain in my ass, but Nik...you saved me. And I wanted it to be you. I *chose* you. But you didn't choose me back." Her voice had been reduced to no more than a whimper. Getting to voice the feelings she'd buried for so long and so deep was an ache like nothing she'd felt before. And now she finally stood to bare her whole heart to him. "I stayed by your side because every time you pushed, it was only halfway. And I couldn't figure out why. Why would you want to keep me close when you had no desire for anything more between us? And like a pitiful fool, I couldn't let you go. Not while—"

"You are my silent war," he hushed out as though he knew exactly what she thought. Tauria couldn't suppress her wince. "You're the war I've fought for over a century. One I can't ever win."

"Why?"

"I love you, Tauria."

Her breath stilled. The silence of the air was tense and electrifying. That pull between them became so strong she had to fight it with physical resistance. Only, she couldn't be sure whether she wanted to kiss or slap him.

"You don't get to say that to me. Not now." She meant to hiss the words, but they tumbled out with the quietness of a plea.

"I'm irrevocably *in* love with you. I have been for a very long time."

"Stop." Now it was a beg. Because his words twisted and twisted the dagger in her chest, and she couldn't be sure why he was hurting her past the point of no salvation.

"I can't. Because you deserve to know why I pushed you away all this time—yes, only halfway, because I need you, Tauria. In whatever way I can have you, I need you close. I'll never forgive myself for how selfish I was that I couldn't let you go to find the happiness you deserve."

Tears of anguish slipped past her defenses. "You did let me go."

Nik shook his head. "It's not real. Nothing with Samara is real. Only a means to silence any speculation about my feelings for you that could put you in danger here."

She couldn't stand it. The half-truths, the suppression. She'd dealt with it all for so long, but he'd finally broken her. "I wish I had never fled to High Farrow."

Her words seemed to hit deep. Nik was masterful at steeling his expression, but she learned every flicker that gave away his feelings behind the mask. This was more than a flinch; there was a tightening in his whole demeanor. A slight shrink that told her he was hurt too deeply to fight back with anger.

"You don't mean that."

Did she? There was so much conflict battering her mind she could do nothing but own her words. In that moment, she realized this night would change everything between them, but she was uncertain whether it would be for better or worse.

Tauria had to turn from him. She paced to the dark, sad firepit, focusing on her deep breaths to reel her composure—which was threatening to shatter all at once—back in. Was this the night they would finally let each other go?

She felt Nik's approach from behind, felt him slowly closing the distance between them at her back. She knew he was getting too close, but she couldn't stop him. Not when she felt the echoes of his warmth. Not when he hesitated mere inches behind her. Tauria inhaled a breath that was a partial whimper when his body pressed to hers, hands grazing her arms. She couldn't stop him. She couldn't find the strength to step away.

"Tell me it's not real," Nik said, his low voice traveling like sand down the column of her neck.

"I can't," she got out, fighting against the *need* to lean into him and angle her head in response.

"This night, right now, decides everything." Nik's hand moved from her arm to travel over her abdomen. Slowly. Precisely. As if he knew the map of her body to trace the perfect path. "Tell me you don't love him."

Tauria meant to shake her head, but she couldn't be sure any movement had been made when Nik drew her closer, tight with anticipation, skipping a pulse of her heart. "Why does it matter?"

His nose grazed the tip of her ear, and she could do nothing but submit to his cruel game. He had her ensnared. "I need to know I'm not taking anything from you before you hear what I have to say."

It didn't make sense, but she wasn't even sure she cared anymore while she focused on his touch, his warm breath. Nik was a drug that could kill her, and she forgot all her reservations. Forgot why this was so wrong. Forgot everything bad that came of submitting to the feeling in his presence.

"Do you love him, Tauria?"

"No." She let the truth slip, but immediately her lips tightened shut. She found the will to pull out of his grip and turned to him with rising anger. "Is that what you want to hear? Does that make you feel good, Nik?"

Anger shifted his jaw. "I've not felt *good* since that night you were mine."

"Don't," she warned. Or maybe pleaded.

"And I was yours."

"You don't get to pretend that I wouldn't have given myself to you again and again. You used me, and you left me. I was the fool for believing I was anything more to you than the dozen others who took my place." Her chest rose and fell deeply. Her throat burned. The freedom of her decades-long torment came at the price of a pain so crushing she wondered how she was going to make it out alive.

"There is not a soul in any realm who could take your place."

Tauria shook her head. She was faltering, her fool's heart clinging to words her mind rebelled against. In the end, her anger triumphed. "I might have loved you once. But now I think I *hate* you."

Nik gave no warning, no hesitation, as he closed the gap between them. His hands took her face, and his lips crashed to hers.

Tauria answered to it. Spirits be *damned*, she did. She couldn't stop the response of her body as it came alive with his touch.

He pulled away abruptly, eyes wild and blazing. "Say that again. But say it like you mean it, Tauria."

They stared off in challenge as he held her still, matching hard breaths of anguish.

"I *hate* you, Nikalias."

"Not convincing enough." He brought his head down to meet her once more, and they collided in a battle of love and hate, decades of warring feelings she couldn't suppress, until enough of her rational mind had returned to strike her with fear. Tauria gasped as she pulled away, her hand on his chest to keep him from kissing her again while she scrambled to remember where they were—*who* they were.

"What are we doing?" Horror swept her. Guilt twisted in her gut as she thought of the unaware second parties in all this, right within trespassing distance.

The desire in Nik's eyes was claiming. Tauria swallowed hard, struggling to regain her composure as she put a step of distance between them.

"It's not real," he ground out. "The worst torture has been watching you believe it so easily."

"*You* made it easy!" Her heart pounded furiously. "I waited for you.

For decades. You made it easy for me to believe you didn't want me. You had others—"

"They were all just a front too. I don't care how pitiful it sounds to admit none of them gained anything except an empty reputation with me. Because I wanted you to hate me if you thought I had no regard for how much that night meant to me. I wanted you to forget me on your own when I didn't have the strength to push you away for good."

"And Faythe?" The vile, resenting thought slipped past her lips in the heat of the moment, one she'd never allowed to see the light before. But the truth was…Tauria had agonized over it for far too long when she first found out about their ventures together. She loved Faythe and surfaced no judgment of her for following her human heart in the moment. But Nik knew…

His expression twisted with pain then fell with defeat. He didn't look away from her, owning his next words. "In my selfishness I needed to know I could feel something again. And I did. Faythe helped me to *feel* again. I never intended for it to go as far as it did, but it was like this strange curiosity between us," he confessed.

Tauria had to break her gaze, wishing she could steal her last words back. Perhaps ignorance would be a bliss in comparison to the deep wound of the truth.

"But in her I saw you. Your resilience. Your defiance. Faythe needed help, and I knew I was the only one who could assist. We became close as naturally as if I'd known her for a lifetime. I can't explain it."

Tauria's cracked heart splintered a fraction more. Because she understood that pull toward the impossible human.

"I can't justify why I gave in to those awakened feelings with her. I can't ever justify all the ways in which I've wronged you. And her. She knows everything."

Tauria recoiled with embarrassment. "For how long?" How long had Faythe tiptoed around her with the knowledge?

"Only since she visited me through Nightwalking. You had made up your mind to leave for Olmstone, and I had to tell her—"

"Tell her how much of an idiot I've been for pining after someone who doesn't want me!"

"I want you," Nik snapped. His breaths came harder; his fists trembled at his sides. She couldn't be sure what he was restraining himself against—anger or the impulsive need to give in to the gravity between them. "So badly that it often doesn't feel like a want. You are a *need*, Tauria. Like air to breathe and a heart to bleed. I feared for a long time what I would become when the time came to let you go once and for all. And when the news came about your engagement…"

She swallowed hard. In her mind, she was exhausted. His words conflicted with his actions, and she didn't know what to believe.

"You could have had me." Her voice fell, tired from all the emotions he'd dragged up at once that she'd spent so long suppressing. "Why did you push me away?"

Nik was warring with himself, a look she was all too familiar with. She didn't think she'd survive the strike of disappointment this time. But then…defeat. His posture faltered; his face turned ghostly as though he'd committed a heinous crime. This side of the battle he fought she had never seen before. But his opposition was not happiness or love or triumph. It was a force darker and stronger than any other.

"Because I'm destined to kill you."

A violent chill swept her. They were just words. Ludicrous, near laughable in their incredulity. But accompanied by the pale look of terror that washed his skin and glittered in his emerald eyes, any instinct to ridicule the notion was smothered by a blanket of ice.

"What are you talking about?"

"I learned it not long after we—" Nik's breath slowed. "It's always been you, Tauria. Since before I even realized who you were to me. I chose you the day I met you. For your stubbornness that wasn't afraid to challenge my far from warm reception. For your effortless laughter that brought me so much joy when I didn't deserve it. For your resilience in all you faced and overcame. I would have chosen you until the end… and then I learned that to love you was to condemn you. That by my hand, the one I was soul-bonded to was destined to die. And suddenly, nothing else mattered. Nothing but keeping you safe from me. I know you. You wouldn't have believed it, and even if you did, I knew you would have wanted to take that risk. But I couldn't. I have many regrets about how I treated you in the height of my fear, in my foolishness, thinking I was protecting you by hurting you. Because I believed it was nothing compared to the final *unfathomable* way I could hurt you if we were together."

She heard the words, but her feelings couldn't translate them. Make *sense* of them. "You truly believe you could harm me?" Because she couldn't. Not for a second.

"I don't believe I would ever lay a hand on you in malice. I would sooner end myself if there was ever a moment of doubt."

"Then it means nothing."

"Faythe confirmed it."

Tauria was both surprised and unsurprised at the mention.

"The creature who damned me with the knowledge, Faythe had encountered one before, and what she was told came to pass. Caius…"

Tauria's mind sprinted to the conclusion that drew a gasp from her. *Gods above.* If Faythe knew her friend was going to die… Tauria breathed through the guilt that she hadn't known the burden of her loss.

"I thought that by keeping you at a distance you would be safe from it. From me. That without the mating bond complete it could never come to pass. But now—" His words stopped. Her heart might have too. Along with time, gravity, and anything else that anchored them to this world. "It's the only thing I can think of to save you right now. To know you're safe here while you figure out what you have to. And for High

Farrow, possibly even Fenstead, both of which are at risk of falling to the same evil as my father without this security."

"What are you saying?" She knew. But she wouldn't let that slither of hope mark it as true or real.

"Varlas was just as prepared for us as we tried to be for him. He's blocking me from being able to Nightwalk to you. I assume it's in your food or something else you could easily figure out with a little time. But if he discovers you're no longer taking it and I have ties to you, I don't want to imagine what he'll do. Then there's my reign. I discovered a document signed by my father and many of my nobles that favors Lord Zarrius as next in line for the throne should I pass before my time. It places a deadly target on my back, and my life aside, I won't let High Farrow fall to malicious hands again. The threat against me, against High Farrow, won't be so prominent if there's an overruling candidate for my throne should anything happen to me."

Tauria's hand went to her mouth. How could she not have thought of it sooner? Because in her own misery and heartache, while she was being fed the tales of Nik's courtship in High Farrow, she had so easily believed it was him who'd cut off all communication. *Wanted* something to blame him for in her feelings of abandonment. "Oh Gods," she muttered, reeling over everything.

Nik came a step closer, taking her hand away to hold her chin. "I haven't stopped thinking about you. Not for a damned minute. I'm sorry I didn't realize it sooner, but I wanted to believe you were happy here, that you had found happiness without me and you were blocking me from being able to see it. It was an entirely selfish and pitiful way of thinking, and I left you in danger because of it. But not anymore."

"Who can overrule Zarrius's right to reign if it's written in a law passed by your father and nobles?"

"It was Marlowe who discovered it. She's utterly brilliant, and it didn't take her long to find a loophole in such a decree. An ancient law that grants one other the first right to reign should a monarch fall."

There was a pause of thickening silence as though he knew she'd figure out the answer before he had to say it.

"A mate," she breathed.

Nik nodded. "A soul-bonded partner. It is not a law of High Farrow, but a law of Ungardia, forged so long ago in agreement that there could be no better match for a fallen monarch than their mate. An equal in power. If we were blood-bonded, they would have to dare to take us both down to lay rightful claim to either throne. But Tauria—" Nik seemed to be fighting a conflict that had been tearing him apart for so long. Knowing she was the cause almost pulled the world from under her. "It is dangerous. I won't ever force your hand, and know that before I suggest this we can always find another way. We can leave tonight. I want you to know that I would go to war for you. Because you are Fenstead, but you are also High Farrow. And no matter what you choose, I am yours. Even if you cannot be mine."

Her hand closed around his at her cheek, and her face pinched at hearing the words she'd craved for a lifetime. "What is your plan, Nik?"

His eyes were full of terror. And longing. And desperation. Then his words, like a verse of a long desired but forbidden love, stilled her heart.

"We claim the bond."

Silence. Still, suspended silence.

"Tonight."

CHAPTER 44

Tauria

Tauria jerked away from Nik with the shock of his statement. She thought it over. And over and over. She wanted it. *Gods,* there was never anything that sang with so much glee and pleasure within her. She'd wanted him since that first night. Before the bond, Tauria realized she'd chosen him back. But they were never two souls who were free to surrender to such a blessing without danger following in its wake. Judgment and fear chased the path of their happiness.

"If it works…it's also the only communication line that can't be stifled. They can't take it from us even when I'm back in High Farrow. The mating bond is the only thing strong enough not only to maintain communication, but to allow me to feel if you're in danger."

"They would know," she breathed, trying to scramble together the rest of Nik's plan that would make their mating bond acceptable.

Nik's eyes fell to her wrist, and Tauria's followed, to the bracelet she wore, an *engagement* gift from him. "Marlowe has been practicing spell magick," he said. Tauria's brow rose at that, unsure of what conclusion he was about to draw but bewildered to learn her friend was capable of such things. “It conceals my scent on you. On the balcony yesterday, you should know I never intended to try it out so recklessly. My scent was already on you from the dance, but afterward…no one detected what we shared beyond that.”

Her cheeks warmed in reflection, flashing her desire, and Nik might have sensed it with the shift of his eyes.

“I’m hoping it’s strong enough to conceal the scent of the mating bond. As infuriating as the mere thought is, because I want the world to know you belong to me, and I to you. That you always have and always will be mine.”

Tauria blinked at the item. The brilliance of it wavered with a slight note of uncertainty. Should it prove not to be strong enough magick for the bond…this would condemn them both to fight their way out of here instead. A huge, frightening risk.

“We don’t have much more time tonight,” Nik continued softly. “I wish I could give you more time.”

The fear in his voice, his eyes, buried the root of the reality of their situation. The completely life-changing, irreversible choice she had to make in that moment. She captured those emerald eyes. Of her friend. Her savior. Her protector. Her lover.

Her *mate.*

“Yes,” she said, no louder than a quiet whisper. Because she’d always known…

His face creased, and silver lapped in his eyes. It was her turn to close the distance between them. Tauria’s palm met his face, and Nik’s closed over it.

“I don’t need time, not another second, to know that I choose you, Nikalias. That I will fight for you. For us, and for our kingdoms. Until my last breath, I want to be yours.”

“If I knew of another way…”

“I don’t want any other way.”

"I don't deserve you."

Tauria strained on her toes until their lips brushed. Her next words were freedom from a world of misery. "We deserve this." Defiance against a twisted prophesy. "Each other." Forgiveness when enough time had been stolen and no time was promised. "No matter how long it took to get here."

Nik began to relax, and she treasured the rare lift of his burden. His arm circled around her.

"I love you, Nik. From that first day, I chose you."

Their mouths collided, and what erupted within her the moment they joined in liberation felt like the first night they surrendered to each other; the alignment of a constellation they'd charted but never followed. Not until now. Every yearning feeling that had been suppressed for so long was unleashed in a passion as furious as it was devouring. She couldn't contain herself—not her movements against his body, not the unchecked sounds he drew from her. Tauria prayed to the damned Spirits his enchantment would work to silence them beyond these walls, and she begged for time. Time they deserved to fulfill this moment.

What became of them beyond this…

Was a fight together.

Never parted, never alone again.

Nik didn't break from her as he fumbled for the clasps of her jacket. Her own fingers were clumsy to aid him, desperate to feel his hands on her bare skin. It fell from her shoulders, revealing Tauria wore nothing beneath the leathers.

"I haven't stopped thinking about the first time I had you," Nik groaned, taking a second to trail his heated gaze down her half-naked body. "The sinful things I want to do you, Tauria Stagknight. I plan to worship every inch of you, inside and out, as my queen."

"Then have me, Nik. You've tormented me for too long."

She untucked his shirt, and he swiftly pulled it off. Tauria's mouth watered with the flex of his muscles, his arms, every sculptured inch of him that was *hers.*

"I plan to make it up to you. On my knees, between those thighs, every day if that's what it takes." His hands gripped her hips, pulling their bodies flush together, and Tauria gasped in surprise. The hard feel of him tipped her head back, and she ground against him, one hand fisted in his hair as his mouth met her collar. "I never thought I would have this." His voice fell with a note of pain, but his lips continued to plant kisses over her shoulder. "But if I ever did, this isn't how I imagined it would be. You deserve far more time to allow me to adore you before I claim you. We'll have that time, I promise you. We will have eternity."

"This is perfect," she whispered. "You're here. You came for me."

"I will always come for you." His mouth trailed back to her neck. Her veins throbbed, every instinct and desire flushing her skin, pulsing in her blood. Blood that was his to claim. The exchange that would bind them eternally.

Tauri's need for it was maddening. She was teetering on the edge of a climax, and he'd barely unleashed a fraction of what she knew he was capable of. His hardness ground against her lower belly, and she was so lost in the moment she didn't know what she wanted.

His mouth to claim her.

His hardness inside her.

His hands to worship her.

She needed it all.

"Nik, please," she moaned, desperate for some release.

He growled low, and her breath hitched when he leaned down, hooking his hands under her thighs. The coolness of the wall as her back met it was a blissful shock in contrast to the smothering heat that encased her body.

"You're mine," he groaned. His hips jerked against her core, and her head fell back with the friction. "Say it."

"I'm yours," she panted, unable to straighten.

He moved against her again—long, torturous stokes that almost had her begging him to release what strained in his pants. "I'm too close to losing control." His voice was strained, near unrecognizable, while his hard breaths formed primal growls that shook her internally.

"I want you. I've always wanted you." She knew what she needed to say, and there would be no more precious words she would utter in her life. "With the Gods as my witness and this by my will, I claim you, Nikalias Silvergriff. I am yours."

What followed fractured and reformed her world. Just as she reached her release, Nik's mouth opened and closed on her neck, the pinch of his sharp teeth sinking into her skin nothing compared to the pleasure that erupted within. Bliss devoured her, *them*, lifting them from that room entirely. Her hand fisted tightly in his hair as Nik drank from her, and it was a pleasure like nothing she had known or would know again. Not without him. Tauria came again. And again. The waves of trembling release exhausted and exhilarated every nerve cell. Her nails clawed into him, and she knew then why he'd used the wall for aid while his arms clamped tightly around her violently shuddering form.

When he pulled back, Tauria reached the pinnacle of absolution before she fell. Ecstatically and all at once. Her chest heaved as the stars dispersed to bring back her vision. Something new and brightly pulsing had kindled within her, something she would treasure until the day she faded on. But it wasn't complete. Not until she claimed him back.

Nik was panting hard when he rested his forehead to hers. His lips gleamed ruby-red, and there was barely any emerald to break up the darkness of his eyes. Her neck throbbed where his mark was, warm and tingling, but it was the sweetest pain.

"You taste…better than I ever imagined." He peeled her from the wall, carrying her over to the long lounge chair where he sat. She straddled his lap. "We don't have enough hours in this night for me do everything I desire with you. But I will, Tauria." His hands gripped her hips, coaxing her to move on him again. The clothing that remained between them was torturous. He licked his lips right before his tongue lapped over her breast, and she moaned. "Many times. In many places. There are no bounds to what I want to explore with you."

His words, the sinful thoughts painted in her imagination, sparked over her breasts and down between her legs. *Gods,* she didn't know how much more she could take, but she didn't want him to stop. Her hands flattened on his chest, and his powerful gaze lifted to her with the signal.

"I need you," she said, never breaking eye contact as she slipped from his lap.

Nik stalked her every movement as she went for the buttons of her pants, her spine curving as she unfastened them. The attention he fixed on her felt utterly empowering, those eyes of adoration he owned for her, and her alone. Fully undressed, Tauria eyed the hard strain in his pants expectantly. Nik's face was trancelike as he continued to watch her, devouring her, while his hands went for the buttons, reading her signal.

Tauria almost came undone at the sight before her. Nik, perfectly sculptured as he reclined effortlessly, naked and glorious. A battle-honed warrior. A fierce protector. A powerful king.

My mate, her mind chanted, rejoiced. *My mate. My mate.*

Nik kept still, waiting, allowing her to choose every movement, every path this would take. "Make me yours, Tauria." His voice was but a husky whisper, and her eyes fluttered with the sensations that trembled through her.

Tauria's thighs spread over him as she climbed back onto his lap. There she came alive. Her bare skin against his was electrifying, a response that could be matched by no other—one that had ached inside and tormented her since their first time. She watched her fingers trace every mark of battle, every perfect contour of his chest and shoulders. Her golden skin against his pale tone was entrancing. She marveled over him as if this reality could blink out as just another cruel dream at any moment.

Nik was here. He had utterly surrendered himself to her. And there remained only one final step before they were bound for eternity.

Her eyes settled on his collar. The sharpness of her canines scraped across her bottom lip as she imagined tasting him. Leaving her mark.

"You're mine," she whispered.

His lips claimed hers. "Yes," he said against her. "Always." His hardness between her thighs grew the ache of emptiness. Her hips rocked against him, and he groaned, his forehead buried into her neck. Their movements were teasing both of them to madness. But this night, this moment, she didn't want it to ever end.

"Just like that, love."

Tauria chased a new high as she moved on him. Then his tongue traced his mark on her neck, and she couldn't bite back her loud cry as her head tipped back. It was so raw and new, and the sensation of it brought her right to the edge of another climax. She reached between them, taking the length of him in her hand. He watched her face as she drew a soft moan, and she couldn't help but marvel at the feel of him, moving her hand in slow, tight strokes. His face was pinched with desire. Breaths came shorter through his parted mouth.

"I need to be inside you." His voice was pained, and she needed nothing more than that admission before she pushed up on her knees, positioning him at her entrance.

Tauria sank her hips down slowly, adjusting to the size of him. Inch by inch she took him, a smooth glide with her arousal that coated them both until he filled her completely. Nothing had ever felt so full, so *right.* And while every instinct roared at her to move, to get Nik to unleash what she knew he was capable of, she had to take a still moment with him fully seated inside her to remember her own gods-damned name.

"Tauria," Nik rasped, glancing at where their bodies joined, his eyes wild. "Every piece of you fits me so perfectly."

Tauria watched him fighting restraint. He was holding back in surrender to allow her to decide the pace this would take, and she knew why. His beautiful face blurred as memories flooded her. Over a century by his side…and she had never known the burden of knowledge he carried.

When he looked up, he noticed her teary eyes. Nik's arms circled around her, bringing her chest flush to his as he straightened. "What's the matter?" he asked gently, ready to stop everything if that were her wish.

"All this time…you wanted me?"

Nik's eyes closed briefly in relief. He kissed her jaw. "With everything I am."

"I'm sorry."

Nik pulled back, frowning, but not with sadness or surprise. He was angry with her apology.

"I didn't see it. All this time, I thought you didn't want me. You—"

His lips pressed firmly to hers. "Don't ever apologize to me. Not for that. I can't bear it when it was me who led you to believe I didn't. Every minute from this day, Tauria, I vow to make it up to you. Now that I can."

"I love you," she whispered. Because it was all she could voice when the love she felt for him was so strong words would never be enough to release the beautiful pain of it.

"I love you, Tauria. As eternal as the moon, I love you."

A grin broke on her face with a joy so overwhelming nervous laughter escaped her. Nik mirrored her expression, his thumb tracing her lip.

"I've missed this," he said. "Smile for me again."

His words alone triggered the upturning of her mouth, and she was so euphoric in that moment bliss made her forget all that lay beyond this forgotten room. She didn't care about crown or country. War or conflict or peace. All she cared about was him. The rare joy on his face that took her back to that first night they'd shared together. Unburdened.

Tauria moved on him, and the reminder of his fullness stirred her lust and set a pace. Nik's hands on her hips aided the friction, but it wasn't nearly enough.

"Nik," she panted, needing him to take control.

He'd warned her once before about how passionate he could be, but she'd been given everything she didn't know she craved. And right now, he was everything she needed.

Nik's hands took her breasts, and then his mouth closed around one, his tongue lapping the peak and emitting unchecked sounds from her as she leaned into him, a silent beg for more. He chuckled darkly. "I love it when you beg for what only I can give you. But one of us has to remember where we are. So while I plan to give you everything, every time you desire it, tonight has one meaning above all."

The awareness that she still needed to claim him was an instinct so strong his reminder had her thinking of nothing else. Nik leaned back, and Tauria's eyes fell to his neck, irritated that her mark wasn't there. Not yet.

Her palms flattened on his chest. Her face creased. She couldn't help the need to feel him moving inside her, much as she needed to taste him. Tauria moved her hips, rocking toward abandon, and a new release formed in her stomach, making every nerve ending in her body tremble. Nik met her stroke for stroke, but it wasn't enough.

"Harder," she rasped, her thighs sliding further apart. "Please."

Nik swore through gritted teeth, adjusting his grip to keep her in place. Then he took control. Tauria could do nothing but claw at his chest, his shoulders, grappling anything as the tension shot though her body with his hard thrusts. It was pure, wild abandon. She was close—so close. And his groans of pleasure quickened, amplified, signaling he was nearing his end too. Tauria's fingers fisted into his hair, and when his head inclined, exposing his neck to her so eagerly, it was all she could do to bring her mouth to his collar. Her sharp teeth punctured it with ease, and his blood flowing down her throat was the single most exhilarating taste in this world. A euphoric personal drug that became her lifelong addiction in that second.

Nik slammed into her in one final powerful motion as he roared his release, and Tauria cried out. Fully seated, his hold verged on the edge of pain. But she loved that. Loved the near feral unleashing of him.

Tauria's own end shattered through her, and she trembled blissfully. When she pulled her mouth away and gleaned the mark she'd made at his collar, she struggled to collect herself. Remember who she was, where they were, and what they had just done. All sense of reality and reasoning was distant as she rode the most incredible high.

Both of them were panting in each other's grip, their skin flushed and slick with sweat. She didn't want to let him go, and for a second, she feared they'd passed the point of no return…and he might regret it.

They were mated.

"Look at me, love," he said gently. Tauria read his own fear in his tone as though their thoughts aligned. Or was it within that she felt that mutual uncertainty? This bright channel that opened wide between them. They were two hearts, one soul. Only death could come between them now.

She didn't respond or move straight away, keeping her head angled into his neck while the world came crashing back down around them. Every dark and desolate thing they were to face that cruelly overshadowed their moment. Nik's hand curled around her nape, the other idly stroking her spine, and she shuddered with the sensation of it now the coldness of the dark room had come back into her awareness.

Tauria found the will to pull back, and when their eyes met, something ignited and pulsed in her chest. The bond flared to life with the promise of an eternal flame. Nik's emerald eyes glittered with a fear so haunting as his thumb brushed her cheek.

"How am I supposed to let you go now? How am I supposed to

leave you here with them, with *him,* and return to High Farrow without you?"

She couldn't believe her eyes when pools lapped against the emerald and a single tear fell down Nik's battle-hardened face. Tauria reached up, her thumb brushing it away.

"We have to do this. Because we also have kingdoms to protect. There are people who depend on us."

"We might have a fight against evil on our hands, but whatever they're capable of, I'm not afraid to become far worse if they lay a hand on you." His hardened gaze rattled her body. There was promise in those words. His fierceness chilled but also strengthened her.

"It won't come to that." It was all she could offer in a weak attempt to console him about what they had to do next. The ache of his leaving made her clutch him a little tighter.

Nik moved, finally slipping from her, and she moaned in protest. She was utterly spent, her muscles weak, but she couldn't explain the need for him that wanted to go again and again until they blissfully destroyed each other. He cradled her to him and lay them back, the width of the lounge chair only enough to accommodate them in entanglement. But even if they had endless space, she wouldn't want it in place of this as she lay on his chest and closed her eyes in contentment.

"No regrets?" she whispered.

Nik's hand idly smoothed her hair. "Only one," he confessed. At her stiffness, Nik's lips pressed to her head. "That I denied this for so long. Thank you, Tauria."

"What for?"

"Waiting for me."

Her brow pinched, and her fingers stretched over his abdomen. There was nothing more to be said, but his terror was thick and palpable.

And she knew why.

Nik believed in his heart that he was destined to harm her. *Kill* her.

Yet there wasn't a fraction of her heart that did. Maybe she should be more wary, at least consider the risk, but she couldn't. Not when she'd embraced all that was good and right in her life.

Tauria didn't know how much time had passed, but tiredness swept her as she clung on, snapping her lids open against the frequent fluttering, and Nik's gentle touch only aided her need to drift off. But every second was precious when she didn't know when she would see him again.

"What do we do now?" She forced her question past her denial that they'd be separated beyond this room.

"We make them believe we rejected the bond." His pain couldn't be hidden at the thought. "It's the only way. Tomorrow, after the meeting, I'll announce what you are to me." Nik's fingers hooked her chin, angling her tired eyes up to lock onto his. "We were born and taught to act our whole lives. What's one more role to play?" He kissed her, and it sparked her back to conscious need. But then he pulled away and captured her gaze with a fierce darkness.

"If I get one faint feeling this is going to shit, I'm coming back for you. The spell on your bracelet will weaken if the bond is used excessively. Conversation will have to be short for a while so as not to risk it, but those bastards won't ever get the chance to hide you from me again." He took her hand, guiding it to his face. Nik planted a single kiss on her palm before resting it against his cheek. "But I also need you to promise me not to close off your emotions entirely. You're smart. I know you'll figure out how to soon. But if you're ever in immediate danger, I *need* to be able to feel it. And if you don't respond to me with a convincing enough reason for any flicker of fear, I don't care what it takes—I'm coming for you."

She knew he would. But the mere thought of him risking everything to defend her was more damning than warming. Nik needed this.

"I promise."

Nik leaned down to graze his lips to hers, and he swept her with a searching stare. "I'm so proud of you, Tauria," he said, hushed. "I don't think I've ever told you how gods-damned strong you are. Resilient. Unbelievably brave. You challenge me, and I love you for it. You push back, and I adore you for it. It stills me with a fear so dangerous, a want to kill them all instead of leaving you here again. But you should know I have every confidence in you. To outsmart them, to figure out what the dark fae could be planning. I know you can do this."

Tauria rolled until she lay partially over him. Her hand began to trace his chest. She would never grow tired of the feel of him. "I'm proud to be yours," she said, silently mapping his torso with a pinched brow as she acknowledged it'd be some time until they had another moment like this. "Thank you for believing in me as you always have. You make a great king, Nik, but I never doubted you for a second. I can't wait to rule by your side. As Fenstead, and as High Farrow." At his collar, she couldn't help the urge to run her fingers in awe over her mating mark. Raw, mesmerizing. He stifled a groan in his throat as his whole body turned stiff. Tauria smiled, her eyes flaring at the satisfying reaction. She wanted to lay her lips there. Or her teeth. Gods, the thought of tasting him again sparked the fires of her desire once more. And along with their clouded scents of arousal, the hard feel of him at her thigh did nothing for her growing ache.

But Nik's hand took up a tender trail along her spine, relaxing her muscles in a way that made her head feel so heavy she had to lay it on his chest. There was more to be treasured here than in any number of hours they could exhaust in lust. Togetherness in such a simple, calming embrace.

"I hope you're ready, love," his voice rumbled under her ear, "to put on the greatest performance of our lives."

CHAPTER 45

Present Day
Nikalias

"IT WORKED."

Marlowe echoed his thoughts as he stepped into the back of the compound to greet her. She could hardly suppress her triumph as she rummaged through the shelves, and it unnerved Nik, as it often did, to know she saw him coming.

He smirked. "Did you even have a little doubt?"

"Of course I did." Yet her feline smile said the humble brush-off was a lie. "But you didn't seem in the best of spirits when you returned. I almost feared you'd chosen differently."

This brought his attention to an infuriating side to the situation. Instincts so strong he couldn't help that his temper teetered on a razor's edge at leaving his mate in another kingdom where danger circled. He had to be strong for her.

"It's difficult to explain—"

"You don't have to," Marlowe offered warmly. "I can't begin to understand what it feels like to be separated right now, especially given the circumstances. It won't help, but I have every confidence in Tauria to have planned a way out if need be. She'll come straight home."

Nik nodded his appreciation. "Yes. She's incredibly smart and brave," he said, picturing her face with so much pride it flared light inside him. He had to divert the conversation before he risked surfacing his pent-up agitation at the danger and separation. "Where's Jak?" Nik observed the space, knowing Jakon would be off-duty at the late hour. He'd used the cloak of nightfall to sneak out and catch Marlowe finishing up and was genuinely surprised to find her alone.

"He's, uh—" Marlowe tried to use her idle sorting of tools to bide time as she sought an answer. "Seeking something for me."

Nik hooked a brow and let the silence call out her lie. But Marlowe spun to him, her face cheerful.

"What did you come all this way for?"

His eyes narrowed at her avoidance, but he supposed he owed an explanation for his visit rather than probing into their private affairs. "The Phoenix potions—I came to see how they were coming along."

Marlowe blew out a breath. "I've tried twice now, and I'm close. I can feel it." Her expression twisted. The disappointment in herself was something Nik couldn't bear.

He crossed the distance to her, placing a hand on her arm as she leaned over a desk. "There's no pressure for you to do this," he assured her. "We'll manage without it."

She shook her head. "You said magick has a well, and that well has a bottom, yet I can't find it. It feels depthless."

He knew Marlowe well enough that she wasn't willing to accept defeat. As much as it riddled him with dread to keep helping her.

"It is. The gift of magick will test its bearer. One too consumed by the powers they have will push past the limits, and magick will rejoice in claiming their life for greed. You need to recognize your own bottom and know when it's time to stop." Nik was swept with a sense of déjà vu as Marlowe's hopeless eyes shifted to his. A flash of memory saw gold eyes instead of blue. There was a time Faythe had looked just as lost as Marlowe did now, desperate to master what she was capable of. And it was then Nik realized it was never just the potions that drew him back to Marlowe; it was that she needed help, encouragement, and Nik couldn't settle knowing he might be able to offer wisdom to her, however small.

"Then I don't think I'm strong enough," she said, barely a whisper, as though she didn't want to admit the weakness.

Nik was conflicted about what to say to her. He wanted to insist they didn't need the potions. After all, what they were attempting to create had been outlawed millennia ago for good reason.

"You remind me a lot of Faythe," Nik reflected, thinking back on the long days he'd spent helping her train through her frustrations. "There were many times she was ready to give up or accept defeat, wanting to silence her magick instead of seeing what she could be with it."

"She's very stubborn," Marlowe said lightly. Nik curved a brow, and his silence had her catching his eye and reading his expression. "I am *not* stubborn."

"I didn't say you were." Nik chuckled at her defensive claim. "But it's also not a bad thing. Faythe is stubborn, but her bravery often turns it into an admirable determination. She's not arrogant; her flaw is that she can be hopeful beyond her means. Determined beyond her capabilities."

"So you're saying I should give up."

"I'm saying that it's okay if you can't do this. No one is expecting you to, and even in touching magick you never knew you could. Creating the Blood Box, it is enough."

"Not for me it isn't."

Nik understood. The need to prove—not to anyone but herself—what she believed herself capable of. He came around the bench, eyeing the books and vials Marlowe had spread out. "Then let's try again."

CHAPTER 46

Jakon

JAKON HAD FINISHED his duties hours ago, and while he made his way to the blacksmith's compound, something unsettled his mind. Neither of them had told Nik of their plans to have him keep eyes on Zarrius. After each shift in the castle, Jakon spent some time enlisting younger servants whose silence he could buy to be his eyes in private places. They didn't tell the king as they couldn't be sure Nik wouldn't oppose the idea for the blatant act of spying it was. Or for the risk to their lives and his reputation. He couldn't be involved.

Jakon found Marlowe leaning over a bench. Under her lamplight, he caught the glistening red vials of Phoenix Blood. She frowned down at them with an adorable sternness, and he couldn't help his smile.

"Keep it up. They might just yield answers for you," he said, leaning his hands by hers on the desk from behind and planting a kiss to her temple.

Marlowe sighed as she straightened into him. "I'm going to try again tomorrow. Nik came by yesterday. I think I have a new tactic to attempt."

Jakon went stiff, awash with dread as he remembered the weakness and illness that followed her last attempt to bind magick to them. "Are you sure you've recovered?"

She twisted, looking up at him with those large ocean eyes filled with determination. "I know I can do this. I'm just missing some slight shift of spell. I can feel it close."

It pained him to watch her in turmoil. Her will to keep trying was what he adored about her. Marlowe's confidence in her skill was both nerve-wracking for the boundaries she could push and awe-invoking for her courage. His hand grazed her chin. "I know you can do it too." His lips met hers, and Marlowe leaned into him.

They moved together like two waves of the same ocean. Aware of the bench, Marlowe squealed in surprise when he lifted her onto it, barely breaking apart. It was she who pulled out of the kiss when he was seconds away from scattering the books and tools. Her fingers trailed over his collar, tracing the gold embroidery of his jacket.

"Have I ever told you how highly attractive you look in uniform?"

Jakon smirked, squeezing her thighs. "It's not the impression I get when you're usually so quick to remove it."

Marlowe bit her lip, but the deviant look on her face had him contemplating climbing onto the table with her. "I would say that's a testament to it." Her tone shifted with a seductive caress as her fingers began to undo the buttons. "Did you find anything today? It's long past your shift."

Jakon stifled a groan at the switch of conversation, but he knew it was necessary. "Zarrius has been very cautious with who he meets within the castle. Many times he's headed out to the woodlands, but I won't send someone to follow him at night on their own. There are far darker things to be fearful of out there. I'll need to go myself sometime.

But today…" He trailed off, his brow pinching as he tried to figure out what he'd gathered.

"Today?" Marlowe coaxed, her hand on his face bringing his gaze back to her.

"I did what you suggested: I paid off two servants who were supposed to be tending to Samara this evening."

"Supposed to be?"

Jakon nodded. "They said Samara dismissed them, claiming she was dining with Nik tonight and they were taken care of. But Nik claimed earlier he was taking the night to himself."

"Perhaps it was a last-minute agreement."

Jakon wanted to accept that simple explanation, but something didn't sit right in how both the lord and lady's plans seemed to change so often and suddenly. "There's a pattern," he thought out loud as he frowned, staring at nothing in particular, thinking over the elusive knowledge he'd tried to gather. He hadn't been able to gain any solid confirmation there was foul play from either of them, but their whereabouts was enough to keep his suspicions on edge.

"With who?" Marlowe asked gently. Her gentle hands slipped under his jacket to slide it off his shoulders. She set the guard's coat aside.

Jakon shook his head with the puzzle that seemed to be right in front of him, one shift away from being complete. Until…

"Both of them."

Their eyes met, their mutual conclusion communicated through that look.

"You think there's still something between them?" Marlowe spoke their thoughts.

"I can't accuse her without solid evidence. After all she's told Nik, I don't think he's in the best mind to discredit her story either. Maybe it's not by her will, but I think we need to find out what her goal is. If she's still a threat to Nik."

It was Marlowe's turn to lose herself in thought. Her vacant face showed her brilliant mind at work. Jakon couldn't help but reach out to brush a loose strand of hair from her face, tracing her cheekbone while her hand absently closed over his.

"I don't think Nik's the only one in danger here," she said, her brow furrowed, her eyes searching and calculating. Jakon saw the moment she figured out whatever it was she pondered. Her face smoothed, but it was not triumph she wore; it was a ghostly realization when she looked at him. "If Samara has still been telling him of Nik's plans, staying on both sides, Zarrius knows his secret spy is compromised no matter how expertly she can fool Nik."

"Yet he's still playing along."

"For now. But Zarrius is not one to leave loose ends that could expose his plans. Nik found out about Samara, and if Zarrius knows…"

Jakon drew the conclusion on his own. It wasn't that he cared what became of the fae if she was foolish enough to play two sides. His horror came in realizing if Samara loved so fiercely as to go against a king, there was no telling what she would do with Zarrius's whispers in her ear.

CHAPTER 47

Tauria

"It's the last bed," Tauria said with both triumph and sadness. "What do you think we should plant here?" Twisting to the young princess, she found Opal lost in thought, staring at the perfectly turned soil ready to be peppered with color.

It was over a week since Nik's departure, and Tauria had immersed herself in the pavilion garden completely. No one bothered her. Even Lennox was silent, and she'd been left to grieve as they all assumed was necessary.

Tauria rolled her neck, a subconscious habit she prayed no one had picked up on. The high necks of her gowns to conceal Nik's mark were torturous. It grated on a primal irritation that she should have to hide it. But all would be over if anyone found out the truth.

The suspense was crushing as she waited to see if the spellbound bracelet Marlowe had crafted would conceal the strong essence of their mating bond. It was remarkable the blacksmith was capable of such things, and she pined after her friend with the longing to express her gratitude. Tarly had given no indication he had the slightest suspicion when he met her on the balcony, and over the days, she began to relax in the knowledge it was working.

The bond was silent, closed off on either end unless a strong enough emotion was provoked to pierce through. It ached in her chest that she longed to speak with him, feel him, like she knew she was capable of through the bond now. But out of fear it could dampen Marlowe's spell, they'd agreed to keep contact very limited.

In the garden, on the days when Opal had classes and wasn't able to join her, Tauria used her ability to accelerate the progress that had led them to being almost finished restoring the wondrous space. No longer was it a wilted, neglected space. Now, she caught many beyond the glass doors stopping to gawk at its beauty. Flowers of every color, brilliant greens climbing the perimeter wall. She'd even managed to convince Lennox and a few other guards to paint the pavilion a new brilliant white she decorated with climbing vines and flowers.

"Violettas." Opal perked up.

The dual-toned purple flower she'd only seen a few of in her lifetime. They were particularly marvelous against snowfall. Tauria raised a brow. "How is it you know of them? They only grow in the cold, mostly sighted and picked in Lakelaria."

"It's Tarly's favorite," she said casually. "Because it was his mother's favorite. He talks about her sometimes."

She felt a pinch in her chest, and Tauria's face fell. "I can plant them, but they won't last very long with the heat. We may need to keep replacing them or plant something more accustomed to this climate."

Opal pouted. "I think he'd like to see them, even if for a little while."

Tauria smiled, a warmth filling her chest at Opal's adoration for her older brother. Without another thought, she began to bloom the violettas. Some she created and gave to the princess to plant herself, and while at work, Tauria sped up the process by using her magick to sprout them directly from the fresh soil.

Once the bed was full, Tauria beamed and got to her feet with a wince at her dormant bones. Side by side, her arm folded around the princess's shoulders as they admired the whole garden. Opal let out a squeal of glee, and they chuckled in awe of the beauty.

"It's nearing midday, Your Majesty," Lennox gently interrupted.

The princess's face instantly fell from its joy. For once, Serena hadn't escorted Opal here and stayed. It was up to Tauria to deliver her to her classes.

"What are we going to do now?" Opal asked as they walked inside.

Tauria was humbled that her tone seemed to sadden at the thought they'd have nothing else to occupy their time together. It warmed her to see the garden had become something of a safe space for her. "Well, it will need maintaining, of course," Tauria offered.

Opal beamed up at her at the assurance she was always welcome there.

After escorting the princess, Tauria knew where she was headed that afternoon. Since his mention in the garden, she'd found herself *missing* the prince. On her way to his rooms, she bloomed a small bunch of violettas, which she scrutinized over the whole way there. Was it childish to present them to him? Her racing thoughts were halted when she detected a presence down the hall, along with her steps in her shock at who she witnessed leaving Tarly's rooms.

Serena pulled at the bodice of her dress as if adjusting it after…

Oh Gods.

Tauria spun on her heel, nearly knocking into Lennox, whom she didn't look to before she was storming back the way she came. Her heart was wild. It shouldn't come as a surprise; Serena had implied she had a history with the prince before. Tauria felt…nothing. She had no right to be jealous with the secret she harbored. All she hoped was that her near run-in had gone unnoticed as she was sure to be tormented with it later, among the ladies.

By evening, Tauria sat alone on the balcony for supper. In the summer, the days were long, and she watched the glorious sun setting, burning the stone around the courtyard so many wonderful warm hues. She idly stirred her tea, knowing what was within it would block her subconscious mind when she fell asleep later. Just as it had every night to keep her from Nik. She smiled to herself. The spoon clinked off the rim of the teacup, and then she set it aside before curling two fingers around the handle and bringing the cup to her lips.

Tauria tried not to think about Nik in other ways, suppressing the memory of their mating for when she was truly alone in her room in the dead of night only. She couldn't risk her scent shifting with thoughts of him that threatened to undo her. It was an effort to keep her focus on anything but him.

This wasn't how it should be after a mating bond was established. Torn apart. But all Tauria could be grateful for was that it was real.

"I didn't expect you to be out here."

Tarly's low voice tore her eyes from the horizon to catch him strolling out. Over the last week, she'd taken to eating alone in her rooms rather than with the prince. It was part of maintaining the guise. Despite the bond rejection being met with agreement by those they fooled, she was still expected to need time to recover from the painful experience.

"I've wasted enough time as it is. We have preparations to make."

Their *preparations* weaved a silent meaning between them. It was not wedding arrangements and petty party details they had to dive into;

rather, it was the far more ominous and sinister task of discovering what the High Lord Mordecai had to gain from their union.

Tarly took his seat opposite her, his face devoid of emotion. She was growing used to his grumpy reception, finding it wasn't usually a reflection of his company or surroundings; it was a constant shadow. "Taking time to heal is not wasted."

Tauria dropped her gaze to her plate with the twist of guilt. She wished she could tell him, but it was too big of a risk. They couldn't be sure Tarly would remain on their side and go against his father if the worst came to pass.

"I was looking for you earlier." She diverted the topic.

"You didn't find me."

"Clearly."

Tarly hooked a brow, and she realized her tone had switched to accusation. She set down her cup, sparing a quick glance to be sure the guards were far enough away not to overhear the conversation.

"What you do and with whom you do it is none of my business. But I hope you're keeping her silent about the affair that won't go down well for any of us if your father finds out about it."

His face fell to a frown. "What are you talking about?"

Did he really think her a fool? She leaned forward in her chair. "I went by your rooms just as Lady Serena was leaving," she said plainly, trying to keep her tone level to assure him she bore no judgment. "But if word spreads, not only will I appear a damn fool for standing by you before we're even wed, but I can't imagine you or she will be safe from Varlas's wrath."

A long stretch of silence fell between them, and Tauria tried to study his expression. Cold, harsh. As he stared at her...she even thought she caught a flicker of betrayal. No—*hurt.*

"When did you see her leaving my rooms?"

"Is there such a string of meetings that you can't keep track?"

His jaw flexed, but before he voiced the darkness that flashed in his eyes at the remark, they fell to the table by her plate. "Where did you get those?"

Tauria followed his line of sight, knowing what she would find. Only, the prince's anger seemed to heighten. "Opal thought you would like them," Tauria ground out. "Because they remind you of your mother."

Tarly braced his hands on the table and rose slowly. The warm air chilled with the depthless look he targeted at the purple flowers. Then he pinned her with it. "She shouldn't have told you that," he said icily.

Tauria couldn't be sure if she wanted to match his bitter mood or succumb to the pain she felt for him. Even after all this time, she didn't know how to approach the prince. Nothing seemed to be good enough.

"If there are any of them in that damned garden, I want them gone."

"No."

Tarly's eyes narrowed at her defiance, but Tauria didn't balk. She stood too.

"It was your mother's garden, and in her memory they're staying. It would also break your sister's heart to know how much you hate them."

"Don't speak of her," Tarly warned. "Don't speak of either of them again." He pushed off the table and made to leave without touching a single thing from the supper spread.

"You have no one because you push away any ounce of kindness offered to you."

Tarly halted, and though her heart pounded, she couldn't stop the words. If kind gestures and a tentative approach weren't going to work, she could only think to *push back*. Because she'd been through this before. Tauria hadn't given up on Nik, and not because of the bond. She wouldn't give up on Tarly as one who needed a friend but didn't know how to open himself up to one.

The prince turned to her, and Tauria braced at the challenge that rolled his shoulders. She didn't think he would harm her, not even for a second. It was verbal blows they would exchange until they tired each other out. He opened his mouth to begin unleashing the wrath on his face, but a guard's voice called out to them instead.

"Your Highnesses, the king requests your presence in the throne room."

CHAPTER 48

Nikalias

A KNOCK SOUNDED at his door, unexpected at the late hour as Nik glanced up from his desk spilled with candlelight. He called for them to enter, but he already knew the face he would be greeted with by her scent.

Samara entered his council room tentatively. Nik rose immediately, catching the redness around her eyes though she tried to keep her head bowed. He was in front of her before she could retreat, and he caught her chin.

"What happened?" he asked carefully.

Her lip wobbled, stirring his anger with the possibilities that rushed through his mind. What could cause her such upset? *Who?*

She shook her head. Fear sparked in her blue eyes, and it ground his teeth. "I can't help you if you don't tell me," he coaxed, letting his hand fall.

"He's a powerful male. You don't know what he's capable of."

"You forget who has the most power in this castle, Samara."

"He says you don't," she confessed. Only out of terror that Nik wouldn't be able to protect her. If that was what she'd come here in the hope of. "He says that you're merely a face for the people. Until the time is right for him to take reign."

"Is he planning something?"

"You were right."

This caused him to back up a step, forming a guard of caution. Nik extended his senses to beyond the hall, outside the windows, to be sure there were no lingering bodies and that Samara wasn't playing two sides in an attempt to trick him with his sympathy.

"I don't love him. Everything you said that day, and then watching you with Tauria in Olmstone, made me realize love was never what we shared. I've known Zarrius for a long time. He is close to my father, who might have encouraged the lord's advances on me. I was young, doting, and naïve, and Zarrius was powerful, handsome, and a favorable match to my father and mother. I've always been a prize to them, born and raised to be nothing more than a highly titled courtesan ensnaring the wealthiest suitor."

Nik was stunned. Admittedly surprised, but wholly in awe that she felt safe enough to trust him with her past. He motioned for her to take up one of the chairs by the fire, offering a drink, which she declined, so he passed her a handkerchief instead as she sniffed intermittently.

Carefully, Nik lowered onto the seat opposite her, staying silent so as not to spook her, giving his full, undivided attention so she knew he'd listen without judgment. Her eyes briefly fell to his wrist, then to her own, where she spun the bracelet there.

"I take it the enchantment worked." She diverted the conversation.

While Nik was keen to hear more and get to the bottom of what influenced her visit, he found himself fidgeting with the metal adorning his wrist. "Yes. It was brilliant. Marlowe is brilliant for being able to replicate the spell Zarrius put on yours and his to conceal your scents."

Samara gave a small, broken smile. "But you never…mated?"

Nik's body tensed, an instinctual protective shield forming for his mate. He hadn't told Samara everything, and he felt no guilt for it. While he wanted to believe her entirely, he wouldn't take a single chance where Tauria was involved. If Zarrius found out…

"No," he answered. "We shared a moment on the balcony away from the party, but that is all. I only asked for the bracelet out of fear I wouldn't be able to stop myself, but nothing beyond a kiss happened." It wasn't entirely a lie. He tried not to think about how she'd come undone for him so beautifully. The utterly enchanting noises she made. "I'll wear it until I can be sure her scent isn't on me to rise suspicions about us."

They took a short pause of silence. Samara's face pinched, but he couldn't place her feelings.

"Will she still marry the prince?"

Her question grated on his primal, possessive anger, but he had a role to play. "I believe so," was all he said.

Samara nodded, seeming to accept the information, but Nik kept his caution around her. There was no one except Jakon and Marlowe he could confidently trust right now.

"And Tauria—is she safe?"

Nik smiled, pained but grateful for the question. "She can look out for herself."

Samara nodded in understanding. Relief smoothed her face before her eyes fixed down to fiddle with her materials again.

"What happened tonight, Samara?"

Her brow furrowed as if she fought a new round of tears. "I told him I didn't want to be with him anymore. I think he believes my feelings for you have grown true. Maybe it was foolish, but after my rejection of his advances tonight, he—he didn't take it very well."

Nik's hand curled around the arm of his chair, a reckless heat of anger creeping over his skin as he asked carefully, his voice ice-cold, "Did he harm you?"

The sob that escaped her was all the confirmation he needed to make him shoot to his feet. Samara flinched as he did, and his rage pulsed so palpable it took everything in him not to storm from the room and find the lord that second to wring his hands around his neck. Nik breathed deep to see sense and figure out how to handle the situation. After a few seconds of deliberation, watching her broken fear, he knew she was perhaps too out of her depth to feel fully at ease with him. Another intimidating, powerful male.

"No one knows you're here. You're safe."

He was halfway to the door when she called with a hint of terror, "Where are you going?"

His face relaxed. "I'm not going to Zarrius right now, but he will pay for any harm he has caused you this night or any that came before it. I'll be back in a few minutes. You're safe in this room."

Nik propped his chin in his hand as he watched Marlowe perched on the floor by Samara's chair, offering distracting words of comfort while she tried to coax more information from the lady. He knew the blacksmith could offer the softness and ease he couldn't, but there was a moment of uncertainty as he went to ask for her help as he remembered their first rocky encounter and Samara's prejudice.

Yet Marlowe had been nothing but eager to help despite the fae's initial lack of warm reception. Samara's upbringing had made her ignorant to the humans as anything more than lower-class citizens, just as many of the humans were brought up to believe the fae were nothing more than power-hungry elitists. Neither notion was true. And watching the two females now, smiling and accepting of each other, he hoped to pave the way toward a better High Farrow perhaps sooner than he dreamed.

"Where is he now?" Jakon questioned.

Nik wanted to cut in that he should ease his tone as the human hadn't stopped staring at Samara with a look he could only decipher as suspicion.

"In his rooms, I believe—"

"You believe, or you know?"

"Jak—" Nik tried to cut in.

"Why let him rest another night? Let's go confront him."

Nik stared at Jakon as if he'd lost his mind, unknowing of where his brazen determination was coming from. "That is not how we're handling this," he laid down firmly, beginning to feel the rise of opposition that felt wrong when directed at him.

Yet Jakon wasn't backing down. He took a step toward Samara, and Nik couldn't help but follow it with a warning, a flare of protection the human clearly couldn't detect. "And where does he *believe* you would have run to and left him?"

Samara's mouth floundered, her gaze casting to Nik with fear. A vulnerable plea.

"I think you should leave, Jakon," Nik said carefully. "It seems it was my mistake to come to you."

This seemed to ease the human's expression. Marlowe rose tentatively, exchanging a look with Jakon that was a partial reprimand, but Nik had witnessed enough of them to know there was also some unspoken agreement between them. Jakon deliberated his next words.

"All I'm saying is it was reckless to come here. If Zarrius suspects your feelings are coming true for Nik, it only amplifies his desire to see him dead."

The explanation made sense. At least it would to Samara. Nik couldn't understand Jakon's hostility or lack of trust toward the fae who had so far displayed her cooperation when Nik needed her most.

"I can take it from here," Nik emphasized, dismissing Jakon once again.

The human's gaze snapped to him. The hardness wasn't entirely foreign to Nik, who had seen it before. Jakon's courage was admirable;

he was never shy to back down or speak out no matter who or what threatened those he cared for. Nik had even felt Jakon's hard will to protect directed at *him* long ago where Faythe was concerned.

"Thank you for coming," was all he said when the humans hesitated. Against what, he couldn't decipher.

Jakon extended an arm to Marlowe. Her expression twisted in concern, but she offered a smile as she passed, and they left without another word. Nik watched the door for a few long seconds, contemplating the odd night.

"Once again, I must say I do not understand why you allow them to speak to you as they do." Samara broke the silence, her voice quiet but no longer wobbling with fear.

"And how might that be?"

"They undermine you."

"They challenge me. It is what friends do."

"They question me. I do not feel safe in their company."

Nik's fists tightened as he turned to Samara. This was not a conflict he wanted to have, and it was becoming more of a fleeting dream to imagine coexistence in his kingdom. "You are not quick to trust them. Do not expect them to be quick to trust you."

Her lips thinned. Her small nod was a relief that lifted some of the tension in his shoulders. Yet he couldn't shake the unsettling feeling Jakon had left behind.

"I'll have two guards escort you to your rooms and stand watch outside." Nik paced to the window, sliding his hands into his pockets as he looked out over the sleeping city with scrambled thoughts.

"Would you not escort me, Your Majesty?"

Her desire for his company didn't feel right. Not when she knew of his feelings for Tauria without knowing of the bond.

"Jakon was right about one thing," Nik said. The thought of being in the intimate setting of her rooms even in consolation… He shuddered with the wrongfulness. "We can't have Zarrius suspecting you're gaining true affections."

"And if I am?"

Nik stiffened completely. It was little more than a whisper at his back, but it grew on a rippling discomfort. He took a second to compose himself before he faced her.

Samara stood casting shy doe eyes while her hands were clasped tightly. He didn't expect it. Not even once did he get the impression she was gaining feelings past their ruse.

"You're not," he said firmly. He took no pleasure in the wince it earned from her. Nik's gaze softened from his instinct to close off entirely in the presence of another advance. The bond that ran through him roared to seek distance from her. "I could never give you want you want, Samara. What you deserve."

"But now that your bond—"

"Stop."

Samara flinched at the bite of his tone. Nik's fists clenched tight; his jaw flexed. He couldn't offer sympathy with the flash of hurt that stole his breath. Because what she believed—that the bond had been severed—had once been so close to reality he couldn't bear to hear of it.

He took a few seconds to calm down, relaxing as he watched her shrink and shuffle under his gaze. "You have my protection, I promise you that." Nik had to look away as he dismissed her once more. "The guards will escort you to your rooms."

CHAPTER 49

Tauria

Tauria marched painfully stiff with the pent-up agitation she didn't get to release on the prince beside her. It took effort to appear content around him as they headed to the throne room. Inside, Varlas occupied the grand stone throne, with Keira seated beside him. Tauria's gaze caught on the hand she laid on his arm, her body angled toward the king, ever the obedient, adoring queen. Tauria stifled her bitter thoughts to plaster a smile on her face when they stopped before them.

"I trust you are well, Tauria, after what you experienced last week."

She squared her shoulders, slipping fully into the convincing role. "I am well, Your Majesty. I'm just glad for it all to be over so I can start looking forward to our future union." Against all that screamed and protested within her, Tauria angled herself toward Tarly, slipping her palm over his chest. Her body pricked; her heartbeat picked up. *Wrong.* She had never felt the urge to retreat so strongly that her stomach churned with nausea. But she forced her gaze to meet his, and Tarly played his part with a reluctance only she could feel as they shared an adoring look, his hand closing over hers in a show for the monarchs. *Not your mate.* She swallowed hard, returning her attention to Varlas, whose mouth had upturned a fraction. Not a smile of joy for the happy couple; it shadowed the cunning gleam of someone who eyed a grand trophy. A darkness crept down her spine at that look.

"I invited you both here to let you know of the upcoming arrangements for your wedding."

Tarly's arm slipped around her, and she believed his protective act of assurance was real considering all they knew. He spoke when she couldn't with her rattling nerves.

"We don't wish to rush this. We only just announced the engagement and have all the time in the world."

"I'm afraid not," Varlas sang darkly. "Nothing in the alliance is binding without the marriage. Time is not a luxury any of us can afford. We cannot be certain what Valgard's movements are, and the sooner we can join the three kingdoms, the stronger we become."

Tauria's teeth slammed together. To keep the powerful accusation from pinning the king who knew *exactly* what Valgard's next move was. And she intended to find it out before they became prey to it.

"Your wedding is being prepared as we speak and shall commence in two weeks."

Tauria's hand fell from Tarly, but his grip tightened on her waist. She said, "With all due respect—"

"It is not up for discussion." Varlas rose, and Tauria imagined the cool look of loathing Tarly would be wearing without stealing a glance. "In truth, I thought you both would be happier. All the preparations are being taken care of. There is no expense spared, and it will be a day to remember for millennia."

Images of the dark and ominous ceremony room flashed in her mind, along with the wraithlike dark fae and their gruesomely sawed-off wings. Tauria's vision swayed, and Tarly likely sensed her spiral as he drew her subtly closer, taking more of the weight that threatened to collapse her.

It wasn't much time. Despite what they might figure out or not... Tauria hadn't thought of a plan for afterward. Her escape. Would Tarly still be safe if she left?

She didn't know why her eyes felt compelled to shift to the queen. Keira's smile was off, pained with a cool loathing that shot unwittingly at the king's back, and Tauria wondered if anyone else caught the hostility in her posture. As though she were riding the wave of a tense argument before she and Tarly arrived.

Guards surrounded the perimeter of the throne room, but they could be mistaken for statues—not a flicker of expression, not a slight sway or shift of movement. Tauria chilled as she observed their unnatural stillness, wanting to be anywhere else.

"We are very excited," Tarly said tightly for both of them. It was all they could do. Tauria mustered a convincing smile to accompany his words. They couldn't risk arousing Varlas's suspicions by protesting more. Fast weddings weren't uncommon for engaged royals, especially those who claimed to be as hopelessly in love as they were.

"As are we all," Varlas said with a dark undertone.

"Is that all you wished to inform us of?"

"For now." Varlas paced back to his throne, casting a gaze that narrowed on Keira with warning.

The queen smiled. "Congratulations to you both. It will be an enviable ceremony indeed." Her words were enough to set the confirmation in Tauria that whatever the alternative plan was, Keira knew about it. Yet she sensed the queen wasn't entirely in agreement.

"You are dismissed," Varlas said without looking at them again.

Tauria didn't know if she should pause or bow. She was spared from doing either when Tarly's arm wrapped her waist, steering her with him. He didn't let her go as they swiftly left, and she felt the tracking of the king's eyes like a hot brand. As though one slight movement could unveil her shocking secret. As though if she locked eyes with him for too long, he would see right down to the depths of her soul and discover the other half entangled there for eternity.

They arrived at her rooms, and Tarly dismissed the guards for a moment. When Tauria met his stare, the cold shield had returned to them, the ripples of their interrupted conversation returning thick and suffocating.

"I don't know what your problem is—"

"You're my problem, Tauria."

All her anger dissipated with those harsh words. He was cold and sometimes cruel, but not usually this blunt.

"You should never have come to Olmstone. I thought you were smart, but you buy into court gossip just like the rest of them and insert yourself in situations that are too big for you alone. You're my problem because it's becoming a damn headache to keep safe a lamb so willing to prance around the wolves' enclosure."

Embarrassment flushed her face. Anger tingled over her body. "I didn't ask for your help."

"Nor am I offering it. Don't you see? We're in this together whether we like it or not."

Tauria's expression remained set, but she didn't believe him. Contrary to his words, his actions, he'd followed her to the rooftops many times now, sometimes only to talk the restless nights away. He'd enlightened her to the path that was her one sure escape route if she got in danger. Tarly had helped her whether his stubbornness would admit to it or not.

He took a step away from her, twisting to leave. "We're going to the Livre des Verres tomorrow."

Tauria wanted to counter, simply not give him the satisfaction of winning the petty squabble that felt far from over. But she couldn't because Tarly's thoughts seemed to align with hers. She'd intended to suggest visiting the library at supper before everything happened. She put her frustrations instead into the slamming of her door. But within the confines of her rooms, away from prying eyes, all negative feelings left her. Because in here, she was free to think of the one thing that brought her absolution in her tense situation.

Tauria wasted no time in unfastening the high neck of her gown. Pacing to the balcony door, she stared out at the twinkling night. Her hand reached up, and in touching Nik's mark she bit her lip to suppress her longing whimper at the warmth that embraced her within.

"Do you remember when we were younger—what you used to say?"

A soft noise did escape her at the sound of Nik's distant voice in her mind. Sparingly, they exchanged a few words. A compromise to be sure she was safe.

"No," she sent back.

"Liar."

Tauria released a short laugh.

"Do you see the moon, Tauria?"

The question was incredibly soothing. Knowing they stared up at the same sky coated her with comfort while he was so painstakingly far away.

"Yes," she whispered, overcome more than usual with the pain of their being apart.

"What shape is it?"

"A quarter."

An amorous stroke on her senses made her shiver. Like a warm internal embrace.

"You used to tell me that you create the wind in your sails. That you would create mine too. I think without realizing it, you always have."

Tears blurred her vision. She wanted so desperately to be home. To be with him.

"I miss you."

"Soon, love. I know you can do this. And once you find out what we need, I'm coming for you."

She nodded and stared up at the moon, knowing he was too, back in High Farrow. Home. The kingdom would forever be her second home even after she took back Fenstead. She clung to the image with new hope and determination. It was wonderfully strength-invoking to imagine the day they'd rule over two mighty kingdoms side by side. She would do anything for that future with him.

CHAPTER 50

Jakon

IT WAS THE dead of night, an utterly ludicrous time for Jakon to be perched on a precarious high tree branch in the Westland Forest. He'd slipped out while Marlowe slept soundly. Though he didn't doubt he could leave the castle and city without hassle, Jakon was stealthy in getting here, taking the underground route and keeping to the shadows. It was near the hour he hoped to catch his target.

From his findings, this was the one time and place consistent with Jakon's belief that it was routine for Zarrius to meet someone out here. He'd sat for some time now, barely moving with the questionable balance he had on the branch. His hope was beginning to deflate the longer the night remained peaceful and tiredness swept him. His lids began to slip shut.

A few more minutes passed before the first sound to disturb the silence jerked him wide-awake. Branches cracking. Someone wandered below. Jakon had hopefully climbed high enough that his scent couldn't be detected, being deliberately careful in the obscure route he'd taken through the trees.

"You're late. I have been here for some time," a voice grumbled.

Jakon stiffened completely, as if holding his breath could make him vanish while he eavesdropped.

"You work for me, *darkling.*"

It was him. Zarrius. From the height and through the dark, Jakon could hardly make out the silhouettes below. He put all focus into simply listening.

"And you work for *them.*"

A choked sound resounded, and Zarrius's voice fell threatening. "They'll have to find a new messenger if you can't watch your tone."

The harsh shuffling indicated he'd been pushed back.

"Now, I believe you have something for me, and we can part once again," Zarrius drawled, bored.

After a disgruntled huff, all Jakon could distinguish was an exchanging of something. He caught a faint clink. Something made of or concealed in glass. He squinted and scanned, trying to lean forward to catch a glimpse, but the branch gave a faint crack in warning. He stilled, his heart leaping, waiting long seconds in anticipation as he wondered if they'd caught the movement with their fae senses.

"Excellent. Tell them our plans will be progressing."

Jakon's stiff shoulders eased as Zarrius continuing to talk signaled he was still safe.

There was a pause, nothing but the distant creak of nighttime creatures.

"If that was all, my lord," the other male said.

Zarrius hummed and didn't deign to give a response before footsteps crushed the fallen foliage back the way they'd come. It was a short exchange, and as Jakon sat in wait for enough time that both of them would be long out of range, his mind reeled with the knowledge Zarrius had gained something from whoever *they* were. More questions and no answers, leaving him only with frustrations heightened by the fact he'd forced himself away from his fiancée to be here.

Jakon began to carefully make his descent. Halfway down, the branch he stepped on gave way, and his wild grapple with the trunk was futile. He was falling, hitting various branches as he did, some more forgiving than others with gravity's claim.

Slamming to the earth took the air from him completely. All he could be grateful for while he lay there in pain was that he hadn't fallen from high enough to cause serious injury. Jakon lay still while the impact throbbed in his head and back the most. To distract himself while the aches subsided, he tried to glimpse the stars through the thick canopy and let his mind drift.

For that reason, he didn't detect the presence that pounced on him. Jakon tried to react, reaching to his side for the blade there, but the coolness against his throat was a halt against it.

"Are you a *spy?*" The male pressed a knee to his chest in a near crushing force.

"I don't think I'm qualified for that title," Jakon wheezed.

His hood cloaked his face in too much darkness for Jakon to be able to catch a glimpse, but he recognized his voice as the one who'd been in conversation with Zarrius. He was so damn screwed.

"Who do you work for?"

"I can't—" Jakon tried to gesture to his chest through his painful breaths, barely registering the movement before the male roughly grabbed his hood and yanked it down. Then the pressure finally eased, but not completely.

"Human?"

"Tragic to you, I know."

"Whatever the king is offering you, I hope it's worth the price of your life."

Jakon couldn't help himself. He chuckled. Though it quickly turned into a choke when the pressure grew on his chest and the blade almost cut his skin. He acknowledged how dangerous his position was. He didn't doubt the fae would end his life without much thought.

"You really think the king would trust a simple human to be his spy?"

This seemed to make him think. A small consolation. In his distraction, the fae didn't track Jakon reaching for his blade. The fae eased off a fraction, and Jakon attacked, swiping his blade and catching his assailant's cheek. He cried out, and Jakon used all his strength to roll. It pinned the fae beneath him, but not for long. He struggled against the fae's strength as they tumbled. Jakon lifted his blade while he straddled the fae, but he was severely outmatched. Near effortlessly—Jakon couldn't help but gasp with embarrassment—the fae landed a punch to his gut that sent him sprawling. He'd barely got his first draw of air to recover when hands clamped around his throat. Jakon clawed at the vise grip, his fear beginning to edge toward the very real terror he might not make it out of the forest alive.

All he could think about was Marlowe. How he wouldn't have the privilege of finally making her his wife. Against all odds, he would fight for her.

He scrambled helplessly in his mind while his airways were restricted. But he didn't have to do anything as the fae wailed loudly before falling off him. Jakon gasped and gulped for breath, rolling. He didn't forget his assailant as he scrambled a few paces of distance away.

"Are you out of your *damn* mind?"

Jakon could have collapsed with relief. He did. Falling onto his back, he let go of an incredulous laugh before his head rolled and he matched the voice to its face. "Saved by the King of High Farrow himself," he panted. "I wonder who will believe me."

Nik lowered his bow, but even though his hood made it difficult to see his face, the livid outrage he'd revealed in his voice didn't give way for humor.

"The king?" the fae said with piqued interest.

Nik marched over to the fae, his hard strides triggering fear as he shuffled back despite the arrow protruding from his shoulder, until he sat propped up against a thick trunk. "Who are you? Nik asked darkly.

Jakon groaned as he got to his feet, limping over, the pain in his leg he believed to be from the fall, and rubbing his chest from the attack. "He met with Zarrius," Jakon offered.

Nik turned to him, but his eyes were unyielding. "Is that why you thought venturing alone to the woods in the dead of night was a fine idea?"

Jakon didn't take the reprimand well. "Someone has to keep track of underlying threats to our precious *Majesty.*"

"Don't give me that bullshit."

"Wake up, Nik. You've been too consumed by your mate to pay any real attention to what's going on within your very walls—"

"Stay the fuck down," Nik snapped at the fae who tried to stand, freeing the blade he pointed down but never breaking eye contact with Jakon.

"You think I want to be out here risking my life when I have a fiancée to consider, and Faythe, who I certainly plan to see again?"

"Then why are you taking reckless matters into your own hands?"

"For you, dammit!" Jakon exasperated. "If we lose you, we lose all hope of everything."

"I see."

"But also because while you are a royal pain in the ass…you're a friend," he added in a grumble of reluctance, even after all this time.

A few seconds of silence ticked by. Then a small smile tugged on Nik's face.

"What?"

Nik chuckled, shaking his head. "You have no idea how alike you and Faythe are sometimes."

A cough brought their attention back to their captive. Nik turned to him fully.

"You didn't answer my question."

Jakon barely had a second to register Nik's movement as he reached down, gripped the arrow, and ripped it free. It seemed he wasn't in the mood for mercy. Jakon winced at the fae's shriek of pain, but he watched as Nik observed the bloodied arrow tip. When it caught in a ray of moonlight, Jakon frowned, believing his human sight was too restricted in the dark to show color.

"Black blood." Nik mumbled Jakon's first thought. "Never mind who…" He was calculating as if the answer were right there. "*What* are you?"

Jakon scrambled with snippets of information he'd heard before. "Your sword," he said when it clicked.

Nik arrived at the same thought as he followed his line of sight. The mighty blade sang free, and the fae *balked.* Nik raised the lethal point toward the male, so slowly it was clear he didn't intend to strike, but the fae grew fearful, trying to shrink further into the tree. When the metal touched the skin of his neck, he cried out.

It fell into place with a haunting clarity.

Nik eyed the length of the dark blade. The Farrow Sword was crafted of Niltain Steel.

"Dark fae," he whispered, locking eyes with his target to read the confirmation in his hard look.

The assailant said nothing.

Nik bared his teeth. "How did you cross the borders without being detected?"

The dark fae laughed. "Your borders are like a picket fence to a bird of prey."

Jakon shuffled over to them. "You have no wings," he observed.

It seemed to strike a chord, and he found it odd to watch the male who looked so ordinary express emotions. He wasn't like the gruesome creature Jakon had heard of in the caves below the castle… If Nik hadn't seen his blood, perhaps he might never have known what the male truly was. That fact set a daunting sense of unease through every nerve in his body.

"You're up against far worse than you know, *king,*" the dark fae spat.

Nik flared at the challenge, not removing his blade. "What did you speak of with the lord tonight?"

"Nothing and everything."

Nik applied pressure with his sword. "I really don't have patience tonight. Tread wisely."

The dark chuckle that came from the surrendered male vibrated eerily carefree. "If you kill me without hearing what I have to say, you most definitely are the fool they believe you to be."

"Who are 'they'?" Jakon asked, his attention grabbed by the mention once more.

"Forces darker and more savage than you can prepare for. Ones that have already begun to breech your walls and prepare the attack from the inside out. It is only a matter of time."

"Valgard?" Nik scanned his clothing, but he was dressed in simply a thick black hood. He adorned no sigil.

"After all this time, do you still truly believe one kingdom is the driving force in this war? You are all going to fall if you don't start looking between the lines of battle. The clues have always been there."

It didn't make sense that this fae—this *dark fae*—would be here for any other reason than by enemy command. They shouldn't have even allowed him to breathe for as long as they did. If they were smart, they would've killed the threat without hesitation.

"You don't have long to live. I suggest you choose your last words very carefully," Nik warned.

The dark fae smiled. "I was wondering how long it would take for you discover your lord's plan. I must admit, I fear for you already."

It didn't make sense, but Jakon realized something. "You knew I was here the whole time?"

Depthless eyes switched to him. "I did."

"Yet you said nothing to Zarrius."

"Trust me or do not, it is your choice, but choose wisely, king. There won't come another chance like this again."

Nik was reluctant to let his guard down. "You would turn against your own kind?"

"They are not *my kind,*" he spat. "Do you know nothing of history? Or magick? You have to learn, and learn fast. Nothing is as simple as it seems. You'll find there is far more to the dark fae, to Valgard, to the Spirits, than anyone could have predicted. They are always one step ahead, and that is how you will lose if you don't catch up."

Jakon watched as Nik began to lose his patience and gain irritation. He watched his arms rise a fraction, seconds away from recklessly ending the dark fae's life before they got to the end of his riddles.

"Why would I believe you are any different than them?" Nik seethed.

"Because I was once like you. I was once fae."

That stilled them both. Jakon studied the dark fae—his hollow eyes, his slumped posture that had given up caring for the blade at his throat. Killing him might give him exactly what he wanted.

To Jakon's surprise, Nik backed away, lowering his sword. He, on the other hand, wasn't so keen to stand unprotected, not having the reflexes to match. He took the bow from his back and nocked an arrow instead. The dark fae didn't look at him at all.

"I don't have wings. Not because I can glamour, but—"

Jakon applied more tension to the string as the dark fae moved, but he reached for the ties of his cloak, not any weapon. Jakon's strain on the bow slackened, his eyes widening as the material came away and the dark fae turned. His stomach rolled at the gruesome sight.

"They took them from me. Permanently."

Two long, serrated stumps marred his shoulder blades. If he'd once had mighty wings, they'd now been sawn off, and seeing the hideous breaking and splintering of what was left behind, Jakon knew it wasn't by any method of painless mercy.

"Who did that to you?" he asked. Despite the dark fae being the enemy, he couldn't ignore his slither of sympathy.

The fae shrugged back into his cloak. His black eyes were dying. "They call them the Masters. They oversee the Born and the Transitioned. That is what I am. Fae. Turned dark fae."

Jakon could have buckled at the information. Yet it wasn't entirely new. Marlowe and Aurialis had already enlightened them to the fact the dark fae could possibly be advancing their numbers by creation. Being confronted with one only put the scale of the war into world-shifting clarity, and Jakon didn't know what to make of it. This was bigger than defending a kingdom. More to battle with than they were capable of handling alone.

"Why are you here?" Nik's question barely sounded as a whisper. It seemed his mind was reeling.

"They took everything from me. As they have done to many others. I had a family in Dalrune whom they slaughtered. I don't remember much, but I was cursed to remember that. They didn't make it past the Transition. They took my wings the first time I tried to escape. It is what they do to anyone who tries."

"So they allow you to be their messenger now?" Nik's caution seeped back.

"What other use am I to them now? If you think what you see in me is what you will meet when they rain down their forces, you are wholly unprepared, *king*. It will be a slaughter."

A chill rattled Jakon's very bones. All he could picture with a surge of hot desperation were those he would defend no matter the odds. Marlowe and Faythe. Damn, even Nik and Tauria crossed his frantic mind.

"But there is a network running beneath the mountain. The Masters may reign, but in their arrogance, they haven't been smart enough to see what works against them. Around them."

"You've still failed to tell me why you risk telling us this. What could you, or any others, stand to gain from warning us?"

"There are those among both the Born and Transitioned who are not what the Masters paint us to be, king. Like the humans and the fae, evil lies only in the heart. Don't be a fool to see us as all the same."

"What did you give Zarrius?" Jakon asked.

The dark fae shook his head, those eyes filled with *pity.* "You have to start looking within your walls before it is too late. But that is not why I hoped you would be smart enough to figure out the lord's meeting point and come here."

Nik hissed through gritted teeth, "Then why?"

"I came to tell you she is not safe."

The air fell ice-cold.

"Who?" Nik dared to ask, but like Jakon, the face had already appeared in his mind. One who was so damningly far away.

"You've sent Tauria Stagknight right into their waiting arms."

"How…?" Nik breathed, and Jakon's chest twisted for the turmoil that would wreck him with the warning. "How do you know all this?"

The dark fae raised his chin. "Because the High Lord Mordecai has been waiting for her. For you all."

Nik *stumbled* back. Jakon had never seen him so lost and ghostly.

"They don't wish to kill her, only use her. The queen is powerful. She is Fenstead's pride. Though she is not the only one in danger. Fear their desire for all those who bear a crown with royal blood."

"Why? Why would you sacrifice yourself for this—for us?" Nik was pacing, his rage palpable.

"I can't even remember my own name. I remember I had a family, but I can't picture their faces anymore. They gave me wings and tore them away. I now live with the curse of an insatiable bloodlust for humans. I didn't choose this. All I have left is revenge. I had to give the lord what he needed. Be careful, as there may come a time where telling friend from foe becomes far more difficult. Look to the eyes, as the Transitioned's have no color. But the Born…you must test their blood. Silver blood flows in their veins, but there are many with the ability to glamour their wings and makes themselves appear no different from you."

Jakon's mind spun, but he collected the information. "The other *Transitioned*—they're like you?"

The dark fae shook his head. "Some have Transitioned to nothing but savagery. Merciless killers. Some don't even resemble any form of humanity in appearance anymore. They are monsters. But there are those who can be saved. Have patience for them—it is all I ask once I'm gone. Don't see them all as the same as it will take caution to distinguish those who are beyond saving. Both the Blackfair and Silverfair lines have those who fight a war because they have been led to believe it is kill or be killed. It will be up to you—all of you—to convince them there is another way."

Jakon tried desperately to piece together what he knew. One thought screamed over all else: Orlon had known about it all. The creature Nik and Faythe encountered below the passages… What if Zarrius planned to see through whatever it was Orlon had started? Creatures with blood-lust and savagery.

Oh Gods.

Yet as for the one before them, there was *humanity* still within his onyx eyes. Enough to make his final plea with Nik. He had to have known his life would be forfeited by being caught.

He did, as he offered it to Nik. "End me now, king. I have been ready for some time."

Nik's fist tightened around his sword. His chest heaved, and Jakon had no doubt there was one piece of information above all else that flared his wrath. The threat to Tauria.

As if Jakon had spoken it, Nik lunged so fast that all he could do was watch as he kneeled, driving his sword straight through the dark fae without a second thought. He watched the king breathe still and heavy. The flash of merciless violence was something he had never seen before on Nik. Chilling, but he had to admire his protective spirit that didn't hesitate for those he loved and his kingdom. No matter what it might settle in his soul once it was over.

The dark fae choked as his life faded. "Thank you."

Nik stood abruptly, pulling the blade free, and the body slumped. Turning, his turmoil was written on his face as he paced away.

Jakon stood rigid to stifle his trembling from a coldness that had nothing to do with the temperature. He broke the silence with a vacant question. "What do we do now?"

"Now," Nik said through a hard breath while his fist clamped tight around his sword, "I'm not above declaring war on Olmstone if they've harmed her. I'm not above killing whoever stands in my way to get her back."

CHAPTER 51

Tauria

WALKING THROUGH THE streets of Vesmire now felt far more pleasant than the first time. As she linked arms with the prince, the people of the city looked to them with adoring eyes rather than their initial wariness and distain. She supposed now they were a symbol of new prospects for the kingdom. Hope. But Tauria tried not to meet any of their wonder-filled gazes. All she was to them was a false promise.

Within the library, Tarly was quick to put distance between them out of the public eye. Tension from their encounter still ran between them. Above all else, she was irritated with him. The constant switch of emotion was becoming more than she could tolerate.

She diverted from the prince as they went about their own tasks of research. Tauria lost herself between the high cases of books, and her attention was wholly swayed from looking for historical texts when she found herself among endless rows of fiction. Perhaps she could spare an hour for a little leisurely reading before the grueling task of researching the harrowing and the damned…

Tauria ran her fingers along the spines until one set of books caught her attention by its title. Her cheeks flushed as she spared a glance around. No one was nearby. Plucking one of the romance novels, she was quick to find a small reading area, where she settled on a lounge chair. Tarly could get a head start for them both to find any information they could about the dark fae.

Hours passed, and Tauria couldn't turn her pages fast enough, desperate to cram in as much of the enrapturing tale as she could before she was found to be slacking. Over halfway through her story, she had to pause to gather breath. She had expected romance, something passionate and twisting from the title "An Immortal Heart of Vengeance," but the detail that had begun to unfold…

Tauria extended her senses, feeling utterly scandalous for what she read in a public space. With the need that gathered between her legs, she wished she'd opened it in her rooms instead. When she didn't detect the prince or anyone nearby, she couldn't stop herself from opening the book back up.

Just a few more pages.

She couldn't be sure how much time had passed that allowed her to devour the rest of the book with no regrets. The pent-up lust it roused set her irritably on edge. But the ending left her heart racing in splinters. It had been so long since a story gripped her so fully that it drifted her from reality long past the final words and left her thinking. About the thin line between good and evil. About what was right in the face of wrongdoing.

"There you are."

Tauria had never closed a book so fast. The thump of it disguised her squeal of fright as the prince crept up on her. Tarly wore a frown of annoyance as he stalked to her, and all she could answer with was a sheepish look, caught utterly red-handed in the act of slacking. But he didn't need to know for how long. Before his eyes could target the book to identify it, Tauria shifted it out of sight. But it seemed that wasn't enough to conceal the genre as Tarly inhaled deeply, his features smoothing out in surprise while her whole body torched with the knowledge he'd detected the lustful shift of her scent.

"What are you reading?" To her surprise, Tarly dropped all his insufferable sternness. But she decided she would rather his reprimand than the mischievous smirk he tried to fight.

"I just took a break. I haven't gotten that far into the book."

He stalked to her in slow steps, his brow lifted in amusement. "You're an awful liar."

"You're insufferable."

"You don't need to be embarrassed." Tarly stopped in front of her, and something in his demeanor changed. A darkening of his hazel eyes. He lowered to a crouch in front of her, and Tauria's pulse picked up a rapid sprint.

Oh Gods, what was he doing?

"Does it all have to be for show, Tauria?" His voice dipped to a low gravel.

She didn't know how to respond, or how to act. His closeness was wrong. *So* wrong. The bond within her detected Tarly's slow advance, churning her stomach with the need to find distance. But in her shock, she planted still.

"Tarly, this is hardly the place." Her voice shuddered with nerves.

Pinning her with that heated stare, Tarly didn't move. "No one is around."

His hands fell to her knees, and she drew a sharp breath. And held it. She should push him away, but maybe she feared his reaction. All she could think about was not letting an ounce of her feelings slip through to Nik, as every suggestive touch from Tarly felt like a sickening betrayal to him.

When she didn't speak, Tarly's hand came up to her face, tenderly cupping her cheek. "We never got the chance to share that kiss at the solstice ball. You wanted it, didn't you? Before we were interrupted." He began to inch forward, and her mind screamed to retreat. Yet her body betrayed her thoughts by locking in place. She had wanted it, and it would be a lie to deny what he already knew. Yet she couldn't be sure what enticed him to act on it now.

Wrong.

Not your mate.

"It can be our secret," he went on, still moving to an intimate distance. Inch by inch he closed it until his face was level with hers. His fingers trailed down to her neck, a fraction closer to her collar. So close to Nik's mark that it snapped all her senses back into place.

But before she could react, Tarly's breath blew across her lips. "You're good at keeping secrets, aren't you, princess?"

She was seconds away from pushing him until he moved faster than she could react. Tauria gasped when his fingers hooked under her collar, tearing the ties as he pulled the material away to expose her neck. Disbelief widened his hard eyes as he slowly backed away from her. He didn't meet her frantic gaze as she breathed hard, doused in ice.

Tarly fixed his rage on Nik's mating mark. "I hoped it wasn't true," he said with a dark vacancy. He took a couple more backward strides as if preparing to flee.

Would he run straight to his father?

"Tarly, please, let me explain—"

"The two of you put on a spectacular show, I'll give you that. You truly are made for each other." There was hurt in his tone, and she knew she deserved the guilt that rocked her.

"I didn't want to lie to you."

He huffed a bitter laugh. "I don't know what his reasons were, nor how you're concealing his scent"—his fists were trembling at his sides—"but I hope he knows he's signed your death warrant with that mark."

Tauria blinked, recoiling at those words.

I'm destined to kill you.

A shudder of something so dark and cold swept through her. She hadn't heard the exact words the Dresair prophesized to Nik, but riddled with a sense of foreboding, regret rose that she hadn't returned with him when she had the chance…that perhaps the prophesy could be fulfilled by wrong choices rather than his hand.

She shook her head. No. It was just a coincidence. It had been her decision to stay and see this through, not Nik's. Tauria wouldn't fear the supposed prophesy that had tried for so long to keep them apart.

"Please," she begged, standing. She could do nothing but plea with him. "Varlas can't find out."

"You'd better pray to every damn God that he doesn't!"

Her heart rattled the cage of her chest. Her eyes burned. Because above all, she couldn't stand the look of betrayal that slithered through his anger as though he were trying to hide it. "I'm sorry," she whispered. "It was the only way to talk to him. Varlas has been blocking his Nightwalking."

"He put your life on the line to *talk?*"

"I chose him, Tarly."

That seemed to strike him, raising a wall that she detected in his closed-off posture. It pained him to hear it, but she hadn't meant for it to sound like a battle between *them.* As though Nik were *better* than him. But at the quick look of hurt and defeat on the prince's face, Tauria's mouth fell open to salvage her poor choice of words.

Before she could speak, Tarly's hard voice cut in like a shadow. "You'd better hope my father has been far more preoccupied with other matters to have seen what is glaringly obvious to everyone," Tarly sneered. "At the ball, you have no idea what you did. What everyone saw between you two that was so undeniable that the only way to silence the rumors was to kiss you and then keep you close. To try to convince every person in that room my damn *fiancée* wasn't sleeping with the King of High Farrow behind my back. The way you moved on that dance floor as if he knew your body better than you did…like you could answer to his every touch before it was made."

Tauria recoiled at the harshness. But she deserved this. They had been reckless and selfish, and she had gotten what she wanted without considering how it would impact Tarly.

"How did you know about the bond?"

Tarly shook his head as though it were the most obvious thing and she were a fool. "It was there the moment you stepped out of High Farrow's castle. The time I spent having to pretend I couldn't detect his scent wrapped around every inch of you… If you hadn't bathed and changed before we arrived, it would have been over. Even then there were still notes of him, of something deeper than a few heated touches. I kept my distance from you, only entertaining what I had to. I couldn't figure out what you two had planned, but if it was with malicious intent to my kingdom, I was fully prepared to do whatever it took to stop you. But then I discovered there was perhaps a bigger threat—one you had walked right into—and that's when it all turned." A softness he battled not to show slipped into his harsh expression. "I didn't want to care for you, but I did. All I could think about was how it wasn't safe for you to be here, and the only way to keep my father at bay was to entertain you. Us. But maybe it was more than that all this time, much as I was horrible to you in my will to deny it. My feelings that grew for you."

The silence became heavy, and her pulse throbbed wildly. Guilt dried out her throat for not seeing it sooner.

"I had my suspicions about what Nik was to you for a while. He's a dominant, territorial bastard, but he's particularly insufferable around you. Only, I couldn't understand why he'd kept it from you for so long when it was clear he pined after you like a pathetic puppy-dog. But he chose the worst time to finally come out with it and claim you. I didn't like him before, but I despise him more now for the danger he's up and left you in."

"It's not like that—"

"I might hate him, but I know what it's like to lose a mate."

Tauria lost all her arguments to guilt and sorrow, so crushing in that moment as she had been so horribly selfish. All this time, she'd flaunted everything he'd lost right in front of him as if he were a fool. And Tarly had stayed silent.

"Why didn't you tell me you knew right away?" He owed her nothing, but she was desperate to try to atone for all the ways she had wronged him.

He didn't answer immediately. His guard slipped as he looked at her face, revealing something broken in his. "There were moments I felt for you, allowed myself to wonder what it would be like for you to want me instead of him. I knew you never did and never would. Even during those days we spent together in High Farrow, he had you. And you had him."

Her emotions cleaved deep and raw. "I'm sorry," she choked. It wasn't enough, but she didn't know what would be in that moment.

"I don't resent you for it," he said, voice devoid of emotion. "I pity you. Your secret is safe with me. But I don't wish to stick around to see how it ends."

Tarly began to walk away.

"Where are you going?"

He halted his steps, not turning to her as he said, "I think it's your turn to see what you can find out about the one thing that will help you leave this damned place before it's too late." He called back as he left her, "I'll send in your guard to keep you company."

CHAPTER 52

Tauria

Tauria filtered through the pages of yet another historic volume. The table was covered entirely with splayed texts as she dove right into the knowledge, desperate for anything to distract her from the need to go after Tarly. To beg him to let her explain herself and apologize. Occasionally, the wicked dark seed of fear churned in her gut that he could betray her, just as she'd betrayed him.

She had no reason to distrust Tarly. She didn't. He was many things, but she hadn't once believed he was vengeful or spiteful. He needed space from her, and that ugly thought had been enough to keep her here long into the evening. Her stomach churned with hunger as they'd already skipped lunch to come to the library as soon as possible. Time was no longer in their favor. After she'd foolishly allowed herself to be stolen away by dark, romantic tales, Tarly was right: she had some catching up to do, so she'd declined Lennox's invitation to escort her back for supper.

"This is hopeless," she exasperated.

Lennox came over with a new stack of books. She'd sent him on the task of retrieving anything he could find on the dark fae while she combed through the books she'd already found. But hours later, all he'd brought her were tedious histories she already knew, tales of kingdoms establishing, the few mentions of the dark fae all of a time long before they became the lethal force they were known as now. Nothing Lennox brought her shed light on the Dark Age enough for her to find any weakness in the force they could come up against. If history was repeating itself, she needed to learn all she could about that time.

"I'm sure you'll find something," Lennox encouraged her. He stepped away, and she barely paid him any notice as she read the titles of the books he'd brought this time.

Tauria shook her head. "They're mostly carbon copies of what I've already read." She'd had enough and decided to stalk through the bookcases herself.

"Where are you going?"

"I appreciate your help, but I need to look for myself. There must be a section you've missed."

"I'm confident I've looked through every case in this place over the past few hours." His snide chuckle added an undertone to his words that she found odd.

"This place is huge. I doubt anyone would be able comb it in its entirety in a day. It would take several days, maybe even weeks."

"Then I'll continue looking for you tomorrow."

"I need a moment away from reading anyway. I'm starting to gain a headache."

"We should get you back to the castle."

Tauria halted her march, Lennox's persistence grating on her nerves. As she twisted to him, he dropped his gaze from her as he usually did. "Is there a reason you don't want me to look for the volumes myself?" she challenged.

"I only wish to help you, of course."

She couldn't be angry with him, and admittedly, her irritation had only risen so quickly because her nerves were still teetering on a razor's edge after Tarly's swift exit. "I won't spend much more time here," she promised, twisting on her heel to begin her quick pace once again.

She traveled up and up and up, not realizing just how high the levels were and figuring it would be best to start from the top so she could mark which rows she'd covered should she have to come back. Tauria scoured the whole top level in just over an hour. She knew this by sparing a glance at the sundial over the balcony. Daylight began to dull, signaling short hours till evening, but she couldn't give up. There had to be *something* in the greatest library supposedly to exist in Ungardia. If they couldn't find any information in such a well-guarded place, her mind spiraled with the dread that they would never come to find anything that would enlighten them to what the dark fae were planning.

On the second highest level, fatigue began to weigh on her lids and grind her frustration. But then she halted when her eyes caught on a door down the next row of bookcases. She didn't hesitate to storm for it.

Lennox trailed her at a distance. "You shouldn't—"

Tauria knocked before he could finish and brushed off his stupid overprotectiveness. There was nothing that could harm her in here. No weapons were allowed in the library, and she doubted the occasional elderly scholar would pose any great threat.

When silence answered, Tauria brazenly tried the handle. It was locked.

"We should go—"

Tauria conjured her wind, strong and precise enough to blast straight through the keyhole, and the door clicked after a few careful rotations in the lock. "Not my first time," she said triumphantly.

Surprisingly, the room was illuminated. What was more, it wasn't magick cobalt flames that danced in the lanterns, but mundane amber fire. It only alerted her to the fact the room was in use, and whoever its occupant was had only intended to leave for a short while to risk leaving a burning flame unattended around so much alluring tinder.

"I don't have a good feeling about this," Lennox said apprehensively.

"Then leave." She brushed him off. "Or keep watch."

The room was small and closed in, only a quaint study space with no windows. The walls were lined with bookcases, and a few volumes littered the desk and small lounge space beside an unlit fireplace. Odd. A shudder swept through her body, but she had to focus.

Tauria made quick work, moving along each wall, her eyes darting across them all with her rising adrenaline. She couldn't be sure why she felt both hopeful and giddy with dread that she might come to find something of use in the locked room.

"You shouldn't be in here."

Tauria whirled in fright, having been too lost in thought to detect the presence. In her shock at who she found, she couldn't cast her accusation at Lennox for not being alert. The old voice was befitting of the frail being that shuffled, hunched over, into the room. A human man who looked to be living on borrowed time. Tauria didn't expect the mortal, pleasantly surprised the kingdom would give a human such an esteemed role in the great library. From his robes, he was easily identifiable as a scholar.

"Sorry, I'm looking for some specific texts and had no luck in the main library." She paused, biting her lip. Did the human have the influence to speak and be heard if she disclosed what information she sought? The risk of Varlas finding out was too great. "Never mind." Her shoulders fell in defeat as she made to leave.

"What is it you look for, child?" The man's voice was soothing and warm, unexpected considering her intrusion. His gray irises filled with intrigue as he eyed the door, then her. "How did you undo the lock?" he tried instead, gauging her reluctance to trust him.

She saw no harm in sharing that information. Instead of answering with words, Tauria's hand moved elegantly, creating a small gust of wind that danced with her hair and rustled the loose parchments on the man's desk.

His gaze lit up with wonder. "A Windbreaker," he admired. "The Spirits have blessed me to meet one before I see my last day. As I hear, there aren't many of you left."

Tauria had never wondered, and in her sheltered life, she hadn't come across any other aside from her father.

"Did you know," he began, pacing over to the nearest wall of books, "that the abilities have a way of passing down through generations depending on their rarity? If an ability seems to be dying out, it will awaken in the bloodline and begin to pass down once more. Often, if both parents have different abilities, it is the one that features least in the world that will pass on."

Tauria's interest piqued. Her mother was a Florakinetic, and there had been several with that ability in Fenstead who kept the lands enviable and thriving. "What if neither parent has an ability?" she pondered. The question came from her thoughts of Nik. Neither of his parents had been gifted, yet he was exceedingly powerful in his Nightwalking.

The man passed her a smile, seeming to delight in her interest as she got closer. Maybe he even valued the company she imagined wasn't easy to find for someone of his standing. He hummed curiously. "It is possible for abilities to manifest from farther back in an individual's bloodline, I suppose, but not entirely common."

"What if one came to harbor great power?"

"Then I wouldn't ignore such a mighty interference from the Gods."

Tauria straightened, the knowledge striking her with a sense of...*pride.* Because Nik was powerful and brilliant, and she was his mate.

The man hooked a curious brow at whatever he read on her face before hobbling over to his desk. *"To see the end the Mortal Gods must stand,"* he began, his voice a song as he recited words that gripped her so entirely she tremored as if he spoke of something great to come. *"It is not without them that power is true. Fall one, fall all. Find friend in foe to see it through."*

Tauria's heartbeat picked up. "What is that from?"

Behind his desk, the man casually sorted through parchments. "It is the beginning of the end, my dear."

Her eyes scrunched shut with thoughts, questions, distractions. She had a bigger purpose right now, but his words…she couldn't shake the need to find out more. Before she could ask, his voice perked up.

"Now, are we acquainted enough that you will tell what it is you sought to gain from breaking in here?"

Tauria winced sheepishly and found herself sparing a glance at Lennox. He stood in the shadows by the door but didn't object. "Can I trust you not to speak of it?"

The man's wiry brow twitched with amusement. "Who would you expect me to gossip to? I am the only human here, but even the fae scholars don't engage with each other much. We are the keepers of the library, nothing more. The king does not bother with our affairs. I assume that is who you fear, Tauria Stagknight."

She blinked. "How do you know my name?"

The man chuckled. "I may be old and human, but with the knowledge I have acquired, it's not hard to see it in visual form when it comes to me."

Of course. She hadn't considered there would be scripts on her in Fenstead's histories.

"A remarkable fae you are indeed, even more so in person. It is a blessing that I get the honor of meeting you."

Her cheeks flushed. "I'm not that great if you ask around."

His humble laughter brightened the room more than the single lantern ever could. In that moment, she decided to take a chance on him.

"I'm looking for any volumes on the dark fae."

The man's smile instantly fell, and it rattled a chill to watch fear fill his wrinkled eyes. "Whatever you're looking to find out, I assure you, it will not be good."

"I'm not expecting it to be. But please. It's important."

His hesitation gave away that he knew something.

"Many lives could be in danger. Including my own."

Sadness was etched on his tired face. Sympathy. She tried not to feel it like a condolence for what was to come.

"I have what you seek," he offered with low reluctance. Tauria was endeared that it seemed the old man wanted to protect her from the knowledge he would present. As he shuffled to the back of the room, Tauria's sights caught on a set of black spines. The man reached for the thickest one, but before he could struggle to pull the heavy book down Tauria had crossed the space.

"This one?"

He nodded with a grateful smile, but it was a partial wince.

Hooking her fingers over the spine, she carefully took it from the shelf before laying it on the desk. The title was embossed in metallic gold.

Book of Enoch.

"Everything you need to know about the dark fae should be in here. Along with things that may interest you about your own creation and that of other species."

Tauria's eyes slid up to the other books that looked like they were of the same set. Seven more of them, their titles all one word in a language she couldn't decipher. The man followed her interest.

"Tell me, do they still school young ones on the Seven Gods?"

Tauria tried to recall. "Most believe the Gods to be a myth now. We were taught there has only ever been the three Spirits. Though one was cast out from duty a long time ago."

The man huffed. "And who do they say placed the Spirits here to watch over the realm?"

"They are Divine beings. They came from the Realm of the Spirits to grant order."

"The Realm of the Gods, child. Do not think they are one and the same."

"It's not as if it matters," Tauria near snapped. "If there were once Gods, they have long since abandoned us to the mercy of those *They* created."

His gray eyes met hers, something in them sparking with awe and wonder. He watched her, *studied* her, as if she were one of the texts. "Perhaps not," was all he said, but his words were distant like a slipped thought.

Tauria turned taut under the attention that began to prick her skin. To distract from the creeping unease, she came around the desk to the Book of Enoch, opening it up to no page in particular. She tried to engross herself but couldn't absorb a single word while the man lingered nearby, looking over his books but occasionally lingering a gaze on her. She opened her mouth to voice her gratitude to him for the knowledge, but the close appearance of Lennox made her jump she'd been so lost in thought.

"You shouldn't be reading this," he said, his hand coming over the book as if to close the text, but Tauria slammed her hand on the pages.

"What is your problem?" she snapped. His strange behavior wasn't sitting right, and as she glanced at him, he was quick to avert his gaze. But his face had taken on a hard edge. Anger tightened his jaw, and his breaths quickened. A chill swept her that had nothing to do with the temperature.

Tauria cast her attention back to the text, moving to turn a page. Once again, Lennox went to take the book from her, and as he did, she pulled it harshly away. He hissed as he caught his fingers on the paper's edge. Her face fell as he retreated having been cut by it, but her apology lodged in her throat when she looked at the pages. The ink was black, but she swore it hadn't bled onto the edges before where there was now a dark spot.

Her pulse stilled as alarm rang in her ears, but she couldn't be sure why. A tremble shook her fingers as she reached over to trace the edge and confirm what her mind wanted so desperately to believe. But when she touched the dark spill, she found it wasn't dry. Not centuries-old, mistakenly spilled ink.

Tauria upturned her hand, finding the dark liquid still wet on her skin.

Time slowed to a crawl while her mind screamed to run but her body froze in place. Her eyes fixed on her fingers until she found the courage to turn to Lennox. He stood with his back to her, hunched over and clutching his hand. His shoulders rose and fell deeply. She couldn't speak. Couldn't find the words to confirm the impossible that she refused to believe was the truth, hoping he'd turn to her with his usual kindness and brush off the superficial wound.

"Lennox," she choked. Because his silence was dangerous.

"You shouldn't have done that." His voice rumbled dark, unrecognizable.

Tauria's eyes snapped to the man with a terror so consuming. "Run—!"

But it was too late.

Lennox targeted the man just as she screamed her warning, and there was no hesitation as he lunged. Tauria stumbled back in horror, crashing into the bookcase. Her arms raised to protect her head from the tumbling tomes that rained down. But when she beheld Lennox… her whole world stopped. Locking eyes with the old man, all she could do was watch in cold-set disbelief as Lennox's teeth punctured his neck and he drank the man's life right before her. She held those grey eyes utterly helplessly and watched him fade. But despite his pain and being moments from death, the man mouthed one word that returned her to her survival instinct.

Run.

She hoped he saw the apology in her eyes as she strained agonizingly against leaving him. He was already too far gone to be saved. She choked back her whimper at the thought he'd bought her time.

Tauria swiped up the book and shot to the exit. Her wind followed her to slam the door shut just as she heard Lennox pull away from the man with a guttural growl. As before, she worked her magick through the lock in the nick of time, but she knew it wouldn't be an obstacle for long.

Racing down the aisles, her pulse drummed, but guilt and heartache at the life lost doused her adrenaline. An ear-splitting blast of splintering wood rang with the signal Lennox had torn through the feeble door with little effort. She winced, her heart skipping a beat, but she didn't stop running. Couldn't stop picturing the black blood…

Lennox is dark fae.

It didn't make sense. Her mind sprinted as fast as her feet.

Lycus recognized him from Fenstead.

So that couldn't have been a lie.

Tauria wound down long sets of stairs, unable to extend her senses to track how close he was while she focused on heading for the exit that seemed too damn far away. Her thoughts rushed to figure out how foolish she was to have missed it.

She halted abruptly with a cry when a dark shadow landed a stretch away from her.

Landed.

As if she couldn't be rendered any more surprised against such damning odds, Tauria's eyes drifted over his shoulders, trailing up, until she got to the end of his towering, taloned *wings.*

Gods above.

"How?" she breathed.

How had he hidden them all this time?

"A glamour," he sang cruelly, not sounding an ounce like the male she'd come to know dearly. The male she trusted. One of her people. It had all been a lie, and the stab of betrayal was too much to bear. "One of the many superior advantages of becoming dark fae." He took slow steps to her, the kind that displayed arrogance in the knowledge he'd trapped his prey but there was fun to be had.

"How could you betray Fenstead?" Tauria tracked him while she tried to figure out her next move. Running would be futile with the short distance between them.

"Fenstead betrayed me!" he seethed. "*You* betrayed me. And so many others when you fled and let so many of us become captured by the enemy. Did you enjoy sitting prized and pretty in High Farrow while your people were slaughtered?"

Nausea and guilt overcame her. He didn't need a trap or steel or wings; the weapons he broke her with were far more powerful. Words. Truths. She would die here, and she would deserve it.

"Tauria, what's happening?"

She gasped as she heard Nik's voice within, realizing in her terror she must have slipped the shield on the bond. Tears pricked her eyes.

"I'm okay."

Gods, she was grateful to hear him. And with his words of comfort he soothed her. Just for a few seconds. She wasn't alone.

"I'm coming to get you."

"You can't. I'm—I'm going to be okay. I promise."

She had to make it out of that damned library. For him. For Fenstead and High Farrow. This was not the way she would die. She had to block out feeling Nik's desperation and anger.

Lennox continued to advance, and she kept retreating. "I don't remember my life before they made me dark fae, but I'm grateful for it. Fenstead's conquer was the best thing to happen to the kingdom to rise it stronger. But don't worry, Tauria. They still plan to see you rule over it..."

Her back met with a dead end. She'd retreated all the way to the balcony.

"As one of us."

That haunting statement froze her to her core. But then it awakened a defiance so strong she did the most impulsive thing she could think of in that moment. With a battle cry, Tauria cast her hands out, and the air answered to her. Drawing them together, it took such great strength that she clenched her teeth, bracing her legs, to conjure the necessary blast. It worked. Lennox turned too late before the tall bookcase came crashing down with a rain of heavy books, triggering a domino effect of resounding booms as others followed. She didn't have the spare emotion to feel bad for decimating the sacred space when her survival hung in the balance.

Tauria didn't waste a second, using the distraction to hoist herself onto the balcony.

Then she was falling.

And falling.

And falling.

Her stomach flipped as gravity claimed her, and without her staff, she wasn't confident she could break her plummet so smoothly. A tornado encased her to brace against it, and she cursed the sentiment of no weapons allowed in the library.

Her shadow grew against the sundial, and she cast her wind down to break her fall at the last second. She didn't land as well as she'd hoped, but it wasn't the first time she'd sustained an injury from her ambitious testing of her ability. Tauria cried out and rolled on impact, clenching her teeth against the searing pain that shot up one of her ankles. Swiftly, she was rising to her feet again, and she quickly realized the peril that had become of her when she tried to bear weight on her injured leg. Running out of here wouldn't be an option now, and a part of her acknowledged it was over.

"You're hurt. And if you don't tell me who, I won't be responsible for my actions when I get there."

"Your overprotective bullshit isn't helping."

"Neither are you."

"Don't do anything. I'm just…dealing with something."

It was a huge downplay of what she faced, but how could Tauria explain her situation? Being stalked by a dark, evil being who'd posed as her friend all this time was still something she was in denial of herself.

She continued to think of him. Nik. The time they didn't have together after finally becoming one. She would fight until her last breath for that time.

Beyond her, the compass of light around the sundial was eclipsed in darkness. No bookcases. Nothing. Her fae sight adjusted to spy an opening in the far wall that filtered faint light. But before she could hobble another step, a dark form swooped down.

Lennox landed right in front of her, and the feral rage on his face was frightening. She stared into his eyes, which were fully blazing at her. It was the first time she'd been close enough to see…

His eyes were a depthless obsidian. Like the color of his blood. Tauria screamed when he lunged for her, but he didn't attack with teeth. From his grip on her neck, she was sent soaring into the darkness before she skidded harshly along the floor. Lennox stormed for her, and she shuffled back to gain distance, her scraped flesh stinging. He was too fast.

Faster than any fae. Stronger.

Human blood.

Pieces were coming together, but every new thing she scrambled to remember from her vague knowledge of the species only sank her further into helplessness.

"Is it Tarly?"

"He's not here."

"Then who?"

"No one I can't handle."

"This isn't the time to be arrogant."

"This isn't the time to distract me!"

Nik's thinning patience and rage rippled to her.

"You're hurt—badly. Please don't tell me you're alone and in danger."

"I'm not—"

Lennox caught up to her, and she gasped when he kneeled and his hands clamped around her neck. The wrongness of his vile touch against Nik's mark was something she couldn't shield from her mate. It churned her gut with guilt that Nik would feel it all as she clawed at his vise grip.

"Tauria." Nik's voice was so broken, so desolate and helpless, it cleaved something soul-deep. Because there was nothing he could do. She was faltering, and he felt every second of it. Perhaps if Lennox had chosen any other method to kill her, she could have blocked him from the pain. But the grating against the mark that bound her to Nik blasted that channel wide open.

"It's okay." She attempted to soothe him, but she knew it would be futile.

"Hold on, love. Please."

Her vision began to blur, but she clung desperately to consciousness. She reached and grappled with the tether to her mate that slowed her from falling completely.

"Just a little longer."

She choked and spluttered, but her energy dwindled until she couldn't physically fight back. All she could do was tune in to the soothing notes of Nik's voice that lifted the cold from the stone floor and eased the burning in her airway.

"I'll love you forever, Tauria. We'll have many centuries for me to show you in this life, but beyond, I'll find you. I'll follow you. Always. Tell me you'll have me. Against all we've faced and all I've done, tell me you want that life."

Tears slid from her eyes.

"I'll always want you."

"Good. Because you're stuck with me now."

She wanted to laugh—out of desolate joy that he hadn't left her.

"Fight, Tauria."

"I can't. He's—" She choked and spluttered some more when Lennox backed away from her all at once. Rolling onto her side, Tauria gasped to fill her lungs, clamping her eyes shut with the waves of dizziness that threatened to pull her under.

"I'm right here with you." Nik calmed her. His strength echoed through to her, striking her will to survive and snapping her back to full consciousness. *"You are a survivor, Tauria Stagknight. You always have been."*

"Don't leave me."

"Never."

She managed to rise to her hands and knees, glancing over to make out the dark form that towered over her, pinning her with such powerful hatred she couldn't believe she'd missed it all this time.

"What did they do to you?" she rasped, her throat tight and painful.

"They made me stronger," Lennox said ominously, pacing forward a few steps. "I can't kill you. They need you. But I will have to tell them all that you know." He halted, the smile that he turned to her with crawling over every inch of her skin. "The full moon isn't far off. I'm sure they'll lock you away until then. Unless you decide to cooperate. Choose to see that this is the only way to better the world, strip it of weakness. You will make a fine dark fae royal, Tauria. One we will all be blessed to bow before." He crouched down, head tilting with sinful amusement. "If you survive the Transition, that is."

Her blood ran cold. The stone beneath her was ice. It wasn't true. He only sought to frighten her.

No. What would he gain from such games?

Oh Gods.

"What about Tarly?" she dared to ask.

The curl of his mouth grew, and the ground was pulled from under her.

The prince was to meet the same fate.

His own father would put him through such a heinous, forbidden magick. That much she distantly remembered from the Spirit of Life in the cottage, so long ago now.

But why?

Without a second thought, Tauria used Lennox's proximity and awkward crouched stance to her advantage. Her wind blasted him back, and she rose to her feet. She had no staff, but it wasn't as if she could make much movement anyway with her injury. She could still attack.

She worked the motions of her arms, not feeling the air as powerfully as she was capable of wielding it with her restricted movements, but she hit. Again and again.

Catching on, Lennox splayed his large wings, attempting to shoot upward to get away. Tauria stole the air from his flight then wrapped him with it. When she cast her arms down, he came crashing to the stone faster than gravity could have claimed him. His scream resonated in her ears, drowning out the snap of his wings from his awkward landing. Tauria lost focus with the need to clamp her ears against the shrill sound that was not of man or fae.

"You worthless bitch queen," he snarled, crossing to her faster than any fae she'd ever seen before. He bared his teeth and eyed her neck. The horror of what he intended to do shot so deeply that the mating bond within her roared to be protected, unable to stand the thought of another male's attempt to defile it.

Tauria screamed. Agony ripped up her throat, but she couldn't stop. Not as something loud shattered overhead. She didn't stop until her wind had blasted the dark fae away from her and she'd fallen to her knees.

CHAPTER 53

Tauria

"I'*m right here, Tauria. Don't be afraid.*"

A ringing filled her ears. She didn't uncurl from herself. Nik's voice was gentle, coaxing her to answer back. One trembling hand went to her neck as tears fell. His mark was still intact.

She didn't want to know what would have happened if Lennox's vile teeth had punctured over it. All she could think was that it could have taken him from her. And that was a thought as haunting as death itself.

Tauria glanced around herself, and only then did her senses start to return. She felt the swirling wind. Casting her eyes up, she couldn't believe what she saw. In her desperation to protect herself—protect the bond—she'd encased herself in a strong sphere of air that spun impossibly fast, but that wasn't its only lethal element. Shards of glass circled around her in a strong tornado from the shattered dome roof.

She was safe. Anyone who tried to step through it would be torn to shreds. What was more baffling was that she hardly felt the exertion of using her magick. It hummed and heated her veins as usual, but she knew it should take far more to conjure and hold such a forcefield.

Then she felt it.

"How are you doing that?"

Nik's magick. He was extending his well to her through the bond that made the most powerful blast of her ability feel like gentle play.

"I'm not entirely sure. I felt you scream—" Nik paused, the ripples of his rage mixed with terror.

"You can let me go now. It must be harming you."

"I'm fine. Are you still alone?"

There was a strain she felt that he brushed off like a selfless bastard.

"Yes, but I can handle it from here."

"Where is he?"

Nik didn't know who, perhaps even *what,* was after her, but her pulse quickened at the question. She could barely see anything through the gale of reflecting glass.

"Dead," she answered anyway, because Nik had to let go or he risked burning himself out. *"I'm okay, Nik. Let go."* Tauria was confident she could hold the wind and glass shield on her own, but not for long.

"Not until someone comes for you."

"No one's coming, Nik."

But her words were countered when she heard the distorted call of her name. Tauria whirled toward it with a gasp. Faintly, she made out a silhouette. Not one with wings. She'd already detected the voice to be…

Horror gripped her entirely at the shadow that lurked toward the prince.

"Tarly, *run!*"

It was too late. All she could make out was the quick movement of the pair engaged in nasty close combat. They had no weapons, but Lennox didn't need them. Not when his diet of human blood made him the ultimate predator even to the fae.

"Drop the shield, Nik. Tarly's in trouble."

"No."

She ground her teeth and pushed back. From within, she tried to cut him off. But he was so deep into her well of magick that his and hers had become entangled, and he wasn't letting go.

"Nik!"

"Trust me."

"He won't survive against him!"

She tried again, crying out with the pain of trying to sever her tie to him. But they were of equal power. Matched. They would kill each other before either would win.

"Please," she whimpered.

Nik stayed silent. Tauria cursed him over and over, jogging to the edge of the wind shield. It shimmered with lethal beauty, a silent dare to try to pass and survive being ripped to shreds.

She reached out a hand.

"What are you doing?"

"If you're going to force my hand, I'll force yours."

"Stop."

Her hand touched the shield, and she instantly cried out, retracting her arm. Tauria examined the injury. Only a few superficial cuts bled. If she were quick enough with a blast of her wind…

"So help me, Tauria," Nik snarled, reading her intentions.

"You said my will to challenge you was something you admired."

"This is not what I meant. You're putting your damn life at risk."

"I won't stand by and watch him get hurt when I could do something." Tauria backed up a few paces, carefully eyeing the wind and glass shield as if she could calculate the right moment to throw all sanity away and attempt to pass through.

"Please," he begged, and she took a slow blink, feeling his misery that he was helpless to stop her.

"I'm sorry."

Tauria halted. She didn't get the chance to rise her adrenaline to a reckless force. Rushing in through the stone gap, more silhouettes poured into the darkness. There was a split second of terror that it was all over; Varlas had found out and sent his guard to finish them. Or silence them. But at seeing the distinguishing tower of wings, she couldn't bite back her whimper of relief that they were here to take Lennox down instead. His shrill cries pierced through her protective shield.

Like the gentle release of a strenuous tug-of-war, Nik finally began to retreat from her power. Tauria seized back full control. Her arms tensed, and she clenched her teeth against the strong currents of her magick to hold the shield, only to release it slowly. Glass fell to the ground, shattering to crystals. The air became still once more. When she released it entirely, she didn't feel the cuts on her palms as she fell, breathless as everything caught up to her all at once.

"Your Majesty." A voice approached, and she jerked in fright.

The fae raised his hands but kept advancing slowly until he crouched to meet her. Tauria scanned him for any sign of the uniform she expected, but he appeared no more than one of the city fae. He reached up to his jacket, every movement so slow so as not to spook her. When he peeled back the fold, she blinked at the brass pin emblem he revealed to her.

Not the two-headed Wolf of Olmstone.

Not the side-profiled Stag of Fenstead.

It was the mighty Griffin of High Farrow.

She couldn't comprehend how in that moment as the bond fell silent. A groan stole her attention, and her eyes snapped to Tarly. He lay on the ground but was slowly peeling himself from the floor with the aid of three other fae who were dressed simply like the one by her. Tauria winced as she quickly got to her feet and tried to bear weight on her foot. The fae offered aid, and she didn't protest, needing to be sure Tarly was okay.

She fell by his side. There was a tear at his shoulder that drew crimson to the surface. But his hand raised to it before she could examine the wound. Tauria helped him to sit instead, her face pained at the state of him.

"Why did you come back?"

He winced, trying to get to his feet. "I'm sorry I left you here. I had no idea—" Tarly's gaze fell on the fallen heap of wings and flesh.

It all plowed into her at once, and her hand shot to her mouth. Despite everything, Lennox was one of her people. *Transitioned.* It was an immeasurable guilt, and she risked spiraling into helplessness as she imagined how many others could have suffered the same fate. Both of them winced and shuffled to stand, but Tauria didn't release him as he looked around their unexpected band of saviors.

"I still don't like him," Tarly muttered, seeming to have realized these were Nik's fae who'd helped. "But damn it, I guess I owe the bastard."

"Thank you," Tauria said to the males.

They all gave a nod as one said, "We got here as soon as we could."

Tauria would figure out Nik's methods later. Awareness returned to her as she remembered the chaos she'd erupted on the great library, starting with a whole level of bookcases and ending with the shattering of the dome roof. The ancient, peaceful space that knew no violence had been defiled in minutes.

"Varlas is going to know," she breathed in horror.

"He won't." Tarly's hand fell on her back, a comforting gesture of what she dared to believe was genuine friendship. "I'll deal with my father. You were attacked, that is all. He won't know about Lennox. He won't know that we're onto him."

Her heart was pounding, struggling to comprehend the ordeal. But Lennox's words about the dark fae wouldn't silence. Tauria's eyes landed on the discarded Book of Enoch, and she didn't look to the prince as she whispered, "I think we're both in more danger than we thought."

CHAPTER 54

Nikalias

NIK BRACED AGAINST his desk, but even that couldn't help his balance as he lowered to one knee. Agony tore through him, swaying his vision and slicking his skin with dangerous heat. The closest he'd ever come to a full burnout that could have claimed him entirely.

Yet it would have been worth it to save her.

Reaching to merge with Tauria's power was something he didn't believe possible. He knew some mates harbored power so matched they could merge, but with their distance, without physical touch, it shouldn't have been possible. At hearing her scream, something unexplainable had overcome him, and before he knew what he'd done or how, it was as if he were there with her. Harnessing as much of her power as he could while she was still in danger. Now, he couldn't be certain he was safe from the consequences of testing their magick's boundaries. Nik panted with his head bowed low, but all he could think about was her.

"Are you safe?" he tried when too much time had passed in silence since she confirmed his guards had arrived.

"We're heading back to the castle now. Tarly is hurt, but he's taking care of the story of what happened."

It was a mild relief, and Nik closed his eyes. A darkness began to creep over him, but he blocked it all from Tauria. After everything she'd emerged from, this wasn't a concern he could burden her with.

"You were so brave, love."

"Are you all right?" Her concern slipped through, and he knew he had to let her go now.

Nik nodded even though she couldn't see it. *"I'll be fine."* He hoped. For her, he fought. *"I'll check in with you tomorrow. But if anything happens before then, please—"*

"I'll tell you," she promised.

It was all he needed to hear. And though the fear gripped him that he couldn't be sure he would emerge from the oblivion that taunted to claim him, he couldn't stand the thought of her turmoil if she knew when they were so helplessly far apart.

"Our forever…it knows no realm or time."

Her agreement was wrapped with love and promise, a wave of bliss against his misery through the bond. *"Or trial or prophesy,"* she added quietly.

Nik smiled, allowing himself to drown in her comfort before closing off the bond.

Then he let go. And his body fell.

CHAPTER 55

Nikalias

Something urgent awoke Nik in a darkness flickered by cobalt flame. A tugging within. His mind was a haze, and his vision blurred. His body lay against something solid and unforgiving, but a new feeling eased over him. Nik groaned as he shifted his head, his sight adjusting, but he winced at the quick glare of flame glinting against…

His eyes snapped open, and instinct drove his movement to catch the wrist plunging a dagger straight for his chest. But he was so weak, barely able to fight off the assailant he struggled with through clenched teeth. Tearing his eyes from the lethal tip of the blade, horror doused him as he met a cold look of hatred and determination, so foreign on the delicate face he knew.

"Samara," he rasped. His throat was hoarse, his skin too hot. The memory of what he'd done to help Tauria flooded him, alerting him to his weakened state. He couldn't be sure how much time had passed, and despite the threat to his life in that moment, his concern for his mate in the aftermath of what she'd been through was a surge of urgency.

Samara said nothing as she straddled him, adding more of her weight to push down against Nik's attempt to hold her off. He was faltering, and that tip inched closer to his throat.

"You don't want to do this," he tried, trembling with exertion. Magick was still punishing him, but the fact he'd woken up was a sure sign he could pull through it with proper rest and care.

Yet neither would be granted if Samara succeeded in her attempt to kill him.

"This will gain you nothing," he panted, yielding another inch and feeling the phantom scratch of the blade. *Gods,* talking was difficult. But he couldn't accept that she was beyond reach. She was naïve and driven by disillusioned love, that was all.

"Neither of you love me!" she cried. "At least this way, Zarrius will be king. If I kill you…"

Nik tried to shake his head. "No. Without my coronation, he has no guarantee. If you killed me, the throne would be open to any high noble to stake their claim. It would be blood and chaos. Zarrius knows this." His head was pounding, and he struggled for consciousness. It didn't make sense. He thought he'd bonded with Samara on some level. Her betrayal was unexpected, but what did Zarrius have to gain from sending her to do this? "You're a liability," Nik groaned in realization, knowing he didn't have much left in him to fight off her weight much longer. "It's not me he hopes to kill. It's you."

His words settled enough that the pressure of the blade slackened. Nik took his chance. His survival instincts snapped into action. There was agony in every movement he forced, but Samara cried out when he twisted to pin her down instead. Her fingers didn't loosen their clamp around the dagger. He panted, unable to bear his weight or keep her restrained to prevent her from attacking again when he fell sideward.

Samara didn't waste any time before she was kneeling over him again, but with the blade raised she halted. "All I've ever been is a pretty pawn. To you, to him. You're both fools."

Nik fought for consciousness. Breathing deep was painful. He lost the fight against the heaviness of his lids as they fell closed, yet he knew how dangerous it was with Samara's unpredictability. "I'm mated, Samara," he got out. "If you kill me, Tauria will take my throne."

"A desperate lie," she sneered. But Samara's voice was laced with uncertainty in her own words.

"Think about it." He peeled his eyes open, head falling limp to look at her. "You know too much on both sides. All you are to him now is a loose end. Something he doesn't take chances on, no matter how pretty or loving you are. He knows an attack on me will silence you by forcing my hand to detain you."

Anger was etched on her face, but it was no longer hateful; it was cold and sad, and despite everything, Nik pitied her. Her eyes glistened in the blue firelight. Her grip tightened on the blade, and Nik didn't have the chance in his weakened state to react as she pulled back her arm.

"It's a *lie!*"

He braced for the plunge of her dagger. All he could do was whisper his apology to his mate. Picture her beautiful face. And as he thought of the time they didn't have, he fought for her. With the dregs of his strength he shifted to avoid a fatal stab through his chest, but fire erupted in his shoulder instead.

Samara's eyes were wide and horrified, but her trembling hands didn't fall. She looked around, and Nik wondered if she was in search of another weapon. There was no going back now.

Before he could move…

The door kicked open, and the first person to catch his eye inspired a surge of relief and surprise. Nik blinked a few times to be sure he wasn't delirious.

Several more guards filed in behind Jakon, and Marlowe rushed across the short distance to him.

Samara cried out as she was detained. "I did it for him," she sobbed, tears streaming down her face as she scanned the guards as though expecting Zarrius to be among them as her savior.

"Take her to the cells, but no one sees her without my say-so." Nik put all effort into steadying his voice enough to deliver the command, lifting to prop himself up on an elbow while his hand went around the submerged blade. It was in that moment he was done allowing his leadership to be questioned, his authority judged. He was the King of High Farrow, and he would own that title without reservation or apology. "Not a single person," Nik warned them all with a tone that fixed every guard's attention on him, his weakness subsiding just long enough to make himself perfectly clear.

There would be no mercy for those who chose to stand against him. And that meant those who'd sided with Zarrius behind his back.

He didn't have to bear his weight for long as Marlowe slipped behind him on her knees. Tiredness began to sweep over him, dulling the agony of his shoulder where the knife remained. Nik tried to reserve his strength to ensure none of what he felt and endured echoed through the bond to Tauria.

"What happened?" a voice bellowed.

Nik winced, his eyes fluttering with a wrath he was unable to unleash. He managed one dark look toward Zarrius, who put on an epic display of outrage and horror as he stormed into the room. Never before had Nik felt such raw, murderous tendencies toward someone.

"You're going to be okay," Marlowe said quietly, reaching into her pocket.

Nik shook his head as he caught the glow in the vial. "What did you promise, Marlowe?"

She didn't answer him as her fist closed around the captured yucolites. Her face was hard as she cast her attention to Zarrius instead. "We need a healer," she said, and any other time he would have warned her against using such a tone toward the lord. He wondered if she'd seen something, or perhaps she'd figured out on her own that Zarrius was conspiring behind his back. By Gods, was he grateful for the two humans regardless. "Now!" Marlowe ground out when no one was quick to move.

Zarrius warred with reluctance, but it was a surprise when he nodded with a glance at Nik's wounded shoulder and the guards began to shuffle out. Yet just as the lord turned from them, Nik swore he caught the slight upturn of his mouth. He'd triumphed this time. And Nik was a damn fool for not seeing Samara was still enthralled by him. He'd wanted to believe her innocent heart wasn't capable of what she'd attempted that night.

A heavy blanket creeped over his senses to pull him under. Of emotions, thoughts, and so much pain it began to beckon a welcoming darkness.

"You can let go, Nik. You'll be okay," Marlowe reassured him.

It was all he needed, yet his fear still rang true with the face that entered his mind. He had to pull through for her. He had to know Tauria was still safe. He couldn't—*he wouldn't*—fail her again.

Nik awoke with a pounding headache, but his consciousness surfaced naturally. Taking a long breath that no longer felt like inhaling flames, he slid his eyes open.

The first sound to enter his senses stilled him completely. He slowly propped himself up, blinking against the dizziness that swayed his vision. Then his head twisted back to find the source. Nik suppressed his smirk at the sight—and at the fact their dull human senses hadn't detected his movements enough to halt their passion.

"Don't mind me, just coming around from near death." Nik's voice was strained.

Marlowe gasped, pulling out of the heated kiss she and Jakon shared.

"Do you know how many ancient fae monarchs have pondered fates and kingdoms at that very desk?"

He'd never seen such a deep shade color her pale cheeks, but Jakon was otherwise unbothered as his hands slipped from her. "We knew you'd live," he mused. "And we couldn't leave in case Zarrius found some other tragic soul to finish the job of ending you."

"His intention wasn't to kill me." Nik winced as he sat up. "I don't think he anticipated her getting so close." He tried to move his dressed shoulder, wincing at the tenderness. He didn't have it in him to be bothered by his bare torso.

"You'll be left with a nasty scar, yucolites aside, but I should think you'll be perfectly fine in a few days."

Nik's face fell as he remembered what she'd acquired to save him. He wondered how she knew she'd need the yucolites. But Jakon cut in before he could even thank her.

"I must say, I'm still wondering how she got so close myself."

"I was weakened," Nik defended quickly at the amusement that danced in his friend's eyes. Yet he couldn't find the words to explain what he'd been through. "Tauria needed help, and somehow, through the bond, I was able to reach her power. It took me to a very dangerous limit."

"Reach her power…" Marlowe caught on, her frown thoughtful. "From so far away? I didn't think that was possible."

"Neither did I. But I was desperate."

"And she's safe?"

Marlowe's question skipped his pulse. His eyes slid to the window, where he found the sun was setting. Even if they could tell him how many days he'd lain unconscious since they arrived as his savior, he couldn't be sure how much time had passed since Samara's attack.

"I hope so," was all he could offer. He needed to try to reach her. Before he insisted they leave, Nik dreaded to ask, "The yucolites—what did you promise for them?"

Her eyes wandered—only for a second before she plastered on her usual heartbreaking smile that shielded her burdens from the world. "Nothing of concern. And nothing I can tell you about—as part of the condition."

His chest wrenched. Nik spared Jakon a glance, realizing he didn't look as if he knew either. "You saved me," he said, not knowing how he could ever repay such a debt.

Marlowe linked her arm through Jakon's as a signal to leave. "We kind of need you," she mused. "Let's just not make it a habit."

CHAPTER 56

Tauria

TAURIA PACED HER balcony. Her pulse was fast, and nausea had settled in her stomach. It had been three days since the terror in the library. Three days…and she hadn't heard from Nik once when he'd promised to check in the following day. Every time she tried the bond, it was silent. Dark and distant, but still there. Her mind had been unable to focus on anything else until she could confirm he was safe. The Book of Enoch had occupied some of her time, but between every harrowing discovery she made and her sickening anxiety for her mate, Tauria was descending into a helpless spiral. She hadn't slept since the most gods-awful feeling dragged her back to consciousness last night. She'd clung to the bond, screamed it down, desperate for some reply to quell the sense of dread that hadn't left her since. She watched the sun setting now, yearning to be home. Tarly had checked in once two days ago, only to assure her he'd spoken with his father on her behalf and Lennox's body had been buried in discretion, with respect, at her request. She'd wanted to go to the prince, but she couldn't. Not until she heard from Nik.

Tauria halted as the world stopped. Time slowed, and relief almost collapsed her when she felt it.

"Nik," she breathed in relief. *"What happened? Are you all right?"*

"I'm so sorry, Tauria."

At the sound of his voice, Tauria braced her hands on the railing and closed her eyes, forcing back the sting.

"Zarrius made moves on a plan of his, and I was injured, but Marlowe and Jakon intervened."

Her fingers curled painfully into the stone, and her rage must have slipped through the bond as it was answered by a soothing internal caress.

"How injured?"

"I'm fine now. How are you, love? Are you still safe?"

His selflessness was tearing her apart, but arguing with him to get more information wouldn't help either of them. She needed to finish what she'd started here, and then she could return to him.

"I'm safe," she confirmed. *"I'm just so glad to hear your voice. I thought—"* She couldn't finish her sentence. She didn't need to. No amount of reassurance could stop the ache to be with him. Tauria had to divert the conversation before she risked crumbling her bravery. *"How did you get those fae to us so fast?"*

"You didn't think I would leave you there unprotected, did you?"

Tauria said nothing, but her heart beat so full.

"They were difficult to find, but I tracked down three Shadowporters and bribed them enough to be posted an equal distance between us so I could travel my signal as quickly as possible if I thought you were in immediate danger. A small band of guards are posing and living as Olmstone citizens, not to be detected unless they're called upon."

Tauria was speechless. Her face creased with the overwhelming desire to feel him. Nik was brilliant. And protective. And she loved him so fiercely it became a physical ache.

"Come home, love."

Her brow pinched with a wave of emotion at the thought. She wanted it so badly. To be safe and in his arms. To have the time they were robbed of after their mating. *"I will. Soon."* She took a long breath, calling on her courage to see this through to the end.

There were less than three weeks until the wedding, and she was dangerously running out of time. As soon as she got to High Farrow territory she would be protected. But Tarly…

"I have to go."

"Do you see the moon, Tauria?"

She twisted her head back toward the balcony, concluding what she already knew.

"The sun is still setting."

Nik chuckled softly. *"I love you."*

At Tarly's rooms, Tauria knocked and waited, trying not to give away her anxiety in front of her new guard. She felt as though everyone knew the knowledge she harbored—the truth of what really happened to Lennox. She balanced a stack of books, spines pressed tightly to her rib cage. They couldn't discover how close they were to figuring everything out.

The prince's door swung open a moment later, and her eyes widened at his naked torso. His strong physique was clear through the fitted clothing he usually wore, but she hadn't expected just how defined he was.

"I can come back—"

"No need." Tarly stepped aside, and she couldn't deny the urgency of what they needed to discuss. They'd already wasted precious days.

Inside, she placed the books among the many others on the dining table. Turning to him, her attention fixed on the bandage tied around his shoulder just before he pulled on a shirt. "You're still hurt." She quickly paced over to him to examine the injury, but Tarly backed away from her.

"It's nothing."

Tauria wanted to insist, but his hard face warned against it. It had to be deep for it still to require a dressing after days. His eyes fell to her ankle, fully mended with the help of a healer.

"Good as new," she said, shuffling her weight between her feet.

His shoulders relaxed before he blew out a breath. "Let's just find out what we have to. If Lennox was…" Tarly paused, a ghostly *fear* paling his tanned skin.

"Dark fae," Tauria finished. She went for the black book. Heavy, but not in weight. There was a haunting trove of knowledge within. With the power to both enlighten and damn. "Lennox was one of my people," she confessed. Dipping into her dress pocket, Tauria laid the stag pin on the table. "He was quick to make that known, for what better way to gain my foolish trust than to dangle that kind of hope before me?" She hauled open the book, flipping through the pages to distract herself from the self-disappointment and what Tarly would make of her weakness having invited danger to walk by her side all this time.

"It's not your fault they used that against you, Tauria." Tarly's approach was careful. "You're devoted to your kingdom and your people. No one could have predicted this."

It didn't ease her defeat.

"How is it possible he was dark fae?"

The mere name shuddered through her. "They call them the Transitioned. Ordinary fae turned into dark fae. But I think it comes at a dire price for the victims." Her first few findings confirmed what she had come to suspect. "They depend on human blood to survive. And most of their memories of their previous life are wiped, but I think that can vary. Lennox truly believed he was better for what they'd done to him."

"Perhaps not all are the same."

It was a small attempt to console her. She knew if many of her people had endured such a heinous violation, they may be beyond salvation now.

"All this time, he's been keeping an eye on me. I confided things in him, thinking I could trust him, and my mind has been scrambling to figure out what he might have shared with Varlas that could condemn me." Even right now, she was running over everything she could have said to Lennox. "He knew about Lycus," she said.

"We all knew about Lycus."

Tauria shook her head, her chest tight with horror. "Lycus once came to me in trust. We thought we were alone as we didn't consider Lennox a threat when he'd been so convincing that he was on Fenstead's side."

"What did Lycus tell you?"

Breathing became difficult. "He offered me a way out. Lycus told me he knew how to get me out of Olmstone undetected. All I had to do was give the word." She found the will to look at Tarly, but he stared away from her with a frown of disturbance. "What if Lennox told Varlas and he did something to Lycus to make sure I didn't have that escape?" It was a notion so unbearable it had kept her from sleep. If something had happened to him…

"I'll try to find out what I can," Tarly offered. "In the meantime, we have to focus on the threats against you now."

This brought her back to another sinister discovery she'd made in her days of isolation. "It's not just me who is in danger. Tarly…" Tauria had to brace her hands on the table as her panic rose. "I think they mean to perform the ritual on us."

A silence so cold and condemning settled. She turned her head to gauge his reaction. There wasn't one. Tarly's eyes were vacant as they stared off to the side. His thoughts were reeling, but she couldn't decipher a single one of them.

"He wouldn't," Tarly spoke at last, but his tone betrayed his words.

Her heart ached for him as he learned what his own father was willing to do to him. Tauria had spent every minute of the days following the library attack trying to piece it all together, everything she couldn't make sense of or struggled to believe. Bit by bit, the conclusion had come together.

"The Transition would wipe my memories. I would be at the mercy of the High Lord, but no one would suspect a thing. Fenstead would believe their queen had triumphed in taking back the kingdom, and they would bow before me. I'd have wings, but maybe their intention would be for me to glamour them as Lennox did. Or to convince my people it was of my own will so that many would follow in their *want* to attempt the Transition at seeing their queen's success. But it wouldn't be me. Not anymore." Her heart pounded because she would wish for anything else in place of that sinister fate. Even death.

"Why force the marriage? Why involve me?"

"Two reasons, I believe. We will be bound before the Ritual, and should I not survive it and you do…well, you will already have been declared king consort of Fenstead. My people would have no choice but to embrace you as their rightful leader. Or should I survive, it would strengthen the alliance, and both of us would have an allegiance to them as dark fae. Fenstead's armies would be Olmstone's. Finally, in negotiating with Nik, High Farrow would break the treaty if they didn't answer a call to attack."

"I followed you until the end there. Call to attack?" Tarly probed.

She was shaking her head, wanting so badly to deny what was right in front of them. "The one kingdom that has never fallen. Varlas has sunk too far in his vengeance to let it go now even if he wants to.

Mordecai has him, and I think they plan to strike Rhyenelle with the entire might of what they've been gathering for millennia, once and for all."

"By the Gods."

All Tauria could think about was her dear friend. Faythe had to know the scale of what they could be up against. Agalhor had to start preparing his defenses—not only for the ground, but the skies. For the savagery the dark fae could rain down upon them. They were no ordinary army of man and fae.

This was a new dawning of the Dark Age.

"You need to leave—tonight."

"I can't."

"It's not safe here for any of us. But especially not for you."

"I won't leave you, Tarly."

He huffed a laugh, but it lacked in humor. "Now is not the time to pretend. Save yourself. If not for you, then for him." Tarly knew the chord he plucked, but she stood firm.

"I won't leave you."

His fingers flexed. "Don't be a hero. It's pathetic."

"Don't be a prick. It's old."

He strode the two steps to get to her, and she almost gasped when his hands latched onto her arms, but his grip was surprisingly light. Tarly captured her with his hazel eyes, and she saw so much vulnerability in them it imprinted on her. In those few seconds, he was stripped right back into someone she'd never seen before. Perhaps the fae he was before every tragedy that befell him. Real, vulnerable, loving. He would never admit it, but Tarly *cared* for her. And he didn't have to voice it.

"Do us all a favor, Tauria Stagknight, and save yourself. For your parents' sacrifice, go back to your mate who may be the only bastard left who can aid Rhyenelle and *fight back*. You still have armies waiting for you, and all of this demands you live, gods damn it."

Her tears spilled before she felt them form. "Come with me," she pleaded.

Tarly shook his head. "High Farrow is not the place for me."

"Are you really that set in your stubbornness you'd rather stay here than accept Nik's refuge?"

Against the tensions that rose and the darkness that consumed them, Tarly chuckled, deep and genuine. "Believe it or not, it has nothing to do with him."

"Then why?"

"Don't worry about me. Please."

She'd never heard him plea for anything, and it was as surprising as it was defeating. Tauria couldn't stop her feet that moved of their own accord. Her arms circled around the prince who went utterly rigid against her. "It's called a hug, Tarly. You're supposed to relax and hold me back."

He didn't laugh, but Tauria bit her lip against her own chuckle that threatened to escape at his grumbling instead. After a few seconds, he relaxed and embraced her.

"See? You're actually kind of good at it."

Tarly huffed and pulled her away from him. Tauria smiled through her tears, the thought of leaving him here so painful she risked damning it to find another way. As his arms dropped, Tauria caught the wince he tried to suppress. Her gaze targeted his shoulder, thinking she saw his skin darken where it peeked through from the shift of his shirt. Noticing her attention, Tarly was quick to fix it, and then he made a display of rolling his shoulders to convince her it wasn't of concern.

"Have you seen a healer?"

"Yes. She assured me it would be as good as new within the week. It's nothing."

She took his words with suspicion, but Tarly's face fell pained and serious before she could press the matter.

"Take the book. You figured it all out, Tauria—what my father and the High Lord plan. Now you need to act and go to those who can help."

"Thank you." She wiped her face as Tarly stood watching her as if in conflict.

"Damn it," he swore and pulled her back for a final embrace.

CHAPTER 57

Jakon

By nightfall, Jakon's exhaustion from the day's duties in the castle had faded away with the awakening notion he'd get to see his fiancée. He wasn't long past the archway that brought him into the humble setting of the outer town, where he'd head to the blacksmiths to escort Marlowe back to their rooms in the castle.

After all this time, one thing about Marlowe was certain: this life, this world, was not enough for her. Books, they were her freedom. To wander farther than any soul could, bound solely to this world, and bring wonderous tales back to share. Knowledge was her weapon. And Jakon admired her greatly for it.

The streets were somber as the town settled for the night. Whenever he drifted by the hut, no matter how much time had passed or how many times he walked this road, Jakon could never stop his eyes from trailing over the abandoned structure as if in acknowledgment of every memory he'd treasured inside the bricks and mortar. Every time, it clenched his chest with childhood memories of Faythe, and he'd spend the rest of the walk through the town wondering how she was thriving in Rhyenelle.

Since Faythe's departure there'd been a part of him that felt sharp and on edge, but manageable as he found distraction in Marlowe and helping Nik. But since the solstice, whatever overcame him had planted a new bud of urgency to be back by her side. Knowing Marlowe felt it too was his only consolation. Jakon trusted her, and piece by piece she shared things with him that were foreboding and frightening—but he would harbor it all if it meant she was not alone with the knowledge.

Faythe was in safe company, that much was certain. He didn't know the general well, but the protection he radiated for her, and the trust Faythe had in him…

He shook his head with a smile of disbelief.

Jakon halted rather than passing the hut as usual. He knew it remained unoccupied. Since they'd vacated it, he'd never gleaned any movement or glow in the windows.

But the door was now cracked open.

The hut was still dark, revealing no sign anyone had retired inside. And no right-minded occupant would fall asleep with an unlocked door, never mind one left ajar. Jakon freed a dagger as he approached the hut cautiously. His steps were careful and silent. He still adorned his royal blue guard's uniform and only hoped if it was some nighttime bandit that they might fear him for his assumed authority. There was nothing left of value inside, but Jakon couldn't stand the thought of some burly thief defiling the space before anyone else got to call it home as he once had.

Jakon winced as he tried to slide in through the gap, but the damn creaky hinges signaled his presence when the door caught on his cloak. He raised his dagger, eyes darting around every inch of the front room at the slightest possible movement. Yet all was dark and still. He was about to relax until a quiet voice sounded from the bedroom.

"I'm in here, Jak."

His heart leaped up his throat in fright, a rattle down his spine making every hair stand on end. Then urgency had him storming across the room, immediately identifying the voice in shock. Jakon burst through the bedroom door, his relief whooshing out of him all at once at finding Marlowe unharmed.

"What in the Gods are you doing here?" It came out rushed in his breathless surge of panic.

Marlowe sat on the edge of Faythe's old dainty cot, now coated in a layer of dust. A book was splayed out over her lap, and she didn't immediately look up to him. Jakon's alarm returned, and he looked back out to the front room in confusion.

"How did you know it was me? By the Spirits, Marlowe, I could have been someone else entirely, and you're not even armed."

Marlowe closed the volume. Jakon glimpsed the title as she set it on the nightstand: "The Forgotten Goddess." He'd seen the book before—it was one he often found Faythe immersed in though she'd refused to pick up a book since losing her mother. His heart sank, thinking perhaps Marlowe was here out of loneliness, the book being a reminder of her and Faythe's time of bonding.

Instead of meeting his worried gaze, Marlowe's blue eyes looked out of the small box window. The moonlight kissed her face, the image of her ethereal and breathtaking. Yet there was a distant sadness swirling in the ocean of her irises, and her expression was hollow.

Jakon's concern piqued. He took his steps slow until he dropped into a crouch before her. He reached for her hands. "What's the matter?"

Finally, her gaze fell to him, and Jakon's knees met the ground with the pain felt in them. "I haven't seen anything in weeks," she said quietly.

Jakon wanted to embrace his relief, yet the fear in Marlowe set the motion off in him too. "Why do I get the feeling you're not happy about that?"

"It's not about happiness. I think…it's happened."

Jakon trod carefully. "I can't decipher your riddles."

"It is all I am left with," she said in exasperation. "Riddles. Answerless questions that I feel so close to, yet now it's all silent."

"Enjoy the time to rest, Marlowe. This is a good thing."

Frustration pinched her forehead and bowed her head. "We're on our own now."

A cold silence shuddered through him at that. He stood, dipping onto the cot that squeaked with age. His arm went around her, and her warmth eased the shadow of fear. "We have each other. That's all that matters."

Marlowe's arm wrapped around him slowly. "I'm afraid," she whispered. As if it were a confession.

"What of?"

"Time."

His hand caressed her arm. "We'll have all the time in the world. However many days we have, they will be spent together."

Marlowe didn't speak for a long moment, but he read her silence as thoughtful. Whatever loose ends she struggled to find a resolution for on her own would consume her. Her head peeled from his shoulder as she looked over his face. "Do you remember anything else? After what you told me about your vision at the solstice?" Her eyes longed for something he wished to give her, yet all he could do was shake his head in honesty.

"I don't remember anything else yet."

Something of a puzzle was right there in her expression. "You and Faythe—" Marlowe halted.

"What have you seen?"

Marlowe shook her head. This confusion he'd witnessed before when she was working on a puzzle with missing pieces.

"If she's in danger, Marlowe—"

"Jak…" Her quiet voice was pleading. His thundering heart was the only sound against the still night. "I love you, Jakon. No matter the curse of time, I will always love you."

"I love you." Jakon angled her face to kiss her, and Marlowe clutched him tight. "Marry me, Marlowe. All we need is right here; the others will understand. I don't want to wait any longer."

She began to shake her head, but Jakon kissed her again, and the soft noise that came from her made him want to damn the cold, grim surroundings and take her here. But she deserved better. More than what he could ever hope to give her, and the weight of that fear bore down heavy with her hesitation.

"This is real, Marlowe," he said against her lips. "You and me, this is real. I vow to be yours forever."

Her soft hand trailed over his cheek. A conflict of love and pain pinched her brow, but her small smile expressed joy. "I want to have forever with you, Jakon. More than anything, I want that."

Yet there was a lingering hollowness that planted a dark seed in the pit of his stomach. If she'd seen something, he couldn't press for it. Sometimes it would consume her—fear, pain, frustration—and all he could do was be there for her. But what killed him within was that he could never truly take that burden from her, only offer comfort. His hand smoothed her hair, knowing his one wish in this life would be to set her free from it all.

CHAPTER 58

Tauria

HER PACK CHALLENGED her movements as she danced across the rooftops, solely for the dark book tucked within it. Tauria climbed and climbed, reaching the highest peak. She hid behind the pillar where an Olmstone flag billowed and sifted through her pack while stealing cautious glances at the guards below, waiting for them to turn their backs. She took her opening with a racing pulse, tying the green material she prayed would be disguised as purple to anyone else.

Then she had one final flare.

Taking a deep breath, she switched her stance, locking her legs in place. She closed off all her senses except for one. Her wind. Casting out her arms, she circled them above her, aiming skyward, and her eyes closed as her hands slowly came down. Tunneling. Tauria focused on nothing but reaching into her well of power, gathering all she could for her biggest test of endurance yet. The wind stirred against nature, answering her call. Through every vein it heated like sweet fire, but in her chest it raged in a wild storm. Her loose hair whipped around her, along with her cloak. More—until her calculated stance began to tremble. Pushing—until her teeth clamped tight against the need to release. The howling and whistling of the tornado she built started to get canceled out by a dangerous ringing. A warning. Tauria held on for as long as she could, testing herself more than she ever had before.

Then, with a fierce cry smothered by her wind, she let go.

Her hands cast out in front of her as her eyes snapped open to witness the powerful blast she sent hurtling west. The backlash of pushing her magick made her fall to her knees. Tauria panted harshly but watched the fleeting trees defy the pull of wind. Foliage whipped across the evening as it fell.

Tauria took a few long minutes to collect herself from the exertion, waiting until her pulse calmed and her skin cooled.

There was no more time to waste.

Adrenaline quickened her pace back down without giving way to her fear of the fatal height. She slipped inside a familiar window and made her way into the forgotten room.

Her escape.

Her steps pressed on despite her will to go back for the prince. To save him from the danger she was leaving him in. All that kept her moving were his fierce words to get her to think like a leader. And the thought of heading to her salvation. Her mate.

She didn't spare a glance down the vent where she knew the ominous room would be set with everything to host both a wedding and funeral as one. It would rattle her composure too much to glimpse the fate that could befall her.

Tauria was near jogging down the dark passageway, not having to make a choice about which direction to take. There was only one destination, and freedom was almost hers.

The fresh air hit her first, and she was running then, breathing it greedily. Tarly had further instructed her on where it would lead out to. The stables. But she wouldn't risk a horse—not yet. Her endeavor out of the kingdom required her to be as small and hidden as possible. At least until she was out of Vesmire.

Light filled her vision, and she could have whimpered in relief. Tasting the clean air, feeling the warm evening, Tauria was almost there.

Until…

Her steps halted as the light was filled entirely by tall silhouettes.

Tauria froze still as if they hadn't noticed her. As though her presence could be denied entirely.

She blinked hard, her pulse racing too fast for her shallow breaths. The forms started toward her, and she backed up a careful step, seconds from twisting on her heel and sprinting. To where, she could figure that out on the go. But a voice halted her mid-turn.

One that pulled the ground from under her feet.

One that held no emotion.

One she knew all too well.

But her mind struggled to believe; she needed her sight to confirm it. Against all that screamed at her to run…Tauria turned back to face him.

"This doesn't have to be a harsh arrest if you come back with me willingly."

The distance closed in, and when some of the moonlight filtered across his face, she knew she wouldn't be able to fight.

Tarly looked at her with dead eyes. Flanked by four guards.

"Why?" It escaped her lips as disbelief, but she knew she wouldn't be met with an answer. Tauria couldn't look away from him in her utter incredulity. Locking eyes with her ultimate betrayer. She couldn't even look away when two others passed him to approach her. A coldness sharper than ice latched around her wrists, and only then did her stare break from his in horror to look down.

It wasn't just pain; a dark *wrongness* silenced something soul-deep. Her magick. Cut off by a heavy blanket that diminished her senses. The iridescent magestone was a flash of torture that almost brought her to her knees.

"Just a precaution," Tarly explained, not a single flicker of expression on his face. Not an ounce of any emotion in his tone. It was like she had been retrieved by the living dead.

"What are you going to do to me?"

Tarly didn't answer, turning from her as he began to walk away. Two guards hooked their arms around hers to drag her along.

"Oh, and a word of warning, princess. I suggest you keep silent for now. Don't believe death is the only thing that can break it."

His message was cryptic, but she heard the meaning glaringly in a surge of sudden panic. Her mating bond. Tauria's mental walls turned to impenetrable steel to prevent any of her desolate feelings from slipping through to Nik. He couldn't know it was all over.

All this time. First with Lennox, and now….

She couldn't believe her own naivety. The warning signs had been there. She'd extended compassion for his past, for losing his mate. Had that been a lie too? Only a story to tug on her greatest weakness.

Her heart.

Soon, the guards let her go. Because she could do nothing except vacantly follow while she bowed her head pitifully in defeat.

She had no magick. Her staff at her waist would be useless with bound wrists. Her fight had dwindled.

It was over.

Tauria only knew they'd left the stables to join the street when the guards moved back behind her and Tarly came up to her side instead. Her shackles were draining, and she found even the walking to be too much. His touch repulsed her, but she couldn't shake it off as tiredness swept her, so she relied on him to take some of her weight. Her vision occasionally caught glimpses of adoring citizens who gushed at seeing a happy couple, not a captured bride, while her cloak hid her magestone bonds.

Her wrists burned. Not hot, but an icy stabbing that she wanted to claw off. She couldn't tell if her rapidly draining energy was from her sheer heartbreak or the metal. She had no choice but to be folded into Tarly's side as his arms circled around her. Her wet cheek pressed to his chest, and she closed her eyes, allowing him to guide her back.

"How could you?" It barely escaped her as a whisper. Not from her stolen strength, but her obliterated heart. After all they'd been through, he'd been silently advancing toward this moment. He'd opened the door to her cage and encouraged her to run, only to delight in the triumph of dragging her right back to face every evil he'd coaxed her to discover.

Tarly didn't answer, but she tried again.

"Was any of it real?"

Still, the prince's lips remained sealed. Instead, Tauria tuned in to his heartbeat. Strong and warm. A guise of nurture and care when it withered with so much coldness. She wanted to tear the deceit from his chest.

Tauria wept silently when she opened her eyes and saw the castle. Far more terrifying now she knew the evil it was home to. The prison it had always been, and she'd walked in willingly. Tarly's warning was all she could focus on as she reinforced all her barriers within.

Nik couldn't feel her total devastation, or he'd know she'd been caught.

And he would come for her. Just like he promised.

If it was too late for her, she would never let them have him. Tauria found absolution in that purpose. Fenstead would have him for their ruler as her mate, and she embraced solace in that. No matter what they forced upon her or what torture they inflicted, she would always protect him until the very end.

She wasn't led straight to the cells far below the castle. Instead, they wandered familiar halls all the way, until her mind raced to the destination, but she couldn't be certain of why they were taking her to it. In front of the glass doors to the pavilion garden, Tauria found enough of her will to attempt to halt, to pull away from the prince, before she took one step closer to the fae who awaited them.

Varlas stood observing the garden, hands folded behind his back as though he were lost in innocent thought. Her mind raced along with her pulse, but Tauria didn't get the chance to succumb to the wave of dizziness that threatened to collapse her as Tarly pulled her to him again, forcing her to walk while she continued to struggle.

"Well done, my son," Varlas praised. "You've played your role well to know exactly which route she would take to escape." He spoke of her as though she were no more than a dog on a leash, and her rage boiled to rally the dregs of her strength.

"You're a traitor," she hissed at the king. "My father would be disgusted by all you have become." Hot tears rolled down her face because he wasn't controlled by magick or Transitioned against his will; Varlas's choices were all his own. Yet when his eyes finally fell to her, there was nothing in them. A ghost of the male she knew. No remorse or love. But there wasn't evil or hatred either. He was nothing. She couldn't stand it, wanting his fury in place of the *pity* that twinged in her chest for him. Her voice was as smooth as ice as it delivered her final blow. "Freya would be glad to have been spared a life by the side of such a vengeful monster."

There it was: a vehemence so raw it could barely settle on his face before he lunged into action. Tauria didn't have time to flinch when she was torn from Tarly's arms by large hands that gripped her throat. The king's grip was a fraction away from crushing her windpipe. Agony choked her.

"Father."

Tarly's voice became distant. Her knees gave out, but Varlas held her upright in his vise grip, piercing her with daggers as he debated her life in those few searing seconds.

Then she was released with a harsh shove that sent her sprawling by the prince's feet. Her head cracked off the stone as her bound hands were unable to break her fall. The world drifted away from her. A drift of mercy that took her pain as she entered a darkness so inviting in its numbness.

Her snap back to the present was hideous. A drum banged unrelenting in her head, which felt wet and warm. She was bleeding. Hands fell on her, and as awareness encased her, she knew it was Tarly who crouched down, lifting her head from the cold stone. She wanted to launch herself away from his touch despite the stabbing ache, but she was saved from having to do anything when the shudder of Varlas's voice traveled over the ringing in her ears.

"Leave her."

Tarly didn't move straight away. She didn't know why he hesitated. Perhaps the damage his father inflicted would put a dampener on the prince's own fun later on. All along, she'd been nothing but a plaything in their pen. The prince helped her to her knees—a small step up in her degrading situation. Then Tarly stood. They all looked out over the beautiful garden, infused with moonlight that sparkled against the magnificent flowers.

"I watched you here sometimes," Varlas said, seeming to lose himself to memory once more as he let go of his anger so abruptly. "You reminded me a lot of her. The passion you pour over the flowers, the joy it brought you to watch life thrive. So pure, unburdened. One wouldn't imagine any ill fate could befall such a person with so much selfless care for the world. A blessing."

Tauria stayed silent, but she could feel nothing. Varlas didn't even allow his sorrow to slip through as he spoke of his mate. As if she were someone who had never existed at all, only a dream, and perhaps that was how he tried to go on.

"You're aiding the ones responsible for her death," Tauria said, not taking her eyes off the scenic sight that soothed her terror. "The ones who only know how to destroy and take and harm even the purest of souls. She didn't deserve to meet her end the way she did."

"No, she did not. But you are wrong, Tauria, and I hoped you would see that. I didn't want it to come to this."

Two guards shuffled behind her, and she braced in fear, believing she was about to be hauled off to wherever Varlas desired to hold her prisoner. Instead, her sight caught on the flickering amber torches they held as they passed her by.

Something wasn't right.

Her heart stilled with cold trepidation.

She figured out their intentions too slowly, far too late, and her eyes widened with a plea that thrashed in her rib cage and tore at her throat, but only silence left her parted mouth. That bright flame was brought down upon the vibrant garden, and the lethal force rejoiced, lashing out to devour all that lived and thrived around it. Claiming, destroying. It erupted within her. Pain so scorching she screamed internally. Fire consumed the beds of flowers, feeding itself to grow, licking up the wood of the pavilion. It enjoyed that the most. And in the space of a minute that floated as suspended time, an inferno collected.

"Stop," she breathed in denial.

But the more nature it devoured, the faster the burning within her intensified. Her mother's ability, while stifled beyond use, cried for her to save it. To stop the destruction of something so teeming with life and promise.

"Please."

Tears streamed from her eyes. She was helpless to do anything.

Then Tauria wasn't there anymore. Not present. Not in Olmstone. She was projected right back to the scene of devastation that would haunt and torture her for eternity. As she watched the fire blaze, she watched Fenstead fall all over again. Powerless. She was so lost and helpless to save anything. Anyone.

"Why?"

Finally, Varlas spoke. "Because nothing good in this world is ever safe."

She watched the flame flicker in his glassy eyes for a long minute until he cast them down to her.

"Let her watch it all burn. Then take her to the cells."

He turned to leave, but Tauria called desperately, "What are you going to do with me?"

Varlas barely turned his head back. "I'm going to give you all you've ever wanted, Tauria. Your throne. And in doing so, I will honor your father."

"At what cost?" Her desolate, defeated eyes slid away from the unfolding carnage to view the monster who lit the flame.

"Whatever it takes." No remorse. She didn't know the male who looked down at her, a shell of who her father trusted.

She shook her head. "You know nothing of honor, Varlas."

"It will all be over soon, Tauria. You won't remember all that you have lost, but you will be grateful for all that you will gain."

"I will kill you, Varlas. I won't ever bow to you."

"Not me, princess. We will all bow to the one who will change the world."

CHAPTER 59

Tauria

TAURIA WAS FLOATING. A warmth embraced her, and she didn't want to surface from the peaceful darkness. Not until the scent that wrapped around her brought reality crashing down on her all at once.

Her eyes snapped open. Tarly held her, carried her, but only because she'd succumbed to her emotional and physical exhaustion at watching a cruel blaze torch everything she'd spent the summer growing. It wasn't wasted time that tore her heart; it was the merciless, cruel form of punishment of being forced to *feel* the nature dying. Every root, every bud. She'd created it all, and she'd felt it all die.

Before she could damn the pain and embarrassment to jerk out of the prince's embrace, she was lowered onto a cot. As Tauria's eyes adjusted to the dark, she knew exactly where he'd brought her to. Four walls. Solid stone. Not a single window. Only a small, barred hole was cut into the door as the sole way out. The confinement tightened her throat, a panic so raw it rose her adrenaline to snap her wide-awake, and she lurched forward.

Tarly took her arms to pin her down. "There are six guards beyond this door, and you have no magick."

Her eyes snapped to his, but her dread didn't leave room for anger in that moment. She couldn't be trapped in here. The cell was barely big enough for the lone cot within it, the only gap for air too small. She would suffocate.

"Please," she begged. It was all she had left. "Don't leave me in here, Tarly. Please."

Something disturbed his blank expression. In her desperation, she clung to it as sympathy. Even if it was a tiny kernel of hope that maybe there was enough care left in the prince she could grapple to.

"I'll do what you want. I'll marry you. Just—I can't stay down here."

His eyes tightened. That care winked out in an instant, and she bit back her whimper.

"You'll be okay. There is enough air, trust me."

"Trust you?" she repeated though an incredulous breath.

"Or don't. It is your choice." The prince got to his feet. In her spear of desperation, she followed, but he'd already made it to the door. Time slowed as she watched the guard step forward to pull the stone closed. The way it ground against the floor vibrated every inch of her skin sickeningly. It shuddered her next breath.

She was trapped.

Not enough air.

Tauria made it to the door just as it slammed shut, and her palms stung against it. "Open the door!" She slapped it again, but she couldn't feel it. *Not enough air. Not enough air.* "Open the door, Tarly."

Open the door.

It was all she could repeat. As if it would offset the resonating click of the lock that echoed mockingly around the stone cage. The chill that seeped into her bones and drew breaths of ice in her throat.

"Tarly!" she screamed, her fists pounding the stone until they stung and bled. Straining on her toes to look through the small bars, she saw him through blurry vision.

"You'll be okay."

As he turned to leave, Tauria began to sob. Against the stone her flesh tore as she slid down the length, hoping she wouldn't meet the ground but rather the earth would open up and swallow her instead. Anything was better than the confinement they'd locked her in.

Not enough air.

She was drowning. Her throat was so tight her eyes stung.

Pulling her wrists apart, she cried out at the bite of magestone that separated her from her magick. Being unable to reach her wind only convinced her mind further that there wasn't enough air to sustain her down here.

Her vision became peppered, and panic fogged her mind. Tauria curled against the freezing stone floor and wept into the dark.

When the nightmares of her waking state outweighed those in her sleep, Tauria knew she'd truly come full circle. This helpless terror was real. Just like when she'd fled from her lands of defiled blood and ash. It had taken a century to heal. To be able to feel again. To find her courage and believe she could see her people home.

But she had failed.

Perhaps she was a fool to ever think she was enough. Strong enough. Resilient enough. To think she possessed even a kernel of those traits that had radiated so powerfully from her father.

She lay in her cold, feeble cot, numb in her complete exhaustion.

It was no sound that woke her. Her cell was dark and empty, and beyond it was still, as far as she could detect. What coaxed her from sleep was a gentle pull from within. The first flutter of anything warm and safe.

She lay there for a few minutes despite Nik's call to open the bond. She couldn't let him detect her desolate feelings, her tormenting thoughts. Tauria was ashamed of it all. She couldn't stand the thought of disappointing the one person who'd believed her more fiercely than anyone before. If Nik could see her now…

Instead, she focused on her physical senses as they started to come to awareness. Her bones were brittle ice. Clenching her teeth, she whimpered when she tried to use her hands to lift herself from the cot but pain scorched her bound wrists. Nik wouldn't stop until he got through to her—or worse, he'd assume something had gone terribly wrong and march to Olmstone without hesitation.

Her vision was restricted in the dark. Enduring every agonizing movement, she awkwardly folded the pitiful cover around herself with gritted teeth and took a moment to breathe. To settle her raging nerves. Tauria focused on nothing but taming her stirred panic. She closed her eyes and forgot the stone walls that formed around her. She pictured the vibrant, lush Fenstead meadows. She thawed her frozen heart with love for her mate. She recalled joyous memories with Marlowe and Faythe. Then, when she'd sealed all else behind a vault in her mind, she opened herself to the bond.

"Did something happen?"

His first message creased her face. She hated lying to him.

"The destruction of an ancient library, I was hunted by a dark foe…need I go on?"

The internal vibration of his chuckles formed tears behind her lids.

"Do you see the moon, Tauria?"

She opened her eyes, and those tears rolled down her face as she tipped her head back. They'd imprisoned her in eternal night, and through the darkness she imagined not stone but a vast, open sky where they would both stare at the same brilliant moon.

"Yes."

There was a stillness before he asked, *"What size is it?"*

She thought for a moment. Tried to calculate how many nights could have passed since she last saw the true moon. What she knew was that the spell of Transition required it to be full. Tauria had to go with her best assumption.

"It's a half-moon."

Nik was silent for long enough that it spiked her with dread he might've closed off from the bond. But when she reached, she felt him there, and the ripples of the embrace he sent back.

"I wish I could see you." The ache slipped past her defenses.

"I'm right here, love. Always."

"I know."

"Close your eyes."

She did without hesitation.

"Do you remember our first night together?"

"Yes."

"You read to me. Now I'm going to return the favor."

"You'll risk the spell wearing off if we talk for too long."

She assumed Tarly had told his father and the guise was up. But Nik couldn't know. Her fingers traced the bracelet just below her shackles as the only physical thing she had of his.

"It'll be okay. Let me take you away for a while. Picture that night for me, love."

Her brow pinched tight, suppressing every desolate emotion that threatened to undo her. Because they wouldn't get another night like that again.

With the image she painted, Nik filled her senses. She could smell him, his scent always reminding her of vanilla infusing through the meadows she grew up in. She could feel him, how his skin was soft but peppered with beautiful scars. Taste him in the way his lips harmonized so perfectly with hers. Tauria devoured everything he could give her to relieve the agony.

Then Nik began to read, his voice a sound that soothed every terror and ache. Many words blurred as all she could treasure were the gentle notes of his voice that filled her with warmth against the barren cold of the room. She didn't know how much time had passed, but she feared letting him go.

"Nik," she whispered to halt his soothing story. In case it was the last time, she had to tell him. In case they succeeded in making her a monster enough that she wouldn't remember him… It was a fate so torturous she wished for death in place of it.

"No matter what happens, I love you. Everything can be taken from me, but not that. It was never because of the bond. It was you. Only you." She swallowed, wincing at the growing lump that tightened her throat.

Silence settled, and she wondered if she'd spilled too much and given away her terror. That there could come a day when she would face him as someone else entirely. Dark, unforgiving. Loveless.

"You are my life, Tauria. There won't be a realm or time that exists where I won't love you. As eternal as the moon, remember?"

It was a promise. And he wouldn't realize just how much she needed to hear it with what she faced. Tauria wept, knowing he would fight for her. Even past the point of no return. If the bond was severed in Transition. If she became the enemy. Nik would fight for her. It was both relief and agony to imagine.

"I still have the world to give you in this one. Hold tight, love."

CHAPTER 60

Tauria

TAURIA'S RAW FINGERS scraped across stone. The clank of her chained wrists had been the only sound to disturb her silence in countless days. When she met the corner, she turned and continued to trace the wall.

"I am Tauria Stagknight, rightful Queen of Fenstead," she echoed aloud.

You betrayed me.

A sharp tremor shook her body with the echo of Lennox's words. She paused, choking on her sob, biting the inside of her cheek until a metallic tang could be tasted on her tongue. In her loneliness, the darkest, most tormenting demons came out to play. She continued.

"I am Tauria Stagknight, soul-bonded to Nikalias Silvergriff."

Did you enjoy sitting prized and pretty in High Farrow while your people were slaughtered?

"I'm sorry," she whimpered. Because Lennox was not the monster he had been forced to become. He was her people. "I shouldn't have been the one to live. Fenstead deserves better. Nik deserves better."

From her mouth came the words that had threatened to spill in the face of Lennox's harsh enlightenment. She'd been an arrogant fool to believe she was ever fit for the crown she'd deserted. At the back wall, her palms and forehead pressed to the cold stone.

"I am Tauria Stagknight, and I'm afraid I am not enough."

In the maddening silence she'd been left in, the shuffling beyond the door sharpened her senses and triggered the race of her heart, which she'd forgotten still held a beat. Then there were keys. Tauria lifted herself from the bed, succumbing to her terror over who it could be and backing up against the wall. But that distance wasn't far.

She winced at the scrape of stone with the opening of the door, then against the sting of her eyes as flickering cobalt flame flashed across her vision. She curled into herself like the pathetic captured prey she was.

"Tauria."

It was Tarly. His voice was unexpectedly soft and cautious. Her stiff muscles relaxed. He was the better of two evils at least.

Two forms approached her, spiking her panic as they reached out to grip her harshly.

"She's hardly a threat," the prince snarled. His voice drew closer, and she flinched when his hands reached for her as the guards released her.

There was a pause, and she realized her eyes had clamped shut in anticipation of a strike like the one his father had dealt. She peeled her lids open. Maybe it was the dancing light across his firm face, but there was a disturbance creasing his brow for a second. It was gone when his touch fell on her. But he was gentle. His arm curled around her and guided her to walk, ignoring the guards completely. Her fear tried to resist in the stiffening of her legs.

"You'll want to cooperate, princess."

"Burn in the Nether, *prince.*"

They walked—or rather, Tarly took much of her weight to lead her with her stolen strength.

"Your spirit still lives. Good. You had me worried there for a second."

"I doubt that."

He chuckled, but it lacked humor.

"You never showed me the way out," she reflected. In her days of solitude, all she'd had was time to agonize over her time with the king's greatest weapon. "You showed me your perfect plan in case I discovered too much. You sent me there only to capture me and earn praise from your father."

Tarly said nothing, and she glanced at his emotionless face. No remorse. Empty. It boiled her blood with a tingling heat that prickled her skin and flashed in her vision.

Tauria snapped.

He thought her weak enough to need his assistance to walk, holding her so close that all she had to do was catch him unawares. Reaching her bound hands up, straining on her toes, her maneuver was faster than he anticipated, and he cried out when the magestone chain hooked him around his neck. When she crossed her wrists the prince choked, and they both crashed to their knees, their faces deadly close, but she blazed at him with nothing but cool rage.

She heard the guards move, but to her surprise, Tarly raised a hand to stop them. Tauria could kill him—she was almost confident of it—but that wasn't her goal. To her frustration, Tarly didn't fight her. He didn't reach for the blade like she hoped he would. He wouldn't spare her by the only means possible now from the dark fate set to befall her.

Her anger subsided as she searched his hazel gaze, wanting so desperately to believe some of it was real. Anything of the prince she thought she'd glimpsed in the time she'd dedicated to getting him to open up to her. Her face smoothed out as he stayed still.

"Please," she said quietly, so the guards wouldn't hear.

Tarly's frown faltered. But it wasn't long before a hint of horror folded with realization flickered in his gaze. His head shook, teeth clenching against the chains she could tighten enough to strangle him any second.

"Please," she gritted out again. It was the only way. A small mercy she begged of him.

"I won't kill you, Tauria."

She cried out, pulling her wrists, and Tarly's eyes widened on a choke. Once again, the guards advanced.

"Your Highness—"

"Stay back," he hissed though a wheeze.

"You're a coward," Tauria seethed. Agony filled her eyes, and she blinked it back.

"You need to see what's at stake before you settle on your request."

That had her slacking her hold. Tarly gasped for air, but he was still under the threat of her chains. A chill seeped her bones.

"What's at stake?"

"If you're done threatening me, and yourself, you'll find it's where we're headed now."

Dread doused her still. "The wedding."

"Is still in four days."

"How do I know you're not lying?"

"It would make for a rocky start if I had to trick my bride down the aisle." His attempt at humor was so incredulous she didn't know what to do with it.

"The chains and promise of death won't?"

The damn bastard chuckled. "You have a fair point. But you don't really have a choice but to trust that is not where we're headed now."

Trust was so far from what she had in him, but he was right: choice wasn't her luxury.

"Where are you taking me?"

"If you would be so kind as to let me go, I'd rather show you."

Tauria clenched her teeth to bite back the retort that itched her throat. With a huff of frustration at herself for thinking of no alternative, she untangled her chains, and Tarly quickly ducked out of them. But as he did, his hands closed around her forearms. She was about to snatch herself away from him, but the fury in his eyes made her hesitate. His gaze fixed on the ruin of her wrists. They were raw, bleeding, cuts covering far up her wrists from the constant movement. He said nothing.

Tarly stood, effortlessly taking her with him, and she didn't protest.

She watched. She listened. She had to calculate some plan in her grapple for defiance. It couldn't be over. Not while she was still herself.

She would never stop fighting.

As Tauria climbed the stairs, her heart picked up hope that she would taste fresh air, that she was being led out of the underground tomb. She could have cried in relief when the brightness of real light filtered through her vision. Despite still being caught in a snare, the purple tapestries were a comfort to see. They walked familiar halls once bustling with guards, servants, and cheerful courtiers that were now ominously empty.

So Varlas's people wouldn't witness what they'd reduced their foreign guest to. A princess who'd sparked hope in his walls for the illusion of a promising future with the wicked prince who captured her now.

Tauria gathered where they were headed, and it was with new terror that her steps began to resist. The doors to the throne room were wide-open. Varlas Wolverlon wore the guise of a mighty king well upon his throne, yet all she could see was a pitiful coward who faltered under the weight of his crown.

Tarly muttered something to the guards. She didn't need to hear what he'd said when their actions followed. One wrist was freed, and Tauria bared her teeth as her arms were twisted behind her. Then the shackle was replaced. Her powerful gaze of hatred she'd blazed on the Wolf King slid to the prince just briefly as she tracked him to where he lingered by the dais. His lack of triumph or disturbance or *anything* ground on a murderous anger. She would rather he wore his betrayal. Owned it.

Tauria fixed her mark on the king and yielded no wince when she was forced derisively to her knees before him. The silence around them was heavy. Varlas was as still as the stone statues that surrounded them passing silent judgment.

"Believe it or not, I hoped it would not come to this," he said at last.

Tauria had to force down her incredulity. Despite all he'd taken from her—name, title, dignity—in forcing her to bow for him, Tauria raised her chin.

"Your crown," she spoke coldly. "It wears you, Varlas. I pity the fact you've lost sight of yourself under the weight of it."

A guard approached from behind, and Tauria bit back her cry when her head was yanked back by her hair. Varlas rose with slow fury. Tarly shifted a step, and a low growl vibrated across the hall. Tauria's attention was drawn to Katori. Her lips pulled back frighteningly over her teeth. The wolf tracked her steadily, and it was the only thing she feared in that room with a sadness. She'd come to care for the beast that had turned on her too.

"Silence that thing, or I will," Varlas warned Tarly.

The prince backed up a step toward Katori, his look sending a silent command that made the wolf submit.

"All you had to do was play your role here, and this could have ended far better. If only you'd complied with the obedience that is expected of you. It is not I who is unfit to lead, Tauria Stagknight. It has always been you."

Each step he took down the dais locked her spine straighter. Varlas spared one glance at the guard whose fist tightened in her hair. She was released harshly, but not once did she drop her eyes from the king.

"Fallen Fenstead princess. Ward of High Farrow." Varlas's stalking was predatory until he halted, peering down at her with cold nothing. His hand rising was the first thing that wavered her confidence. It wasn't to strike her, though she wished for that in place of where his fingers lingered instead. There was nothing she could do but direct every ounce of her strength into the shield she'd placed on the mating bond. Against all that screamed to let it fall and call to him.

With Tauria at his mercy, Varlas undid the high ties of her ruined jacket before peeling it back to reveal Nik's mark. "Mate of King Nikalias Silvergriff," he drawled, eyes fixed with a rare darkness. "You thought you could play us all for fools. Though it has been entertaining to watch."

Humiliation heated her cheeks. "You can do what you want with me. Change me. But if it's the only thing I remember, I will kill you."

His smile was ghostly. "I have always admired your fighting spirit. Even as a child you had that resilience in you." A cry escaped her when his hand wrapped around her jaw tightly. "This changes nothing. The wedding will go ahead, but don't worry—your mate will be there. As you will call to him to come for you."

Varlas released her, but she didn't feel the pain beneath her coating of horror. The king stepped back, watching as though waiting to delight in her reaction. Her chest heaved with a defiance so strong.

"No."

Varlas opened his mouth, but she wasn't finished.

"I dare you to try, but I will not break. Not for that."

"Your protection of him is admirable. I understand."

"You could never understand. In everything you've done since her death, you have betrayed your mate."

The back of his hand connected with her cheek in a force that would have had her sprawling if she hadn't anticipated it. A copper tang filled her mouth, spilling over her lips.

"Everything I have done has been for her." His voice rose for the first time, booming through the hall. "I look forward to watching your Transition, Tauria. Then your mate's. Dark fae royals with a power unmatched on the continent. The world is changing. You'll soon find honor in being a key part of it."

"He was here. Why didn't you capture him when you had the chance?"

"The timing was unfortunate. Before the next opportunity for the ritual, his armies would have descended. The plan was to urge him back by sending you to him piece by piece. Until my son enlightened me to a discovery he made about your *mating.* I'll admit, I'm impressed. Your ruse was highly believable for some time. Though what you intended to outsmart us with has become your downfall."

"I won't tell him to come."

"Perhaps you misunderstood."

Just then, commotion ensued by the back entrance. Tauria's mouth parted with what she witnessed. She shook her head in denial while reality slowed. This wasn't real. This wasn't real.

She blinked hard, her balance swaying, as the sight was one that would haunt her until the end.

"It wasn't a request."

Tauria wasn't present anymore. Not when a body crashed to his knees before her—not by force, but with the fading life he seemed to grapple to.

He was unmistakably there.

Guilt. So much guilt. It consumed her entirely, and she wished right then that it could kill her. She would deserve it.

His head bowed to the ground, so still she believed herself to be staring at a corpse. But time slowed to a crawl when his head began to lift. Their eyes connected, and his were so filled with agony that a new dagger pierced her chest with each second she couldn't tear away from that broken gaze. Her throat was so tight she could barely utter the whisper.

"What have they done to you, Lycus?"

CHAPTER 61

Tauria

TAURIA'S TREMBLING HANDS rose, hoping this was some kind of dark, horrific nightmare while she stared at the broken sight of her longest and dearest friend. Her general. Whom she believed had abandoned her. Guilt wasn't enough to describe what ripped through her.

When her palms slipped across his dark skin, she let out a whimper at the icy chill. In sight and in touch, he kneeled there as the living dead.

"Let him go," she pleaded. Whatever it took, she would give it to them. "I'm so sorry."

Lycus tried to shake his head, but he was weak. So weak. Tauria shuffled closer as if any heat from her body could help bring some life back to his broken state.

"You know how to make that happen," Tarly said.

Tauria whipped her head around. Tears of disbelief and betrayal battled her wrath. "All this time?"

Tarly didn't have to confirm he'd known of Lycus's capture. It was there in the way his chin rose faintly, the flare of his eyes... The plummet in her chest stole the air from her completely.

"I don't doubt your resilience when it comes to your mate, Tauria. But will you allow your general to suffer in your defiance?"

The high pitch of steel rang with desperation.

"Give them nothing," Lycus rasped.

"Stop," she breathed, a hollow word, as guards approached and she could do nothing but watch with foreboding. One rested a sword along the back of his neck. "Stop!"

"Oh, it can, if only you surrender. Call to him, Tauria. Call for Nikalias to save you."

She was trembling violently, straining against every muscle that blazed in her to fight. She couldn't do it. It darkened her heart, damning her soul to the Nether. "I'm so sorry," she whispered, repeating it over and over. Nik had to stay away. For their kingdoms, he was the only one left. And because since the day she met him, Tauria would always choose him.

"It's okay..." Lycus's labored breaths were tearing her apart. "This is not your fault."

It was. All of it. Starting from the day she'd fled and left her people to be caught and slaughtered. Her mind was frantic. Words. Thoughts. Solutions. Her pulse raced to draw conclusions that seemed right there to grasp. Then...

"If you kill us, he won't stop," Tauria thought out loud. Her breathing was hard as her plan came together slowly. She had to buy time. *Gods,* it tore her apart to imagine what her death would cause Nik. "Your path of vengeance will be nothing compared to what Nik will unleash if you kill me. Don't think *Transitioning* is any different. You'll have three great armies to answer to."

Nik, Faythe, her people. High Farrow, Rhyenelle, Fenstead. It was strength-invoking to imagine them uniting to fight back once and for all.

They would, but Tauria planned to stand on the front lines of war with them.

"If that were a threat, they would have attacked Valgard to take back your kingdom by now."

She shook her head. "The wrath you'll cause in wake of my death will be enough." He had to see that. Even if it only granted hesitation in Varlas enough to take the fear to Mordecai.

"You will not die. You will become stronger."

"I don't need to Transition to swear fealty."

"Tauria—" Lycus strained to protest, but this was the only way.

"I'm powerful. Fenstead only awaits my return." Her throat constricted against everything she so desperately planned. It was the only way. "Tarly is already sworn to you. My marriage to him gains you nothing more. Tell him…" She couldn't believe her proposal, the only thing that might save them all… "Tell Mordecai I'll marry him instead."

"No," Lycus growled, struggling against his guards, but it was all wasted energy.

It was for him she had to do this.

"My only terms are that no Fenstead citizens are harmed, Lycus will be freed, and I will not be Transitioned. Nik—" She had to pause, to breathe and maintain her composure for the greatest betrayal of all. "The bond can't be broken, but perhaps it can work in our favor. Despite everything, he would never harm me. He wouldn't lead an attack on us. His fealty is as good as sealed." It was coming together piece by piece. A condemning fate, but it would save them all. Tauria's heart obliterated her where she kneeled. "Nik can't know until it is done."

"You don't have to do this." Lycus's voice was so heavy with defeat it was an effort for her confidence not to crumble.

"I want to do this."

"Why?" She had Varlas's attention, and she sank her claws into it.

Tauria began to pull her leg out from under her, until guards shifted to force her back down. Varlas's hand raised to halt them. Her adrenaline was racing and hot, but she slowly rose, unflinching at the pain that shot through every muscle and her wrists that burned with ice. She stared off with the Wolf King, and she was not afraid.

"I want my kingdom back. Marrying Mordecai gives us both what we want. All that remains then is to ally with Rhyenelle, and I believe I can be of influence to see that happen without bloodshed. They can be tricked into a law-binding treaty with Fenstead before they know Mordecai is king consort. Truthfully, I'm disappointed he has not seen this for himself."

Every traitorous plan spilled like acid from her mouth. To everyone Tauria loved, this was the ultimate betrayal. Nik wouldn't attack. Faythe wouldn't attack. It was brilliantly in the High Lord's favor, and all it would take was condemning her soul to stand by him. Sacrificing her morals to save blood.

"I will take your proposal to him, but there is no promise."

Her head bowed in relief, but nausea churned, and she fought everything within herself to remain steady as a face flashed to mind. The sin that followed his shadow. Wings of lethal allurement. The thought of facing him as his bride…it was almost enough to break her.

"Take her back to her cell," was Varlas's last chilling order before he left the hall.

The guard removed the blade from Lycus's neck, and she shuddered with a cry of reprieve. Despite being so weak, Lycus struggled with gritted teeth against the guards who held him too, still with a flare of loyalty and protection as he blazed at the ones who approached her. They were led far underground once again, and she noticed the prince had followed. It was energy he wasn't worth to shout or cry or spill the many dark thoughts she had about him. Just before they were about to be torn apart again, Tarly's voice rang through.

"Put them together, but do not remove their chains."

"The king said—"

"*I* say"—Tarly's tone was unrecognizable in its sharp authority—"my father does not wish to be bothered by the prisoners. He has left that duty to me. It is on your life if you want to go confirm this with him."

Tauria's bones rattled to watch him, but in her surge of hope that she wouldn't be alone in that tiny cell, she stayed silent.

The guard nodded, and it was the first dose of mercy since the dire fate that had befallen her. Escorted to the cell, they were all but thrown inside like sacks of wheat. Tauria's hands shot out fast enough to slap against the stone of the back wall, but Lycus didn't have that strength left. His grunt of pain flared her rage as he fell, and she shot down to catch him. Her heated glare met nothing but unblinking eyes as the guards left. She didn't see Tarly again to question his motives in putting them together. There was no strength or strategy they could gain from it, only comfort in a desolate situation. Tauria reached for the feeble blanket before folding it over Lycus to share her warmth.

"I'm sorry I believed you had left me." It was an immeasurable sorrow.

"I would never leave you." His voice was a croak that deepened her frown.

Tauria's head leaned carefully on his shoulder. "I should have known."

"Let's not waste time on that. We're together now, though I wish to the Gods we weren't. Not here. We have to figure out a way to get you out."

"There is no way. And I'm not leaving without you."

"You are not marrying him," Lycus said firmly. "Not while I live are you being forced to marry him."

"Listen to me, Lycus," she pleaded, taking his face in her hands. "I can do this, and I need you to trust me. This may be the only way to see us all alive, not just you. I can't let them have Nik. I can't let them Transition me. I won't remember…any of you, anything of my past. If this is what it takes to keep my memories and everyone safe, I need you to accept it."

He tried to shake his head, but she clutched him tighter.

"I can't do this without you. Please understand why."

They shared a desolate stare. Two people who could see when hope was lost. Who knew what it was like to admit to a surrender that would never ease in the heart.

"The prince told me about you and Nikalias," he confessed. Tauria was stunned as she pulled back. "But I had my suspicions about what you meant to each other long before now from spending so much time with him during the Great Battles. I couldn't figure out his reasons for keeping the mate bond from you considering how close you became. It was not for me to pry when I found you here and it was clear he hadn't claimed you yet. I figured maybe he'd told you, and perhaps you both agreed against the bond, but I was waiting for you to open up about it."

"It's complicated," was all she could offer.

He gave her a weak smile. "He won't let you go. Even if you are wed to Mordecai, he won't stop trying to get you back."

Tauria leaned back, casting her eyes to the ceiling as she tried to picture the moon. It was unbearable to think of. "I know," she whispered. "I won't ever let him go either." But she couldn't allow her sadness to cloud her determination. Tauria doubled back. "Why would Tarly tell you about Nik?"

"I can't decide if I trust the bastard or not," Lycus groaned as he shifted a fraction.

"I would say absolutely not. He tricked me."

"Or he saved you from something far worse."

Tauria couldn't stop the anger that flushed her body. If she weren't so frail and in need of their shared warmth, she would have pushed away from him. "He did this to you. To *us*." Her chains rattled as she held them up.

"I agreed to write that letter to you, Tauria."

That was an unexpected blow, and she winced. "What?"

"I begged him not to tell you what had happened. It was the king who ordered my arrest. I gave him the perfect opportunity to detain me, and he knew because of what happened between us it was a lie you would easily believe. That I'd chosen to leave you and head back to Rhyenelle. Tarly came to me, and I told him I would write the letter the king asked for, but only if he kept you safe in return. If he helped you to escape before—" Lycus seemed to realize that his own defense faltered in the end.

Tauria shook her head because one thing didn't make sense. "I did what you asked, thinking it would bring you to meet me. In the letter—"

"Good," he cut her off quickly. He spared a look at the door, and she realized her error in the possibility they could be overheard. "I knew your brilliant mind would figure it out."

She couldn't ask more. Tauria was so tired. She shifted impossibly closer, tucking in tight where they huddled together in the corner of the barren cell. She closed her eyes, willing herself to think of anything that would relax her mind enough to find rest for just a few hours.

"The only thing that got me through the decades apart was imagining you on Fenstead's white antler throne and knowing I would have the privilege of watching as you reclaimed it all."

The mighty throne of legend she'd gawked at and admired as a child. The one that had seated her father triumphantly so many times. To picture herself in his place…

Tauria's eyes tightened. "It's a wonderful image," she whispered.

"Don't lose hope yet, Tauria Stagknight. As long as I live, it is a future I promise you."

It was all they had. So Tauria allowed herself to cling to it.

Lycus declared, "As long as I breathe, I won't lose hope for both of us to see it."

CHAPTER 62

Tauria

Too many days had passed. When they came for her this time, she was sure this was it. In the darkness there was light as she spent her precious time with Lycus reflecting on their joyous past. Beneath the cold, there was warmth in the days they'd spent being able to hold each other.

Now, she was ready.

"I'm so proud of you," Lycus mumbled as they heard shuffling footsteps. She embraced him a final time. "Whatever happens, we'll fight together."

Her arms squeezed him weakly. "Always."

Tauria didn't succumb to tears. She'd exhausted them all. She didn't torment over her betrayal of her mate, already anticipating the wedding that had been prepared for her was where she was being taken now, and it was the worst of all evils she would wed.

In the room she was led to, Tauria felt barely present. The brute, unforgiving fae who dragged her there were replaced by far gentler human hands. She tunneled and tunneled, moving as no more than a vacant doll while three handmaidens bathed her, scrubbed her, and fixed her hair, and she didn't once look at her guilty face in the mirror.

Then she was left standing in front of beauty embroidered with sin. Stark black material that glittered in the fleeting daylight. A storm was gathering, reflecting her dire mood with anger rolling in the clouds and sorrow close to breaking into rainfall. A shadow that chilled curved her spine. Tauria didn't turn to the presence that joined her. Out of fear, out of dread, she was rooted in place.

"I must say, your proposal was unexpected."

A voice she would never forget.

"But rather brilliant. I am so impressed by your willingness to do what it takes for your kingdom. Maybe we can come to find more common ground than we first believed."

From the hairs that rose over every inch of her skin, she knew he was closing the distance between them. Her robe felt too short. Her body froze still. *Wrong.* Tauria pinched her eyes closed while her back remained to him.

"It is not customary for the groom to see his bride before the wedding," she said, mustering every last dreg of strength to see this through.

"I had to see you, Tauria Stagknight. I am not one to make decisions based on echoed words." He appeared in her periphery like a snake primed to attack.

"Is this not your acceptance of me?" She didn't take her eyes off the magnificent gown fit for the most elaborate funeral.

His chuckle was dark and smooth, stiffening her body. "Won't you look at me?"

Her heartbeat risked betraying her fear, but Tauria raised her chin then turned to face the dark fae king of legend. Mordecai was everything death embodied. Roguishly beautiful. But he was less intimidating than when she first laid eyes on him despite his closeness, and she realized why.

"No wings?"

His dark brow curved. "I thought it might ease your nerves, princess."

"How considerate of you."

Shadowy delight danced in those onyx orbs as he took a step toward her. Then another. Tauria remained painfully unmoving at his advance. His hand raised, and she held her breath as his unexpected light touch caught her chin.

"You are far more beautiful than they say," he said as though releasing his thoughts while he assessed her. "But how exquisite you would be as dark fae."

Her blood ran cold. "That wasn't part of the agreement."

"A shame," he drawled, but her dread wouldn't give way to relief as his eyes trailed up over her shoulder. A shudder ran through her at knowing what he was imagining there.

Wings.

"You mask your fear well."

"Who says I'm afraid?"

We were born and taught to pretend our whole lives. Even now, in the face of her betrayal, she grasped Nik's strength and wisdom. Her whole life she had been a master in the making in preparation for this moment.

Mordecai continued to look over her face while she wore her mask of steel. Then he seemed to find satisfaction in whatever he pondered as his hand fell away. The step back he took delivered new air to her throat.

"I shall see you at the altar, Tauria Stagknight."

What erupted in her chest was nothing short of fire straight from the Nether. It scorched soul-deep at hearing the wrong voice speak those words. In a blissful world, it would have been a song to hear from Nik, but in this twisted reality it came from her worst nightmare. She said nothing, but her nod was weighted like iron. She kept her head bowed low as he left like smoke on the wind.

Alone, Tauria took three calming breaths to calculate her next move. Then her gaze slipped past the mannequin at last and fixed on the balcony beyond.

CHAPTER 63

Tauria

THREE THINGS PUT Tauria's skills to the greatest test and laid her life on the most perilous line. The first, and what she considered the tamest, challenge was scaling the rooftops with her hands bound in front of her. With the bite of the magestone numbed in the cold, this felt like the time she convinced Lycus to tie her wrists in a mock trial as she ran through Fenstead's castle, a day of childish arrogance. The second challenge was the weather, which was a merciless bitch that made her bare feet slip dangerously too many times. Her final test threw all regard for modesty out the window. Literally. With the black robe her only cover-up, Tauria Stagknight had officially lost her damn mind.

She could be glad for the pouring rain, only because it made the material cling to her skin, shielding her from exposure to the harsh wind. With gritted teeth, she eyed the next steep slant she had to climb. Urgency didn't leave enough time for calculation, and as she leaped, Tauria could already feel the tumble her error would result in. Her fingers were just shy of hooking over the edge when her feet slipped against the wet stone, and with bound wrists, unable to react on instinct, her face hit hard.

Tauria was falling.

And falling.

For a second there was bliss in the movement as her element was the only thing that encased her.

Then her body slammed into something unforgiving. Agony was a pulse that surged through her until the world drifted away all at once.

"What are you afraid of, my child?"

Her father's voice trembled through her, and Tauria gasped, eyes snapping open. Around her, beautiful mists of white and green whirled, and she lifted a weightless hand. She wasn't in pain anymore.

"I'm afraid I am not enough," she whispered, turning to the King of Fenstead, her brow creased to suppress an agony worse than any possible flesh wound. This ran deeper with eternal grief. Because while she didn't know where she was…Tauria knew he was gone.

If this was the end, he had come for her.

"I failed."

But the king shook his head. "You are only just getting started."

A whine caught her attention. Her head whirled sideways, and Tauria blanked, stunned by the great white wolf that approached. She blinked hard, shaking her head, when another materialized from it. Two wolves. Identical to Katori.

"Enemies fear each other truly because they can identify when they are matched," her father said, but she couldn't tear her eyes from the magnificent beasts.

The wolves were staring at something on her other side, and Tauria felt compelled to follow their gaze. A short sob left her at who she saw.

Tarly…but the one who caused her ache of longing was Nik beside him.

"You love them both."

"I never loved him," she said bitterly, hatred pouring into her gaze though she knew Tarly's image wasn't real.

"It is okay to care for him."

"No."

"There are many forms of love, my child. You know this."

She remained defiant. "He betrayed me."

"Love can provoke wrongdoing just as easily as evil."

"Stop!" she shouted. She couldn't take it. She couldn't bear to look at him and clamped her eyes shut. "Where are we?" she whispered, hoping for some relief to her torment.

"Your mind, Tauria. This is all you. Your brilliant thoughts. Your treasured memories. You'll figure it out. But it's time to wake up now. Your kingdom needs you. Your mate needs you. *Fight*, Tauria Stagknight. *Fight…*"

She inhaled deeply in shock, crying out against the stabbing in her head, her ribs, her leg. Tauria blinked the rain from her eyes while she lay there gathering deep, painful breaths. The dream from which she'd emerged was a striking call to go on. Even if it flared her mind with confusion, it was strength.

She'd landed on her side, only having fallen a few feet down onto a flat ledge. The rain drowned her, forcing her to stay down, and she was almost willing. Rolling, she yelped, clutching desperately at the narrow ledge, one wrong shift from falling the far deadlier height and meeting the ground.

Gods, she was hurting, and hardly in any state to battle the storm that was collecting. It terrified her. But her father's words pulsed in her mind, drawing the might to get to her knees. The wolves inspired a will to protect what she still had left. Seeing Nik, even in a vision…she had to go on.

Tauria was breathless on her feet, taking a moment to regain her balance and calculate her next move. Her head turned to spy a window. She couldn't be sure of where it led to, and it likely wasn't to her hopeful destination, but she couldn't risk tempting death again.

Adrenaline coursed through her as she made the few quick maneuvers against all that burned relentlessly in protest. Tauria didn't have any stealth left as she tumbled in through the window, rolling onto the ground with zero grace. She didn't care. She was finally free from the storm, and she took a few seconds to collect herself.

"Oh, my dear."

The voice that greeted Tauria locked her still. She couldn't believe her string of sheer, damning bad luck. She didn't have the energy to muster much else, but she let her head fall to glimpse the one she expected.

Keira approached her slowly, dropping to a crouch that fanned her gown. "What a terrible fate you've met with."

It had all been for nothing, yet she couldn't even be angry with herself. Tauria had enough dignity left to get to her knees, her teeth bashing together with the ice that began to coat her. Keira spared a glance behind her, and Tauria's gaze followed to land on a guard by the door. To her surprise, whatever he read in the queen had him unfastening his cloak, and Tauria didn't know how to react when he gave it to Keira. The queen fixed it around Tauria's shoulders, and in her desperation for warmth, she didn't even flinch as she clutched it tightly around herself.

"What are you doing?" Tauria asked.

"I think you should be asking yourself that." Her slender fingers touched Tauria's temple, dragging back some of the wet hair that clung to her face, and she hissed at the sting. Keira examined the blood on her fingers. "You poor thing." The sympathy in her gaze was crushing. As though Tauria were already a corpse. "I tried to warn you, Tauria Stagknight. He's never felt love for me either. I too am someone to prize and conquer. A means to bear him a new son when he could barely stand the presence of the one he already had for the semblance he bore to his lost mate."

Tauria felt the first skip of her heart, which she'd long tuned out of in the presence of her desolation. "Why are you telling me this?"

"Because we are all just beautiful pawns in a mighty king's game."

"There is nothing mighty about Varlas."

For the first time, Keira smiled. It wasn't a smile of goading or conquer or seduction; it was agreement. It fell again as her hand rose, and Tauria couldn't stop her instinct to flinch as though she were going to strike her. But the queen gently cupped her face, searching and seeing someone else entirely.

"I love my daughter, Tauria. Despite what you may think of me, I would never allow harm to come to her. I watched you two many times—how she adored you, looked up to you." A slither of coldness, perhaps jealousy, as ludicrous as that seemed, folded in her knitted brow. "She has never looked at me that way. But regardless, I would never allow Varlas to have her. Not to do what he plans to with you. I tried to get you to leave, but you were so ignorant in your defiance. You saw opposition as a challenge, not a warning to flee. I tried to tell you about Nik in the hope you would go back to him before he wed another. I tried to convince you that Tarly would never be faithful. Still, you stayed here like a trapped deer, and prey is exactly what you have become. You are very smart, Tauria Stagknight, and I hoped you of all people would see that sometimes cruelty can be kind."

Tauria's heart thumped as Keira released her. She was stunned into silence as she relayed her words. Over and over. "You didn't care about me," she breathed in denial. "You only cared that I was a risk to your throne."

"Do you think I wanted this life? Bound to a male who didn't have a heart left to give? Not even on our wedding day did he show affection. Opal was a conception of duty, nothing more, but she is the greatest gift life could have given me. To his cruel dismay. A daughter was not what he wanted, and I tried to conceive again, but the Gods had other plans. So instead, he crafted his own cunning plan to cut us out completely. I look at you and see what Opal could become. A leader of heart. But I wouldn't wish it upon her at the price Varlas seeks from you."

"The Transition."

Keira's eyes filled with cold *fear.* That look shivered down Tauria's spine. "Yes. It is so heinous and evil I wouldn't wish it upon anyone."

Commotion sounded in the hall beyond the room, and Tauria's panic spiked. They were searching for her. Her time was up, and she had achieved nothing. Staring wide-eyed at the door the guards could charge through any minute, she didn't detect Keira's movements but stifled a scream of shock.

Keira fell, but not before hooking an arm around Tauria that left her with no other response than to straddle the queen. She gripped her wrists, forcing Tauria's hands around her throat. Then something solid and cold slipped under her robe, wedged under the flexible corset she wore beneath it.

When they stilled, Tauria was too sunned to move. Then Keira screamed, calling out for them to find her. Everything happened so fast she didn't register the door kicking open or the hasty shuffle of bodies. All she could do was stare and stare at the queen, wondering…*why.*

"Make them pay, Tauria Stagknight. Make them all pay."

CHAPTER 64

Tauria

THERE WAS NO pause for her to heal. Tauria was dragged right back to the room where they would resume dressing her to be wed. The servants who tended to her were gentle at least. Soft hands warmed and dried her, salvaging what they could of her hair and cleaning the blood, though the wounds from her fall wouldn't fade as the magestone dampened her fae healing. She didn't really care about her appearance or the fresh gash at her temple anyway. Mordecai would only see fury after her attempt to escape him.

Tauria wore a dress of night, crafted with a darkness that devoured any light that tried to shine on it. Beautiful death was all she could think of as she braved the mirror, staring at the black crystal sleeves and bodice while silk with a high slit flowed down her legs. They affixed a shadowy veil to her hair as the final piece to cloak her in darkness.

Though it swept her with foreboding, Tauria clung to her relief. That the dress would match what she considered this day to be. Her dying day. She found solace in the fact that while she was not to meet him at the altar, she had fulfilled her dream and desires even on borrowed time.

Nik.

His name, the echoes of his touch, and the memory of his voice were home. She clung to everything about him that soothed every terror at what she was about to do. She wanted that joyous life with him that had been glimpsed but never promised more than anything she would ever come to desire in one existence. With or without their crowns. For however long they lived.

But she didn't succumb to the desolate thought they wouldn't have that time. She embraced all they did have with nothing but gratitude. For the time they'd stolen to completely and wholly belong to one another.

Now, as she stood staring down a dark aisle that was not formed of love and purity but death and evil, where marriage would be the ultimate imprisonment, Tauria's steps halted at seeing him. Mordecai, towering wings and all this time.

A fae shuffled over to her, head bowed, and extended something to her. Flowers. But Tauria's blood ran cold as she glimpsed the deep red center of the white blooms. Spindlelillies. It was a despicable, sickening ploy to have her hold Fenstead's mourning flower as she headed to her death. If she hadn't embraced her numbness, she might have surfaced rage at the mockery. In her defeat, Tauria accepted the flowers but didn't look down at them. She cast her gaze up, chin poised. Confident.

Mordecai awaited her, but he didn't turn to her as the many cloaked and hooded figures filling the benches of the ceremony room did. She didn't pay any of them attention. Her eyes—cold with the icy promise of revenge—targeted the king poised on the elevated dais facing her. He accepted her stare, chin raising a fraction as if acknowledging her silent words. That she would find a way, no matter how, to find vengeance for his betrayal. And she would unleash the might of the Nether on his kingdom.

Something sharp and cold pinched her back, straightening her spine.

"Best start walking," the guard sneered.

Tauria did. Not out of obedience or fear, but because she was ready. Her apologies had been spoken, her love was locked and protected. Her mind steeled in the face of what she had to do.

The black river of her gown followed, death cascading in her wake. No joyous music, only ominous silence, rang through the dark hall. No adorning stares, only daggers of hate from wraithlike forms.

Tauria Stagknight lived to walk herself down the aisle of her own funeral.

At the bottom, she halted side by side with Mordecai, still not turning to him, and neither did he to her.

"You made a grave mistake, princess," he said, a whisper of darkness.

Her bravery quivered in his presence. She couldn't respond. Tauria listened to him turn, her pulse racing at a dizzying speed.

I am Tauria Stagknight, rightful Queen of Fenstead.

"Face me, bride." His voice triggered a stiff tremble with its threat.

She obeyed.

I am Tauria Stagknight, soul-bonded to Nikalias Silvergriff.

"You could have had it all your way." His hand took her chin, slowly applying more pressure until she whimpered. "Now, we do this my way."

I am Tauria Stagknight, and I am enough.

"You took everything from me." Tauria was silent, careful not to chime her shackles. The spindlelillies disguised her reach to a fold of her dress. "This is only the beginning of me taking it back."

Dropping the flowers, Tauria's maneuver was quick. Her hands gripped and twisted. Once. Mid-size. Twice. Full-size. Her finger found the trigger without falter, and the click of the blades didn't finish resonating before her staff whirled between her hands. She slid one foot back to brace, thrust forward, and then her aim made its mark.

Niltain steel. She couldn't have thanked her brilliant blacksmith friend for the creation more in that moment as Mordecai spluttered, wide-eyed, glancing down at the spear through his chest.

All went still. Silent. Then something darker than rage shadowed the High Lord's features. His hand roughly grabbed her staff, and Tauria let go, stumbling back. Black blood poured from the wound, yet he tore it from his chest with a growl that wasn't of man or fae. Tauria thought he would lunge straight for her, but he fell to one knee as the Niltain steel did more damage than ordinary steel. He threw her staff out of reach, the only sound that echoed through the hall.

"You are a fool," he seethed, but his labored breaths bought her time. "I cannot be killed by your mortal means."

"I wasn't counting on it," she breathed in a panic. "But it was worth it to see you kneel before me." Tauria's gaze snapped up, landing directly on Tarly for the first time as she registered his presence. The prince's usually tanned skin had been washed pale, as had Varlas's as everyone seemed to process what had happened.

Mordecai's laugh was dark and breathy. "When you Transition, you will be mine willingly, Tauria. The future you painted of us is one of power and leadership, and I can't let it go."

Her skin crawled at the sickening notion.

"Detain her," Varlas ordered.

Guards advanced, and Tauria cursed, having no other plan to follow her reckless attempt to wound Mordecai. She had to act. She had to—

"Allow me."

A stab of despair halted her reeling mind. She tracked Tarly as he made his way over, face devoid of emotion, ever the obedient prince. *Gods,* she wanted to hate him, but her heart broke at watching him close in to bring her down once again. He stopped right in front of her, freeing a blade from his side. In her utter conflict of loathing and sadness, she could do nothing but stare into those lost brown eyes, searching and searching for the warmth she'd slowly been easing from them. Yet the point of his blade aimed at her throat.

"I may have underestimated you, son, but you have proven your loyalty to the cause in all this. Your mother would be proud of us."

Tauria blinked her blurring vision, just in time to catch the slow turn of Tarly's head. But him looking at his father wasn't what made her tears dry up and a chill rattle her bones. It was the shadows that formed in that gaze.

"You never deserved her." Those words had barely departed the prince's mouth before the glint of steel went hurtling toward the king.

Tauria's mouth parted, eyes wide as Varlas grunted, shocked. He stared at Tarly in bewilderment but was met with nothing but an emanating fury, a century of wrath unleashed by the prince all at once as he went for his sword. But it wasn't a lone blade that sang through the hall. Commotion ensued behind them as guards became armed. The prince, however, was fast, standing before his father in a heartbeat. He halted, seething through his teeth as he braced to plunge the length of steel through his father's chest.

"You won't kill me," Varlas rasped, his hand raised to the hilt of the dagger, hissing through the agony that washed his face. She couldn't be sure if it had sunk deep enough to be a fatal blow. "Your mother—"

"Don't speak of her!" Tarly's voice rumbled over the ground. "All this time you've sought revenge, but never in the real person to blame for her death." Tarly's stance was wide, rigid, to stifle his trembling. Despite his loathing of his father, the prince wasn't a cold-blooded killer. Despite all the ways in which the male had wronged him, this was no easy confrontation for him.

Tauria stilled in her stupor, shocked by the turn of events, but perhaps there was always a part of her that refused to believe Tarly was evil. He was hurting. More than anyone she'd known before, Tarly

Wolverlon was a tragically broken soul, and she didn't know if it was possible to heal such deeply carved wounds.

"Tell me it's not you." Tarly's hard voice slipped with sorrow. "Tell me they have a hold on you as they did with Orlon. That none of this is your doing."

They stared off for a long, agonizing moment, father and son in a battle of love and loathing. Tauria thought she caught a flicker of remorse on Varlas's face, however faint it was, before his features cut hard.

"I cannot." Varlas spared a quick glance to his side, but it was all that was necessary before guards approached her, hooking their hands around her arms.

Tauria clamped her teeth tight to bite back the cry of agony from her frail bones and magestone chains.

"This Transition will happen. What you do to me won't change that. I did this for you. To make you stronger," Varlas said, and for a moment she thought she detected the plea in his words. That it was all wasted energy to fight.

Maybe there was some part of the lost king's heart that was *sorry.* For the well he'd fallen into so deeply. His spiral of betrayal had started with himself and ended with the one person he cared for most in this world. His mate. Their son. Because they were one and the same.

"This a blessing for you, Tauria."

Her vision peppered, her skin flushed, when his gaze slid to her. Her wrath rose at his unapologetic stance.

"I planned to make sure you got everything back. Everything you have longed for. Without this, you are a princess with no kingdom."

"No, she is not."

That echo through the hall was a declaration that halted time. For the voice that disrupted far behind Tauria caressed her neck and raced down her spine, until that phantom touch traveled within, stroking her senses with exhilarating awareness. *His voice.* Tauria's breath shuddered out of her.

"She is a queen with two."

Tauria turned slowly, pulse quickening, and her skin broke out in a thrilling shiver. Her mind taunted he wasn't real. He couldn't be here. But her heart found him without falter. Guiding her eyes up to land on a cloaked figure among the masses on the balcony, she confirmed his presence undeniably when the people parted and he pulled down his hood, unclasping his black cloak to let it fall.

There he was.

The King of High Farrow.

Her mate.

He had come for her.

Nik effortlessly hoisted himself onto the railing, and there was little pause before he leaped, landing in a graceful crouch that vibrated with an electrifying awakening under her feet. As he straightened, Nik brushed off his impeccable jacket nonchalantly, but everything about his demeanor was threatening. Cold and calm, as if he'd collected a storm just waiting to be unleashed. His green eyes blazed at the guards who held her.

"I will warn you to take your hands off my mate," he said, voice so dangerously low, "before I paint this wedding red. Or"—Nik's fingers grazed a black rose—"discover if you'll match the pretty décor when I tear the heart from your chest."

Tauria shifted with the urge to go to him, and the resonating clank of her shackles in the silence drew his attention to them.

"Are those chains on her?" But his question didn't leave room for answer as he seemed to quickly detect they were not of any ordinary iron. His gaze traveled to Varlas with a promise of death. There was no rage, but a calculating, chilling wrath. His voice was sharp as ice as he said, "You dare to take away her wind?"

Nik stalked to them, and it were as if the darkness followed. A predator who didn't fear the opposition in the slightest—not even the High Lord he was yet to grant an ounce of his attention. Nik's form was powerful, dominating, and he rippled with a violence so palpable it shook her whole body.

She had never seen this side to him before.

Among petty lords and occasional snide ladies, he was never shy or hesitant to come to the defense of who or what was dear to him. But this…it was a darkly possessive air. Unapologetic for what he might become. Unhesitating to do whatever was necessary to protect. And it laced her spine with a dangerous thrill.

Mordecai began to gather strength, groaning as he shifted as if to stand, and Tauria's heart leaped. Yet he halted at the unmistakable tension. Glancing up, she couldn't believe it when the front line occupying the balcony braced with arrows aimed at everyone below.

"You might want to stay down," Nik said to her as shadowy fury twitched the High Lord's face. She didn't know how he'd breached the castle undetected with them all, but *Gods,* Nik was brilliant.

Along the rows of benches, cloaked onlookers *balked,* shuffling away from him as he made his way down the aisle without acknowledging a single soul. The guards finally released her, taking a few steps back. The Olmstone king's resentment and rage choked the air, battling the wrath that grew with every step of distance Nik closed.

He finally tore that darkly piercing gaze from Varlas as he came to a halt and turned to her. Nik's emerald gaze softened like the flick of a switch. As though they were alone. His small smile made that wish all the more tangible as it fluttered in her chest and soothed her terror. Just for a moment. His hand raised to her face, and his skin grazing her cheek released a breath of contentment that pinched her brow despite their harrowing surroundings and many seething eyes. That first touch made her forget it all.

"Hello, love."

She bit back her whimper and the overwhelming desire to have him hold her. She'd missed him so much it was a cruel taunt of a reunion. Bound, restrained, and stuffed into the most ridiculous funeral gown she could have imagined. Nik reached for her veil, plucking it from her hair. He tossed it aside while his other hand dipped into his pocket. Light glinted off the emerald-jeweled comb as he held it up with a tender smile despite everything.

"I believe I promised to return this to you."

He slipped it into place, and she was hit with treasured memory and consumed by a love that would never know full expression.

"It took you long enough," she hushed out.

Nik almost broke a grin. Then his hand eased from the back of her head and grazed her temple. His jaw flexed a few times in silence at her injury. As his gaze fell to the discarded spindlelillies, his rage turned tangible, like a crawling heat through the room. He spoke to all their enemies but didn't grant anyone the attention of sight.

"Your first mistake was imprisoning her." Nik looked her over carefully, studying every mark. "Your second mistake was making a mockery of something sacred to our kingdom."

Tauria's chest burst with pride and warmth at his words.

Our kingdom.

It sounded so wonderful, so hopeful. She grasped that treasured future with the striking will to see them both make it out of here.

"Your third mistake..." There wasn't a second for her to brace when, with gritted teeth, Nik reached for her shackles and snapped the chain that joined them. She gasped in a shock that numbed the pain. "Was taking away her wind." His hands softly took one of her shackled wrists, and his voice lowered to her personally. "Eyes on me, love."

When she looked up, Nik eased her nerves with that emerald stare and then hooked his fingers under the magestone, the pain of it written on his face. With a strain against the energy-sucking material, he snapped the lock. Tauria wasn't spared of searing injury against her raw wrists with the force it took, and Nik knew it. His command for her to hold his eyes was the best distraction he could offer. His hands went for the other magestone binding.

"How did you know?"

"Not important," he answered, and with a wince, the second lock broke and echoed as it hit the stone. Nik took her wrists, revenge hardening his expression as he glanced down and saw their abrasions.

"I'm okay," she said to him within.

Nik's fingers curled under her chin as if refraining from bringing his mouth down on hers. *"I'm going to kill them all for what they did to you."* Then he turned to where Tarly still surrendered his father on his knees. "You want to know how we easily breached your defenses?" Nik mocked, spinning on his heel toward the door. "In fact, I'm sure he'll tell you."

Tauria picked up on the thundering footsteps at the door before two guards burst through, halting abruptly, hands darting to their weapons after a quick scan of the room.

"You—Your Majesty," one stuttered, clearly debating if the information he held was of urgency compared to the compromised position of his king he'd stumbled upon. "They've begun to siege the city."

"Who?" Nik prompted, amusement slithering into his tone. Then his gaze flashed back to her, and Tauria knew. She'd been heard.

"The Stone Men," she answered.

The letter she'd entrusted Lycus to see out of the city. She wasn't entirely confident her voice would be heard by the chief.

The guards at the door were too stunned to pick up on the threat at their backs. A sword ran through each of them, and Tauria winced at the lack of mercy. She didn't know what she envisioned with their notorious name, but the bodies who shuffled into the hall were striking. Men and women. Humans, to her utter disbelief, and she didn't know how she could have missed that detail in her readings. They were garbed in beautiful handmade wears with vibrant headwear. Their feet were clad in what could be mistaken for sandals but on closer inspection were reinforced shoes, structured to endure combat. They were equipped with spears and wooden shields, bows and arrows. They were awe-inspiring.

"We were intercepted on the way here. Though sieging the city is a little dramatic when the gates were open for us to walk straight through," a voice rumbled, so deep she felt phantom vibrations. "I must admit we've been waiting some time for an excuse to…*urge* you along, King Varlas."

Her mind screamed as it reached its conclusion on who he was. Chief Zainaid of the Stone Men. He was so large for a human, built broad and dominating with dark, tanned skin. He walked down the aisle as though strolling through summer sands. His blue eyes slipped to her.

"When the winds gale force from the east…" He recited the words of her letter, and she released a breath of pure gratitude. "Tauria Stagknight, I presume?"

The pride in Nik's gaze thumped in her chest as she nodded. "I didn't know if you would believe me," she admitted.

"I didn't," the chief was quick to say. "You also have her to thank."

At the door, a large beast of brilliant white fur and silver eyes stalked past the others. Tauria blinked, her head snapping back immediately, because she was sure she'd seen—

There were two of them. Katori behind her moved as if to meet her twin. Tauria spared Tarly a look, but his confusion only sank her disbelief further.

"She showed up precisely as we felt the tail blast of your wind—a sudden disruption to the otherwise still air of the day. Asari is her name, if you did not know. It was unpassable as a coincidence that she should show when you called and caused a stir among our own packs." The chief tracked Katori with his eyes, a thick brow rising when he seemed to sense something no one else did. His assessment flashed from the wolf to the prince. "A powerful bond you have made with a powerful beast, Your Highness."

"You are all fools," Varlas said, not with malice or hatred. Tauria might have deciphered his wavering voice as *fearful.*

Chief Zainaid spoke calmly. "If you want a final sign it is over, Fenstead armies heard the call from their queen. Along with Rhyenelle, they're prepared to attack from the south if given the signal. This does not have to end in bloodshed."

Tauria couldn't believe it. Fenstead had answered her. Agonizing over Lycus's code in his letter had led her to believe he'd left her instructions to tie green to Olmstone's flag as a way of summoning him if she got into danger after he left. It was true, though selflessly, he'd known it wouldn't bring him but the might of their armies instead. He'd kept them thriving for this very moment.

"You might want to rethink your plans." Mordecai's voice would never fail to turn her stomach.

Tarly remained poised to take his father's life in a second. Nik shifted, only to be closer to her. The two wolves whined. The Stone Men were still. A rise of thick tension choked the air from her lungs.

Mordecai caught the eye of some of his dark guards by a side door, giving the most subtle of nods that triggered their shuffle from the room. "We must make the most of this night," he drawled as though he were surrounded by no hope of triumph, not even for him.

Tauria picked up on the distant cries before the shuffling feet entered the room. She had already pinpointed the wails of distress before she laid eyes on her. It wasn't only the queen who was dragged in disgracefully… Tauria's heart came close to matching the deep strike of terror in Keira's as she watched the small, terrified form get escorted in by a different set of guards.

"No," Tarly snarled, but it lacked wrath under the blanket of his own horror.

Opal's usual sun-kissed skin was washed pale and ghostly. She wasn't dragged as her hollow steps guided her to stand before the dais. Tauria's spine curved tight at Keira's heart-wrenching wails from where she was restrained at the side of the hall, fighting against the guards.

"You promised!" The prince's loud shout snapped her eyes back to him. Both his hands shook around the hilt of his sword, ready to plunge it straight through Varlas, but his desolate face gave away his hesitation. The king was still his father. Still a male he had early childhood memories of joy and love with despite the harrowing turn of fate that had befallen them both. "You gave your word that if I brought her to you, Opal would be spared!"

Tauria's knees weakened, threatening to pull her into a darkness so tormenting at his words and what she concluded in them. She should have thought of it sooner. She should have *believed* in the prince. Yet in her anger and hopelessness, it had been so easy to paint Tarly as the villain.

To see him as his father.

Yet it was not a beast but a broken savior whom she had come to know throughout her time in Olmstone. A prince who, despite all that cursed him with a melancholy heart, still held onto what was once pure and alive in him. He only buried it deep to protect what little shards were left.

"Please—she's just a child!" Keira's voice was unrecognizable in its choked plea, eliciting nothing of the arrogant guise that saw her through courtly life. Stripped of crown, title, and wealth, all she was in this moment…was a desperate mother. "She won't survive it."

This inspired Tauria to act. She slipped out of Nik's protection to run to the young princess who trembled in terror. The guards shifted but didn't stop her as she made it to Opal, and the princess immediately clamped her small arms around her waist.

"You're going to be okay," Tauria whispered down to her. Smoothing down her hair, she met Keira's wild, pleading look. It was a promise. Tauria would do whatever it took to see the princess spared.

Nik was close at her back, and Tauria targeted a cold gaze of fury at

Varlas on his knees, about to unleash her words of hatred that he could be capable of inflicting such evil on his own children.

But that wicked voice of darkness spoke first.

"You are a foolish prince to believe your father's hollow words held power. Though I hope it grants you some peace to know it is not your pitiful father's will to do what is necessary." Mordecai let out a long sigh as if boredom had overcome him. "You will all come to thank me soon enough."

Tauria was still tunneling into her well of power. Her skin was flushed, but she focused to maintain control against her rising panic.

Commotion ensued from the side door again, grabbing everyone's attention. When she saw who was dragged through this time, everything Tauria believed about getting to go home required sudden reassessment.

Lycus could barely stand his weight, hauled in by a guard on each arm. The second person she was stunned with fear to see…was Serena. Then two other males she had never seen before, but equally, they were all pulled into the sinister ceremony against their will. Lined up in front of the dais, the four hostages were forced to their knees.

"A life for a life. It is the cost for the powerful species you will become."

Tauria wished for time to stop so she could comprehend his meaning. She looked over each terrified face that had been brought here for slaughter. One for each of them. It was a thought so sickening she couldn't believe the evil. She had to put in every effort not to fall apart, so she didn't look down at the hostages. She didn't look down at Lycus, who she knew would collapse her composure in his desolate state.

"The only life on forfeit tonight is yours, Mordecai," Nik said.

Tauria's eyes followed the commotion to the balcony, where behind the archers still poised to release their arrows, High Farrow warriors braced on the stone flat, ready with swords to descend on the dark fae below. To aid the Stone Men who made a formation to attack.

"As much as I would enjoy getting a head start on ridding the world of you, I'll give you the chance to allow us to walk out of here." Yet there was something about the subtle way Nik braced that let her know that was never going to be the way they left this place. They would have to fight. Nik knew, and he was reaching for his sword.

"I need you to run, Tauria."

She shook her head, but his tug of urgency within almost made her gasp.

"Not to flee, but to fight. You're the only one who can get the princess to safety."

"I can't." Her heart raced with an ache to defy him. *"I won't leave you and Lycus."*

The silence in the room was tense and thick. Calculating. Even as she spoke, she knew the choice she had to make was cruel.

"We will be right behind you. I promise."

The assurance Nik wouldn't forget about her friend and general eased the burden she felt at not standing to fight by their side. Nik broke, spiking her into combat senses. Lunging forward, he retrieved her staff, and her arm extended to catch it. Yet as soon as the vibration of her weapon shot up her arm…

Tauria couldn't run.

Not yet.

Chaos erupted in a song of steel and cries. Conflict erupted in a dangerous beckoning for her to have her revenge.

"Now, Tauria."

She snapped her gaze to her mate. Nik didn't look at her, fixing his dark wrath on Mordecai as they faced off.

Despite his urgency, Tauria turned her head…

To the King of Olmstone.

Settling a calm wrath on Varlas—still surrendering on his knees while Tarly battled with what to do—she realized she could spare the prince's soul and have her revenge. It was a thought so sinister and foreign, but her magick answered to it. Tauria felt the air, extended her reach where she stood, and drew every breath from Varlas's lungs. The king choked, and Tarly stumbled away in confusion, but she could pay him no attention as she took slow steps, *relishing* in the king's bulging eyes as he clawed his throat for phantom hands. For all he'd put her through.

"You betrayed my father," she said, uncaring if he heard, perhaps only needing to soothe the pain that trembled her bones with what she was doing. "You betrayed your own children."

"Tauria—"

Her hand lashed out on instinct as if the prince sought to stop her. She had to do this. It was for him she would do this.

"You betrayed *me.*" She didn't tear her eyes from watching vines of red rush through the whites of the king's, and for a second, she might have believed the apology in his dying look. But she couldn't feel it…not when it was only remorse risen in a terror-filled soul's final moments.

He would have let them all die. He would have made them all into monsters.

"Tauria, you don't have to do this," Tarly tried again.

But she did. In time he would understand that.

"You're not a killer, love." Nik's voice crept through the conflict that had begun to tremor through her body. The tight grip on her staff tried to ease the pain that raged within. In that moment, she didn't know who she was. *What* she was.

"You don't know everything he's done."

"I know you." He was so gentle it tore her apart. No matter what she did, he would stand by her. *"Your heart that forgives even those who have wronged you truly."*

A sharp sob escaped her. There were only seconds to decide before his fate would be sealed. An eternal tarnish that would brand her soul for taking a life.

Then she chose.

Tauria unleashed half her rage on Varlas, seizing the wind and air she choked from him, her palm pulsing with warm energy before she cast her arm out to send the powerful blast into him. The king was airborne for a few seconds before he slammed against the wall with such force she couldn't be certain it *wouldn't* kill him. She didn't have a second to spare, didn't even witness his body fall, before she adjusted her stance, whirled her staff between her hands to collect a new storm, and, turning, aimed the second dose of her wrath at the queen. It was a precise effort to control its direction to avoid it barreling into Keira. Instead, it hit the two guards beside her. Tauria's teeth clenched to continue sending the wind that erupted chaos on the black petals and décor.

"Run!" she yelled to the princess.

Opal did without hesitation when Keira's arms flew open. Tauria spared a look and was relieved to see Lycus had risen and somehow found the strength to wield a weapon as he joined Nik, closing in on the dark fae king. Against all that resisted her steps away from Nik, against the warm embrace that lingered as she passed him—pride, love—Tauria forced herself to run.

Keira grabbed Opal's hand, and without looking back they slipped through the side door, leaving death and destruction behind. Her steps surged forward with the knowledge that all she had to do was see Keira and Opal make it out alive. The stables. Once they were on horseback, Tauria would return. She would never leave them.

"Do you know the quickest way to the stables?" Tauria was focused and alert, never allowing their pace to slow.

Keira nodded. "Through the throne room. The back door will take us close to the nearest exit."

Tauria couldn't confirm it, and she cursed her lack of time spent getting to know the layout of the castle. She followed the queen anyway, racing down halls, until she knew the way herself and the grand doors came into view. Tauria stilled her mind and braced for the guards they might find protecting the space. The doors were open, and as she steered them sideways, her steps halted abruptly.

Not in the face of guards.

Not a mass of foes.

These were perilous odds all the same, yet she couldn't be sure why.

Upon the throne sat one figure. A creature of flame and beauty was all Tauria could think, yet something about her was of sin and malice. She sat so elegantly it was as if she were a Goddess. Her vibrant red hair waved like fire against the blood red of her gown. Her eyes…

Tauria blinked long and hard. She had seen them before, yet the gold irises of this female were ablaze. *Alive.* The conclusion was glaring, yet she couldn't believe it.

"I have been waiting for you, Tauria Stagknight."

Her voice was power in itself, conflicting as it willed her to bow or run far and fast from its grip of allurement. The female's bright amber eyes slid beside her, and that almost shifted Tauria into defensive mode until she spoke again.

"Thank you for leading her to me. As promised, you are free."

She couldn't believe it. Tauria's breath fell from her as her head bowed with the delivery of betrayal. Silence vibrated through the air for a few long seconds before the queen began to back away from her.

"I had to protect my daughter," Keira confessed.

Tauria knew. She didn't look at Keira or Opal as she gave a barely-there nod of understanding. They would be safe. That was all that mattered.

"I won't go without Tauria," Opal said, defiance in her pure heart. Tauria clamped her eyes shut against the cries that began to echo from the princess, making out a short struggle as though she fought her own mother. "I'll stay with you!" Her small voice of devotion was agony to hear. Tauria couldn't turn around or open her eyes.

The crying faded slowly. She wasn't sure how much time had passed before silence settled once again. Condemning silence.

Tauria looked up, just as the red-haired fae curled a cruel, seductive smile and rose perfectly from the throne, taking her first steps that crawled across Tauria's skin with echoes of haunting. She was fae, except…there was something *more* about this female. Power and dominance radiated so effortlessly from her, lapping in the waves of her blood-red gown, forged in the tresses of her burnt umber hair. Every movement was elegant and snakelike. Poisonous but undeniably beautiful.

"Do you know who I am?" she asked smoothly, with a delight that already knew the answer.

Tauria's rapid heartbeat couldn't match her breaths, which she tamed to focus on the fae. "I do," she said with all the bravery she could muster in the face of the greatest threat of all. The master behind everything.

Her gaze was nothing short of blazing triumph. "This is going to be so much fun."

CHAPTER 65

Nikalias

NEVER BEFORE HAD Nik's rage pulsed so tangibly. He couldn't stop seeing the marks on her wrists, the wound on her temple, the mockery they'd made of her. His mate. Never before had he harbored such murderous tendencies. There was a small bliss in knowing she wasn't among the battles they fought valiantly around him as he fixed his wrath on Mordecai.

"They call you High Lord because you are not fit for the title of king. Not anymore," Nik taunted.

The flex of Mordecai's eyes told him the words were a weapon. Yet his opposition was strong.

"There will only be one ruler of the continent. One queen."

That caught his attention, and realization slipped into place. "I see." Nik huffed a mocking laugh. "You are nothing more than her puppet." He braced to engage with the dark fae in combat to unleash the storm he'd gathered since learning of Tauria's capture. His hand tightened around the Farrow Sword as he watched Mordecai's hand raise a fraction—

A pull from within stopped the world.

Something wasn't right.

The High Lord watched his stance falter a fraction, and the faint upturning of his lips was a strike of cold dread Nik wasn't prepared for. He didn't know what was wrong, but Mordecai did. He tried to call through the bond, but Tauria wouldn't answer. Not with words to explain the gods-awful ripple that hollowed his stomach. She was in trouble, and his vengeance silenced with the urgency to go to her.

"Let's end this bastard."

Nik's head snapped to Lycus. Despite the weakened state of him, the general wore an admirable defiance as he clutched a blade, ready to fight by Nik's side.

"She's in trouble," Nik breathed. Nothing else mattered.

Lycus met his look of calculation with fear. Before either of them could speak, Nik caught the movement just in time to raise his blade against Mordecai, who took their distraction to his advantage. Teeth clenched, he pushed off against his blade, but before they could clash again, Lycus stepped in front of him to take the next blow.

"Go to her!" he barked, engaging in a battle with the dark fae that built toward ruthlessness.

Nik couldn't debate staying to aid him, not when Lycus had bought him his escape in distracting Mordecai. But he couldn't think of his life if Tauria's was the alternative.

He didn't hesitate to make sure that bought time wasn't wasted.

Movement was numb; sound was nonexistent. All he grappled to was his tether to her that he could follow in the dark. That he *would* follow until the end of his days. Every time she called. No matter what. He didn't expect the destination it led him to, but as he stormed into Olmstone's throne room…

There she was.

Nik panted, scanning the room urgently. She stood just below the dais. The moonlight shining down through the glass dome roof made every black crystal on her glitter where she stood poised with her staff.

"There you are," he said, still frantically scanning her for distress or injury as he slowly closed the distance. "What are you still doing here? Tauria, what's wrong?" He couldn't place it. Something still screamed within him.

"Nik..." Her choke pierced him like a dagger of anticipation, locking his spine with dread.

"I'm here." He edged toward her.

The shake of her head was tight, barely-there. The sob that escaped her echoed through the room with a rattling chill. "I'm so sorry."

She moved in a way he never could have anticipated. Never could have prepared for. Tauria shifted in a familiar stance, and he was too late to detect it, but the lick of her wind was a warning.

She attacked.

The blast of her wind hit him. Fully and without mercy. It sent him flying back before he braced for impact on the unforgiving ground. Pain shot through the side of his body. Nik groaned when he stopped skidding, but he rolled, wincing as he shot to his feet on high alert. His sword clattered away from him, and as he locked eyes with Tauria, incredulous, he lunged for it, and she ran toward him.

A hairsbreadth from being impaled by the lethal arrow of her staff, Nik gripped his sword just in time to intercept its spear. Tauria didn't pause. Nik honed in on her to deflect the blow despite his utter shock.

"This isn't you," he rasped, stepping methodically around her maneuvers.

She said nothing, her full focus placed on the incredible speed with which she danced. That was what watching Tauria in combat was: a dangerous dance of lethal passion. Yet he'd never been on the receiving end of all that she was capable of. It was both terrifying and mesmerizing. His pride was conflicted with the threat she didn't relent in the slightest.

He tried to reach her within. He had to hear her.

"You can do better than that," he taunted, trying some other method to provoke something. *"You're slowing."* She wasn't in the slightest. But her brow pinched at that. Not in anger, but fear. *"It's going to take more to kill me, love."*

Her staff pushed off his sword, twisting expertly between her hands, and Nik knew what was to come next. A second too late, all he could do was lock his body. She gathered a gale, turning, and Tauria cried out as it unleashed from her with the vertical strike of her staff, which aimed for him as she dropped into a beautiful crouch.

Nik was airborne for a long time before he slammed into the wall. Agony hit the tip of his spine first, shooting fire through every nerve cell, before he fell, palms slapping the stone. His arms trembled, threatening to give out while he fought for consciousness. *Gods,* she was powerful. He would have basked in his pride were it not for the awareness she was stalking toward him, far from finished.

"Just feel me, Tauria. I'm right here," he tried. With everything he was he embraced her from within. *"Please, love."* He forced himself to stand, miraculously still clutching the Farrow Sword. Her face remained emotionless, but her eyes…they were desolate. Nik kept channeling his thoughts to her, until finally, she spoke back.

"I can't stop."

Hearing her voice was a wave of relief despite all she unleashed on him. They crossed staff and sword once more. He didn't attack, only deflected as best he could while trying to calculate a maneuver that would stop her without harming her. She was so fast, so precise, it was difficult to find a safe opening.

Tauria twisted around him. Her staff knocked into the back of his legs, hitting a nerve she knew would force his knees to buckle. Nik hissed as he fell, but right before she could plunge the iron tip through his back he twisted, hand lashing around the wood she had aimed for his heart.

Tauria was strong, and he'd been weakened. Nik trembled with the effort to push off the full weight she leaned into him.

"You've really been holding back all these years," he strained through the bond.

"I'll kill you, Nik." Her voice broke, and he couldn't bear it.

"I'm sure you've wanted to plenty."

Her breath stuttered from her, an ache echoing through their connection. *"You shouldn't have come for me."*

He held those desperate hazel eyes. Despite everything, Nik smiled at his world. *"I'll always come for you."*

Tauria was shuddering from within. She was fighting. Nik sensed the moment her inner turmoil was distracted enough for him to catch her off-guard. His grip on her staff jerked sideward, throwing her off-balance. Nik caught her as she fell and didn't allow her to take a breath before he rolled, pinning her beneath him, while her weapon clattered out of reach. His hands clamped her wrists.

"You put up some fight, Tauria Stagknight." He breathed hard. "Is it wrong I find it so damn attractive?"

"I can't—" Pain clenched her face as if she were fighting an invisible control with everything she was. She tried to thrash beneath him, but he held her tight. *"She's in my mind, Nik."*

"Shh." He wrapped every piece of himself around her senses, soothing everything he could. *"So am I, love."* Nik leaned his forehead to hers and closed his eyes. He listened to the drum of her heart, and like he had done infinite times in sleep, he arrived at the block on Tauria's mind. Her lips parted, and he felt her breath across his lips. *"I need you to let me in."*

"How are you—?"

Nik put every focus into finding a way past the barrier he was all too familiar with without harming her. It was an odd sensation, similar while also different to his Nightwalking, and his own fear that he wasn't experienced enough in this and could hurt her threatened to make him retreat. But he had no choice.

"You can do it," he coaxed. *"Just show me."*

Having to restrain her against her forced movements tore him apart. Her physical and mental pain was a helpless torture he'd never endured before.

Nik let go of his power. He wrapped Tauria in it, sending all he could through the bond that was so strong he'd reached her from kingdoms away. He would reach her over sea and through realms. They were one.

Tauria took her first full breath. Something so small but so liberating, as it was the sound of her feeling them merge. With that gasp, there it was. Nik saw his opening and seized it entirely. Within her mind, with their power combined, the shadow that seized her in its claws hissed and retreated all at once.

Nik pulled back, adrenaline coursing through him with the most unexplainable high, and they stared wide-eyed at each other.

"How did you do that?" she rasped.

They didn't get a moment to collect their thoughts.

"What a happy little reunion."

The melodic threat of that voice forced Nik to act. He straddled Tauria and took her with him now she'd gained full control of herself once more.

They rose together carefully to face her.

"I must admit, I am a surprised by the revelation, but it was highly entertaining to watch two lovers in battle."

Nik's eyes landed on her easing out of the shadows like a tendril of flame. He didn't know what he expected, but those eyes… It was a conflict to fear the glittering gold of them.

He didn't have a second to brace or anticipate her attack. A familiar but far more powerful force infiltrated his mind like talons, sinking deep, and his lost control locked his spine, curving his back. Tauria gave a similar reaction, the peril that had befallen them feeling helpless and cold.

"I am the Spirit of *Souls,*" she drawled, stalking toward them with seductive triumph. Her ethereal irises marveled at him and Tauria. "I can take the essence of one soul and plant it in another. I can shatter a soul so one might never find their other half. And best of all, I can break a completed mating bond as easily as snapping my fingers."

Then it was as if the world stopped. Nothing mattered. Nothing but her. Them. This beautiful, wonderful bond that ran between them. Nik had loved her before it, and he would love her for eternity without it. But that didn't make the thought of having it broken any less despairing.

The red-haired beauty spared a twist back as two guards marched in, each drawing blades as they approached. Nik stayed still, channeling all he could into Tauria to soothe her panic as the guards' daggers came to rest against their necks. He had to bide his time to create a new plan for all he never could have prepared for.

Shuffling sounded behind them, but neither could turn to look as they faced the stone throne. Then a voice called to halt everything. One he expected, but not here, facing off against the foe they weren't prepared to meet. She spoke with unwavering confidence, calling out the name he'd so far refused to speak in his denial, and for a second, Nik had to wonder if she *did* know who she would face this night.

"Marvellas."

CHAPTER 66

Tauria

Marlowe couldn't be here. It didn't make sense for the delicate human to walk straight into the scene of death and destruction when there was no way out. Yet even though Tauria was unable to make any movement to confirm the ocean eyes and honey hair she expected to find, it was undeniably Marlowe's voice.

All Tauria could do was watch Marvellas's reaction and extend her senses to gauge what was happening at her back. The Spirit's eyes widened. Not with surprise, but in glee. Almost as if she knew…

"Marlowe Connaise," Marvellas drawled in recognition.

Maybe it shouldn't have been a surprise that Marvellas knew who she was, that she could have been watching them all for far longer than they imagined.

"It's Kilnight now," she answered.

It was her friend's voice, yet the confidence…the cool collectedness despite all she walked into, didn't match the timid, wondrous person

Tauria knew. Joy or surprise couldn't even settle with the confirmation she'd married Jakon sometime since Tauria left.

The Spirit chuckled, an alluring sound that pricked every hair on her body. "Oh, child," she taunted. "What a tragic fate."

As Marvellas passed them, her command on their movements released all at once, and Tauria would have fallen forward were it not for the threat of the blade still pressed to her throat. She and Nik were turned around by their guards, and her eyes fell on Marlowe with a wash of dread. As if there were a still kernel of hope she'd been mistaken.

The blacksmith stood poised, confident. Yet she was not the blacksmith in that moment. She wore a familiar face, not a blonde curl different, not a slight change in the hue of her eyes, but there was something far *more* to the person who faced off with the Spirit without a flicker of fear.

Marvellas's next step as she stalked to Marlowe was halted by an arrow whizzing through the air, striking the ground in front of her where her next footstep would have landed.

Everyone's gaze snapped up to the balcony, and the sight was as awe-invoking as it was incredulous. Jakon Kilnight, an ordinary human, stood poised and balanced on the stone rail above, a second arrow already nocked to target the unparalleled threat that approached his wife.

"The husband, I assume?" Marvellas sang with mocking amusement. "Human. Mortal. I suppose it would be contradictory for me to fault you for your choices. Yet I hoped with all the knowledge you bear, all the twisted stories of history you know the real truth behind, you would not make such damning mistakes."

Confusion was an unexpected twist to the suffocating fear and threat. It flinched on Jakon's hardened expression too. Yet Marlowe…all her face bore was *pain.*

There was a long moment of suspended silence, as though the Spirit expected Marlowe to have an answer to her mocking gibe. Then Marvellas's shoulders squared, eyes darting between Marlowe and Jakon, even sparing a glance back at Tauria and Nik, but whatever she read on their expressions rumbled dark laughter in the Spirit.

"They do not know," she delighted. As if she thought this a brilliant climax to the entertainment. "Are you afraid of what they will think, Marlowe Kilnight? Or are you afraid to break his heart with the truth?"

Marlowe's expression was etched with defiance and a sharp anger. "It means nothing."

Marvellas chuckled. "It seems not even the smartest of us, not even the one who has seen as much to know nothing good will ever come of trying to repeat history, will learn from past mistakes." She took more steps toward Marlowe, and the groan of Jakon's bow was heard but no arrow loosed before a choking gasp left him. Without even sparing him a glance, Marvellas had seized his movements.

The Spirit stopped at a deadly proximity, but Marlowe didn't balk. Tauria was stunned at what she witnessed, not recognizing the human before them.

Marvellas cast her eyes up to Jakon. "It's a tragic twist of fate when a mortal"—her gaze fell down, and so did the weight of a revelation so crushing Tauria's mouth opened on a silent gasp—"falls in love with an immortal."

"I'm not immortal," Marlowe quickly hissed in defense.

"In comparison to him, you may as well be."

Nothing in that moment felt real. Marlowe…the quiet blacksmith who didn't seem capable of harming a soul…who was so full of joy and love and forgiveness. *Immortal.* Human, but with a lifespan that would clearly outlast that of her species.

Was anything beyond the impossible anymore?

Marvellas looked around them all. "Did you really think an oracle would be content to live and die in a simple length of mundane human existence?" The Spirit's eyes sparkled with wonder as they trailed over

Marlowe. "But you are so much more—aren't you, child?" She lifted a hand.

"Don't touch her," Jakon hissed with malice.

The Spirit barely cast him a glance as she said, "Why don't you come down here and join us?"

Jakon, not by his own will, dropped his bow, and it clattered to the ground. He straightened, braced to jump, and horror drew a breath of helpless adrenaline, the whole room stilled, because it was far too high for his fragile human form to fall without breaking bones. Or killing him.

"Stop!" Marlowe shouted, the first wavering of her bravery as her gaze snapped up to Jakon.

"I would be doing you both a favor," Marvellas snarled. "Ending this pitiful union to spare you from a strung-out heartbreak." Then something changed on the Spirit's face. Understanding settled. "I've known about you for some time. Like you, I also get visions. Did you see me before, just as I saw you?" Marvellas took hold of the blacksmith's face. She didn't flinch, but her nostrils flared with a foreign harshness.

Jakon's struggle could be heard above.

"We could do so much together." The Spirit spoke as if she were airing her thoughts without a care for her response. "With the magick you harbor, raw and unformed, who knows what you could be capable of?"

Tauria wanted so desperately to aid her friend. There was never a more helpless, soul-damning feeling than to watch, unable to do anything, under the threat of the blade. Not only for her own life, but for Nik who remained silent beside her.

Then his hand brushed hers, and Tauria inhaled a shallow breath at the tingles that shot up her arm with the contact. The blade on her throat slackened just as his palm fully slid into hers and their fingers entwined.

Stunned the guards hadn't moved to stop him reaching for her,

Tauria found the will to twist her head to Nik. He didn't look at her, so she spared a quick glance up. The guards…they were *livid.* Veins protruding in their necks, bodies giving off a stiff tremble, as if they fought…

An invisible control.

Yet it didn't make sense for Marvellas to have seized her own soldiers.

"This is not going to be clean, and it's not going to be easy." Nik's voice was calm, preparing her.

"What is happening?" A warm vibration started to travel up her arm, over her chest. Her magick surfaced, but not by her awakening. It was him.

"I need you to be ready to fight. Can you do that for me, love?"

Adrenaline quickened her pulse, incredulity filling her mind, as there was only one impossible conclusion to the guards' stillness at their backs. If it wasn't Marvellas…

"How are you doing that?" she breathed. She *felt* the waves of power emanating from him. More than what she knew—more than what he should be capable of. Nik seemed to harbor his own well of power. To call upon at will, but not to consume him with burnout. And he was extending that power to her through the bond, making her feel…unstoppable.

"I'll explain later. But right now, do you think we can do that thing?"

"We have a thing?" She caught his internal smirk. And despite the fear that gripped her still, it was a welcome contrast.

"Many things," he said, accompanied by a desirous stroke on her senses. *"But I mean the one that will give us a fighting chance out of here. Take the power—I know you can wield it. Just like we did in the library. Seize the wind, love. Bold and without restraint. Unleash the Nether on them all. As Fenstead…"*

A strength straightened her spine, racing through her as she braced for what they had to do. *"And as High Farrow,"* she promised.

"I have a proposal," Marvellas announced suddenly, but her eyes were fixed on Marlowe. "You come with me, join me without resistance, and I'll let them all go."

"Not a chance in—" Jakon's snarl was halted, his speech claimed.

But Marlowe…the question didn't surprise her.

So many questions threatened Tauria's focus as she began to harness the height of her ability, aided unexplainably by Nik.

"Why do you think I'm here?"

Tauria's dread was a blanket of ice. Shock. Her magick pulled back at it. Nik's hand squeezed hers again, and she grappled control of it once more, summoning the power and preparing to unleash it all.

Marvellas's red mouth curled in triumph, her bright gold eyes blazing as though she were eyeing a grand prize. "So willing… I like that. You had to have seen me coming, yet you walked right into this fate. Tell me, is it simply to save these pitiful lives, or have you seen the better world that will become of my creation?"

"You will create nothing but false superiority built over the bones of anything good or true. You will spill the blood of pure hearts, only to give life to pure evil. You will create beasts, not beings. What you seek is a world of power against power that will make your triumph short and your downfall of your own making."

"You are wrong." Marvellas seemed unfazed by Marlowe's passionate speech. Her gaze traveled up to Jakon once more. "One human at a time, if that is what it takes. There won't be another trap for those as powerful as us to fall into for the weaker species again."

Jakon shuffled closer to the edge, and panic paled the blacksmith's face.

"You said you would let them all go!" she yelled.

"I'm doing you a favor, Marlowe. The others will be free to leave."

He wobbled forward as if straining against everything he was not to tumble headfirst in a fatal fall. Tauria's heart was wild. She had to act now.

"Not yet, love," Nik echoed to her as if anticipating her break.

"We can't let him fall!"

Nik soothed her from within, but she was incredulous he was still holding back.

"You were once all-powerful." Marlowe spoke with a dead, cold calm. "Now, you're almost just…fae."

It happened so fast, but Tauria was alert to everything in anticipation. Marlowe reached for something that was hidden under her cloak. The echoing chime of metal and stone was one she would never forget, but it was confirmed by sight when the glittering black cuffs clamped around the Spirit's wrists and she cried out.

"Now."

Tauria didn't hesitate, and a sharpness of instinct had her whirling back instead.

Mordecai appeared, blade raised as he neared Nik. Tauria cast out a hand, blasting him back before her fist clamped tight, choking the air from his lungs. Her other hand was still entwined with Nik's, and she felt him from within, reaching to merge with her.

With time bought, Nik let go of her hand only to take her waist, and he braced.

Tauria's arms cast out as Marvellas hissed with the most lethal sound, snapping the chain between her cuffs effortlessly. *Gods above.* Despite her being a fae, it shouldn't have been a shock to learn magestone didn't harm the Spirit the same. The air stirred as Tauria kept her focus and controlled her movements. The wind answered, swirling around the room, and everyone began to shield their eyes with the force that collected. Tauria's hair whipped across her face as her tornado grew. Nik's hold on her tightened, and their power together…

It erupted chaos.

A deafening boom blasted through the space that would have taken them out too were it not for Nik's aid. When the domed roof shattered and rained down a deadly waterfall, she caught it in her wind, but it was

Nik who focused on making sure not a single piece could harm any of them.

Tauria's teeth clenched tight. It was a force so strong to keep from letting go of the deadly current that would surely hit them all if she lost control. And she was slipping. Never before had she wielded this velocity of pure power that raged like flame through her body.

"You can do this." Nik pressed into her from behind, a welcome aid to her trembling form that wanted to give in and collapse. *"You are born of the wind. Don't fight it; become it. You are more than enough."*

She had to close her eyes, feeling his words like a gentle release of burden. Her breaths cooled, slow and calculating against all that wanted to erupt within her. And like the calming of a thrashing sea, Tauria's gaze snapped open, and she suddenly knew exactly what to do.

I am enough.

Her eyes targeted Marvellas, marking her, just as the Spirit snapped the cuff of her second shackle. Her gold eyes were nothing short of a fire so scorching it was an effort not to balk under their heat as they marked her right back. Shifting her stance, Tauria began to release her tornado. Then all at once she let it go, redirecting only wind to shield them as glass rained down. The scent of blood curdled in her stomach. Because something about it was…*wrong.* Sparing a quick glance behind her, she saw the two guards had fallen, and she'd been too caught up in her ability to notice they hadn't been spared of the glass shards. Black blood coated them and the beige stone floor, and her stomach twisted.

Nik twisted with her, his arm around her bringing their bodies flush together, and despite everything…he smiled. With pride and awe. Love. "You are incredible," he murmured, right before bringing his lips to hers.

It was a short kiss as the threat was far from over. But when he pulled back, the flutter of her heart was a surge of strength. His eyes flashed over her shoulder, and it was as if they'd communicated a whole plan through that seconds-long stare.

They moved as if knowing the precise steps the other would take. His hands encased her body as he stepped around her, and all she caught was Mordecai choking before she honed her entire focus on Marvellas.

An arrow whizzed past, glinting a dark gray before the cry of Mordecai rang out from behind them. Niltain steel. A quick glance at the door confirmed the humans were safe. Together. Jakon had made it through the castle to be down here and was already letting go of his next shot. It made its mark. And she couldn't help the triumphant look she stole at seeing the dark fae in agony, wings pinned by Jakon's shots at the throne while Nik stalked to him with a calm, lethal fury. It was his turn now, and it made her blood race to watch him.

Then Tauria's sights met with Jakon as he lowered his bow, his arm reaching around Marlowe instead, knowing the fight was beyond them now. They'd done all they could, and this would become no place for mortals. Despite whatever Marlowe was, her flesh and bone healed just like them. Humans. She would cut and break just like them too. And Tauria was far from done unleashing the storm inside her.

Jakon gave a nod of acknowledgment and farewell just as she did, and watching the humans slip out was a temporary reprieve.

Tauria targeted her wrath on Marvellas. A face of lethal beauty that charged flame in her eyes. Seizing her wind, she had to be fast. Collecting shards of glass, Tauria sent them hurtling toward the Spirit. Like flame she moved, gliding around Tauria's darts as though she knew the path of each one before it was made. Glass shattered off the pillars, marking deep scars in the walls, but she didn't stop trying.

Then it clicked.

Tauria divided her focus, throwing up her mental walls and putting effort in to reinforce the barrier. Then she attacked. Again and again, until the sound of victory rang in her ears. Marvellas cried out, her hand raised over the large serration of glass protruding from her abdomen. Without hesitation, Tauria used her wind to wrap around another shard, and as if it were an arrow, she loosed her shot and watched it strike the Spirit's shoulder.

Marvellas fell to her knees.

Tauria's name was called on repeat before a sickening crack tremored her spine and curdled in her stomach. She turned to be sure it was Nik in triumph against the High Lord, yet what she saw instead froze her blood and fell the world. Time was a luxury as instinct took over with how fast the seconds ran. But even though she knew there was no other way, the consequences of the action she'd had to make had already marked her soul and obliterated her heart.

But in that second, she chose him.

She would always choose Nik.

Wrapping a shard of glass in her wind, there was no pause to consider what she was about to do before she sent it soaring toward Nik, who had his back to her, looking down at the heap of wings and flesh. It hit its mark, and his grunt of pain was swallowed by the ringing in her ears at what she'd done.

Lycus's hand, which gripped a blade high, seconds from taking everything from her, fell limp as his knees gave out. Tauria trembled stiffly, her mind blank, and she didn't think she was present anymore at the sight of her longest and dearest friend and the glass protruding out of his back.

She didn't have a choice.

Her feet moved while her mind struggled to believe what she'd done, but as she fell and caught Lycus…she knew this was no dream. It was a living, breathing nightmare.

"Oh Gods," she whispered vacantly, scanning his horror-struck face. His dark skin was slicked with sweat, as if he'd used everything in him to try to stop the control Marvellas had over him while she entertained Tauria's display. Tauria was so lost in her anger that she hadn't heard him arrive and wondered if that was the Spirit's intention.

"It's okay," Lycus panted. "I'll be okay."

Tauria couldn't be sure. Blood flowed from the wound. He needed a healer. Now. She would never be able to live with herself if she killed him.

Nik fell beside her, offering a huge relief. A sense of calm she grappled so as not to lose her composure.

"You foolish child," Marvellas sneered like poison at their backs. "Did you really think you could defeat us with your silly magick?"

Glancing at the Spirit, Tauria saw she'd removed the glass she impaled her with, gliding to them as if she'd never been wounded at all. Marvellas's golden gaze fell on Nik, and Tauria's wind flared in defense.

"I am rather surprised by the revelations of the night." Her head canted curiously at him. "How is it you bear the gift of my kin?"

Nik's hand slipped over Tauria's back before curling around her waist as Marvellas continued to walk to them. Tauria couldn't deny it was a question that stunned her still.

"We're not afraid of you, Marvellas," Nik said calmly.

Her chuckle was smooth but predatory. "Your bravery is admirable, Nikalias," she mocked. "But it will not save either of you."

Marvellas raised a hand, and with that movement Tauria gasped, her spine curving. Not from anything physical—something within pulled so hard with a pain like nothing she'd felt before, a hideous violation. And she knew what it was because everything within her screamed to protect it as Nik gave a similar reaction beside her.

Marvellas stroked a dark touch on the tether that bound them. Their mating bond—that precious, absolute thing—became as vulnerable as the delicate string of a harp. The Spirit plucked at it without care, testing its strength and resistance, and Tauria whimpered, fighting with everything she had to wrap some protection around their bond. It was something only to be treasured and shared between them, invaded by the Spirit of Souls who had them at her complete mercy.

"I spent my entire existence as a Spirit guiding souls to one another. Watching as they fell in love and adored each other, their magick thriving, their offspring strong. But sometimes, there would be those ungrateful for their match, rejecting what I presented." Her gown lapped the ground like blood spilled in her wake. "I'll admit, there was always a part of me that wondered why they would give up the perfect match I brought to them. Until I followed the severed bond to see what became of them. They did not live on in misery or heartache or longing. Most of them found happiness with one who was not their mate, but in turn, there was another soul taken from its match. Every untrue pair created two severed bonds. It seemed...tragic. Love—it is the ultimate weakness. Those who rejected their bond rejected the power that I gifted them to be strengthened in their union. It was their foolish hearts that chose to disregard all that could have been." She took the steps slowly up to the dais, and all Tauria could do was watch. With a terror so stilling she feared one movement could snap the bond. "But look at you two. In all my thousands of years, very few have come close to such a powerfully perfected match."

Nik's palm slid against hers, and their fingers entwined. Tauria gripped his hand tightly. *"As eternal as the moon."*

She nearly choked with the emotion that clenched in her chest at his promise. No matter what happened here, that would never change. Their love could not be broken.

Marvellas flexed her fingers, pulling at their bond as though they were puppets in her grip. Tauria whimpered, and Nik tried to soothe her with a caress on her senses.

"But as dark fae, you will not need each other. Love will never be used against you. Look how easily it puts you at my mercy. You must see that I am not the villain, but the savior of this world that has been led by *love* for far too long"

With the next harsh tug on their bond, Tauria cried out. Nik pulled her to him, and she leaned into him, allowing his scent to drown her fear. She was ready to accept that this was it. But it had been worth it. She would do it all again. Waiting. Hoping. Longing. It was cruel to have it taken from them so fast, but she would endure it all again for what they had glimpsed together.

Something other than the hard beat of Nik's heart caught her hearing in the silence that settled. A faint whisper, chanting words she couldn't decipher—but that didn't matter, because the voice…

"You loved once, Marvellas," Marlowe said as clear as day, and Tauria's eyes snapped open to find the blacksmith crouched halfway down the aisle, her fingers finishing a tracing she'd made in crimson on the floor. Blood. Marvellas's blood. "You don't get to tear down a realm on a broken heart."

Jakon stood firm with an arrow aimed at the Spirit. Marlowe rose as the final ancient words spilled from her mouth.

Nik gently pushed Tauria away and stood while Marvellas was distracted. Then a wave of power blasted through the room, and Tauria folded into herself.

Her head snapped back up just in time to watch Nik make it to Marvellas. Her heart leaped up her throat, and her mouth parted on a silent scream, but Nik was fast. She could only stare in shock as he reached her, and with no hesitation, Nik snapped her neck before she could turn around.

The thump of her body to the ground wasn't enough for Tauria to believe this was real. She breathed, staring and staring, on her hands and knees, unable to allow the relief to settle as she waited for Marvellas to launch straight back up and go for him first. *Kill* him first in her rage at the mockery they'd made of her.

Tauria couldn't move. She didn't know how many seconds or minutes ticked by.

"Tauria." Nik's voice was soft and close, yet she couldn't tear her eyes from the Spirit who looked so magnificent, like a curled ball of flame.

Until a gentle hand curled under her chin, guiding her to lock eyes with the most striking emeralds.

Her brow pinched. Her vision blurred. "Nik," she breathed.

He nodded. "We're safe."

And it was all she could do as Tauria fell into him with a wave of overwhelming joy at those words that trembled her with sobs. On their knees he held her, soothing her senses, her body, her mind. Nik was here, and they were going home.

"If I may request to come with you…"

The pained voice behind them stole her attention with a gasp. Whirling to Lycus but unable to let Nik go, the sight of him had Tauria's hand covering her mouth in horror, remembering what she'd done to him. The glass shard was still visible over his shoulder, and exertion slumped his posture as he bowed on his knees.

"We have a healer," Nik assured him, a temporary relief to her crushing guilt. He had to live. "She's not dead. I don't believe he is either despite meeting the same fate."

Tauria's gaze slid to the High Lord, her lips pinched tight against the nausea that made waves in her stomach.

"We need to leave now. Marlowe's powerful twist on the Blood Box spell should seal them both to the castle for a while. Hopefully long enough for us to cross over to High Farrow."

The humans hadn't left. Marlowe—her brilliant, cunning, friend—had saved them all. Drawing her attention, a surge of panic had Tauria rising to find her cradled by Jakon. Concern was written across his face. Marlowe's face was pale, but she managed a small smile up at him, her lids fluttering as she fought for consciousness.

"Marlowe—"

Nik caught her as she began to advance toward her friend. "It's a side effect of exerting her magick. She wouldn't be swayed against it, but she's come back around before."

It wasn't a full reassurance, and she didn't know how they would ever be able to repay the blacksmith for everything she'd risked in saving them all. Tauria met Nik's gaze, which was pained at Marlowe's situation too. All they could do for her now was use every moment of time she'd bought them and get her to the healer.

Snapping into action, Tauria made it to Lycus as he tried to stand, and Nik was by his other side instantly, hooking his arm over his shoulder. Tauria allowed him to take her general as the only one who could really help bear his weight. They began to make their way out. No dark fae stopped them. As Tauria passed Marvellas, she couldn't help the glance down she spared, halting for just a second as the others shuffled down the aisle.

As though she were asleep, her face was smooth and peaceful. So beautiful and delicate Tauria could hardly imagine the evil she harbored within when stripped back to no more than a vulnerable fae. She thought of Tarly, how she'd caught him slipping from the battle of the ceremony room, but she'd had no time to question why he fled. That brought her to the thought of Varlas, and how she didn't know if he still lived or if she even cared. Yet despite all the ways in which he'd wronged her...Tauria's resentment freed itself from her heart. Because there was a time when he was kind. There was a time when he was loyal in friendship with her father. And in his name, she chose to let go of his wrongdoings and remember he was a male who had *loved.* It was the only way to prove Marvellas wrong.

Love was not a weakness; it was strength. It wasn't a bond that brought her and Nik together. Or circumstance that brought Faythe and Marlowe into her life. Or convenience that planted Lycus by her side. It was their love for one another that had bloomed into even the most unlikely of friendships. It was their love that meant they would protect one another. Stand by each other's side.

It was in love and loyalty that they would raise the greatest army Ungardia had ever seen to fight back against evil.

The hearts who couldn't love—she mourned for them.

CHAPTER 67

Tarly

Tarly Wolverlon tracked them for hours, his panic on a razor's edge in case he was too late and something had happened to them. He'd lived this sense of dread before, and his whole world had shattered to find his mate dead.

He wouldn't survive it again. Not with his sister.

But then he began to pick up on sounds, and he ushered his horse a little faster as her scent too grew stronger. Katori raced by his side. He just had to be sure they were headed somewhere safe and that they had a way to remain cared for and hidden.

Until when…he couldn't be sure.

Olmstone had fallen. But it didn't burden him with the dread and heartache it should because Tarly had had a long time to accept his kingdom was plagued by dark forces and an unforgiving king. He would mourn for the Kingdom of the Wolf. His prince's heart would always yearn for it to be restored to the greatness of its past. Yet he couldn't deny the relief that lifted his shoulders. The sense of freedom he gained perhaps by cowardly, selfish means, but it was his.

Leaving the throne room in carnage wasn't an easy choice. But Tauria had Nik, and he'd felt too feeble against the grand scale of what they were capable of to combat the dark threats. Watching his father die…

Tarly had yet to accept it. His mind had been too disconnected from the events since to truly believe he was gone. Above all, he was afraid to admit his *relief.* Not of a loathing son or in triumph. All he clung to was the relief that his father's tormented soul could rest, and he prayed...to the Gods, for the father he knew who once harbored love, he prayed it was not the Nether he met despite his wrongdoings. He prayed he would meet Tarly's mother in the Afterlife and find solace at last in her forgiveness. Because that was always in her heart.

At the child's cry, Tarly pushed the horse to a gallop, nocking an arrow into his bow as he did. It had always been his preferred weapon, a means to silence his unrelenting mind. The bow didn't breathe dangerous life to his constant suppressed rage and sorrow; it honed them, focused and tamed the emotions. And his shot never missed, no matter how far or small or moving. He'd had centuries to master the weapon.

Hearing a struggle, he was already priming a shot before they came into view. The two guards dragging Keira and Opal apart were the reason he'd had no choice but to come after them when the moment presented itself for him to slip away from the castle. His fear that they'd been caught came to life in front of him.

His first arrow fired through the wings of the first male, who released Opal with his cry, but it didn't get the chance to finish leaving his throat before Katori pounced, sending the fae sprawling. He'd seen her vicious side before, during the Great Battles where she'd also stuck by him. Only to protect did she ever show an ounce of the powerful beast she could become.

Tarly dismounted as the second guard released Keira, who cried as Opal fell into her lap. His hands raised in surrender, but that wasn't an option. Tarly's arrow fired, striking through his wrist and pinning him to the tree. His shrill cry pierced through the woods as he reached to pull the arrow free. Glimpsing his next arrow tip as Tarly stalked to the dark fae with a cool sense of wrath, his hand jerked up once again in trembling submission.

"P—please, I—I'll go. I won't tell anyone."

Tarly didn't care. His life was forfeited the moment he went after them. "What did you plan to do with them?" he asked with careful fury. At the dark fae's pause of silence, a white rage flashed across his vision. He spoke to Keira. "Take her out of sight. Cover her ears."

Somehow sensing his plan, Katori knew he didn't need her to finish off the final fae. Her growls quietened as she backed away with Keira, protecting them.

A whimper left the shriveling coward when they stood alone. "We were to bring them back." His voice wavered.

"What use would Marvellas have for a child who would likely not survive the Transition?"

"They believe there's something different about royal blood. They have trialed it with success before. And you all would have become the most powerful monarchs to have lived." The information was chilling, a reminder of the dark fate that had been so close to befalling him. All of them. "You are all fools to pass up such an honor."

"I wouldn't call it as such." Tarly's arrow fired through his foot. The fae's shriek was ear-splitting. "You're Born dark fae." He observed the mesmerizing silver tone of the blood that poured.

"Proudly," the dark fae sneered.

With the pass of silence, Tarly realized something. "Your heart is still."

The dark fae said nothing.

"Yet you breathe. There's warmth to your skin…"

"I was Born this way, *prince.* Without your foolish emotional weakness that leads only to one thing. Your bleeding hearts."

Tarly wasn't really hearing his words because they didn't make sense. "It's just an organ with a beat. One purpose that has nothing to do with the emotions of our foolish *minds.*" He was calculating, wondering. "Why do they want you to believe you cannot feel?"

"Don't speak to me as if I am a fool when you are the weaker species."

"A curse?" Tarly thought out loud, ignoring his wails of superiority. As the stillness in his chest was so unusual, he tried to piece together any knowledge he might have to make sense of it. Even from works of fiction that were often twisted from some origin of truth.

"You are *weak,*" the dark fae spat.

Tarly's gaze locked on him with a shadow of fury. The hatred twisting the dark fae's expression smoothed out the instant he nocked and aimed an arrow at his chest. "Your heart may be still, but I'm willing to bet it has the same vulnerability as mine." He'd planned to end the dark fae's life regardless, but he truly was curious to see if his arrow would pierce straight through the oddly cold organ.

It did.

The dark fae barely choked a cry before his last wide-eyed look glassed over permanently. He fell to his knees slowly, dead but still pinned to the tree by the arrow through his wrist. Tarly stalked around him, confirming the arrow through his chest had exited as it dripped silver blood.

It didn't make logical sense that his heart didn't have a beat, but he stored the finding for now at hearing the soft cries behind him. Whirling around, all he caught a glimpse of was their clothing and shoes from the side of the tree they hid behind. Katori sat patiently as if she knew she wasn't best received by Keira. He walked to them slowly. Though the threat was gone, he knew they would be riddled with fear at the ordeal.

Keira startled with a gasp in her skittishness, but her relief when she looked up was visible in her slumped shoulders. She gently removed her hands from Opal's ears. When his eyes fell to her ghostly, fearful face, it was an ache he didn't know what to do with. Didn't know how to ease and comfort after all she'd been through and witnessed tonight.

Yet Opal scrambled to her feet against Keira's attempt to restrain her, and Tarly fell to a crouch on instinct to catch her as she barreled into him. It was a relief so strong all he could do was close his eyes and hold her small, trembling form as she cried.

"You're all right now," he said gently, unknowing of how to soothe such terror. Not believing there was any consolation for what she had been forced to go through. So young. It was a rage he would carry with him until he had his revenge on the ones who put that stain on the child's memories.

He rose slowly, but Opal still clamped her arms tightly around him. Tarly met eyes with Keira, whom he'd never seen look so utterly *defeated.* He may not like the queen—the *former* queen—but he would not have wished the ordeal upon her either.

"Thank you," her broken voice croaked.

Tarly didn't know what to say. Didn't feel accepting of her gratitude. He'd come for Opal, and Opal alone. Yet it was only to be sure she was headed somewhere safe. His palm smoothed Opal's hair in knowing he would have to part with her. The unsure path he was headed down, with no home and no name, was not one he could take her on.

"There is a farmhouse far east from here. It's home to a man named Kayan. Yes, a human. He's son to a man who gave me refuge when I was gravely injured during the Great Battles. Give him my name and tell him I sent you." Tarly reached into his pocket, producing a heavy pouch of coin.

Keira took it hesitantly. "What are we to do there?"

"Live. Help them and earn your keep. This should be enough to get you through the journey and pay for your stay for some time, but sometimes it's the simple things that offer more value than coin." Tarly unhooked Opal's arms, and she cried in protest, but he dropped back to her level. "There will be so much land to venture, flowers to grow. Everything Tauria taught you you'll be able to practice for yourself now."

"I want to come with you," she cried.

He smiled, mustering a brave face for her though his chest was tight. "This isn't goodbye. I'll see you again soon, I promise. I just have some other things I must do that aren't nearly as fun as where you're headed."

She nodded with pained reluctance, but it was a huge relief.

They backtracked to his horse. Keira mounted as he helped to lift Opal up the height.

"What will you do?" Keira asked quietly, and for a moment he might have believed she cared.

"Don't worry about me," he said, smiling to reassure his sister, whose sad eyes never lightened. "You do whatever it takes to keep her safe. Go where I told you, accept help, and accept the new life you'll have to forge without wealth or title."

"Neither were my desire," Keira said, her words more like a slipped, sorrowful thought. "I'm sorry I wasn't always kind to you, Tarly. I won't blame Varlas for my resentment, as I'm sure you won't blame him for yours." Just before she snapped the reins, he almost missed her last words. "Your mother would be proud of you. As am I."

He watched them ride off through the trees, unable to move, and he couldn't be sure why when his mind was still. Or perhaps too lost to form a single thought. Tarly fixed the bow over his back, finally yielding a hiss with his wince of pain as he moved his injured shoulder.

Weeks, and it had not healed. Pulling back his collar, he tried to catch a glimpse, if only to keep track of its changes as best he could. His tanned skin was gray around the wound. The *bite* wound he hadn't wanted to alarm Tauria with the knowledge of since the library. Truthfully, he had no idea what it meant. A bite from a Transitioned dark fae felt like a very slowly spreading poison. The healer he saw had seen nothing like it before, so completely baffled that all she could do was offer a salve that numbed the pain for a short while but didn't stop the slow spread.

He fixed his clothing again before he took off, not knowing where he was headed, and Katori followed him down that uncertain path. At least for now, and he was glad for it. In every step, he began to let go of all he once was. He prayed for Tauria's safety, and for her sake he hoped the bastard Nik had made it too.

He didn't even feel guilty that he was the one to order the gates open and allow the Stone Men to pass without force. He chose to believe they were the peaceful people he'd decided to learn more about after overhearing Lycus and Tauria in the library. He'd never known of Tauria's call for them, and that settled with sadness. She had never fully trusted him, and he couldn't blame her. But now he was out of his father's tainted shadow.

As he gained some distance, Tarly Wolverlon even shed his own name, wondering with an air of freedom who he would come to be as he left crown and kingdom behind.

CHAPTER 68

Nikalias

"It's not as if I haven't seen every inch of you," Nik teased as he leaned against a tree, his back turned while Tauria removed her torn-up black dress, fitting into riding leathers for their journey. "And that I will every day from now on."

Tauria huffed, rushing, as they knew moments of rest had to be few and far between until they reached High Farrow. They'd only stopped in the first patch of forestland, not even out of Vesmire, for Tauria to get more comfortable for the journey. And for some impending goodbyes.

"You're keeping watch," she said, and he gauged that she was now clothed as he pushed off the trunk and turned to her. "And I'm keeping you from getting any ideas if you were to watch me dress."

A devious smile curled his mouth as he stalked over to her while she fastened her cloak. The sight of her in the form-fitting leathers was almost as alluring as her bare skin. He couldn't stop his need to touch her, and his hands glided across her waist, pulling her to him as hers climbed his chest. "I don't need to watch you dress to spark desire for you," he mumbled huskily. Nik claimed her mouth, and the soft sound that came from her had his hands tightening then roaming. Every curve of her body that arched into him, every taste of her—he would never get enough. The need to be back in High Farrow was infuriating. Where she would lie beside him every night. Where he would announce to the world that Tauria Stagknight was his and he would challenge the Gods to take her from him.

Everything he was, everything he did, would be for her and for their kingdoms. He would bow to nothing and no one else.

Tauria pulled out of their heated kiss when he couldn't. He didn't know when they'd shifted back, but he realized he'd been seconds away from losing control and taking her against the tree that caged her in.

"We'll have forever, Nik," she said quietly, her delicate fingers tracing over his cheek.

Nothing had ever sounded so joyous. But he didn't give way to the darkness that wanted to snuff out that light.

"Yes, we will."

Nik took her hand, and they found their way back to the others who were waiting with the horses. The Fenstead General was still weakened after a healer had managed to remove the glass and stop his bleeding. Because of its depth, the wound would take far longer to heal and leave a scar. Something Nik knew would nurse Tauria's guilt for a long time—and his own.

She had saved him. Without fear or hesitation. Even against someone dear to her. Her loyalty was something he didn't think he would ever deserve, but he'd spend his life making sure she knew there was nothing he wouldn't risk for her.

"I think this is where we'll part," Jakon announced, rising from where he and Marlowe took quick rest.

The blacksmith was still coming around from the large pulse of energy it had taken to cast the spell that sealed Marvellas and Mordecai to the castle. It had all been planned. But nothing was ever guaranteed to go as they hoped, and the fear of losing her was very real. For a moment, Nik thought they would. He believed Marvellas would succeed in severing their bond, and while it was an immeasurable pain to imagine, he knew it would change nothing.

His love for Tauria had never and would never change.

Jakon helped Marlowe to rise, drawing her to him to bear some of her weight. Color had returned to her face, and her smile was reassuring as always to the many concerned faces that pinned her. She was one of the bravest, most inspiring people he'd had the privilege of calling a friend. And he would forever be indebted to both humans for following him down this dark, uncertain path.

But now it was time to part, and his chest pained with that knowledge.

"Let me send the guards with you. At least until you reach Rhyenelle borders." Nik wasn't really offering; he refused to let them go unprotected.

Jakon nodded. "Thank you."

"No—thank you. Both of you. If you ever need anything, just get one word to me. But I have a feeling this is not goodbye. Only farewell for a little while."

Nik extended his arm, and Jakon embraced it, sharing a mutual look of respect and understanding. Not a king and subject. Not a fae and a human. Just two friends from the most unlikely of places.

His gaze fell on Marlowe, and Nik shook his head. "Is there any end to the impossible?" He couldn't get Marvellas's claim from his mind—that Marlowe's lifespan was more than they could have predicted but had been fools not to consider with the ability she harbored.

Marlowe's smile was sad. "I've long since let go of that word."

Nik's arms opened as Marlowe took the weak step into them. "Then don't give up hope. We'll find a way." His eyes briefly flashed to Jakon. His knowing look made him wince, but the unspoken meaning lingered.

They would find a way to align the mortal differences that came to light between him and Marlowe. For once, Nik wished for the seemingly impossible.

Tauria was beside him, and Nik stepped away as they exchanged their words of farewell. Their embrace was tender and long, twisting Nik's chest to watch. He wanted them all to return to High Farrow, but the humans had been insistent it was time for them to go to Rhyenelle at last. There was a part of him that envied them in getting to reunite with Faythe. He longed to see her too, if only to confirm she was safe and well when he couldn't shake the sense of dread that coated him every time she came to mind.

Watching the humans travel away was more gut-wrenching than Nik anticipated. But when Tauria folded into him, her hand effortlessly reaching his chest, it gave him the will to turn away. Because there was nothing more important than seeing her to safety.

"Let's go home," he said softly.

She turned to him fully, hands sliding around him as she pressed her body to his. Her hazel gaze was so full of love. Breathtaking. Then her cheek met his chest, and he embraced her. There was never a more perfect fit in the world. Never a more content feeling than having her so effortlessly in his arms. She took a long, deep breath of contentment.

"I am home."

As the sun blazed promising and triumphant before them, Nik's arm tightened a fraction around his whole world while they rode on horseback together. All that mattered was the defiant stance he took against fate. Destiny mocked his happiness. *To love her is to condemn her.* All that mattered now was fighting that looming darkness. Her heart would come first—her desires, her life. He had to have faith the prophesy was no more than a twisted taunt. Because Nik would strike down anyone who tried to lay a hand on her.

Even himself.

"How did you do that back there?" Tauria's puzzled voice broke their peaceful silence. "With your ability."

Nik reached for the bottle he'd tucked away in his jacket. He raised it in front of her, the crimson liquid sparkling mesmerizingly as it swirled around its container as if the sun had awoken it. "They call it Phoenix Blood," Nik said as she took the vial, examining it with an air of wonder.

"The Phoenix birds are extinct," she pointed out.

"Perhaps. But I had a feather of one that I didn't believe to be real until Faythe was sure, and so Marlowe created the elixir."

"So it granted you an ability akin to Faythe's?"

"Not exactly. It manifested my Nightwalking—not as strong or sure as Faythe's ability, but whatever I could do in the mind at night, I could do so in a conscious mind. We weren't certain it would work. That's the second dose of what Marlowe created. I consumed the other in the hope it would buy us time if I was able to hold Varlas—or whoever else thought to lay a hand on you—while Marlowe slipped out and began to seal the castle exits. Then, when she returned, all she needed was for me to have spilled the blood of who we sought to confine there for her to bind the spell, and it would be done. All I had to do was get you out of the castle walls, and I didn't care what it would take."

"And now, can you still—?"

Her question made the magick still coursing through him hum. "Yes." Since he'd taken it before they arrived, he'd been battling it within. It was like an extension to his well of magick that made it feel endless. Inviting him to take too much could physically burn his body out, a dark chant that dared him to test his new limits. "I don't know when it will wear off. In truth, I'm hoping it's soon."

Tauria's hand caressed his, and the comfort was a warmth that burst in his chest. "I'm sorry I kept it all from you. That I was caught. I couldn't stand the thought of them using me to get to you."

A tugging pain pinched his eyes closed. "I knew you would. I knew…if they ever suspected you and decided to act that you wouldn't tell me." The ripples of her guilt were something he couldn't bear. "I don't blame you. Not ever."

"Then how did you know?" she whispered.

"Every time I asked if you could see the moon, you always answered." Nik's hand began an idle caress over her arm as she reclined against him. "I knew that if you were ever caught, Olmstone's castle didn't have a tower. I knew they would take you underground."

Her disbelief was strong, and he heard her small intake of breath. "No windows."

Nik nodded though she couldn't see. "When I asked if you could see the moon that final time, you answered like always, so sure and confident. Yet it was daylight. If I told you what I suspected, it would only make it worse for you. I feared you would try to do something reckless to save me, or at least it would torment you with the knowledge I was marching for you." He had to pause at the memory of the most damming, helpless situation he'd ever lived through. Knowing her life was in the balance and he was still weeks of distance away. He'd never ridden so fast, nor demanded so much of the legions that followed him. Then, when he saw her…saw what they'd bound to her wrists over and above the mistreatment, he nearly ruined the whole plan to rage and kill them all.

"Look at me," he said softly when he knew she was crying.

Tauria turned to him, her hazel eyes glittering. The sun kissed her golden skin. She was the most breathtaking thing he had ever laid eyes upon.

"We've wronged each other in the past, but I hope you know none of that matters. Everything we've been through that brought us to now has only made us stronger. I don't ever plan on letting you go or being apart from you for a moment. You are so brave. So perfect. You are mine." His forehead pressed to hers while he cupped her cheek.

"I'm yours," she said.

Then spilled from his mouth a question he'd harbored so deep, treasured, never believing he would have the privilege of asking her. "Marry me, Tauria."

She took a deep breath as if in deliberation. Nik's mouth curved before she spoke.

"I don't really have a choice, do I?"

He chuckled, his spirit so light, and squeezed her waist. "Not really, no."

Her head lay back against him, and his lips pressed to her temple. "I want a ring."

Nik smiled in elation. "A diamond?"

"I think you know me better than that."

"Of course I do."

His hand slipped over her forearm until their palms met. After dipping into his pocket, his other hand came around her, and Tauria gasped as the cool metal slipped onto her finger. Adorned with the sparkling emerald, she raised her hand.

"You brought it with you?" she breathed, admiring the reflections off the stone.

Nik's arm tightened from the flash of panic at their narrow escape. "I didn't plan on leaving without you." He took her hand, guiding it to his face, and she twisted on the saddle to look at him. Nik tapped the stone on her finger. "It was in the bracelet before. My mother's bracelet."

Tauria's mouth parted in surprise as her eyes fell to the ring. Then she shifted, reaching into her pocket to produce the item that was no longer needed to conceal his scent.

"I wanted to give you something close to me while you were far, and I asked Marlowe to take out the emerald and replace it with her enchanted stone. But I knew you would have no need for it once we were back together. Then she made the ring, and it was so perfect. It was you."

She brought her mouth to his. A single kiss that said far more than any words could. When they parted, her hand at his face traced his jaw. "Our family names are ridiculous together."

Nik barked a laugh. "You really do think of everything."

Tauria's smile was the brightest light before she twisted forward for comfort. He embraced her in perfect contentment.

"Yes, Silvergriff-Stagknight would be quite the mouthful."

There was a long, thoughtful pause. He had mulled over the concept before but never believed it would see reality.

"How about…we join them instead?" His lips lingered by her ear. "Tauria Silverknight sounds utterly exquisite."

She shivered against him with his breath blowing across her ear, but she didn't respond for a long moment. She didn't need to. The echoes of her pride and joy filtered through him, and he treasured every feeling they shared.

"It's beautiful," she whispered softly.

Nik closed his eyes in contentment. His head leaned down against hers to speak intimately. "Thank you for waiting for me."

Tauria's face twisted until their lips nearly met. She searched his eyes that hid nothing from her. No more guards, no more walls. "You won't hurt me, Nik. I don't know what the foretelling means, but you're not capable of it. I trust you. Whatever it is, we'll fight it together."

Tauria saw or felt the darkness that ensnared him still. That would haunt him for eternity. The world-shattering prophesy that gripped him with a terror so deep: that he could be capable of harming her in the most final, soul-damning way.

He was her protector…yet the shadow lingered that he could become her killer instead.

His lips pressed firmly to hers, and the soft noise that came from her sparked his desire that was already dancing at the feel of her rocking against him with every dip of the horse's walk. Her hand slipped over his face before tightening in his hair. Her need was his unraveling.

They parted to gather breath, and Nik said huskily, "We'll add weeks to our journey if we keep needing to stop for…*relief.*" The scent of her arousal had him stifling a groan so they wouldn't have to make one of those stops right there. But he was eager to take her home. To where she would be safe—in one of their kingdoms.

Tauria diverted the topic. "Our family names have carried on for millennia. We can't allow them to end with us simply to forge a new one."

"We won't. This is just for us. We will have heirs someday. One will come to reign over High Farrow and take the Silvergriff name; another will rule over Fenstead and take the Stagknight name." He wanted the time to be hers alone—time that was stolen from them—and would wait as long as she wished. But it was a future so hopeful he painted it without burden and would protect it with everything he was.

"I like the sound of that." Tauria leaned back against him, her head tucked perfectly under his chin. "I like it a lot."

Nik's lips pressed to her head, taking a second to breathe in her intoxicating scent. "Me too, love."

"I can't wait to marry you, Nik."

Pride and adoration swelled in his chest. He could have this. Happiness. He took hold of it and didn't feel guilty, unknowing of how long it could last.

Because there was a shadow lurking that was bigger than him. And it was growing. A storm that gathered to cloud over the kingdoms one by one. No one would be spared from it; no one could seek safety from it. Nik felt the dark unease as a permanent cloak of foreboding. Sometimes, he knew it unsettled Tauria too. Since the Solstice Ball, the solar eclipse…

Change was coming.

So he held onto his mate tight, because no time was promised with the war that had only just begun.

EPILOGUE

Nikalias

A CENTURY'S WORTH of torment had been worth it for this moment. As he gazed up at the single most precious thing to ever exist, Nik knew he would have waited endlessly for her.

He couldn't help himself. Watching Tauria read aloud so compellingly finally made him break. Nik didn't speak. Wanting to listen to the beautiful notes of her voice but needing to feel her, he shifted, propping himself up where they'd been lying comfortably by the fire in his rooms. He'd set up the position where they'd lost blissful hours to each other. In the days since they'd returned, he and Tauria had avoided confronting the storm that was gathering with all they'd defied in secret to be together. Instead they'd locked themselves away to have the time that was stolen from them after their mating.

Nik's lips pressed to her shoulder while his hand slowly trailed down her back and curved around her waist. He devoured every touch of her bare skin as all that covered them were thin sheets with the amber fire blazing. His second kiss was pressed to the crook of her neck, and her hitched breath made him smile.

"Are we ever going to get to the end of a story?" she sighed, but her head angled in response to his touch.

Nik chuckled softly against her neck, and Tauria's desire filled his senses, stoking a primal satisfaction that wanted to give her everything. "Only our own," he said, a quiet murmur over her skin. "Only together."

Sliding the book from her grasp, he shifted with her until she lay and he hovered above her. The feel of their flushed bare skin was an insatiable craving. His eyes slid to his mark on her collar, a sight that would always make him rage with so many emotions. It was the deepest reminder of how real this was. After everything they'd been through, they belonged to each other finally.

"How do you feel about this…?" Nik asked, trailing his lips down her neck. "Would you prefer we move to your old rooms?"

Tauria had been staying with him for the past few days, and there was never a more content feeling than having her here, within the walls that once homed only torment and loneliness. She breathed a new brightness and hope with her presence. Nights he'd dreamed of having her by his side, and it was now his cherished reality.

"This is perfect," she said breathlessly, arching into him as his mouth descended.

"Or we can pick new rooms together." Nik traveled toward his mark, his sharp canines grazing her skin, and the thought of tasting her riled their mixed arousal.

Her throat shifted with the faint shake of her head.

"Words, love."

Her hands slipped into his hair, a movement he'd come to read as her impatience. Nik smiled deviously, pulling back. Her small whimper was adorable when her head straightened. He braced on his forearms above her, straining against his tethers of control while she lay gloriously bare beneath him. Her hand reached up, tracing over his chest, and he marveled at her every thoughtful touch.

"I like it here," she answered. "It feels right." Tauria's thighs shifted, sliding farther apart before tightening when he was positioned fully between them.

Her silent commands drove him wild. It had become this enticing challenge; him trying to coax her voice while she remained defiant in her torturous silent seduction.

"What do you want, love?" Nik whispered huskily, grazing his lips against hers.

Tauria's hips raised. Her head tipped back, and Nik groaned as she took what she wanted. Her slickness against him almost made him break.

"You're a wicked thing," he said, right as his mouth closed over his mark, teeth sinking into her skin.

Tauria's nails clawed his lower back with a moan that was loud and encouraging. Nik reached between them, entering her in a smooth glide as he drank from her. It was euphoric and utterly primal. His hand massaged her breast as she shuddered, tightening around him in so many ways he forgot his own gods-damned name. Tauria was shuddering and spent by the time he pulled away, glimpsing the raw redness he'd created on her neck.

"Beautiful," he rasped, thrusting into her as he climbed toward his own end. "Again for me, love."

She shook her head, but her increasingly breathless sounds told him she was already close. "I can't."

Nik leaned back on his knees, watching where he entered her, and it was enough to tip him over the edge. But just before he did, his thumb circled over her apex. Tauria unraveled beautifully for him, back arching as she held her breasts. The pure pleasure painted on her face and the golden glow of her skin was the most breathtaking sight as he stilled within her.

He lay over her, panting and filled with so much adoration for her. "I could take you all day."

Her eyes fluttered closed as she nodded. He kissed her flushed cheek.

"Don't sleep yet, love. I'll ask them to fix us a bath."

The servants were quick in their work. He almost felt bad for their shyness when the state of the room left little to the imagination. With the bath heated and ready, he left the washroom to find his mate. Tauria wasn't where he'd left her lying by the fires, and he was surprised. He'd half-expected to need to gently awaken her.

He caught the breeze, and his eyes followed it out to the balcony. Nik was slow to approach, watching her in awe as she stood in the gentle wind she was made of. Her short robe and hair breezed sideward, the moon glowed on her skin, and like a magnet, he was pulled to her. Nik's hands slipped around her, and they looked out over the eternally glittering Caius City together.

"You did this?" she whispered.

His lips pressed to her temple. "You did, Tauria."

What they watched together was a sight so mighty and triumphant. It was a beacon of unity and strength that challenged anyone to oppose it.

Where High Farrow's flag of royal blue adorned with the Griffin had always stood as a proud marker for the kingdom, now another stood by its side.

"We are High Farrow," she said.

"And we are Fenstead. Always."

Her tears caught in his senses, but they were of joy and pride. Nik wanted to bask in their happiness and damn what else was to come. With Tauria by his side, he had never felt such raw determination. To protect against the war to come. To defy against the dark prophesy that shadowed them. To rejoice in the victory that could almost be tasted.

They were ready, and it was time.

"It's time to fight back," Tauria said.

Nik took a deep breath and stepped away from her. Tauria turned, her eyes widening as he took her hands and lowered to one knee before her.

"My kingdom and I are one and the same, but both belong to you. With our armies and our crowns, with my own sword, I vow to take back Fenstead not for you, but with you. It terrifies me more than anything in this gods-forsaken continent to imagine you fighting in the war to come. But it is also with a pride so striking I wonder how I came to be the luckiest bastard alive. And you should know I'm not finished with avenging all those who have wronged you. I have no hesitations, no reservations, because you are right…" Nik rose, his hand slipping over Tauria's cheek, brushing away the tear that escaped.

Then he looked over the balcony once more, and she followed his line of sight. To the magnificent view of the emerald green banner flying the side-profiled stag emblem of Fenstead side by side with High Farrow's flag.

"It's time to take war to them."

SHE WILL RISE

Faythe

IMMORTALITY WAS NOT a gift given kindly.

It was fire-torched blood against ice-kissed bones. It was a peaceful still wave beneath the thrash of a storm. It was dying in agony and the birth of something powerful.

Faythe was suspended in a void she knew few souls had ventured before. Between death and life, with the blessing to *choose.* Let go, and she could embrace a dark, painless end. Let the world cycle days without her, let others carry fate, relieve herself of feeling another heavy burden. Or she could pull back on that tether that ran within, straining toward breaking point the longer she stayed in the veil between realms. The Afterlife called to her with warm arms and a freedom from anything that could harm her. Yet despite the harrowing, the damned, and the foreboding that awaited her if she decided to return…there was a light in the dark. A flicker of silver and sapphire. A scent that wrapped around her and coaxed her to come…

Home.

Taking a stand against the dark force of death was never destined to be a ride of bliss and reward. Time was a precious currency. And Faythe had stolen far more of it than the Gods had planned. She had never desired more time than what was owed to her in mortality, but now it was within her grasp she didn't want to let it go.

Yet it was a cruel taunt. An immortal body on borrowed time.

The hourglass of her days had been turned. Moments of life turned to grains of precious sand that fell with the weight of stones.

For now, she would return. To them, to *him*...she must return.

Reylan

The dark fae had left, but the darkness remained. One of uncertainty—a cruel, merciless taunt that what he grappled was nothing more than his own desperate illusion. Reylan cradled Faythe's still form, willing her eyes to open. Wanting nothing more in this world than to glimpse the beautiful amber of them. The single sight that soothed centuries' worth of torment in an instant.

Come back to me.

He didn't care how pathetic the plea sounded. If there was a small chance she could hear him, he wouldn't stop repeating it in his desperation for her not to leave him. To *choose* to come back. Maybe it was selfish to coax her back to the cruel world that had harmed her so much, but he knew he would dedicate himself to her if only she came back. He swore the next time she left here it would be together. He would fight for her.

Reylan blinked when he caught a shimmer, sparing a glance around the cave as though he would find a source. All was dark save for the flickering of flames in the torches. His eyes fell back to Faythe, and his pulse quickened...because *she* was the source. That beautiful shimmer rippled like the thinnest sheet of iridescent water until Faythe was aglow with the energy it encased her in. Reylan's hand traced over her face in a surge of panic that this was her final farewell, her soul preparing to leave him finally.

He pleaded. More than he ever had in his existence, he pleaded with everything he was.

"We didn't have enough time, Faythe," he whispered, leaning his forehead to hers and pinching his eyes, holding her close as if it would return the warmth to her cooling body. "I promise to stand by you. Until the end of days. We'll fight…we'll fight it all together. Just please come back to me."

Light penetrated the darkness of his closed lids. When he snapped them open, he couldn't believe what he was seeing.

Faythe was still glowing, so mesmerizing and ethereal that despite everything, he wanted to treasure the sight. Because the blood that had dried on her face was gone, the dirt cleaned away. It looked like Faythe, but…*more* somehow.

Then his attention caught on something else that stopped time.

Impossible. Yet with the sight, the tiny tinder he'd desperately tried to keep alive within—it flickered. It grew. So slowly he didn't think he was still breathing to track it.

The flare that came from her chest was felt in his.

Reylan felt compelled to brush the hair from her face, but as he did, it was as if he wasn't within himself anymore. Or present in this room. Or bound by the law of time. His eyes were fixed. His fingers lingered over the delicate pointed tip of her ear. Hope was a wicked torment, but *damn,* if it didn't capture him completely with what he discovered was happening.

Faythe was…

The most treasured sound filled the room, spiking his adrenaline. Faythe's chest rose with a deep breath that would stay locked in his memory for all eternity. Her eyes fluttered, wincing as she slid them open. Reylan remained utterly still as though this were a dream. One blink of movement and she would go back to being the lifeless ghost he cradled. But there was beautiful color on her cheeks now, a new vibrancy in her hair.

Life.

He leaned over carefully, unable to speak. Faythe's head shifted to look at him on his lap. Her gaze studied his face. Her hand reached up slowly. Meeting his cheek, her thumb brushed his skin.

Her face was thoughtful but sad as she asked, "Why are you crying?"

Her voice was a song he'd thought was lost forever. It was only a whisper, but it was enough to confirm this was real. Faythe was real.

His time became measured by the strong beats of her heart, the only affirming sound in a desolate silence. Then her eyes slid to his, sapphire met gold, and the world…

It stopped.

AN HEIR COMES TO RISE NOVEL

- V -

A SWORD FROM THE EMBERS

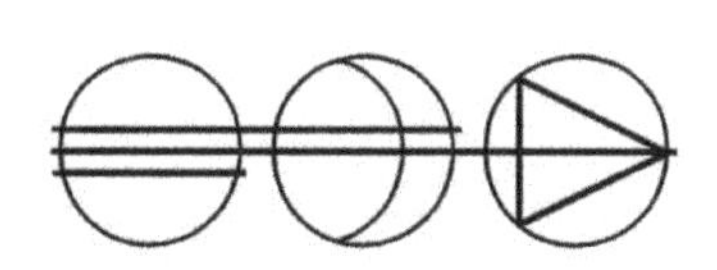

CHLOE C. PEÑARANDA

LUMARIAS PRESS

PREQUEL CHAPTER

A WINTER SOLSTICE

Nikalias

It was all ridiculous. The confetti of color from all courts. The tiresome dancing that barely stopped. The clamor of voices that heightened to irritating wails and shouts from those high on fae wine. Nik was forbidden from consuming the only thing he itched for to dull his grating senses and pass the night quicker. His parents didn't stop him back in High Farrow, yet in *esteemed* company they'd made clear the consequences should he reach for it.

He still planned to, of course. Once the night eased in fully and his parents were otherwise occupied.

"If you could *try* to act pleased to be here, Nikalias," his mother scolded under her breath.

He refrained from scoffing. "I thought I was doing a good job, actually."

A rough hand landed on his shoulder. "This is not a punishment, son. Who knows who you might meet this night?"

His father's suggestion wasn't subtle, but Nik had no desire to seek anyone's company, only to survive the grueling flamboyance, and they would be heading back to High Farrow tomorrow. He'd protested coming here many times, wanting to stay home rather than trek the long distance to Fenstead for their grand Winter Solstice Ball. He could hardly even stand the celebrations they hosted in High Farrow.

"Come—we must greet our hosts," his mother's soft voice encouraged, steering him with an arm around his shoulders as if he might break away.

The King of Fenstead stood mighty upon the dais, greeting guests that seemed endless, yet his bright reception felt genuine. He was tall and broad, his dark skin striking against the emerald green and gold that adorned his clothing. There was no doubt he was a leader of love and compassion, and it was the first time Nik's mood eased from discontent in his awe.

"Orlon!" The male beamed in acknowledgment when he spotted Nik's father.

They embraced forearms before drawing each other in for a hearty embrace while Nik and his mother stood back.

The King of Fenstead's gaze fell to him, and Nik stiffened at the attention as though waiting for assessment and wanting the male's approval. It wasn't often he felt the need to make a good impression.

"Nikalias," the king drawled warmly, his voice deep and smooth. "I haven't seen you since you were far younger. I don't suppose you'll remember me as your father has neglected to visit."

"Has your kingdom run out of horses that cannot bring you north to us instead?" his father countered lightly.

The kings exchanged knowing chuckles.

Nik smiled. "I apologize. I do not remember."

The king's grin broke, adding a whole new brightness to his face. It was effortless to feel at ease in his company. Nik found respect for him.

"You raised him well, Your Majesty." The King of Fenstead bowed his head to Nik's mother, who mirrored the gesture.

"You host a fine celebration. We knew this could not be missed."

"And I hope you will continue to enjoy it long into the ungodly hours of the night."

They exchanged more hearty laughter, and even Nik let go of a small chuckle, delivered so easily from him.

"You must meet my daughter, Nikalias." The king's eyes roamed the room with a frown. "Though it seems she has managed to elude me already."

Nik smiled at that, wondering if she too felt suffocated by such parties, but admittedly, he was glad for her absence to spare the awkward greeting in front of his parents. They would undoubtedly fail to keep from their meddling and insist they latch onto each other's company all night. Nik planned to elude them too. Once they were too drunk to care for his whereabouts and he could find a quiet escape for the night.

It didn't take long.

His parents were lost in conversation with other monarchs after more tedious greetings. Nik didn't have to try to leave them as he was all but pushed out of conversation among the old friends. He took his first opportunity to swipe a glass of wine as he weaved through revelers. It was so hot in here. He downed that glass of wine, set it on a tray passing by, and swiped another, all without faltering a step. Nik eyed a side door, desperate for the clamor to halt for just a moment.

The hallway was a much-needed breath of fresh air, and his prayers were answered further when he spied the open balcony doors after a few turns. The night met Nik with a welcoming embrace. He closed his eyes on a long inhale as he walked right up to the stone railing. He opened them again to the sight of the brilliant moon accompanied by the stars that endorsed it. His breath left him in a cloud at the bitter-cold temperature, though he didn't mind it in contrast to the heat of clustered bodies.

His moment of peace was disturbed by a shuffling above, followed by a whispered curse.

Twisting, he cast his gaze up, eyebrows lifting at what he saw. He should have felt astonishment first, or confusion, or disbelief…yet all he could think was that he was staring at the single most beautiful fae he'd ever seen.

And he hated it.

Snapping back to his senses, Nik said, "What in the Nether are you doing?"

Her golden-brown skin glowed against the moonlight. Breathtaking. Her hair sparkled with a river of emeralds that rivaled the stars. Her dress was extravagant—too much, a ludicrous garment to be wearing—and he wondered with absolute incredulity how she'd climbed to the slanted rooftop in the first place.

"You shouldn't be out here," she snapped.

Nik was taken aback but wildly intrigued. "Need I be the one to point out your location is far more concerning than mine?"

"You needn't point out anything," she grumbled, shifting.

Nik jerked forward, anticipating her fall. She paused her descent with a smirk.

"If I fall, don't bother," she said, continuing her climb down.

Nik tracked every shift of her movements regardless. His steps moved to every one of hers, not entirely of conscious effort.

"I'd deserve to take the impact."

When she stood on a very narrow flat, Nik's head reclined back while they stared off for a few seconds.

"You're in my way."

Nik couldn't fight the slow curl of his mouth. He didn't think she'd land the jump gracefully, but he knew it would be entertaining to watch, and perhaps she'd come to her senses and ask for his help. He took a couple of long backward strides, folding his arms over his chest. They never broke eye contact. Until she rolled hers and braced. Regardless of wanting to triumph in watching her stubbornness result in an embarrassing landing, Nik couldn't stop his arms from dropping, his stance shifting to catch her.

The air stirred so suddenly in the still night, wind building until it became a current his eyes flinched against. The final gust blew past him right on time with her landing. Her impeccable, mesmerizing landing that blew the skirts of her gown just high enough for him to glimpse her long, slender leg that stretched out before ending in the most alluring crouch. Straightening, she dusted herself off nonchalantly. Her coy smile was accompanied by a twinkle in her eye as she canted her head at him.

"You're staring," was all she said.

Nik swallowed hard. "Witnessing a lady descend from castle rooftops in a ballgown—I think it's granted."

"Who are you?" she asked.

"I could ask you the same."

"Do you avoid all questions so childishly?"

For the first time in a long time, the thrill that awoke in him was unexpected but enticing. "Nik," he obliged.

"Just Nik?"

His smile widened, and he gave a shrug. Her eyes trailed him from head to toe. Never before had he turned so rigid under the assessing eyes of a female. Now he wanted to know what she was thinking. Not just about him—about everything. She'd gripped his interest entirely, deeper than what he was used to.

"High Farrow," she observed. The royal blue accents and griffin emblem adorning his shoulder would have been confirmation to anyone.

"Fenstead." He stated the obvious. Green was a wonder on her. "You haven't told me your name."

"Never mind my name," she brushed off. The fae turned, her walk like a glide as she made away from him.

He had an urge to call after her—*go* after her—but he was transfixed where he stood, in a complete stupor at what he'd just witnessed. She turned out of sight, and still Nik stood like a gawking fool. Never before had someone addressed him so brazenly then disregarded him without a care. He could only assume she didn't know of his crown. Back home, he'd let the attention get to his head too much, not realizing the ugly flare of his arrogance now at her dismissal. Her lack of interest.

"I see you met the princess," a cool male voice said. Easing out from the shadows, the unwanted company joined Nik, but the word caught his attention.

"Princess?"

The male's smirk made him feel a fool for not knowing. "Nikalias Silvergriff, Prince of High Farrow. Am I correct?"

Nik's eyes narrowed on him, having never met him before. The male appeared around the same age as him, with dark black hair like his and electric blue eyes. Burnt orange adorned his clothing with the emblem of an owl. His wears…

"You're Callen Osirion, Prince of Dalrune."

He raised his cup. "Guilty." The prince stepped further out, taking a long, deep breath. "I wouldn't take it personally. She's shown no one any interest. Tarly Wolverlon asked for a dance earlier, albeit by the force of his parents, but I doubt he'll try again after the rejection. It was highly entertaining to watch."

Nik chuckled. Tarly was one royal he had in fact met. Only because of the closeness of their kingdoms that had seen their fathers grow into power together. Nik had never been best fond of him, perhaps because their fathers constantly tried to force them to bond despite the two having no similar interests. All it stirred was resentment.

"She's a Windbreaker. I hear there's not many of those left." Nik felt pitiful for his subtle probing for information about the princess in case Callen knew more and could feed his interest.

Setting his cup down, Callen leaned on his forearms against the railing. He flipped his palm, sparking a cobalt flame within. It almost matched his irises. His other hand hovered around it, stealing his own heat against the bitter night. "Not like your talent or mine," he agreed.

It was beginning to show just how little Nik paid attention in his teachings. It wasn't sitting right the amount the prince knew of him when Nik had no counter knowledge. "What do you know about my ability?" he asked.

"You're a notorious Nightwalker," Callen drawled. "Do they fear you as much as they say?"

By "they," he supposed Callen meant everyone. It was true that what he harbored within made people wary. He'd long since given up trying to convince people he would never use his ability for personal malicious intent. Friendship wasn't a term he found familiarity with.

"Their fear is often ignorance," he mumbled, unsure of why he shared it, but Nik began to feel the barriers of his reservation rise.

Callen only shrugged. "I'd be questioning how bad their secrets are for them to want to avoid the possibility of you lurking and finding out."

Nik almost broke a grin. It was the first time anyone had spoken of it that way, swaying the judgment from what he was capable of to the people who avoided his company instead. It was…liberating.

"Will you attempt to win her affections?" Callen diverted casually.

"The princess? I don't have any desire to seek company, only to pass the night." It circled like a lie in his stomach, a betrayal to his mind. Nik *did* want to find her.

"Hmm."

"Will you?" Nik tensed waiting for an answer, unsure of why the thought flared something ugly within him.

Callen smirked. "I'm spoken for, actually. In fact—"

"It's becoming an effort to keep my concern for your absence at bay." A gentle female voice drifted out to them. A beautiful fae wearing white and amber floated out with it. Her eyes sparked with something that look like yearning.

"Allow me to introduce my mate, Lady Katiana." The prince's gaze was nothing short of pure adoration. His fire winked out as she approached, and his arm circled around her. "This is Prince Nikalias Silvergriff."

Her head dipped warmly. "Your Highness."

"Just Nik is fine." He offered the same respect—after all, she was as good as titled the Princess of Dalrune.

Katiana leaned into Callen as he reclined against the railing, and the look they shared signaled Nik's leave. He said nothing more as he headed back inside, but Callen's last words called at his back.

"Good luck, Nik."

Amusement danced in his tone, and Nik wondered if it was so obvious that his intrigue for the Fenstead princess hadn't been erased from his face since she left. All he wanted was to see how she composed herself as what he'd witnessed was so careless and wild. Brazen and free. Even in that short moment, she'd ensnared him more than anyone ever had before. He tried to convince himself it was mere curiosity, something to tide over his boredom until the night was over and he would leave.

The instant need to retreat the moment he stepped into the ballroom was so strong he couldn't falter a step or he risked turning back. It seemed even more crowded than before, but everything was a blur of color and distant music. Without realizing, he was already focused on one thing. Her. The acknowledgment of that ground his irritation. He wasn't some pining fool.

She stood out so effortlessly that he spotted her with little effort.

His steps were already making way to her, as much as his mind screamed at him to retreat. She reached out to take a cup from a tray, but Nik stepped up behind her, brushing her hand to swipe it before she could. Her small gasp awoke in his chest, adding a fluttered beat. All it would take was for her to step back and their bodies would be flush, and by the *Gods*, did his mind rage for it.

"What would you father say if he saw you indulging on fae wine?" Nik mumbled privately. His breath blew down to the point of her ear, adorned with golden accents. It was maddening what he felt in that moment. She turned only her head, enough that her sparkling hazel eyes met his. Ire momentarily faded to surprise. "Tauria Stagknight."

The server left them, and the princess turned fully. "He needn't know." She didn't break his stare in a silent battle as she reached up.

Nik's fingers slackened around the cup as she took it. Her touch lingered, and the challenge that radiated between them was electric.

"Because I needn't point it out?"

She smiled, and for a suspended moment of time he captured that sight, entranced by it.

"Exactly, Nikalias Silvergriff."

He curved a brow. "You knew who I was out there."

Her head canted as she took a sip of wine. "Do you make a habit of allowing the world to know about you while you remain oblivious to the world?"

Nik had never thought about it that way. In a few quick exchanges, she'd challenged him at every angle. He hated it. Yet he adored it. Tauria was winding a net around him without even trying.

The band stopped playing, setting up to begin a new song as people stemmed off to find new partners. Tauria spared a glance around them before her gaze cast back to him expectantly. Seconds ticked by, and for the first time, there was a slight flex around her eyes that indicated irritation. It was deplorable for him to find excitement in it.

"You aren't going to ask me to dance?"

Nik lost the fight against the curl of his mouth. Slowly, he reached for her cup. Tauria let it slip from her grasp, clearly thinking he'd pass it off to a nearby servant and ask for her hand on the dance floor. He would never find out if it was her game to decline him if he did.

"No, I am not," he said, taking a sip.

Her mouth parted, and Nik's gaze fell to her lips, which sparked a flame of desire he didn't expect. In a want to know what they felt like.

"Just as well." She perked up, snapping him from his trance. "I feel I may be too tired after my dance with the Olmstone prince." Her smile was confident as she passed him by, but in an instinctive reaction he twisted, not registering what he was doing until it was too late. Nik reached out, plucking one of the many jeweled combs from her hair.

Tauria whirled to him with adorable incredulity.

"You have far too many of them," he said, only to get a rise out of her, as if this had become an exciting game between them. "They wear you."

Tauria lashed out to grab it, but Nik raised it out of her reach, ignoring the small scowl he found oddly attractive. He pretended to admire the light reflecting off the emerald crystals. At her silence, he slid his gaze back to her, but she'd composed herself to indifference. Nik smirked, holding out the comb. Tauria's attention shifted from it to him, and she poised her chin.

"Keep it. It would match your eyes if you dared to let a sparkle of joy into them."

With that, she turned from him, and he could do nothing but stare in fascination.

Until he followed to where her path led—to Tarly Wolverlon, who stood idly by on the sidelines of the party.

She doesn't want to dance with him.

He couldn't help the bitter thought, the tightening of his hand around the wine. Nik didn't know what to do with the feelings she riled in him that he wasn't accustomed to. Didn't want to feel them and have it further grind his irritation for the damn festivities to be over. He tried to occupy himself by the refreshments, yet his traitorous eyes kept wandering. No—*capturing*. It wasn't an effort to land his attention directly on her each time. He watched her dance with the prince. The way she moved was like the air she was born of—weightless, burdenless, a wisp of emerald that stood out among all the movement on the dance floor. He couldn't bear the itch of his skin every time her eyes slipped to him. It was as if she were goading him to break.

Nik wandered to the side of the hall, leaning against a pillar and facing away from the dancers. The night would be over soon. Several ladies approached, but he couldn't feel bad at using his lack of warm reception in place of his refusal to dance. The songs changed endlessly, and the fight not to turn and see who the princess could be dancing with next was a conscious effort he couldn't shake.

"You've stood staring at that wall for such a long time you must be fair acquaintances by now." Her voice raced a tremor down his spine. He couldn't see her, but he could feel her. Tauria Stagknight leaned on the other side of the pillar.

"Dancing isn't really my thing, though it does seem to be yours," he commented. Nik immediately cursed his error when the princess slipped around the pillar until she was right in front of him. Her eyes sparkled with deviance.

"Have you been watching me, Nikalias?"

Gods, she rattled his nerves like no one before. It was a conflict to want distance from these feelings he had no desire for. He swore he didn't want to find out if her body would mold so perfectly to his as he imagined.

"No more than you've been watching me, it seems."

This time, Tauria reached up to take the cup from him. The battle of their locked stares was becoming a game. He let her and simply watched with a thrill as she took a sip and placed it on a passing tray.

"Dance with me." She wasn't really asking with the demand of her upturned palm. Nik's eyebrow lifted, leaving a pause in which he half-expected laughter and mockery. But Tauria remained still, challenging.

"Shouldn't I be asking you?"

"It didn't seem like you were going to."

"Like I said, dancing isn't really my thing."

"Exactly." Her smile was wicked and daring. "This dance isn't slow or tender. You'll find the dance floor quite bare of those not confident enough in their footing or their significant other to attempt it."

The band started to play an intro to invite all those who would brave the dance to the floor. Nik had watched it performed many times. He'd *participated* countless times. Though he would never admit that to her.

"Are you afraid, Nikalias?"

Something bright and dawning encased his entire body. In those hazel eyes he'd found what he hadn't been searching for, yet he didn't know what it was that stirred within him. Nik's hand took hers, and the touch of their bare skin shot an awakening through him as he led her.

It was in that moment he knew…

No matter what happened beyond this night he'd first laid eyes on her, Tauria Stagknight was someone whose imprint on him would never be erased.

PRONUNCIATION GUIDE

NAMES

Faythe: faith
Reylan: ray-lan
Nik: nick
Jakon: jack-on
Marlowe: mar-low
Tauria: tor-ee-a
Mordecai: mor-de-kai
Lycus: lie-cuss
Tarly: tar-lay
Marvellas: mar-vell-as
Aurialis: orr-ee-al-iss
Dakodas: da-code-as
Ashfyre: ash-fire
Arrowood: arrow-wood
Zarrius: zar-ee-us
Katori: ka-toe-ree
Keira: Key-rah
Zainaid: Zai-nayd

PLACES

Ungardia: un-gar-dee-a
Farrowhold: farrow-hold
Galmire: gal-my-er
Vesmire: ves-my-er
High Farrow: high-farrow

Lakelaria: lake-la-ree-a
Rhyenelle: rye-en-elle
Olmstone: olm-stone
Fenstead: fen-stead
Dalrune: dal-rune
Fenher: fen-er
Ellium: elle-ee-um
Niltain: nill-tain

OTHER

Riscillius: risk-ill-ee-us
Lumarias: lou-ma-ree-as
Yucolites: you-co-lights
Dresair: dress-air
Magestone: mage-stone
Skailies: skay-lees
Fyrestone: fire-stone
Phoenixfyre: phoenix-fire

ACKNOWLEDGMENTS

This was a book to challenge me. There were many times I doubted, but in the end, this book holds a special place with me, and I hope you enjoyed stepping into Nik and Tauria's world for a while. It opens up so much to come, and I can't wait to continue the series with you.

To my mother, as always, thank you for being someone I can count on come hell or high water. I will always call you first, even though it's guaranteed to go to voice mail because you seem to enjoy calling me back seconds later.

To Bryony Leah, each time I get to this page I wonder how else I can express my gratitude for your dedication to these books. Time and time again you strengthen these stories, and you sure helped make Nik and Tauria's the best it could be. Editor extraordinaire.

To Alice Maria Power, prepare for trouble! And make it double! You continue to blow everyone away with these covers, thank you for lending your incredible talent to this book. Go Team Rocket.

To Miranda and Nichole, thank you for being your amazing selves. I can go to you for anything.

To Lyssa, for being with me since book one and cheerleading for this series harder than anyone. Here's to more "take over the world" type stuff.

My dear readers, from the bottom of my heart, thank you for loving these characters with me, for coming back into this world book by book with me. You are more than enough.

Lightning Source UK Ltd.
Milton Keynes UK
UKHW012310060922
408450UK00010B/89/J